CRITICAL PERSPECTIVES ON J. M. COETZEE

Also by Graham Huggan

TERRITORIAL DISPUTES: Maps and Mapping Strategies in Contemporary Canadian and Australian Fiction

Also by Stephen Watson

SELECTED ESSAYS, 1980–90
RETURN OF THE MOON: Translations from the /Xam

WITHDRAWN FROM
KA 0260969 X
THE LIBRARY
UNIVERSITY OF
WINCHESTER

Critical Perspectives on J. M. Coetzee

Edited by

Graham Huggan
Department of English,
Harvard University

and

Stephen Watson
Department of English,
University of Capetown

Preface by

Nadine Gordimer

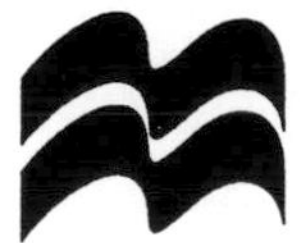

First published by
MACMILLAN PRESS LTD
Houndmills, Basingstoke, Hampshire RG21 6XS
and London
Companies and representatives
throughout the world

ISBN 0–333–56912–1

A catalogue record for this book is available from the British Library.

This book is printed on paper suitable for recycling and made from fully managed and sustained forest sources.

Transferred to digital printing 1999

Printed in Great Britain by
Antony Rowe Ltd, Chippenham,Wiltshire

Contents

Preface

NADINE GORDIMER

It might be better to call this an anti-preface rather than a preface. I understand a preface to a book of this nature to require a preview of the contents in relation of the authors of the critical essays to their subject but I, as J. M. Coetzee's fellow-writer, naturally take the subjective view, which is that of the writer to the critics. Whichever way, the relation is a We/They one; for me, John Coetzee and I are We and the critics are They. As a writer, I must break with the conventional function of the preface and present a view of the written-about rather than the writers-about.

Who is addressing whom in a collection of literary criticism? Is it a dialogue between critic and critic? Between critic and writer? Between critic and reader? Very likely these questions have been the subject of discourses I have not read. My general experience over the years has been that the subject is avoided. We all agree that for the health of literature there must be a canon of criticism, but how it functions I don't believe we are sure or don't care to enquire.

That a critique is firstly a dialogue between critic and critic is clear in this collection, where the pollen of an insight garnered from Coetzee's work is blown through the pages of scholarly journals to fertilise a second generation of insights or mutations in contradiction. The exchange serves as both expansive and corrective in the placing of a work within the confines of current literary theory, which, in the regime of the intellect, arrives from successive intellectual traditions at the linguistic, philosophical, metaphysical and material *possibilities* inherent in contemporary consciousness, rather as in the regime of governments the frontiers decided in past wars, the price of oil and the possibilities of extending human life or destroying for ever its sustenance determine the ethos of sociopolitical power. Criticism, like the literature it propagates itself on, seeks to transcend its time and is formed by its time; this is reflected fascinatingly in a dominant debate in this collection.

J. M. Coetzee's critics almost all seem awed by his textual innovations which, as one puts it, traverse European literary and philosophical traditions. (Though why this should seem extraordinary to those who are well-read by profession is puzzling: perhaps there are vestigial traces, in the critics themselves, of the very phenomenon of colonialism they are hunting down through his work – why, otherwise, should it be more remarkable that Coetzee's writing, rather than that of, say, Kundera, Primo Levi or Danilo Kis, with whom he shares the power of the imagination in its appropriation of forms to its purpose, traverses these traditions?) At the same time, the critics wrestle with whether or not Coetzee's fiction is part of the discourse of colonialism itself, avoiding its stark issues with elegant allegory or whether, indeed, his themes are distilled from that bloody starkness.

His work perhaps epitomises the problem of the critic in South Africa (most contributing to this book are doing so as South Africans within our country). What balance between aesthetic values, regarded as transcending time and temporal engagement, formed in and by time, constitutes achievement in literature? If I were to stray, as I have done occasionally, into the territory of the critics, I should expand on this with my own battery of footnotes from Barthes, Benjamin, Derrida, Lacan, Lukács etc., scraps of paper the Hansel/Gretel critic drops along the pages so that other critics may find their way back to recyclable sources. But I have been asked to preface, not to contribute in the strict sense. I content myself with paying a deserved tribute to the critics I might contend with: it is their theses that have prompted me to think at all of an intervention of my own. And isn't that proof of the value of criticism, between critics in their establishment?

What service is criticism to its subject, the writer and the writer's work? In many instances, the critique imposes the intent of the critic on the intent of the writer. This may be subconscious on the part of the critic, nevertheless the writer receives it as intent. Yes, yes – the critic is seeking out the hidden intent of the writer, but does he/she find it? (Sometimes he/she appears to be distracted by the fatuous on the way. Even though made conditional by the precautionary 'could', one of the critics in these covers quotes his suggestion to students that, speaking of Susan Barton in *Foe*, 'We could fault Coetzee for not letting a woman have access to both authorship and motherhood.' *Could we?*) The critic sets out on this expedition armed with the compass, sieve and latest model geiger-counter of literary theory, but the writer has to forge the literary theory he or she knows, before beginning to write. All labels are peeled away. The writer forgets about the summations of metafiction in order to be in the naked state of grace – no less – in which his/her intent will be worked out. In all humbleness – for it is a humbling and dangerous experience from the point of view of mental exposure – only we know what our motives and purposes are, when we write. *Only we know what we were saying.* I venture to speak for Coetzee because it is obvious to anyone who appreciates his exceptional gifts that he, more erudite than most writers, forgets the language and thought-patterns of literary theory when he visualises a man digging in a municipal garden, a man tracing the worm-scroll of a scar on a waif's eyelid, a woman washed up on a desolate shore. His readers receive these visions directly, unencumbered by any theoretical reflection upon them, by any alienating hint of how they were achieved. He forges categories, analyses, his modes are organic, they are transformations of the imagination growing out of his consciousness and that of his society, as the persistent nurture of the earth, producing growing things, is a theme which sprouts through the sombreness of his work.

What I have said is not to be taken as an attack on criticism; it is meant as a reminder of the limitations of the function of the critique in any assumption there may be of its usefulness to the writer. Most of us ignore the critical debates that go on over our texts. The critic has to accept the fact that when we writers do read a critical analysis of our work it often seems to be some other work that is under discussion, someone else's: the critic's unwritten one. So the question of how much influence a critique may have upon a writer's view of his/her own work is doubtful. Only occasionally – and with gratitude, I may say – does the writer find a critic who has understood exactly what the writer was saying. I hope John Coetzee may come upon that experience somewhere in this book. Only very rarely – and with immense gratitude – does the writer perceive his work to be in the hands of a critic who, starting out from that understanding, discovers for the writer aspects of what he/she was saying that were unknown to him/her. To receive weighty consideration and praise in misreadings of one's work is discouraging in the extreme, for one can't always blame the inadequacy of the critic. Even hermeneutics has to have, on its own terms, something sufficiently lucid to work on . . .

To receive the rap of unfavourable criticisms from a critic who truly has understood and accepted the writer's intention – that is the encouragement, the exceptional resource the writer may receive from the critic. There are some essays in this collection which could fulfil this purpose for J. M. Coetzee.

What about readers? I suppose that every 'ordinary' reader is a critic in the sense that she or he may say 'I like this novel', 'I don't like these stories' although without any occupational obligation to attempt to say why. Yet I find it difficult to accept that any consideration should be given, as it is in one of the essays, to people who found Coetzee's novels boring. This is not analogous to misreadings by professionals. These are non-readers of Coetzee, they have given up; as there is no communication, even of misreading, between them and the writer, I can't see that there is any profit for literary study in attempting to look at his work from the point of non-view. One must grapple with a work, as a reader, in order to validate a claim to be taken seriously by literary criticism. The measure of literature cannot be taken in a Gallup Poll.

I would also raise an eyebrow at, if not take issue with, critical contention that the difficulties of Coetzee's novels require that the reader shall have read the same books the author has. Given that Coetzee has made specific use of cross-fertilisation in his fiction, creating in one novel, at least, an appealing (to me) afterworld where those of us who have lived much in books in this one could meet again and mingle with writers and their creations on the same level of imaginative reality, *all* writers have read a great many books. Echoes of the nature of thought in these books, transliterations of their language usage and variations on their forms, transpositions of their events, acronomic versions of their characters' names – these are part of the creative consciousness of every writer, however far removed he or she takes them in a unique vision. There is an added pleasure, for those of us who know Cavafy, to reflect upon his barbarians' identity with those of Coetzee. There is an added pleasure, for those who have read works of Defoe other than Crusoe, to encounter Amy and Defoe himself, for example, making an appearance in *Foe*; and furthermore (if we are looking to boast of the exegetic pleasures of wide reading), to compare Michel Tournier's *Vendredi* with *Foe*. But does that mean people who know only the Crusoe of childhood storybooks cannot appreciate the beauty of this stunning novel and be led by it into deep self-questioning of human attitudes, those specific to our own country and consciousness and those the world shamefully shares with us? Of course not. All literature is a retelling, endlessly, of human life and its ungraspable mysteries, since story-making began. You don't have to know the provenance to respond to the contemporary version, whether or not it gives over references.

Our contemporary versions, in South Africa, return me to the critic's dilemma: whether, until *Age of Iron*, J. M. Coetzee's fiction has made no mention of South Africa, has been distanced from it. If I may interject, I should like to remark that his fiction could not have come from anywhere else in the world. *Life & Times of Michael K* are the life and times of the millions of black South Africans who were removed, dumped, set wandering, hiding from Endorsement Out under the Group Areas act. Michael K was one of them, all of them. Whether by making him 'all of them', allegorically, Coetzee evaded the demands of his time and place or whether he enhanced commitment to these, in the choice, is something the reader of this collection of essays will find interestingly explored. Coetzee chose and maybe helped to decide for himself, with *Age of Iron*, to do something of what the incomparable Borges did towards the end of his life, turning from the aesthetic and metaphysical patterns of existence to what restlessly resists artistic form, the naming and recounting of lives which apparently stand for nothing but themselves. A half-turn to realism? Realism? Nothing is more unreal than simulation of outward reality; realism, whether in painting or writing, doesn't exist. Art *is* transformation. Coetzee simply took up a mode of art he had not much used before, now perhaps more suited to, demanded by, his theme and his changing sense of relation to his society, where and how he lives.

There is a space round a literary work that can't be filled by explication. Neither yours nor mine. It is a private space for the writer and the reader. The best thing about a collection of criticism is that it should send us, the readers, back to the works themselves. For me, the worth of a work of fiction is proven, finally, only when, alone with me, it imposes the rhythm of its thought processes so that I hear its voice, feel its pulse coursing through my life between readings of it. J. M. Coetzee's fiction fulfils this aesthetic pleasure completely and makes this invasion of the sensibilities, this demand on intellect, morals and mores, with rare authority. If this collection of essays finds a general as well as an academic readership and sends others, as it has me, to reread Coetzee's work, it will have fulfilled its purpose both as homage owed to him and in service to South African literature.

Acknowledgements

Three essays in this collection previously appeared, in slightly modified form, in the following books or journals: Derek Attridge, 'Oppressive Silence: J. M. Coetzee's *Foe* and the Politics of the Canon', in Karen R. Lawrence (ed.), *Decolonizing Tradition: New Views of Twentieth-Century 'British' Literary Canons* (Urbana: University of Illinois Press, 1992) pp. 212–38; Peter Knox-Shaw, '*Dusklands*: A Metaphysics of Violence', in *Contrast*, 4:1 (1982) pp. 26–38; Stephen Watson, 'Colonialism and the Novels of J. M. Coetzee', in *Research in African Literatures*, 17:3 (1986) pp. 370–92. Thanks are due to the editors and publishers of these books and journals for permission to reprint the essays. Thanks are also due to the Hyder Rollins Fund, Harvard University, for subsidising this collection; and to Shelley MacDonald, in Vancouver, for her help in preparing the manuscript.

The editors and publishers wish to thank the following for granting permission to use copyright material:

Penguin Books USA Inc., for the extracts from the following books by J. M. Coetzee: *Dusklands*, copyright © 1974, 1982 by J. M. Coetzee; *Foe*, copyright © 1986 by J. M. Coetzee; *In the Heart of the Country*, copyright © 1976, 1977 by J. M. Coetzee: all used by permission of Viking Penguin, a division of Penguin Books USA Inc.;

Martin Secker and Warburg Ltd, for the extracts from J. M. Coetzee's *Dusklands* and *Foe*.

List of Abbreviations

The following primary Coetzee texts appear in abbreviated form:

AOI	*Age of Iron*
D	*Dusklands*
F	*Foe*
IHC	*In the Heart of the Country*
MK	*Life & Times of Michael K*
WFB	*Waiting for the Barbarians*
WW	*White Writing*

Notes on the Contributors

Derek Attridge was born in South Africa and studied at the University of Natal, Pietermaritzburg. After further study at Cambridge University, he taught at the Universities of Oxford, Southampton and Strathclyde and he is currently Professor of English at Rutgers University, New Brunswick, New Jersey. His books include *Peculiar Language: Literature as Difference from the Renaissance to James Joyce* and a selection of Jacques Derrida's writing entitled *Acts of Literature.*

David Attwell lectures in literary studies at the University of Natal, Pietermaritzburg. He is the editor of J. M. Coetzee's *Doubling the Point* (1992) and has recently published *J. M. Coetzee: South Africa and the Politics of Writing* (1993).

Teresa Dovey has studied and worked in South Africa, Australia and the United States of America. She is currently teaching at Rhodes University. Her book on J. M. Coetzee, entitled *The Novels of J. M. Coetzee: Lacanian Allegories,* was published in 1988.

Ian Glenn is an Associate Professor in the Department of English at the University of Cape Town. He is currently working on a study of discourses on race and gender in early South African fiction.

Nadine Gordimer was born and lives in South Africa. Her novels include *The Conservationist, Burger's Daughter, July's People* and *My Son's Story.* Among her collections of short stories are *Friday's Footprint, Livingstone's Companions, Jump* and *Why Haven't You Written?* She has collaborated with the photographer David Goldblatt on two books, *On the Mines* and *Lifetimes: Under Apartheid* and has also published a collection of essays, *The Essential Gesture.* In 1991 she was awarded the Nobel Prize for Literature.

Graham Huggan teaches post-colonial literatures in the English Department at Harvard University. He is the author of *Territorial*

Disputes (University of Toronto Press, 1994) and is currently working on a book on contemporary anglophone travel-writing.

Peter Knox-Shaw is author of *The Explorer in English Fiction* (1987) and of many critical essays. Forthcoming work includes 'Persuasion, Byron, and the Turkish Tale', 'The West Indian Vathek' and 'The Otherness of Septimus Warren Smith'.

Michael Marais teaches in the Department of English at the Vaal Triangle Campus of Potchefstroom University. His current research interests lie in the field of political metafiction.

Patricia Merivale, Professor of English and Comparative Literature, University of British Columbia, is author of *Pan the Goat-God: His Myth in Modern Times* (Harvard Studies in Comparative Literature) and of numerous essays, from comparative perspectives, on such topics as elegiac romance, apocalyptic (and other) artist parables and the metaphysical detective story.

Kenneth Parker is Professor of Cultural Studies at the University of East London, London. His publications include *The South African Novel in English: Essays in Criticism and Society* (London: Macmillan, 1978), *The Letters of Dorothy Osborne* (London: Penguin Classics, 1987) and (with Elleke Boehmer and Laura Chrisman) *Altered State? Writing and South Africa* (Mundelstrup, Denmark: Dangaroo, 1994); he was a founding editor of *The Southern African Review of Books.*

Benita Parry writes and lectures on culture and imperialism; she is the author of *Delusions and Discoveries* and *Conrad and Imperialism*, essays on colonial discourse and post-colonial theory and is working on a study of the discourse of imperialism.

Stephen Watson is a Senior Lecturer in the Department of English at the University of Cape Town. His most recent books are *Selected Essays 1900–1980* (1990) and *Return of the Moon: Translations from the /Xam* (1991).

1

Introduction

GRAHAM HUGGAN and STEPHEN WATSON

The international reputation which the South African novelist J. M. Coetzee now enjoys is fairly indicated by the many prestigious awards his novels have received over the last decade or so. Among others, he has been awarded Britain's Booker-McConnell Prize, the Prix Fémina Etranger in France and the Jerusalem Prize in Israel. Already his work has been the subject of four book-length studies: Teresa Dovey's *The Novels of J. M. Coetzee: Lacanian Allegories* (1988), Dick Penner's *Countries of the Mind: The Fiction of J. M. Coetzee* (1989), Susan VanZanten Gallagher's *A Story of South Africa: J. M. Coetzee's Fiction in Context* (1991) and, most recently, David Attwell's *J. M. Coetzee: South Africa and the Politics of Writing* (1993). With the possible exception of Nadine Gordimer, there is no other South African author who is currently the subject of so many scholarly articles and dissertations.

Nevertheless, despite the ever-growing critical acclaim his work has received, J. M. Coetzee remains the most elusive of writers, one whose fictions seem almost deliberately constructed to escape any single framework of interpretation. More than this, his six novels to date[1] amount to a phenomenon not all that common in world literature today. Essentially, he is a first-world novelist writing out of a South African context, from within a culture which is as bizarre and conflicted an amalgam of first- and third-world elements as any on this planet. His is a body of work both highly realistic and subversive of realist aesthetics; in which police brutality and postmodernism cohabit; in which South Africa, his native land, appears at once central and marginal to his concerns. More than anything else, his novels would seem to situate themselves somewhere in that space invoked by Ian Glenn when, in his contribution to this collection, he comments on the figure of Magda in Coetzee's *In the Heart of the Country*: 'Between systems, worlds, symbolic orders'. Decidedly, Coetzee writes – to use a phrase from another contributor, Derek Attridge – 'from a marginal location'.

Not surprisingly, then, the critical difficulties are considerable when one seeks to define the particular place J. M. Coetzee occupies as a writer. For someone who has consistently broken down or transgressed the boundaries between what is and is not 'South African', there would be little point in approaching him simply as if he were a *South African* author. Nor, on the other hand, is the character of his work such that it could be legitimately regarded as supra-national, belonging entirely to some or other late twentieth-century internationalism.

Accordingly, the editors of this collection of critical essays have sought contributions from critics resident in South Africa, who are familiar with the most immediate of the historical contexts in which J. M. Coetzee has his place; but they have also commissioned essays from critics elsewhere in the world, whose interest in his work may lie outside this particular context. Needless to say, there is no hard and fast division in this book between 'South African' and 'other' critics. Rather, we have divided the collection into two sections, beginning with essays of a more general nature, followed by an individual essay devoted to each of his six novels in turn. A couple of these – notably the contributions by Peter Knox-Shaw and Stephen Watson – have been published before and pre-date the rest of the contributions specially commissioned for this book by several years. But whatever their particular focus, each essay seeks, in its own way, often using very different critical idioms, to define that elusive space which J. M. Coetzee's fiction has made his own.

Although none of the essays here includes much specific detail on the South African culture from which Coetzee emerged,[2] it is worth bearing in mind the character of this culture in mind in any attempt to understand Coetzee's novels and criticism. His climb to prominence in South African letters began not long before the exact historical moment in that country – the Soweto Revolt of 1976 only just preceded the publication of his second novel, *In the Heart of the Country* – which was to usher in a period of state oppression unprecedented even by South African standards. The impress of this era, the stifling weight of which can be measured as much in the fraught tone of Coetzee's earlier novels as in their other aspects, cannot be underestimated even if, by now, the precise reality of that weight is often subsumed un the cliché that the single word 'apartheid' has long since becom

J. M. Coetzee's particular reaction to this historical moment provides at least one reason for the almost immediate acclaim his work was to receive in South Africa. Almost from the beginning, his novels struck one as ways of escape from the most immediate contexts, the South African, in which they were produced. The human imagination, it has been said often enough, is like the dog in the basket; it has a tendency to dream of hares in the open, particularly when such hares might not exist, nor even the space in which they might subsist. The more oppressive conditions of life in South Africa were to become – and these conditions have hardly relented, even at the time of writing – the more transcendent, one might say, became the formal impulses of his novels, the more profound the misery and revolt of their protagonists. No matter what, it would seem that Coetzee could not help building into his novels certain spaces (or, perhaps, places of refuge) which might or might not exist, but which were designed to elude the dead-weight of South African life in the 1970s and 1980s.

The atmosphere of a prison-house which was a permanent feature of life in South Africa throughout these decades was obviously not confined to the political sphere alone; it was soon to be felt in the cultural sphere as well. For an understanding of Coetzee's work, it is also worth remembering that the tendency of human beings to think in deadening, and even deadly, binary opposites – black/white; friend/enemy; aesthetics/politics – is seldom more irresistible than in situations of extreme racial polarisation and political struggle. This tendency has been all too evident in the critical debate surrounding Coetzee's work in South Africa. Unlike many critics and reviewers elsewhere in the world, a number of South African critics, particularly those belonging to the political Left, have sought to attack Coetzee's novels in terms of an opposition that has sometimes approached the crudeness and reductiveness of racial thinking. Given the priority that these critics attached to political struggle, they were to charge him with an aestheticism which they considered politically irresponsible, or simply irrelevant; they demanded of him an explicit form of commitment which his novels evidently eschewed. Although later critics, like some included in this book, were to counter-argue that Coetzee's narrative strategies involved a radical questioning the very discourses of power that upheld brutal and unjust social systems, thereby making him a more profoundly political writer than any exponent of Agitprop, there seems little doubt that the general level of the aesthetics/politics debate in South Africa was to do little more than add another bar to the prison that the country's cultural life so often appeared to be.

The very simplifications of the debate itself, the oppressive reductiveness of the terms in which it was waged, provide a further explanation, as well as a justification, for Coetzee's elusiveness as a writer, and for the complex independence he has assumed. Between those who have demanded that literature in South Africa serve a political cause solely and exclusively, and their diametrically opposed antagonists, J. M. Coetzee has consistently posited a third, more elusive term. It goes, of course, by many names. It might be called the Magistrate in *Waiting for the Barbarians*, Michael K himself in *Life & Times of Michael K*, or perhaps Mrs Curren in *Age of Iron*. Whether or not this third term exists, whether it is based on delusion or a questionable faith, the need for it – plus a fourth or a fifth – is insistent in Coetzee's novels. Spurning the almost endless series of binary opposites that are so characteristic of South African life, cultural or otherwise, J. M. Coetzee has simply refused to be tied to the terms of the debate. The more oppressively these terms have been wielded by critics, the more fervently his novels have reached after a space elsewhere, a margin of freedom, which they could not fail to posit. As a result, Coetzee has become South African literature's 'elsewhere', producing a body of work which seeks to define, as in all deeply imaginative work, a place which might not exist, for which there is as yet no recognised definition, but which remains, for all that, an indispensable human need.

It is for reasons like these, above all, that J. M. Coetzee does not strike one primarily as an 'anti-apartheid' writer, one of those who has gained his or her world-wide reputation through an exposure of the human outrages for which apartheid has been responsible. Though his allegiances and sympathies are not in question, it is evident that he is, as a novelist, amongst those who would maintain that even a right side (in a political struggle) can impose a wrongful silence, required untruths; even solidarity can be an extension of power – that is, the beginning of the lie. In fact, Coetzee's novels, eluding (as distinct from evading) the numbing conventions of South African culture, might not be considered South African at all. He has had almost as little to do with official versions of 'anti-apartheid' thought and literature as he has had to do with the equally official versions of South African race thinking. As one consequence, he is amongst the least 'reader-friendly' of novelists, making few concessions to even the best-intentioned of contemporary pieties and shibboleths, giving not much more comfort to ostensible friends than to enemies. Discouraging this might be. But it is also why such difficult, qualified freedoms as exist in his novels – such spaces in the open that might suddenly appear in them – seem more than merely rhetorical or the consequence of wish-fulfilment.

J. M. Coetzee is elusive in another respect. He is not simply a *South African* writer; in fact, his work repeatedly calls into question any effort to find an identity for itself in such national terms. He takes for granted what many another South African writer has had difficulty acknowledging: that he is contemporaneous with the rest of the present world and, as such, is not excluded from the intellectual developments that have taken place elsewhere. Thus, from the outset of his career, his novels have not only been marked by any number of indisputably South African aspects; they have also asked readers to acknowledge those defining elements that modernist literature used to insist on, and which had been relatively rare in other South African literature at that time: the difficulty – even impossibility – of meaningful communication; the mutability of things; the contingency and absurdity of human existence; the nightmare of history, past and present; and, not least, the confusion, fear and anxiety that follow from an encounter with any of the foregoing. In short, Coetzee's work possesses a disquieting vision, with those distinctly apocalyptic, even nihilistic overtones we usually take to be characteristic of the era of international modernism.

But there is far more to it than just those characteristic features which have been more the stock-in-trade of European and American modernism than the province of the South African novelist. Like those strands in contemporary philosophy which attack all forms of foundationalism, Coetzee's work is even more contemporaneous in incorporating a radical critique of language, of the forms of authority made possible by language, not only questioning the latter, but challenging our right to such things as epistemological certitude. In much of J. M. Coetzee's fiction we no longer have even the *grounds* for certitude. In short, his novels embrace a scepticism of a thoroughly contemporary, particularly thoroughgoing kind – one, it must be said, that is more in keeping with the period of high modernity (as the sociologist Anthony Giddens would call it) than with anything specifically South African.

This, doubtless, has something to do with J. M. Coetzee's current reputation. There is little question, for instance, that Coetzee is partly admired amongst his small body of readers in South Africa because his work embodies a sophistication, an at-homeness in currents of contemporary thought world-wide, from which the nation has been relatively isolated through the repressive effects of apartheid and the recent cultural boycotts. In this sense, his reputation in his own country has partly been a function of the link his work has continued to provide with the world outside South Africa. But it goes further than this. Corrosively self-aware as they are, consistently self-reflexive, Coetzee's novels are entirely sympathetic to many of the more radical tendencies in current critical theory. In their critique of liberal humanism, their questioning of traditional modes of representation, their undermining of even their own pretensions to knowledge, his novels positively invite criticism, even if, as Ian Glenn points out in this collection, they often pre-empt the efforts of the critics themselves. In fact, there are occasions when it seems that Academe would have invented J. M. Coetzee had he not already existed, so sympathetic do his concerns seem to be to critical theory and many of its current preoccupations. Whether this is an unqualified virtue or not remains to be seen. But what seems certain is that J. M. Coetzee represents in himself a new kind of author, in whom academic critic and writer, formerly regarded as distinct, are melded as never before – even more closely than is the case with, say, an American novelist such as John Barth.

This might well be one additional reason why Coetzee's work will continue to elude whatever critical net might be used to pin it down. Given the unique historical circumstances from which Coetzee writes, as well as his unusual reaction to them, his work has assumed a particularly complex, shifting identity. In this respect, not least, it might well prefigure the kind of identity which could be more the rule than the exception in the future, wherever in the world. Ian Glenn implies as much in his conclusion to a discussion of *In the Heart of the Country*. Referring to Anthony Giddens' recent study, *Modernity and Self-Identity*, Glenn suggests a further reason for the importance of J. M. Coetzee's achievement:

> Giddens' study of the ways in which the modern represents a dislocation of the national and the local leaves us with the possibility . . . that the conditions of modern identity may be first found and most sharply felt in colonial situations, that the colonial, between worlds and systems, is exemplary of the modern. . . . What we see then is that Coetzee's formal innovation is related to the colonial world experience which is modernist in all the terms Giddens enumerates. Coetzee has produced the novel of identity for the multi-national age by focusing on the colonial as a kind of generic precursor of the multi-national.

Does Coetzee's work look forward to an uncertain future, or does it remain entrenched within the past? Does it speak only of colonial atrophy or also of possible renewal? These questions, like so many others, remain unanswered in Coetzee's fiction: either/or categories dissolve into an – often elaborate – play of paradox and contradiction. The essays in this collection probe some of those paradoxes and contradictions. How is it that Coetzee's work engages with history, yet also contrives to elude it? How is that the fiction voices opposition, yet also remains complicit? And how is it that we, Coetzee's readers, enter in spite of ourselves into that complicity?

'Our experience remains largely colonial', Coetzee has said of contemporary South Africa. Yet it is obvious from his work that colonialism extends beyond national boundaries. Colonialism traces lines of collusion between the marginal locations of Coetzee's fictions and the metropolitan centres of Europe and North America where those fictions are consumed. Colonialism is at work behind the rhetorical manoeuvres and language-games of an *oeuvre* which graphically demonstrates the struggle for the word. And perhaps it hides, as well – as Nadine Gordimer suggests in her provocative preface – behind the clutch of critical categories to which Coetzee's work is subjected. For critical interpretation – however grounded – is, potentially, a colonising act. A critic himself, Coetzee is well aware of the multiple ironies involved in the struggle for interpretive authority. In the world of Coetzee's fiction, signs are removed from their usual referents, disfigured by those who have or claim to have the power to control them. In this estranged, often violent world, there is little room for compromise. The text, like the landscape(s) it traverses, occupies disputed territory; it is subject to litigation and the battle for proprietary rights. Readers vie with writers over ownership of 'their' stories – as often as not, the stories are sold off to the highest bidder. Few writers are more acute than Coetzee in their perception of the materiality of language, or of the susceptibility of words and stories to ideological manipulation.

The critical debate carried on in this collection contributes to that perception; it is situated, like the fiction, on – sometimes hotly – contested terrain. Stephen Watson seeks to account for the contradictions in Coetzee's writing by invoking Memmi's notion of the 'colonizer who refuses'; this claim is countered by Ken Parker, who emphasises Coetzee's *privilege* to dissent. Teresa Dovey sees Coetzee's novels as 'locating themselves in history without assuming the transcendence of history'; Benita Parry sees their author rather as attempting to 'detach [them] from their worldly connections'. Parry stresses Coetzee's concern to 'safeguard his fiction from incorporation into a critique of the South African condition'; Patricia Merivale finds his novels to be 'remarkable, if oblique, parables of, among other things, the contemporary political situation in South Africa'. Mike Marais reads the silences of Coetzee's protagonists as expressing resistance to 'political programmes of containment'; Derek Attridge reads them instead as drawing attention to the exclusionary practices of the canon. Ian Glenn links the existential anxieties of Coetzee's novels to the context of South African colonialism; Peter Knox-Shaw critiques Coetzee for an 'existentialism of the armchair' in which context is 'downplayed in favour of a psychopathology of Western life'.

Emerging from this debate is a sense of quandary, of crisis. This crisis is seen, in part, as the result of intellectual stalemate: of a paralysing process by which white South African writers (and/or critics) are obliged to reconfirm their own displacement. This process is seen, in turn, as part of a European modernist inheritance. It is also seen in the confluence of two apparently incompatible histories: 'the history of [the white writer's] discourse, [which is] rooted in the discourses of imperialism, and the suppressed history of the colonised, which has to be recuperated without being arrogated to colonial discourse' (Dovey). Finally, it is seen as belonging to a wider material struggle, whereby South Africa's particular history is linked to the histories of all those other countries who 'participate in the rise of Western capitalism, and the ideology on which it depends' (Attridge).

'One requirement in moving toward a resolution of the struggle', says Attridge in his essay, 'is an understanding of the ways in which the cultural formations that we have inherited through those histories are ... complicit with the daily barbarities that occur in South Africa'. Coetzee's work contributes to that understanding, not least in its interrogation of the hypocritical pieties of Western liberal humanism. Like Gordimer (a writer with whom he is often, unfairly, contrasted), Coetzee is eager to unmask the false universals of liberal ideology. Yet as the essays collected here show, opinions are divided even on this. Thus, while Graham Huggan reads *Age of Iron* as an ironic swan-song to liberal humanism, and Teresa Dovey reads *Waiting for the Barbarians* as a deconstructive allegory of humanism's failure to acknowledge itself as discourse, Ken Parker detects a residue of humanism in Coetzee's work – a residue that links him to a tradition from which he seems unable to escape.

Indeed, the inability to escape is a motif that runs throughout Coetzee's writing, prompting some exasperated critics to see him as indulging in defeatism. Is Coetzee's 'an art that can only reenact' (Knox-Shaw)? Is it condemned, like the Magistrate in *Waiting for the Barbarians*, to reciting a past that it has not understood; or, like Mrs Curren in *Age of Iron*, to 'rehearsing an ending that continues to elude [it]' (Huggan)? Once again, the issue is unresolved; Coetzee's fiction wavers between the unacceptable alternatives of frustrated Utopianism and apocalyptic despair. (Or are these alternatives *interchangeable*? As Patricia Merivale remarks of *Life & Times of Michael K*: 'The book's crypto-pastoral ending, with its ironic paean to the spirit of survival, might be Faulknerian were it not so *doubtfully subjunctive*' (emphasis added).) Critical hypotheses on Coetzee's work seem prone to such doubtful subjunctives. Is this a product of the writer's elusiveness, or of the critics' trepidation? Does it reflect an indeterminate (post-)modern world, or an unreconstructed (neo-)colonial one? None of the usual labels applies, although, as Coetzee's work repeatedly shows, the labels *do* matter. (I say he is a laundryman, Susan Barton remarks of Friday, and he *becomes* a laundryman.) Perhaps Coetzee's work can best be seen, as Mike Marais in his essay sees it, as resisting the reader's attempts to 'assimilate it within a literary system of intelligibility'. Or perhaps we should conclude, with Stephen Watson, that 'at the heart of Coetzee's heart of the country, there is nothing. The solid core of his work lies elsewhere, outside the works themselves, in something that is effaced, implicit, barely alluded to'. It would be churlish, at any rate, to see Coetzee's obliquity as merely a strategy of self-protection. Coetzee's parables yield no obvious morals, yet they are 'ethically saturated' (Lazarus, quoted in Parry). What is most characteristic of Coetzee's novels (and, one suspects also, of their author), is that they brook no compromise: they refrain from uttering 'truths' when they know these to be relative; they uncover the material conditions that produce the lie of 'transcendent value'. The obliquity of Coetzee's writing is the sign of its *precision*.

Notes

1. Unfortunately, this collection of essays pre-dates the publication of Coetzee's latest novel, *The Master of Petersburg* (New York: Viking Penguin, 1994).
2. The reader interested in Coetzee's own comments on this, along with some remarkably candid autobiographical statements, need go no further than his collection of essays and interviews, edited by David Attwell and entitled *Doubling the Point* (1992).

Part I

2

Colonialism and the Novels of J. M. Coetzee

STEPHEN WATSON

I

In an interview conducted in 1978, J. M. Coetzee remarked that he was inclined 'to see the South African situation [today] as only one manifestation of a wider historical situation to do with colonialism, late colonialism, neo-colonialism'. At the same time, as if to underline his sense that South Africa's situation was bound up with a global historical process, he added, 'I'm suspicious of lines of division between a European context and a South African context, because I think our experience remains largely colonial.' This colonialism, he concluded, was evident even in publishing in this country: 'Our literary products are flown to the metropolitan centre and re-exported to us from there at a vastly increased price. . . . That very fact should give people pause before they start talking about a South African literature' (Watson, 'Speaking' 23–4).

Given his particular understanding of the historical process of which present-day South Africa is both product and part, as well as of its importance, it is not surprising that J. M. Coetzee's first four novels should all be situated in colonial times and should deal with one or other of the various aspects of colonialism. Eugene Dawn's narrative in *Dusklands* (Johannesburg 1974) has as its backdrop the attempted American colonisation of Vietnam; Jacobus Coetzee, in some respects a forerunner, is both a product of colonialism and, like Kurtz in Conrad's *Heart of Darkness*, one of its most avid, twisted servants. Magda, the spinsterish cipher whose obsessed, excessive voice dominates *In the Heart of the Country* (Johannesburg 1978), announces at once that she is one of 'the daughters of the colonies'. *Waiting for the Barbarians* (London 1980), to my mind Coetzee's finest novel to date, is a novel of an imaginary empire, of an imperialism which is merely an extension of colonisation. Even *Life & Times of Michael K* (Johannesburg 1983), while it might appear to treat of something rather different, has to do with colonialism. Its protagonist is a man intent on eluding colonisation, whether it be the colonisation of the body (through labour camps) or the colonisation of the mind (through charity). In fact, in all four novels colonialism is treated from both an external and internal point of view. The novels not only allude to an actual historical reality, but they also give us, in fictional form, the type of psyche and psychology that this reality dictates. If colonialism, at its very simplest, involves the conquest and subjugation of a territory by an alien people, then the human relationship that is basic to it is likewise one of power and powerlessness: the relationship between master and servant, overlord and slave. It is this aspect of colonialism that receives the most extensive treatment in Coetzee's fiction.

In its concentration on the ambiguities and cruelties, that combination of sadism and masochism that the master–slave relationship invariably entails, his novels would appear to have much in common with many other novels in South African literature. And not only in this respect. What Coetzee's Magda calls the 'savage torpor' characteristic of life in the heart of the country (or colony) was equally well suggested more than a century ago in Olive Schreiner's *The Story of an African Farm*. There, too, one finds a character (Lyndall) with a frustrated, impassioned hunger for a world with horizons broader than those imposed by the institutionalised mediocrity of the colony. There are other points of contact as well. Anyone familiar with colonial literature, whether from South Africa or elsewhere, will also be acquainted with the figure of the colonial adventurer who, in the well-chosen words of Hannah Arendt, enjoyed in nineteenth-century colonies 'a world of infinite possibilities for crimes committed in the spirit of play, for the combination of horror and laughter, that is for the full realisation of their own phantom-like existence' (Arendt 190). Both Coetzee's Jacobus Coetzee and Schreiner's Bonaparte Blenkins occupy a world that knows no social restraint, a world where everything is permitted because nothing can be punished; one in which both characters have the opportunity to indulge that sadism (combining horror and laughter) through which they assert the reality of their own egos against a wilderness whose very emptiness would seem to mock all human endeavour. Coetzee, like Plomer in *Turbott Wolfe*, also makes use of a conception of Africa which was first elaborated by Conrad in *Heart of Darkness*. The notion that the colonial experiences at the heart of Africa, a void which would seem to penetrate every level of existence, from the biological to the metaphysical, is hardly foreign to him. In all these respects, then, his work is very much a part of a tradition founded by earlier writers like Schreiner and Plomer.

Nevertheless, it is all too evident that even if Coetzee's novels do have something in common with other works in South African literature, then the actual critique of colonialism that emerges from them is hardly conventional. They do not deliver the usual moral condemnation of greed and hypocrisy, something which is all too familiar in the average colonial novel. Indeed, their very distance from this type of conventional 'criticism', their striking difference, might well lead the uninformed reader to question whether they belong to South African literature at all.

When *Dusklands* appeared in 1974, Jonathan Crewe hailed it in *Contrast* as the arrival of the modern novel (what he should have said was the 'modernist' or 'postmodernist' novel) in South Africa for the first time. Never before had a South African novel broken so obviously, even self-consciously, with the conventions of realism and so candidly announced its own artificiality, its own fictionality. In the pseudo-scholarship in which the second half of the novel was embedded, the example of Jorge Luis Borges and Vladimir Nabokov was palpable. The very conjunction of the two narratives seemed to suggest that their relation to reality (and I mean *historical* reality) was problematical, hardly a simple matter of representation or mimesis.

There is no doubt that part of the success of *Dusklands* was due to this modernity. There is perhaps even less doubt that to those who had been brought up on an unrelenting diet of South African liberal realism, with its studious commitment to depicting everything from the flattened vowels of the English South African accent to the contents of its average laundry basket, and having as its controlling centre some bewildered nobody beating his or her moral wings in vain – to such people J. M. Coetzee's first novel had something of the liberating, clarifying force of a genuine revelation. But this was not simply because it was up to date, as avant-garde as anything overseas. In *Dusklands*, and even more so in his subsequent novels, South Africa was transfigured into a place at once clearer and more strange – and not least because Coetzee had so many affinities with modernism.

It was, it should be remembered, perhaps the central modernist project to restore the inert, empirical world to the transfigurations of myth. And it was at once evident that, in one sense at least, his work was a late addition to this project. It dealt in myth, not empirical fact. Or, rather, it transformed the latter into the former. If many people responded to this, it was not only because they were tired of a prose which was resolutely tied to a reality which was either tawdry or bland. In Coetzee's transfiguring myths, in his penchant for situations and characters way beyond the bounds of society, in the very asceticism of his style which gave no place to the 'naturalistic arbitrariness' which Lukács once deplored, there seemed to lurk a quasi-religious impulse which, whether recognised by the reader or not, only made his work that much more compelling.

But his modernism was not the least of his innovations. No reader could have failed to notice the way in which Coetzee conflated historical periods in his first three books, imposing, with a seeming disregard for all historical veracity, an eminently twentieth-century voice and an academic intelligence onto a historical period seemingly remote from it in both time and space. What sense are we to make of a supposed translation of one Jacobus Coetzee's journey in 1760, a man who was an illiterate in actual reality, and to whom the following reflection is attributed?

> The gun stands for the hope that there exists that which is other than oneself. The gun is our last defence against isolation within the travelling sphere. The gun is our mediator with the world and therefore our saviour. The tidings of the gun: such-and-such is outside, have no fear. The gun saves us from the fear that all life is within us. It does so by laying at our feet all the evidence we need of a dying and therefore a living world. . . . I leave behind me a mountain of skin, bones, inedible gristle, and excrement. All this is my dispersed pyramid to life. It is my life's work, my incessant proclamation of the otherness of the dead and therefore the otherness of life. (*D* 84)

Similarly, what are we to make of a colonial spinster who, while living in a world in which some of the realistic props would seem to suggest the nineteenth century (Magda speaks of 'dancing slippers', 'daguerrotypes', and even a 'Weekly Advertiser' and 'Colonial Gazette'), delivers the following meditation which betrays both an acquaintance with certain French surrealists and later commonplaces of structuralist linguistic theory?

> Words are coin. Words alienate. Language is no medium for desire. Desire is rapture, not exchange. It is only by alienating the desired that language masters it. Hendrik's bride, her sly doe-eyes, her narrow hips, are beyond the grope of words until desire consents to mutate into the curiosity of the watcher. The frenzy of desire in the medium of words yields the mania of the catalogue. I struggle with the proverbs of hell. (*IHC* 26)

Clearly, we are a long way from the notion of verisimilitude when, as the second last sentence of the above passage indicates, a supposed nineteenth-century colonial ignoramus, lost in the historical backwater of the South African hinterland, has read Roland Barthes's *S/Z* and can regurgitate some of his reflections on the frustrations of language when it attempts to capture desire and create a verbal image of physical beauty.

In the case of a book like *In the Heart of the Country* there is, of course, an immediately apparent reason why Coetzee should use certain elements of structuralist linguistic theory and some of the devices which Barthes elaborates in *S/Z*. On the one hand, he obviously wishes to register the impact of colonialism not, as is customary in the realist novel, through a series of incidents or events, but at the more basic level of language itself. For this purpose, structuralism, with its emphasis on the creation of meaning through relationship, is a useful tool. In the same way that human relations are opaque and destructive in the colonial situation, so, Coetzee would seem to suggest, language itself fails to signify, to mean at all, under the conditions prevailing in such a situation. The only tongue the colonialist can speak is the circular one of tautology. The presence of Barthes is also not fortuitous. Like *S/Z, In the Heart of the Country* is, on one level, concerned to demonstrate that realism is not real at all, but simply a production of language, a code that people have come to accept as 'natural'. Coetzee wants to create what Barthes would have called a 'writable' text, one which makes 'the reader no longer a consumer, but a producer of the text', one which does not attempt to reduce the potentially multiple meanings, the 'plurality' of the text, by fixing one single meaning for it. The novel is surely constructed on the principle that it is through language itself, through those conventional representations which come to be accepted as either 'natural' or 'universal', that we are colonised as much as by any overt act of physical conquest. The deconstruction of realism, then, is evidently intended, at the most basic level of language itself, as an act of decolonisation and, as such, is very much part of its political meaning.

So much is clear. Even so, this political meaning is by no means transparent. In the first place, by loosening the bonds of historical verisimilitude imposed and indeed demanded by the conventions of realism, Coetzee allows his fictions to float literally free of time and place even in the act of seeming to allude to a time and place which is specifically South African. In this way they would seem to enter the realm of myth, of the archetypal. Moreover, his texts suggest an extremely curious understanding of the meaning of colonialism and the driving force behind it. The long-accepted wisdom on this subject has been put well enough by Aimé Césaire in his *Discourse on Colonialism*. 'What, fundamentally, is colonisation?' he asks:

> Neither evangelisation, nor philanthropic enterprise, nor a desire to push back the frontier of ignorance, disease, and tyranny, nor a project undertaken for the greater glory of God, nor an attempt to extend the rule of law. To admit, once and for all, without flinching at the consequences, that the decisive actors here are the adventurer and the pirate, the wholesale grocer and the ship owner, the gold digger and the merchant, appetite and force, and behind them, the baleful projected shadow of a form of civilisation which, at a certain point in its history, finds itself obliged, for internal reasons, to extend to a world scale the competition of its antagonistic economics. (Césaire 10–11)

In short, both yesterday and today the motive force of colonialism was essentially an economic one. Behind it lay the desire for land, raw materials, cheap labour and the recurrent crises in capitalist production in Western Europe.

Since Coetzee's work is apparently so specific in its allusions to colonialism, one might expect to find some mention of material factors in it. Yet one seeks for these in vain. In *Dusklands*, as Peter Knox-Shaw has noted, there is a 'virtual effacement of economic motive. Nothing is made of the gold dust which Jacobus Coetzee gathered on the banks of the Great River and later displayed at the Castle (indeed the omission is noted)' (Knox-Shaw, 'A Metaphysics of Violence' 28). Magda touches on questions of economics only once and then only obliquely:

> And economics: how am I to explain the economics of my existence, with its migraines and siestas, its ennui, its speculative languors, unless the sheep have something to eat (for this is not finally an insect farm)... There is another great moment in colonial history: the first merino is lifted from shipboard, with block and tackle, in a canvas waistband, bleating with terror, unaware that this is the promised land where it will browse generation after generation on the nutritious scrub and provide the economic base for the presence of my father and myself in this lonely house. (*IHC* 19).

Throughout *Waiting for the Barbarians*, the all-too-material reason for the very existence of the empire is only mentioned in passing when the magistrate is questioned by a newly arrived young officer:

> 'Tell me, sir, in confidence,' he says, 'what are these barbarians dissatisfied about? What do they want from us?'
>
> .....
>
> 'They want an end to the spread of settlement across their land. They want their land back, finally. They want to be free to move about with their flocks from pasture to pasture as they used to.' (*WFB* 50)

But nothing more is heard of this seemingly crucial, if obvious, fact. Coetzee's focus is on something else. In *Dusklands*, for instance, the reader would be far from mistaken in coming to the conclusion that colonialism is primarily the projection of a certain mental aberration located exclusively in the divided consciousness that is a special feature of Western humanity. If the narratives of Eugene Dawn and Jacobus Coetzee are anything to go by, the colonising project of the West was set in motion when this same man embarked upon his Cartesian project of separating subject from object, self from world in a dualism which privileged the first of the two terms and thereby assured his domination of nature and any other obstacle he might confront. The possible reason why Coetzee should be more interested in this metaphysic than the actual material reasons for colonialism will be suggested later on. At the moment it is enough to say that his identification of it is hardly original. It is based on one of the great commonplaces in the history of Western philosophy. The basis of it is to be found in innumerable histories. William Barrett, among many others, has conveniently summarised the origins of this metaphysic of power as follows:

> The modern era in philosophy is usually taken to begin with Descartes. The fundamental feature of Descartes' thought is a dualism between the ego and the external world of nature. The ego is the subject, essentially a thinking substance; nature is the world of objects, extended substances. Modern philosophy thus begins with a radical subjectivism, the subject facing the object in a kind of hidden antagonism. . . . Nature thus appears as a realm to be conquered, and man as the creature who is to be conqueror of it. This is strikingly shown in the remark of Francis Bacon, prophet of the new science, who said that in scientific investigations man must return to the rack in order to wring from it an answer to his questions; the metaphor is one of coercion and violent antagonism. (Barrett 180)

The alienation that entered modern philosophy with Descartes translates itself, in the field of action, into a will to power whose appetite is voracious, limitless, precisely because there is an unbudgeable void at the very heart of it. On the evidence of Coetzee's Eugene Dawn, colonialism is merely one – perhaps the most significant – expression of this void. Just as Western people conquer nature in an effort to conquer their own self-division, so they cannot desist from enslaving other human beings who necessarily confront them as that Other, alien and forever threatening.

With this basic philosophy behind it, it is difficult to escape the impression that for Coetzee the modern era, the era of a continuing colonialism, is primarily the enactment of a certain metaphysics which reaches its culmination in Nietzsche's will to power.

In fact, if there is any spirit presiding over his work it would be that of Nietzsche, not Marx. And it is for this reason that, perhaps predictably, Coetzee has aroused the suspicions and then the complaints of many people on the Left in South Africa, people for whom the most important philosophical and political distinction would still be some line of division between an 'idealism', on the one hand, and a 'materialism', on the other. Michael Vaughan is characteristic. He writes:

> The absence of *industrial labour* is particularly striking in Coetzee's latest novel, *Waiting for the Barbarians*. In this novel, relations between the imperialists and the barbarians are very tenuous, and the imperial project acquires the status of an absurd formalism. There is no suggestion of any *material interests* being involved in this project. Of course, this is characteristic of Coetzee's methodological idealism. . . . Coetzee gives the rationale of the project of world colonisation in an idealist form . . . Coetzee's idealism prevents the possibility of a fiction of materialist realism, a fiction which understands the determination of the present by the past, without essentialising either term, and thereby producing a fatalism. (Vaughan, 'Literature and Politics' 123)

Perhaps Vaughan's disappointment, if not exasperation, is understandable. On the face of it, Coetzee would seem to be a writer obsessed with history to a degree scarcely matched by any other author in South Africa today. The epigraph to the second part of *Dusklands*, Flaubert's 'What is important is the philosophy of history', might stand as a motto for all Coetzee's work so far. And yet in his conflation of historical moments, in his metaphysical preoccupations, his modernist leanings, he cannot help striking one as the most ahistorical of writers at the same time.

Of course, there is one obvious reply to Vaughan and those like him. Coetzee is writing *fiction*, a type of fiction, moreover, which is not realism and which, therefore, does not need to obey the latter's invariable demand that the individual event be related to wider social and economic processes. Vaughan might simply be forgetting that 'the fictional element in literature, including poetry, is definable precisely in terms of our having to supply the missing elements in an act of communication as an absent context' (Scholes 9). What constitutes the fictional in Coetzee, one might argue, is precisely that effacement of the material determinants which we, the readers, are expected to bring to our reading. Even if this were not so, if Coetzee were ignorant of the fact that colonialism was about land, labour, capital (which, I might add, is almost unthinkable given his general erudition), his work would still not amount to an 'idealism'. Although someone like Vaughan is well aware of the value of Coetzee's stylistic innovations, as well as their implications, he may be missing the fact that Coetzee's specific orientation, one which distinguishes his fiction so markedly from that of all his peers in contemporary South Africa, which gives it its singular stamp, is the result of a set of circumstances which is all too material. Of these Coetzee himself is hardly unaware. The problem is that they are only given an oblique expression in the novels themselves. If, for instance, one searches within them, examining their structure, one discovers little more than an artfully constructed void. At the heart of Coetzee's heart of the country, there is nothing. The solid core of his work lies elsewhere, outside the works themselves, in something that is effaced, implicit, barely alluded to.

II

This is nothing other than the fact that *Dusklands, In the Heart of the Country, Waiting for the Barbarians, Life & Times of Michael K, Foe* and now *Age of Iron*, are the novels of a man who is himself a coloniser, at least objectively speaking. The one fact most important for an understanding of the apparent anomalies in his work is that he is not only a coloniser who is an intellectual, but a coloniser who does not *want* to be a coloniser. Even if this were not a matter of historical, biographical record, it would be evident from the novels themselves. With the exception of Jacobus Coetzee, who is determined to play out his role to the bitter end[1] and Michael K as well, all Coetzee's major protagonists are colonisers who wish to elude at almost any cost their historical role as colonisers. All of them (and this would include even Jacobus Coetzee) are wrought to a pitch of desperation in their efforts to escape the intolerable burdens of the master–slave relationship. Eugene Dawn, Magda, the Magistrate, even the medical officer in *Life & Times of Michael K* are all of a piece in their single hunger. If, indeed, there is a dominant moral impulse at work in Coetzee's novels, it is to be found in the insatiable hunger of all his protagonists for ways of escaping from a role which condemns them as subjects to confront others as objects in interminable, murderous acts of self-division. If there is also a pessimism in them, it is because the majority of these characters (Michael K being the exception here) beat against the shackles of their historical position in vain.

For, of course, there is plenty of evidence to suggest that there have been and still are historical situations in which the dissenting coloniser, 'the coloniser who refuses', to use Albert Memmi's phrase, finds himself hamstrung and worse. In fact, the portrait that Memmi provides of this type of person in his *The Coloniser and the Colonised* is far from being obsolete today. But it is a gloomy one. In the case of colonisers who do not (or perhaps cannot) return to their home country and who nevertheless vow not to accept colonisation, the spectre of contradiction, of multiple contradictions, confronts them at every turn:

> He [the coloniser who refuses] may openly protest, or sign a petition, or join a group hostile towards the colonisers. This already suffices for him to recognise that he has simply changed difficulties and discomfort. It is not easy to escape mentally from a concrete situation, to refuse its ideology while continuing to live within its actual relationships. From now on, he lives his life under the sign of a contradiction which looms at every step, depriving him of all coherence and all tranquillity. (Memmi 1974 20)

What is worse is that the passage from the refusal of the role of coloniser to that of accepting and being accepted by the colonised does not necessarily follow as a matter of course, however natural a progression this might appear to be. As Memmi puts it:

> The leftist coloniser is part of the oppressing group and will be forced to share its destiny, as he shared its good fortune. If his own kind, the colonisers, should one day be chased out of the colony, the colonised would probably not make any exception for him. . . . Colonial relations do not stem from individual good will or actions; they exist before his arrival or birth, and whether he accepts or rejects them matters little. . . . No matter

> how he may reassure himself, 'I have always been this way or that with the colonised,' he suspects, even if he is in no way guilty as an individual, that he shares a collective responsibility by the fact of membership in a national oppressor group. (Ibid. 38–9)

Thus, his conclusion is sombre. 'There are, I believe, impossible historical situations and this is one of them' (39). 'The leftist coloniser's role cannot be sustained; it is unliveable. He cannot help suffering from guilt and anguish and also, eventually, bad faith. He is always on the fringe of temptation and shame, and is in the final analysis, guilty' (148).

Albert Memmi based these observations on his own experience in Tunisia three or four decades ago. In present-day South Africa the situation is somewhat different; the position of the coloniser who refuses is not necessarily intractable. Nevertheless, I wish to suggest along with Memmi that a fundamental and wide-ranging ambivalence is common to those who find themselves in the role of the dissenting coloniser and that this ambivalence is only compounded in the case of a writer like Coetzee who also happens to be an intellectual of a quite particular sort.

The specifically intellectual quality of his fiction is, of course, immediately noticeable. It is not simply that he is the most bookish of all authors in South Africa. Quotation is basic to his fictional practice. In the first half of *Dusklands*, for example, one finds a few transposed lines from a John Berryman poem amid other sly allusions to William Carlos Williams, T. S. Eliot and Franz Kafka. In places, *In the Heart of the Country* is a tissue of borrowings. Among many others, one comes across Luis Cernuda's 'Desire is a question that has no answer' and more than one echo of Beckett's famous sentence from *The Unnameable*: 'Many faults I have, but changing my tune is not one of them'. Henry James makes an appearance towards the end of *Waiting for the Barbarians* and, clearly, the very title of *Life & Times of Michael K* makes a bow to Kafka, perhaps particularly to 'A Hunger Artist', whose showman starves because there is nothing in the world worth eating. But it is not only in its use of quotation that the intellectual quality of his work is manifest. His books are steeped in other books. Eugene Dawn himself mentions Bellow's *Herzog* and Patrick White's *Voss*. It is even more evident that Coetzee has read Hegel, is well acquainted with structuralist linguistics, and has a thoroughgoing knowledge of Sartre's *Being and Nothingness*. He clearly knows the latter's definition of man as 'he who is what he is not and who is not what he is,' and, more important, his work is nearly saturated in the Sartrean distinction (ultimately of Cartesian provenance) between Being-for-itself (*être-pour-soi*) and Being-in-itself (*être-en-soi*). In fact, there are occasions in his work when Coetzee puts one strangely in mind of something said by Marlow in *Heart of Darkness*. Like Kurtz, one is tempted to say, 'all of Europe' (and North America) has gone into the making of Coetzee – or at least into the making of his books. He has produced by far the most intellectual and indeed intellectualising fiction of any South African or African writer.

It is just this feature of it which has irritated several commentators. Cherry Clayton, for instance, has referred to parts of *In the Heart of the Country* as mere showing off (Clayton 43). Behind her criticisms, as well as those of others, one feels the sour suspicion that Coetzee is guilty of a kind of inverse provincialism. In his sophisticated manipulation of French intellectual fashions, in his apparent determination not to be outdone by any metropolitan avant-garde, there might well seem to be an element of what Australians have called 'cultural cringe'. The suspicion is that while the novels themselves might be taken as an attack on colonialism, they are the product of someone who has a colonial mentality himself.

This type of opinion is, however, only tenable if one forgets the precise way in which Coetzee is using various intellectual elements in his work. For just as there is nothing really original about the metaphysics of power already referred to, so there is nothing specifically complex or particularly original in these elements as such. They would all form part of a certain type of academic training. Almost all the initial difficulties of his novels vanish when one happens to have read the same books that he has. The real intellectual difficulty of his fiction lies outside the works themselves, in Coetzee's own status as an intellectual. To appreciate the deeply problematic nature of this status it is necessary to remember that he is (again, objectively speaking) a member of the Western-oriented English intelligentsia in South Africa and that this intelligentsia, rudimentary as it has always been, has suffered something of a crisis in the last three decades.

This is not simply because of the large-scale exodus of English-speaking intellectuals from South Africa both before and after

Sharpeville, something which has had an incalculable effect on general intellectual life in the country. Before 1948, as is well known, South Africa was in many respects the virtual preserve of the English-speakers. Economically, legally, even politically, it was their type of society. Given the pre-eminence of this subculture, the function of the English-speaking intellectual was clear. He or she, characteristically standing somewhat to the left of the culture as a whole, was cast in the role of guardian of the South African liberal tradition. The whole English intelligentsia saw itself as a kind of vanguard and hoped that by its efforts and own example a gradual liberalisation would take place in all aspects of South African life. But, as we know, everything changed in 1948. Just as the English lost their political pre-eminence, so their intellectuals suffered a fall. Where it was they actually fell is implied by an observation of Denis Worrall's:

> English South African intellectuals are deluding themselves if they think they have some sort of mediating role to play; apart from the fact that people, however well-intentioned they might be, are, if they have no power base, generally thrust aside in a pinch situation, Afrikaner nationalism has shown that it does not require mediators in its relations with Black Africans. (Worrall 216)

As Worrall suggests, these intellectuals fell nowhere; their traditional role had vanished.

At this point it is worth recalling something written by Arthur Koestler during World War II, an essay of his entitled 'The Intelligentsia'. In it he speaks of the manner in which many a Western European intelligentsia was, in the decade preceding the outbreak of war, increasingly deprived of what he calls 'the responsibility of action'. As a result, 'the bulk of [these] were not wanted, had to remain fellow travellers, the fifth wheel to the cart. The intelligentsia of the Pink Decade was irresponsible because it was deprived of the privilege of responsibility. Left in the cold, suspended in a vacuum, they became decadents of the bourgeoisie' (Koestler 78–9). Deprived of a role, an intelligentsia, like any other social organ, decays and begins to exhibit every type of morbid symptom.

Something similar happened to the English-speaking intelligentsia in South Africa after 1948. It too was increasingly left out in the cold, hunched over that vacuum that had opened up within itself, one which was always threatening to implode. If its decadence was hardly flamboyant, then it nevertheless grew to experience an isolation which many felt to be terminal. This was not merely an intellectual isolation. It was also that impasse encountered whenever the political sphere of life, in which people come together in pursuit of a common goal, is destroyed. And what took the place of this sphere, what filled the subsequent vacuum, was inevitably neurosis.

In the same essay Koestler points out that neurosis is one of the occupational hazards of any intelligentsia:

> The relation between intelligentsia and neurosis is not accidental, but functional. To think and behave independently puts one automatically into opposition to the majority whose thinking and behaviour is dependent on traditional patterns; and to belong to a minority is in itself a neurosis-forming situation . . . . To quarrel with society means to quarrel with its projections in one's self, and produces the classical neurotic split patterns. Oedipus situation and inferiority complex, timidity and arrogance, over-compensation and introversion are merely descriptive metaphors for various deformations with a common denominator: maladjustment. An intelligentsia deprived of the prop of an alliance with an ascending class must turn against itself and develop that hothouse atmosphere, that climate of intellectual masturbation and incest, which characterised it during the last decade [the 1930s]. (Koestler 80)

The relevance of this extract to the characterisation of Magda in *In the Heart of the Country* is undeniable, but it applies equally well to the English-speaking intelligentsia in South Africa in recent times. When Magda herself, imprisoned in her 'stony monologue', cries out: 'There is no act I know of that will liberate me into the world. There is no act I know of that will bring the world into me' (*IHC* 10) she might well be defining its central neurosis and providing a possible epitaph for it.

The predicament of the 'coloniser who refuses' is thus only exacerbated by the predicament of an intelligentsia that has forfeited its role as an intelligentsia. To write as Coetzee does, acutely conscious of both dilemmas, is to inherit a twofold displacement: from what Koestler calls an ascending class as well as from one's own kind. To be in a position like his is, one suspects, to be deprived of responsibility while continuing to feel a responsibility which is as boundless in its guilt and as all-pervasive as those neuroses that breed so easily in the psychological closed circuit of any great impasse. It is to be caught with a severely divided mind. It was Plato who once defined the worst possible psychological condition of any human being as 'division of the psyche'. But it is not necessary to invoke his name in order to appreciate the severity of this condition. One has only to look at Coetzee's novels.

In them one finds over and again an extraordinarily skilful fictionalisation and projection of the divided mind of a certain type of colonial intellectual. This is not only dramatised through the old means of plot and characterisation. Just as the unequal relationship between coloniser and colonised can take many forms, so this divided mind finds expression on a number of levels and, at its very deepest, translates itself into a series of oppositions or opposed needs which at times appear to be the first two terms of a rudimentary dialectic but which never manage to issue in a third or synthesising term. As is the case with South Africa today, so much of Coetzee's work can be viewed as a failed dialectic, a world in which there is no synthesis, in which the very possibility of a synthesis would seem to have been permanently excluded. No doubt this failure may be taken as a metaphor for the human failure of colonialism itself, but in Coetzee's case it is obviously blooded by his own contradictory position as a 'coloniser who refuses' and an intellectual with an essentially romantic and modernist inheritance.

III

The most immediate consequence of this position is a division and then breakdown between thought and action, theory and practice. Coetzee's novels are pervaded by a kind of Hamlet complex, by what Eugene Dawn refers to as the 'blocked imperative of action'; they are literally and quite deliberately 'sicklied o'er with the pale cast of thought', by the corrosive worm of an intelligence that suspects that it is nothing but an intelligence. This self-consciousness is everywhere evident. Even as Magda intellectualises her quandary, she is quite aware that she is mythologising, that the spate of questions and answers that spill out of her with Kafkaesque profusion might be one way of making sense of her world but it is not *the* way, *the* sense. And this, as has been suggested, gives to the intellectualising itself a function which it is easy to misunderstand.

For the most part the intellectualisations – some would say rationalisations – that protrude so blatantly from Coetzee's work are not there because he is being élitist or lacks the talent to let the action speak for itself. Far from it. Thought as such has an entirely different status in his work. It is not there to enlighten, nor for the purposes of understanding. If one looks at *In the Heart of the Country*, for example, one might justifiably ask why Magda gives (among many others) what is so obviously a Freudian explanation for her predicament. Why, one wants to know, does she have to refer to the 'childhood rape' as if she were some glib psychology undergraduate? Why does Coetzee announce so blatantly that he has read Freud, Hegel, Sartre, Kafka, Beckett, and so on?

The answer is surely that, divorced from action and its fulfilment in action, thought itself becomes immobilised, petrified. Deprived of its terminus in action, something which is essential to both personal and political health, even the best ideas of the most eminent thinkers become worthless. Living in a world in which 'nothing happens', in which Magda can make nothing happen except in fantasy, her thought turns back on itself and literally congeals. It is because he wishes to demonstrate just this that the novel is a veritable museum – in fact, graveyard – of the thought and literary culture of the West. This is quite intentional. In the heart of the country, where 'nothing can be done', Freud, like any other intellectual eminence, becomes a relic, a fossil. The entire novel is almost a parody of thought ('names, names, names', Magda intones) in which the very processes of reasoning, of deduction and induction, are mocked by the simple fact that they go nowhere. To think and to think to no end, no purpose, is the typical fate of Coetzee's characters.

In the light of this breakdown between theory and practice, it is also easier to see why the Aristotelian model for literature, with its definite distinctions between inner and outer, real and unreal, past, present and future, beginning, middle and end – in short, the model that is at the basis of Western literary realism –

should disintegrate in much of Coetzee's work. As in so much of Beckett, the lesson of his novels is that reality itself becomes conceptually incoherent when individuals can no longer be agents in the world. In Michael Vaughan's words:

> Realism implies that there is an immediate, effective relation between individual experience and objective reality. The medium of this relation is always some form of practice. With Coetzee, the relation between individual experience and reality – and hence also practice, as a mediating link between the two terms – is highly problematic. Hence his anti-realist aesthetics. (Vaughan 15)

Realism cannot survive a world in which characters are more the powerless objects of the historical process than its active subjects.

There is perhaps an even more important consequence of this breakdown. Although this point is made tentatively, it would seem that, in the same way as the disintegration of the unity of theory and practice entails an attenuation of reality and the ultimate petrification of all thought, so its victims are steadily drawn towards placing a higher value on the notion of 'being' rather than 'becoming'. Whilst this might not always be the case, it does seem one possible consequence of the stasis that characterises the position of the coloniser. Indeed, it would often seem to be no more than the extension of this stasis to the world. In the case of Coetzee's novels, this orientation is registered in the enduring fascination with the interiority of stones (of all things, the stones themselves, 'so occupied in quietly being', are Jacobus Coetzee's favourites) and in an obsessive consciousness of the entirely passive, self-contained world of nature. It is evident, too, in Magda's repeated longings. And it is exemplified in the very existence of Michael K, himself described as a stone, a character who above all embodies what the Jewish philosopher Abraham Herschel once called the 'quiet eminence of being', a quality that stands as a perpetual rebuke to the frenzied participants in historical struggles.

In suggesting this, however, I am very far from claiming that Coetzee is guilty of 'idealism'. On the contrary, I believe that this orientation in his work is entirely logical; it is, one might say, directly expressive of the ambivalent position of the 'coloniser who refuses'. For the latter is characteristically both inside and outside time. Unlike the majority of the colonised who are entirely involved in the world of their struggles, the world of becoming and have no possible choice in this matter, this type of person may be described as existing half in the world of being and half in the world of becoming. As a consequence, he or she cannot fail to feel the wrench of history pulling in one direction and, simultaneously, the opposing pull of a world of contemplation where time is cyclical and knows no irruptions. Moreover, the essence of such a position would seem to be an inability to decide in favour of one or other mode of being. If contemplation is chosen, history will not cease to remind the chooser of his or her irresponsibility and guilt. If he or she decides to act, to enter history, the world of being that they have necessarily left behind will continue to be present to them in the form of an inner hollowness.

On the evidence of his novels at least, Coetzee himself seems subject to very much the same dilemma. His position is further complicated by the fact that the modernism which is obviously his intellectual inheritance has always privileged being over against becoming; this is in accordance with its quasi-religious, mythic bias, its attempt to restore to the world a quality of being emptied out of it by modern political and technological developments. And, as a result, his work is informed, at the very deepest level, by a grave dichotomy. Czeslaw Milosz, in his Nobel Lecture in 1980, spoke of just such a split, referring to the way in which the allegiances of many a twentieth-century writer have been divided between 'being' and 'action', his or her devotion to art on the one hand and solidarity towards his fellow men and women on the other (Milosz 407). Such, says Milosz, was the contradiction for poets like himself, a contradiction 'engendered by the twentieth century and discovered by poets of an Earth polluted by the crime of genocide'. And such, one might say, is the contradiction at the heart of Coetzee's novels.

It is because of this contradiction that there is, for instance, that curious ambivalence in his work, that failed dialectic that has already been noted. It can be seen most clearly in the conception of history itself that emerges from his four novels. More often than not, the ambivalence of the role of the 'coloniser who refuses', along with the contradiction between being and action which those in this role seem fated to suffer, is transferred to history itself.

Typical of Magda's experience in the supposed colony is her

sense that she is 'lost to history', is one of 'the forgotten ones of history'. She never ceases to lament this fact:

> I need people to talk to, brothers and sisters or fathers and mothers, I need a history and a culture, I need hopes and aspirations, I need a moral sense and a teleology before I will be happy, not to mention food and drink. What will become of me now that I am all alone? For I am alone again, alone in the historical present. (*IHC* 119–20)

All of Coetzee's novels contain passages which express a great longing for history. They are unfailing in their desire for a world of event, for a narrative in which there is direction and purpose, a story which has a beginning and end, in which character has some continuity in time.[2] From this perspective, history is nothing less than God: it promises salvation, a release from the purgatory of personal isolation and political stagnation. It may be seen as the particular fantasy of history entertained by all who have, willy-nilly, been excluded from participation in its processes and thereby condemned to all the neuroses – the narcissism, introversion, and so on – that are inclined to afflict those whose position has become redundant in their historical moment.

At the same time this hunger is everywhere contradicted. According to Coetzee, history is not only a saving God; it is also the great Satan himself. In direct contradiction to Magda's fantasies, the history that might confer a pardon is also the history that condemns. This is made explicit in one of the Magistrate's outbursts in *Waiting for the Barbarians*:

> What has made it impossible for us to live in time like fish in water, like birds in air, like children? It is the fault of the Empire! Empire has created the time of history. Empire has located its existence not in the smooth recurrent spinning time of the cycle of the seasons but in the jagged time or rise and fall, of beginning and end, of catastrophe. Empire dooms itself to live in history and plot against history. (*WFB* 133)

Here it becomes only another name for the Fall, a radical loss of innocence. It does nothing but dismember. The torment it causes is even more forcefully suggested by the Medical Officer in his imaginary letter to Michael K, his elusive charge. With obvious envy he refers to the latter as:

> a human soul above and beneath classification, a soul blessedly untouched by doctrine, untouched by history, a soul stirring its wings within that stiff sarcophagus, murmuring behind that clownish mask. You are precious, Michaels, in your way; you are the last of your kind, a creature left over from an earlier age, like the coelacanth or the last man to speak Yanqui. We have all tumbled over the lip into the cauldron of history: only you, following your idiot light, biding your time in an orphanage (who would have thought of *that* as a hiding-place?), evading the peace and the war, skulking in the open where no one dreamed of looking, have managed to live in the old way, drifting through time, observing the seasons, no more trying to change the course of history than a grain of sand does. (*MK* 207–8)

These opposed conceptions of history as God and as Satan knock against each other throughout Coetzee's work. Nor should the lack of a resolution to their conflict be surprising, particularly given his characters' inherent ambivalence and the uncertain position of the author himself. For only to one who felt himself (whether rightly or wrongly) displaced from it, could history appear as very heaven. Only to one who was equally aware that he was actually enmeshed in it, that his existence was continually being accused by it (the coloniser, as Memmi said, is always guilty), could it simultaneously be that hell, that History with a harsh, deified capital *H*, judging and condemning, giving birth to characters, both fictional and otherwise, who are alternately attempting to embrace and to flee headlong from it.

This ambivalence is only reinforced on other levels in his work. It is present, for instance, in the oscillation already mentioned, between what Sartre has termed Being-in-itself and Being-for-itself, two fundamentally opposed modes of being. Again, one does not have to look very long at Coetzee's novels to notice that they contain many an example of the one striving to reduce itself to the other. Magda, for one, is constant in her efforts to allay the anxiety of human existence, the insecurity of being a consciousness always falling beneath its possibilities, never coinciding with itself, by transforming herself into the self-contained being of a thing – a stone that is nothing but a stone. Her repeated attempts to destroy that consciousness which reminds her of her separation from the world of nature, others, and from herself, is merely one transposition of the conflict between being and action. Like other Coetzee characters, she knows that it is only the consciousness never at one with itself that dwells in history and is compelled to make it. That which is complete in itself inhabits a realm blessedly beyond the prison of historical time.

There are times when one cannot escape the impression that J. M. Coetzee is struggling, albeit behind an extraordinary control and stylistic elegance, to combine his Western, modernist literary culture with an African historical reality which is hardly welcoming to it. This would partly explain the multiple ironies in his novels, perhaps also that element of cunning in their construction which so often appears as a form of self-protection. Coetzee, one might say, wants to preserve the contemplative, myth-making, sacralising impulse at the heart of modernism and nevertheless respond to an actual historical moment in which such an impulse could not seem more of an irrelevancy. In other words, he wants to preserve the aspects of both being and becoming. Still more evident, perhaps, is something that follows from his intellectual modernism and his contradictory position as a coloniser who refuses: a tendency to privilege the former term in that opposition. From *Dusklands* to *Life & Times of Michael K* there is an evident pull towards the mode of being, and always at the expense of action. Increasingly, History itself is relegated.

In the light of this, it is perhaps easier to understand why Coetzee's critique of colonialism should be so very unusual, at least in comparison with others. It is not because he conceives the historical phenomenon itself to be without material causes. That is not the question. Rather, I believe it takes its unusual form because he occupies a historical position, like many another writer in South Africa, which combines an unusual number of contradictory elements. Given all the factors pertinent to this position – the most important of which this essay has attempted to spell out – it is not particularly surprising that, in his case, a historical phenomenon with very definite material determinants should become a metaphysical history; that the metaphysics of power at the basis of the modern era should emerge as his chief preoccupation.

Nor is it surprising that there should have been objections to his work. Michael K concludes his life and times by musing:

> Now they have camps for children whose parents run away, camps for people who kick and foam at the mouth, camps for people with big heads and people with little heads, camps for people with no visible means of support, camps for people chased off the land, camps for people they find living in some storm-water drains, camps for street girls, camps for people who can't add two and two, camps for people who forget their papers at home, camps for people who live in the mountains and blow up bridges in the night. Perhaps the truth is that it is enough to be out of the camps, out of all the camps at the same time. Perhaps that is enough of an achievement, for the time being. How many people are there left who are neither locked up nor standing guard at the gate? I have escaped the camps; perhaps, if I lie low, I will escape the charity too. (*MK* 248–9)

To all of which a certain reader might reply: Yes, to have achieved this is some goal; to have written this is to have offered a powerful emblem of endurance, and more. But Michael K only escapes the camps by escaping history altogether. What sort of model does he provide for we readers who have to live in history and could not survive elsewhere? If he can only preserve his pumpkin-like being and slip like a stone through the bowels of the war by refusing to act in history; if being itself can only be preserved by those who are outsiders beyond the pale of society and its necessarily political practices; and if, conversely, a character like Jacobus Coetzee can only enter history and indeed make it at the price of a perpetual loss of being, at the expense of a burgeoning inner vacuum which is compelled to fill itself through ever more terrible acts of vengeance and orgies of destruction – is there not a contradiction here that is finally being evaded? Is Michael K's achievement (for the time being) really enough?

One's own answer to this sort of question will, of course, depend on any number of factors. If, for instance, one demands of any colonial literature that it lay bare the material interests at work in the phenomenon of colonialism itself as well as the ideological practices through which these interests are disguised, then Coetzee's novels will hardly satisfy. It might well seem as if his fictions do no more than give body to a series of myths which mystify no less than the old myths (primarily racist) which went hand in hand with the act of colonisation itself. After all, the argument might go, men seek refuge from history in myth. What they ought to be doing, whether writers or anything else, is dispelling myth by creating history, a new history.

I myself do not happen to take this view. This is, first, because the unique focus that emerges in his novels is definitely grounded in a certain historical position. Moreover, they never forget to call attention to themselves, however ironically, painfully, as the work of a certain type of intellectual and certain type of coloniser. If this entails an ambivalence in focus, then it should be remembered that contradiction as such is not necessarily a limitation. In Coetzee's case, quite the contrary. It is almost always turned to his own advantage. It serves to open up a perspective often ignored: to remind us that South Africa is part of a global historical process and that a certain mental structure created by this process is still rampant, here as elsewhere. In doing so, he has provided more insight into the colonising mind, as well as the dissenting colonising mind, than any of his contemporaries. And if this were not enough, there remains that passionate hunger in all of Coetzee's novels to escape the warped relationships that colonialism fosters. Nobody has given a more forceful expression to this hunger, and thereby delivered a more powerful indictment of all that the historical phenomenon entails.

Notes

1. As he says, 'I have taken it upon myself to be the one to pull the trigger, performing this sacrifice for myself and my countrymen, who exist, and committing upon the dark folk the murders we have all wished' (*D* 113).
2. In this sense Magda is nothing but a voice crying in the particular wilderness of the collapsed system of postmodernism for a world of liberal, bourgeois realism. It is one which, given the conditions in the heart of the country, can doubtless never materialise.

3

Speech and Silence in the Fictions of J. M. Coetzee

BENITA PARRY[1]

I

David Attwell maintains that Coetzee's novels are 'directed at understanding the conditions – linguistic, formal, historical and political – governing the writing of fiction in contemporary South Africa'. In turn, he offers the recent volume of interviews and essays he has edited as reflecting 'on an encounter in which the legacies of European modernism and modern linguistics enter the turbulent waters of colonialism and apartheid' (Attwell, *Doubling the Point* 3). This is an apt and elegant designation of the fictions' moment and space, and I use it as a starting point for considering the ways this fraught confluence is negotiated in self-reflexive novels which stage the impossibility of representation, estrange facility and work, in Coetzee's words, to 'demythologize history'.

The Attwell interviews with Coetzee are remarkable in that a notoriously reticent writer has been induced to speak about his homeless situation as an inhabitant and novelist in, but not of, Africa. One of the primary concerns of this essay is with variations on the theme of white South African deracination in Coetzee's fictions: a deracination upon which Coetzee, as his own critic, has commented. In these conversations, Coetzee disarmingly confesses that South Africa beyond the Cape 'has always felt like foreign territory to me' (Attwell 337); he recalls his apparently failed effort, when a graduate student in the US, to 'find an imaginative (and imaginary) place for myself in the Third World and its narratives of itself' by reading Césaire, Senghor and Fanon (Attwell 338); and he remarks that 'time in South Africa has been extraordinarily static for most of my life' (209) – a reference to the political order dominated by Afrikaner–Christian nationalism in which he grew up (he was born in 1940) and the culture in which he was educated, 'a culture looking, when it looked anywhere, nostalgically back to Little England'.

In identifying as a predicament the possibility of 'European ideas writing themselves out in Africa' (Attwell 339), Coetzee reiterates a problem he had already pursued in a previous book of essays, *White Writing*. Here he had asked: 'Is there a language in which people of European identity, or . . . of a highly problematical South African-colonial identity, can speak to Africa and be spoken to by Africa?' (*WW* 7–8). This is a matter to which he later returned when observing an uncertainty troubling white South African poets about 'whether the African landscape can be articulated in a European language, whether the European can be at home in Africa?' (167). Behind such questions, Coetzee continues, 'lies a historical insecurity regarding the place of the artist of European heritage in the African landscape . . . an insecurity not without cause' (62).

Metropolitan reviewers, as well as those critics whose attention, when reading South African novels, is focused on detecting condemnations of an egregious political system, are predisposed to proffer Coetzee's fictions as realist representations of, and humanist protests against, colonial rapacity in large, and against an intricately institutionalised system of racial oppression in particular.[2] Other critics whose concern is with the radicalism of Coetzee's textual practice, and who foreground parody and reflexivity as oppositional linguistic acts, argue that the authority of colonialism's narratives is undermined by subversive rewritings of the genres traditional to South African fiction – the heroic frontier myth, the farm romance, the liberal novel of stricken conscience[3] – hence opening conventions to scrutiny and confronting the traditional and unproblematised notion of the canon (see Attridge 'Oppressive Silence').

Such readings have come from Coetzee's most attentive critics, amongst some of whom there has been a tendency to construe the fictions as calculated transcriptions of the author's known critical stances on the instability of language and the unreliability of narration. The consequence is that paradox and impasse, gaps and silences are accounted for, not as textually generated through the interplay of the referential and the rhetorical, or by the interruptions of incommensurable discourses, but as the planned strategy of a highly self-conscious practice which displays the materials and techniques of its own process of production. More specifi-  cally, it has been suggested that by deliberately inscribing ambiguity, indeterminacy and absence, Coetzee's fiction registers the author's understanding of his own 'positional historicity', thus effecting a formal and aesthetic encoding or fictionalising of Jameson's premise on the political unconscious, and thereby preempting any effort by critics to theorise the elisions and ideological complicities inaugurated by the texts' spoken and unspoken cultural affiliations (see Attwell, 'The Problem of History').

What I want to consider here is how novels that weave a network of textual invocations traversing European literary and philosophical traditions, as well as contemporary theory from linguistics and structuralism to deconstruction, circumvent, or rather confirm, the quandary of white writing's insecurity or dislocation in South Africa: a quandary Coetzee as critic has detected. For the principles around which novelistic meaning is organised in Coetzee's fictions owe nothing to knowledges which are *not* of European provenance, but which *are* amply and variously represented in South Africa; while their disposals of Western interpretative paradigms are dispersed in a poised, even hieratic prose uninflected by South Africa's many vernacular Englishes.

That Coetzee's novels interrogate colonialism's discursive power is indisputable; through estrangement and irony, they make known the overdeterminations, fractures and occlusions of colonialist utterance, while their excavations of the uneasy, timid white South African liberal consciousness are amongst the furthest-reaching in South African writing. All the same, I want to consider whether the reverberations of Coetzee's intertextual transpositions, as well as the logic and trajectory of his narrative strategies, do not inadvertently reprise the exclusionary colonialist gestures which the novels also criticise. Let me put forward a polemical proposition: that despite the fictions' disruption of colonialist modes, the social authority on which their rhetoric relies and which they exert is grounded in the cognitive systems of the West. I suggest, furthermore, that the consequence of writing the silence attributed to the subjugated as a liberation from the constraints of subjectivity

– a representation to which I will return – can be read as re-enacting the received disposal of narrative authority.

The paradox contained by this hypothesis is that, in the double movement performed by Coetzee's novels, the subversions of previous texts enunciating discourses of colonial authority are permuted into renarrativisations where only the European possesses the word and the ability to enunciate, the lateral routes of the virtually plotless novels taking in nothing outside the narrators' world views and thereby sustaining the West as the culture of reference. A failure to project alterities might signify Coetzee's refusal to exercise the authority of his dominant culture to represent other, subjugated cultures, and might be construed as registering his understanding that agency is not something that is his to give or withhold through representation. Yet I will argue that the fictions do just this, and that European textual power, reinscribed in the formal syntax required of Literature, eventually survives the attempted subversion of its dominion.

Let me now modulate the terms of the argument. Richard Terdiman maintains that 'no discourse is ever a monologue, nor could it ever be adequately analyzed "intrinsically". Its assertions, its tone, its rhetoric – everything that constitutes it – always presupposes a horizon of competing, contrary utterances against which it asserts its own energies' (Terdiman 36). Coetzee's preferred modes, the diary, the journal and the letter – where the disingenuous transparency of the earliest forms of novel writing is problematised – make an apparently uncontested arena available to a speaking subject. In effecting an estrangement of the consciousness she or he articulates, this speaking subject manifests the solipsism of disquisition deprived of dialogue, while intimating another world whose agency is denied, or as in the recent novel *Age of Iron* (London 1990), deprecated for its modality as a violent political struggle. Perhaps, then, these narrative solutions stage the process of occluding contending enunciations, of disavowing other knowledges, of constructing and holding in place a hiatus, of construing a 'differend" between a narrator and its other – Lyotard's notion of a speech act in which the addressee is divested of the means to dispute the address.

But whereas Coetzee's novels enact the discursive processes whereby 'Bushman' and 'Hottentot', in *Dusklands* (Harmondsworth, 1974), the Barbarians, in *Waiting for the Barbarians* (London, 1980), the servants, in *In the Heart of the Country* (New York, 1982), the gardener, in *Life & Times of Michael K* (New York, 1983) and the enslaved black Friday, in *Foe* (New York, 1987), are muted by those who have the power to name and depict them, or whereby, as in *Age of Iron,* they are subjected to acts of ventriloquising, the dominated are situated as objects of representations and meditations which offer them no place from which to resist the modes that have constituted them as at the same time naked to the eye and occult. The question can be differently phrased, however, to privilege the force of an unspoken presence: do these figures, as Derek Attridge argues, register a 'new apprehension of the claims of *otherness,* of that which cannot be expressed in the discourse ordinarily available to us, not because of an essential ineffability but because it has been simultaneously constituted and excluded by that discourse in the very process of that discourse's self-constitution'? (Attridge, 'Literary Form and the Demands of Politics').

Consider 'The Narrative of Jacobus Coetzee' (*D* 1974), where the mimicry of three chronicles of the colonial enterprise is calculated to display the historical record as ideological fabrication and to undermine the commemoration of a colonialist mission. The narrative route moves from a critique of the colonialist calling that emerges from the enunciations of an acolyte alienating his own rhetoric, to a demythologising of the hagiographic mode favoured by historians of Boer expansion, to the diagnostic rewriting of a Dutch East India Company report transcribing an expedition made by an illiterate explorer into the hinterland of the Cape in 1760. The style of the last is that of the official chronicle into which the excited and fanciful mode of travel literature has intruded; its substance is an itinerary of the territory Jacobus Coetzee covered, the rivers and mountains he named, the people and physical landscape he encountered. Already, through hermeneutic revision, this supposedly archival testimony is shown to be a construction of how the observing eye of the European and a European nomenclature map a hitherto uninscribed earth, while the parody of Afrikaner scholarship in the 'Afterword' depicts this same 'Coetzee' as one who 'rode like a God through a world only partly made, differentiating and bringing into being' (*D* 116).

The irony that speaks through this naïve pedagogical version of Afrikaner historical recuperation is exceeded by Jacobus Coetzee's own narrative, where the speaker of a discourse is used by the language he uses in order to enunciate an ontology of white expansion, and to expose the pathology of the colonialist calling –

the speech of an illiterate eighteenth-century explorer being invested here with the linguistic range and speculative consciousness of an alienated twentieth-century intellectual acquainted with the literary canon, the literature of psychoanalysis and contemporary theories of language. In staging a beginning encounter between an explorer and proto-coloniser and a still undefeated and undomesticated Khoi-Khoi community, Jacobus Coetzee's story rehearses the multiple and conflicting enunciations in a colonial discourse. Hence, whereas Jacobus Coetzee details what he had earlier witnessed of the Khoi-Khoi physiques, music, dance, codes, ceremonies, taboos and belief in a creator, his exposition denounces them as a people sexually malformed, without art, ritual, magic, law, government or religion. 'What evidence was there', he rhetorically asks, 'that they had a way of life of any coherence?' Such disavowal is provoked by his perceiving the threat of their having 'a history in which I shall be a term' (*D* 81). Thus, it is imperative that they be found 'a place . . . in my history' (97), a move he initiates by depriving them of an immemorial habitation of the land, and by incorporating them as inconsequential figures into his chronicle of conquest.

The making of a colonial discourse and the process of silencing are dismantled here even as they are rehearsed. But what is there, in a narrative that is explicitly concerned to conceptualise a metaphysics of conquest, to contradict Jacobus Coetzee's doomed discovery that 'in that true wilderness without polity . . . everything, I was to find, was possible' (*D* 66), since the Khoi-Khoin are relegated as being unable to impinge on and participate in annulling the discourse of mastery disclosed by an auto-critique? Is the silence of these 'strange' and defeated people deployed here as a textual strategy which counters the colonising impulse and impudence in simulating another's voice? Might it be construed, alternatively, as a mute interrogation and disablement of discursive power? This second possibility is offered by Derek Attridge, who reads Coetzee's fictions as a continued and strenuous effort to figure alterity as a 'force out there disrupting European discourse', a force which is both resistant to the dominant culture and makes demands on it, not by entering into dialogue but by the 'very intensity of an unignorable "being there"' ('Literary Form and the Demands of Politics'). Or does this narrative muteness intimate a narrative disinclination to orchestrate a polyphonic score, the silenced remaining instead incommensurable, unknowable, unable to make themselves heard in the sealed linguistic code exercised by the narrating self and, thus, incapable of disturbing the dominant discourse?

Tzvetan Todorov, whose discussion of the other constituted by colonialism enlists the work of Levinas, has written that 'one does not let the other live merely by leaving him intact, any more than by obliterating his voice entirely . . . Heterology, which makes the difference of voices heard, is necessary' (Todorov 250, 251). This suggests a notion of commerce with alterity as a contact taking place in an intersubjective space which leaves both 'I' and 'you' separate and intact but enhanced, and where the non-identity of the interlocutors is respected and retained. A text written from within this interval of 'in-between' would register the opening of one's own discourse to strange accents and unfamiliar testimonies, but without suppressing or erasing difference, without pretending to simulate another's authentic voice or speaking on another's behalf, and without imprinting an ontological dissimilarity which simultaneously offers an explanation of, and excuse for, oppression. Such a procedure would engender a recombinant, 'neologistic' idiom, however; because it inscribes alterity not as a dumb presence but as an interlocutor, it would counter what Levinas names as 'the eclipse, the occultation, the silencing of the other'.[4]

II

Within the discussion of colonial and postcolonial discourse, silence has been read as a many-accented signifier of disempowerment and resistance, of the denial of a subject position and its appropriation. Emphasising the ambiguity of silence, Christopher Miller has written that because 'the voice remains our central metaphor for political agency and power . . . silence is the most powerful metaphor for exclusion from the literary modes of production', adding that while some insist on its oppressivity, others 'find in silence itself a different kind of word to be listened to, perhaps a strategy of resistance' (Miller 248, 250).[5] In keeping with this recognition of the multiple resonances to silence, some critics have construed Coetzee's deployment of the topos as if it were notated by the text to be intelligible as an emblem of oppression or to be audible as that unuttered but inviolable voice on which discourses of mastery cannot impinge and, thus, as an enunciation of defiance.

Gayatri Spivak, in her discussion of *Foe*, designates Friday as 'the unemphatic agent of withholding in the text', and Graham Huggan maintains that Coetzee's figuration of silence is an exemplary instance of a postcolonial writing where it is not an absence of or an incapacity for speech, but rather 'a different kind of speech, a muteness to be perceived either as a form of self-protection or a gesture of resistance'. Paola Splendore reads Michael K, the Barbarian Girl and Friday as 'characters who cannot speak or who refuse to speak the language of the foe, but whose silence shouts as if they were a thousand people screaming together', and for Derek Attridge 'a mode of fiction that exposes the ideological basis of canonisation . . . that thematizes the role of race, class and gender in the process of cultural acceptance and exclusion, and that, while speaking from a marginal location, addresses the question of marginality . . . would have to be seen as engaged in an attempt to break the silence in which so many are caught'. Only Debra Castillo, who observes that 'neither of the two narrative voices of *Dusklands* proposes itself as the voice of the other, a shadowy presence at best and one that retains an unreadable silence in all of Coetzee's novels', refrains from attributing intelligibility to the representations of aphonia.[6]

I want to suggest, however, that the various registers in which silence is scored in Coetzee's novels speak of things other than the structural relationship of oppressor/oppressed or the power of an unuttered alterity to undermine a dominant discourse and that these other things are signs of the fiction's urge to cast off worldly attachments, even as the world is signified and estranged. I have already tried to show how in 'The Narrative of Jacobus Coetzee', the process of muting is staged as an act of conquest. My hypothesis about Coetzee's figures of silence in the subsequent novels is that although they are the disentitled, and are therefore available to be read as manifesting subordination to, and retreat from, a subjugated condition, this potential critique of political oppression is diverted by the conjuring and valorising of a non-verbal signifying system.

By observing the texts' correspondence to the templates of psychoanalytic theories, and in particular to Kristeva's propositions on the transactions within the signifying process between the modalities of the 'semiotic' and the 'symbolic' or the 'thetic', it is possible to gloss the textual connections between the trope of silence and the simulacra of woman's writing as two different discourses of the body performed by those who are outsiders to a patriarchal linguistic/cultural order. Shared by Coetzee's protagonists of silence is an absence or economy of speech which is, in all cases, associated with sexual passivity or impotence: the hare-lipped Michael K, a gardener and progenitor of fruits and vegetables, lacks a father, a patronymic and sexual desire, and remains bonded to the mother; it is intimated that the mute Friday is possibly without either tongue or phallus; while the taciturn Vercueil in *Age of Iron* is perceived by the narrator as unable to beget children, his semen imagined as 'dry and brown, like pollen or the dust of this country' (*AOI* 180). These deficits have been read as signalling their location on the fringes of the phallocentric social order, whose dominance through their speechlessness and asexuality they evade.[7]

But although the silence of each of these figures has a distinctive tenor, what all signify is not a negative condition of lack and affliction or of sullen withdrawal, but rather a plenitude of perception and gifts: Michael K's aphasia facilitates a mystic consciousness; the verbal abstinence of the drunken and incontinent Vercueil, who means more than he says, is appropriate to his metaphysical status as the unlikely incarnation of an annunciation – 'verskuil' in Afrikaans means to obscure, conceal or mask; while the outflow of sounds from the mouth of Friday gives tongue to meanings – or desires – which precede or surpass those which can be communicated and interpreted in formal language. It could be argued, then, that speechlessness in Coetzee's fiction exceeds or departs from the psychoanalytic paradigm it also deploys, to become a metaphor for that potentous silence signifying what cannot be spoken – the undifferentiated echo of a Marabar Cave, a presence that is too sacred, revered and adored to be rendered in profane speech, or an event that is too terrible to be told and is told of instead, as in *Beloved,* by 'the holes – the things the fugitives did not say . . . the unnamed, the unmentioned'.

Coetzee's figures of silence are not without a quotidian dimension, and an inequality in social power is marked by the disparity between the obsessional will to utterance in Coetzee's female and European narrators, who literally perform the constitution of the subject in language and are authors of a discourse of the body, and the inaudibility of those who are narrated: Michael K, who is cryptically identified as Coloured (*MK* 96), is a propertyless labourer; Friday is a black slave and Vercueil is a tramp of unspecified race. This incipient critique of how deprivation inflicts silence on those who are homeless in a hierarchical social world is deflected, however, by the ascription of value to the disarticulated body, since the reader is simultaneously offered intimations of a non-linguistic intuitive consciousness, and is invited to witness the fruits of speechlessness that spring from a failure of the dialectic between the 'Imaginary' and the 'Symbolic' or, in Kristeva's vocabulary, between the 'semiotic' and the 'thetic'.

Both surmises can be referred to Michael K (*MK* 1983), who is written as a being without an identity, outside the writ where the Law of the Father runs, and as the exemplar of a mind turned inward. Spoken for in the narrative – his representation depends on 'he thought', 'he found', 'he said' – Michael K is interpreted as being too busy with fantasy 'to listen to the wheels of history' (217); he is 'a soul blessedly untouched by doctrine, untouched by history' (207) who lives in 'a pocket outside time' (82), has access to a numinous condition when he 'emptied his mind, wanting nothing, looking forward to nothing' (74), and attains an ineffable state of bliss on eating a pumpkin he had reared in a parodic act of parental nurturing.

Although the narrative gloss has him likening himself, a gardener, to 'a mole, also a gardener, that does not tell stories because it lives in silence' (248), Michael K is attributed with an ambition to interpret his own solitary, eidetic consciousness: 'Always when he tried to explain himself to himself, there remained a gap, a hole, a darkness before which his understanding baulked, into which it was useless to pour words. The words were eaten up, the gap remained. His was always a story with a hole in it' (150–1). Failure to attain and articulate self-consciousness is not rendered here as disappointment, since silence is privileged as enabling the euphoria of desire unmediated by words; alternatively, if Michael K is perceived as dramatising the inability to achieve a voice in the Symbolic order, then we can note that his 'loss of thetic function' is not represented as a lapse into psychosis but as a path to the visionary.

Because Friday's inner consciousness is not narrated (*Foe*, 1987), his silence is more secret, less available to the attention of conjectural readings, a sign of which is that he is offered alternative futures by the fiction, one within and the other outside the formal structures of language. In her discussion with Foe on how to bring Friday into the realm of representation, Susan Barton protests at Foe's proposal that he be shown writing, believing that since 'Letters are the mirror of words', Friday, who has no speech, can have no grasp of language. For Foe, on the other hand, writing is not a secondary representation of the spoken word but rather its prerequisite: 'Writing is not doomed to be the shadow of speech... God's writing stands as an instance of a writing without speech' (*F* 142, 143). It is Foe's view that would seem to prevail in the first narrative turn, where the prospect of Friday as a scribe is prefigured. Formerly the pupil of an Adamic language taught by Cruso and a pictographic script offered by Barton, Friday, who had previously uttered himself only in the 'semiotic' modes of music and dance, now takes his seat at Foe's desk, and with Foe's quill, ink and paper, and wearing Foe's wig, he appropriates the authorial role.

Friday, whose mouth is likened by Barton to an empty buttonhole, begins by forming Os, of which Coetzee has written 'The O, the circle, the hole are symbols of that which male authoritarian language cannot appropriate' (*F* 411). It is intimated, all the same, that Friday will go on to learn *a*, a portent of his acquiring linguistic competence. There is, however, yet another narrative turn, when the dreamlike quest of a contemporary narrator for Friday's story takes him into the hold of a wrecked ship. This time, Friday does not cross the threshold into logical and referential discourse, but remains instead in that paradisal condition where sign and object are unified, and where the body, spared the traumatic insertion into language, can give utterance to things lost or never yet heard: things whose meanings, we are given to understand, will water the globe:

> But this is not a place of words.... This is a place where bodies are their own signs. It is the home of Friday.... His mouth opens. From inside him comes a slow stream, without breath, without interruption... it passes through the cabin, through the wreck; washing the cliffs and shores of the island, it runs northward and southward to the ends of the earth. (*F* 157)

It would seem, then, that although the various figures of silence in Coetzee's fictions are the dominated and, hence, intimate disarticulation as an act of discursive power, they are not just 'victims' but also 'victors', accredited with extraordinary and transgressive psychic energies. Furthermore, since it is explicitly posited in the fiction that writing does not copy speech and is not its symbol or image, might we not consider whether for Friday, and the other disempowered figures who cannot or will not make themselves heard in the recognised linguistic system, their bodies are to be read as encoding a protowriting?[8] Friday's home is designated as 'a place where bodies are their own signs', and to the Magistrate in *Waiting for the Barbarians* (Penguin, 1980) who cannot understand the gestures of the Barbarian Girl, and who can communicate with her only in makeshift language without nuance, her body is a script to be decoded in the same way as the characters on the wooden slips he has excavated.

It is therefore notable that when Coetzee's novels stage another discourse of the body, it is not in the scripted silence of the lowly and the outcast, whose oppression is also the condition for their access to transcendence and/or intuitive cognition. Rather it is as the progeny of women who speak, albeit uneasily, from a position of entrenched cultural authority, while also articulating their homelessness in and opposition to the patriarchal order. Three of Coetzee's narrators so far have been women, and while he seems to be enlisting the notion of the body as progenitor of woman's language – a notion posited by several feminist theorists (for a critique see Moi, 1985 and Jones, 1986) – it is less certain that the writing transgresses standard usage to register the irruptions of repressed libidinal elements into the performative text.

It is evident, however, that Coetzee's female narrators explicitly represent the body as the agent of language: Mrs Curren, in *Age of Iron*, declares in her letters to an absent daughter that her words 'come from my heart, from my womb' (*AOI* 133), assigning to writing the properties of the genetically communicated code – the phylogenetic inheritance made flesh in print: 'These words, as you read them . . . enter you and draw breath again. . . . Once upon a time you lived in me as once upon a time I lived in my mother; as she still lives in me, as I grow towards her, may I live in you' (120). In another register, Susan Barton, in *Foe*, who asks 'Without desire, how is it possible to make a story?' (*F* 88), asserts that 'The Muse is a woman, a goddess, who visits poets in the night and begets stories upon them' (126), while Magda, in *In the Heart of the Country*, rejects her 'father-tongue' as a language of hierarchy which is not 'the language my heart wants to speak' and longs for 'the resonance of the full human voice... the fullness of human speech' (*IHC* 97, 47).

In Coetzee's imitations of woman's writing, there is a tension between the striving after a discourse of the pre-symbolic and the language of the symbolic in which this is articulated. Magda's search for a condition before the body's insertion into the homelessness of language alights on the speech of the Coloured servants as the repository of a prelapsarian condition (in this reiterating a colonialist conceit); while her utterance of the aspiration to that euphoric consciousness discernible in the figures of silence – 'a life unmediated by words, these stones, these bushes, this sky experienced and known without question' (*IHC* 135) – succeeds where they failed in authoring a story from which, as in the rejected discourse, the testimony of the 'brown folk' is erased. Similarly, Mrs Curren's praise of motherhood, far from being saturated with joy and ecstasy, is delivered in a vocabulary and syntax appropriate to her status as an educated white South African, while her representations of Africans issue in pastiches of naturalist reportage and morally outraged protest writing, modes which Coetzee is known to despise, and which are directed at displaying the banality of a white South African literature which undertakes to write the voice of the oppressed. (Against the grain of a novel which parodies the liberal mode of making known the inner world of Africans by mediating their speech, *Age of Iron* nonetheless registers an African woman's eloquent contempt for the White world, in her laconic responses to the narrator's expressions of sympathy for her servant's grief at the death of a son killed by the police.)

All Coetzee's female narrators resolutely position themselves as authors of their own narratives:

> I have uttered my life in my own voice... I have chosen at every moment my own destiny. (Magda, 139)

> I am a free woman who asserts her freedom by telling her story according to her own desire... the story I desire to be known by is the story of the island. (Susan Barton, 131, 121)

> How I live, how I lived: my story... my truth, how I lived in these times, in this place. (Elizabeth Curren 140, 119)

However, in terms of dis/identification with masculine narrative traditions, each produces a differently accented script. Whereas the recitations of Magda and Elizabeth Curren ostentatiously enunciate maternal desire, Susan Barton in *Foe* (although insisting on her freedom as a woman to choose her speech and her silence) affirms her wish to be 'father to my story' (*F* 123), holding out against Foe in suppressing 'the history of a woman in search of a lost daughter' (121), and thus refusing to write a discourse of motherhood. Alone amongst Coetzee's narrators, Barton articulates a reluctance to exert the narrative power which she holds over those who are muted, when she resists Foe's urgings to invent Friday's story 'which is properly not a story but a puzzle or hole in the narrative' (121).

It is above all in *Foe*, which amplifies its status as a book about writing a book, that the disparate strategems of novelistic authority are conspicuously and self-reflexively dramatised. The dialogue of Foe and Barton condenses a contest between protagonists holding different positions on language and representation. With her commitment to the priority of speech, Susan Barton formulates the task as descending into Friday's mouth, seeking a means to use Friday as an informant in order to fill the hole in her narrative: 'It is for us to open the mouth and hear what it holds' (*F* 142). But to the exponent of writing's primacy and the father of linear realist narrative – 'It is thus that we make up a book . . . beginning, then middle, then end' (117) – it is the author's brief to fabricate another's consciousness and circumstances: 'We must make Friday's silence speak, as well as the silence surrounding Friday . . . as long as he is dumb we can tell ourselves his desires are dark to us, and continue to use him as we wish' (142, 148).

Is Coetzee's fiction free from the exercise of that discursive aggression it so ironically displays, since it repeatedly and in different registers feigns woman's writing? The artifice of the rhetoric perhaps serves to foreground that these texts are artefacts contrived by a masculine writer pursuing the possibilities of a non-phallocentric language. But why, in that case, does a male novelist take the risk of simulating woman's speech, indeed her self-constitution in language – Magda declares 'I create myself in the words that create me', while Elizabeth Curren writes 'I render myself into words' – while this same white novelist refrains from dissembling the voices of those excluded from the dominant discourse (where such voices are audible, their status as written by a white narrator is made apparent), instead elevating their silence into the sign of a transcendent state? If, as I have suggested, both the topos of silence and the imitations of a woman's writing act to transcribe and valorise the body as an agent of cognition, then both the claim that the fiction manifests an identification with feminism and the charge that it consigns the dispossessed to a space outside discourse could be dismissed as irrelevant to the novels' interests. Such an argument overlooks the fact that the effects of bestowing authority on the woman's text, while withholding discursive skills from the dispossessed, is to reinscribe, indeed re-enact, the received disposal of narrative power, where voice is correlated with cultural supremacy and aphonia with subjugation, just as the homages to the mystical properties and prestige of muteness disperse the critique of that condition where oppression inflicts and provokes silence.

It is tempting to associate Coetzee's deployment of silence with the mute Africa of *Heart of Darkness* which, in its 'unknowability' and its own 'overwhelming reality', is resistant to incorporation into European discourse, its unrepresentable presence rendered in an obscure, ornate and obfuscatory language and engendering a crisis in Marlow's adherence to the ethic of work and duty. Were Coetzee's figures of alterity to be read as dramatising the texts' destabilisation by a wholly different discursive realm, then its modality as an otherworldly state beyond subjectivity and the secular would set the same limits on its power to oppose the dominant discourse as does Conrad's metaphysical 'Africa', the space of both novels remaining sealed from that heterology in which the narrative discourses are inflected by the tones, accents and testimony of other voices.

Coetzee as critic, surveying the South African pastoral novel, has written with regret about the ways we now read silence:

> Our ears today are finely attuned to modes of silence. We have been brought up on the music of Webern: substantial silence structured by tracings of sound. Our craft is all in reading *the other*: gaps, inverses, undersides; the veiled; the dark, the buried, the feminine; alterities. To a pastoral novel like *The Beadle* we give an antipastoral reading . . . alert to the spaces in the text. . . . Only part of the truth, such a reading asserts, resides in what writing says of the hitherto unsaid; for the rest, its truth lies in what it dare not say for the sake of its own safety, or in what it does not know about itself: in its silences. It is a mode of

> reading which, subverting the dominant, is in peril, like all triumphant subversion, of becoming the dominant in turn. Is it a version of utopianism (or pastoralism) to look forward (or backward) to the day when the truth will be (or was) what is said, not what is not said, when we will hear (or heard) music as sound upon silence, not silence between sounds? (*WW* 81)

Without reiterating the implications of turning his discriminating gaze on his own fiction, I would suggest that Coetzee's writing, rather than exploring the dialectic between sound and silence, or teaching us to hear sound as trespassing on silence, situates its inarticulate protagonists, who intimate the mystery of enigmatic, non-verbal modes of cognition they are unable or unwilling to narrate, as the objects of another's narratives. This secretion of contradictory meanings suggests that 'what [Coetzee's] writing says of the hitherto unsaid' may be other than what the critics are saying about his silences.

III

I have attempted so far to argue that Coetzee's narrative strategies both enact a critique of dominant discourses and pre-empt dialogue with non-canonical knowledges through representing these as ineffable. I now want to consider whether the noticeable absence of inflections from South Africa's non-Western cultures in the narrative structure, language and ethos of Coetzee's fictions registers and repeats the exclusions of colonialist writing: omissions on which Coetzee has commented in identifying 'the baffling and silencing of any counter-voice to the farmer/father' in the South African farm romance (*WW* 135). The eclipse, the occultation, the silencing of the other, is, after all, what South Africa's settler colonialism, as the self-appointed representative of Western civilisation in Africa, was intent on effecting. Hence, the cognitive traditions and customs of South Africa's indigenous peoples were derogated and ignored, as were those of the practitioners of two world religions whose communities in South Africa were initially brought as slaves from the Dutch East Indies in the seventeenth century and as indentured labourers from the Indian subcontinent in the nineteenth century.

The paradox here is that whereas South Africa's institutional structure has internally duplicated the divide between the hemispheres, and its state apparatus has exercised an imperialist ascendancy over neighbouring and *de jure* autonomous territories, within the orbit of imperialism's global system it was, and still is, an outpost complicit with but on the boundaries of the West's power centres: its mining and heavy industries are dominated by multinational capital, and its white comprador class is deferential to the cultures of the metropolitan worlds. This inessential status in relationship to Europe was registered in the founding novel of white South African writing in English, Olive Schreiner's *The Story of an African Farm.* In Schreiner's novel, the books in the loft belonging to Em's English father, the shelf of books cherished by the German overseer and the books given to Waldo by his French-looking Stranger, are signs of a secular explanatory system imported from Europe into a land which is deemed as having no native resources with which to validate itself – the Dutch too had brought a book with them, but only The Book.

Such subservience was perpetuated, as Coetzee has shown in his essays, in the adoption/adaptation of established European fictional genres by both English and Afrikaans literatures. These, until the 1950s, were overwhelmingly aligned with, and served to naturalise the ideology of, white supremacy and segregation coterminous with Boer, British and subsequent diverse European settlement. Such writing is now virtually extinct, while a literature predominantly in English, but also increasingly in Afrikaans, has positioned itself as opposed to the status quo.

The identification of white literature with the traditions of the first world has been a given for writers: a remark of the expatriate novelist Dan Jacobson, to the effect that settler colonial societies cannot sustain a culture, suggests how resolutely he turns his back on the possibility of this settler society participating in generating new formations through its interaction with the cultures of South Africa's volatile non-European communities, who have been instrumental in effecting transculturation. Consider too that the flight of the Sestigers, a group of young avant-garde Afrikaner writers escaping from the constraints of a militant nationalism, took them during the 1960s, not towards those ethnically diverse groupings resisting the regime and ethos of White South Africa, but to Paris, perhaps in search of their seventeenth-century Huguenot ancestors who had disappeared into the

Afrikaner nation. To culturally insecure, dislocated white South African writers such as these, Europe is the imaginary and imagined homeland from which they have been exiled. And whether it is to classical and modernist realism or to postmodernism that they turn for inspiration and sustenance, these writers have remained dependent on metropolitan modes – although critics are now claiming that the later Nadine Gordimer, and those younger white writers who have transgressed cultural insulation and assimilated knowledges and accents from which previous generations were through circumstance and choice isolated, are on the brink of inventing other forms in their plurally located and multiply voiced 'post-apartheid' novels.[9]

Meanwhile, the predominant mode of the South African novel, white and black, remains social realism, a mode from which Coetzee, in his critical writings, has intimated his distance. Reviewing a study of Gordimer in 1980, Coetzee disputed the author's contention that her writing is 'engaged in undermining the structures of time that the realist novel as a genre embodies', arguing that 'whatever she is, Gordimer is not an innovator in narrative method. *The Conservationist*, technically her most complex novel, does not use any technique that had not been used by 1930'. When, in a later review, Coetzee noted Gordimer's interest 'in herself as the site of a struggle between a towering European tradition and the whirlwind of the new Africa' and commended 'an oeuvre that constitutes a major piece of historical witness', his appreciation in no way reverses his earlier judgment of her modes as conventional.[10]

If Coetzee's own writing defamiliarises the practices of white South African fiction, then its subversions of the representational paradigm also sets it apart from black writing, which, for complex historical reasons, is similarly indebted to established Western modes. Shared by the black novel and the short story, often autobiographical in inspiration, and historically concrete in location and moment, the fictionalised journalism/journalistic fiction first devised in the 1950s by the *Drum* generation, and the populist realism of the prose, performance poetry and drama generated by the Black Consciousness movement of the 1970s and 1980s, which found a home in the magazine *Staffrider*, is an impulse to register the heterogeneous black experience in its own oppositional terms and its own resistant voice. Although spokesmen for the project of a 'new black aesthetic' mooted during the 1970s and

1980s had declared 'we are going to kick and pull and push and drag literature into the form we prefer', recommending a violently innovative diction, dislocated syntax and explosive narrative structures that would produce a literal enactment of social disjunctions and political conflicts, this radical programme was largely implemented in further experiments within an urgent social realism that frequently issued as an extreme 'naturalism'.

The persistence of an overwhelmingly testamentary writing led one critic working in the United States to consider 'why black South African literature remains outside the problematic of a modernist or postmodern culture', asking if a pre-modern literature is not a 'necessity . . . for a dominated and struggling people', and questioning whether to reflect on modernity and modernism, postmodernity and postmodernism is not 'always already ethnocentric because it excludes one important dimension of the current global system of capitalism by concentrating on an issue that belongs solely to the "first world"?' (Schulte-Sasse 5–22). The congruence and incongruence of forces in South Africa's combined and uneven development (a mining capitalism dependent on a pre-capitalist labour force is a striking instance), the co-existence and overlap of different modes of production, multiple vernaculars and distinctive heritages, and the recombined cultural forms and innovative Englishes engendered by the black majority, all suggest the relevance of these issues to the critical discussion. They also suggest that the very disjunctions and contradictions, as well as the transactions and flows, between pre-modern and modern forms, would have stimulated innovatory literary modes.

The designation of black writing as 'pre-modern' could be disputed, however, or even dismissed; for while white South Africa denied itself the pleasures of cross-cultural inventions, the various black communities, because of urbanisation, albeit in situations of planned deprivation, because of participation in high-tech industries, albeit as a massively exploited work force, and because of an educational system designed to keep them in their subordinate place but which gave them restricted access to literacy, have been the agents of transculturation processes in South Africa. If English, the language of the cities, remains the predominant medium of print culture, it has also enabled transnational perspectives, since not only English sources but the writings of European, Asian, African and Latin American novelists, intellectuals and revolutionaries are accessible in translation, making possible the recitations of Césaire's poetry, Fanon's addresses and the prose of Baldwin and Baraka as public events. Nor does a literature of attestation preclude the enlargement of realist form, or the infiltration of pre- and post-realist discourses, procedures which have been effected by the transgression of generic frontiers between documentation and fabrication, autobiography and fiction, as well as by the incorporation of older, oral modes of story-telling within narrative structures adapted from those developed on other continents and at other times.

In these departures, critics argue, the writing of black women – delayed by their more effective separation from the technologies of the text and occupying what one critic has described as 'the ravaged ground where class, race and gender oppression intersect' – has been prominent. Such writing, it is maintained, has challenged the masculine accents of the black literary tradition and the newer fighting literature, both of which protest class and race oppression while continuing to thematise woman's subordination and to project male agency. A writing which negotiates the tensions between the female self, still largely conceived as wife and mother, and the affiliation to being black, within narratives which foreground the immediate conditions and social forces making for woman's multiple oppressions, both criticises patriarchal relations extant within traditional structures and transgresses the preoccupation with the black urban experience by calling upon the epistemological and linguistic resources of new disrupted peasant societies. In forging a link between urban and rural women, black women's writing has broken the silence about the ancestors imposed by the regime's invention of distinct, incompatible ethnic traditions: an invention which has served the interests of segregation through maintaining the fiction of separate African 'nations'.[11]

While the material conditions of oppression generated a literature bearing witness to black experiences and aspirations, the question of why writers turned to the existing fictional forms must be asked. Perhaps the restricted privilege of a liberal education, shaped by a British-influenced academic practice, delivered the ready-made example of the European novel as the unsurpassable medium of social and ethical critique. Certainly such a training brought with it the constraints of a literary aesthetic privileging the organicism, coherence and 'high moral seriousness' of the classic realist text. Noticeably, two prominent black critics of older generations, both of whom censure the limitations of protest writing, appear inhospitable to formal experimentation, recommending in one case a literature that documents 'the vicissitudes of African society at major points of crisis', reconstructing the precolonial past and chronicling the struggle against colonialism; and in the other positing the necessity of producing 'compelling imaginative recreations of hitherto ignored themes and settings'.[12]

The preference for a responsible realism aimed at reclaiming black history and registering black agency, was reinforced on different grounds by 'cultural agendas' devised by the most visible organisations of the liberation movement. These decreed that writers commit themselves to developing a purposeful, expressive and accessible literature depicting oppression, illuminating the struggle, and serving to raise consciousness. Such demands in turn generated a 'solidarity criticism', which by arguing that evaluation should be based on cultural function, encouraged the praise of unmodulated and declamatory prose, poetry and drama, and inhibited the debate on what might constitute a revolutionary act.[13] A climate in which established Anglo-American critical paradigms vied with political programmes for the arts is now changing. This is evident in the founding of at least two journals participating in the transnational debates on critical theory and postcolonial criticism, and in the self-interrogations of critics and writers who, as members of one or other community, are aligned with the struggle, and who, as scholars, are aware that the discussion on autonomy and commitment in the arts in South Africa is in urgent need of redefinition.[14]

IV

It is from within this specific literary landscape that I now want to look at Coetzee's implementation of 'a politics of writing for postcolonial literatures' – his own terms. Detached from the predominant modes of South African writing, obliquely situated to the prevailing intellectual formations of his native land, whether white nationalism, liberally socialist-liberationism or black consciousness, and little touched by the autochthonous, transplanted and recombinant cultures of South Africa's African, Asian and Coloured populations, Coetzee negotiates 'South Africa' as a referent in his fictions through defamiliarising strategies which efface its spatial and temporal specificity, denying it the identity of a social space and rejecting it as a site of cultural meanings. In one of the Attwell interviews, Coetzee, while speaking with admiration about the 'passionate intimacy with the South African landscape' of fellow writer Breyten Breytenbach (Attwell, *Doubling the Point* 377), and the ostensible pleasure which playwright Athol Fugard takes in the beauty of South Africa (369), explains his own refusal to contrive 'nature description' of the Cape on the grounds that this represents no challenge to his 'power of envisioning', threatening 'only the tedium of reproduction' (142).

Such abstinence, I would argue, has further implications. In his critical writing, Coetzee has detected an impulse in the South African pastoral mode 'to find evidence of a "natural" bond between *volk* and *land*, that is to say, to naturalise the *volk's* possession of the land', observing too that 'the politics of expansion has uses for a rhetoric of the sublime' (*WW* 61). It is these connections between landscape and the legitimising narrative of the white nation which the novels sever by ostentatiously failing to register any signs of splendour in the very scenery that has inspired rhapsody.

Hence, the terrain mapped by 'The Narrative of Jacobus Coetzee' constitutes an ideological cartography, the naming by an eighteenth-century explorer and proto-colonialist of rivers and mountains, and the designation of flora and fauna as yet uncatalogued in European taxonomies, establishing the authority of the invader's nomenclature and marking the act of territorial acquisition. Magda, in *In the Heart of the Country*, atones for her confession 'I am corrupted to the bone with the beauty of this forsaken world' (138), by spurning the tropes and topoi of the South African pastoral tradition and by rendering the scene as existentially sterile, her lapses into humanising the spectacle being swiftly followed by recantation. The pastiche of naturalist conventions in the litany of place-names that tracks Michael K's journey through the Cape Province, registers the past occupation of the territory by Afrikaner and British settlement, but screens the meticulously inventoried locations from the infiltration of affect. In *Age of Iron*, the romance and promise with which European voyagers infused their accounts of the fairest Cape in all the world, The Cape of Good Hope, are demystified when the majestically serene and smiling peninsula of legend is configured in a rain-soaked suburb built with bricks made by convict labour, and the drably named 'False Bay' is redesignated a 'bay of false hope'.

In thus estranging and decathecting a landscape named as the Cape, Coetzee's narrators effect a distancing from the historic claim to the land celebrated by white settler writing. But does not rendering a locale as null and void repeat that 'literature of empty landscape' which Coetzee has designated a literature of failure because it articulates a homelessness in Africa? Further, does not restricting the site of the colonial drama to the Cape act to produce a truncated version of the narrative of conquest which the fiction invents in 'The Narrative of Jacobus Coetzee'? Because the beginning colonial confrontation is played out here between Afrikaner and Khoi-San, the so-called Hottentots and Bushmen whose resistance was effectively crushed, whose populations were decimated and whose cultures were dispersed, the boundedness of the staging excludes the violent and prolonged struggles that took place between the white settlers as they moved across the southern subcontinent and the Nguni- and Sotho-speaking peoples, where the military defeat and dispossession of the latter did not entail genocide. And indeed, since Coetzee's fiction only leaves the Cape and its immediate hinterland for the unnamed and unspecified imperial frontier of *Waiting for the Barbarians* and the textually received locations of *Foe,* it might perhaps even be seen as turning its face from Africa.

When Africans do enter the South African present of Coetzee's more recent novel, *Age of Iron,* the passing of so pitiless an era is contemplated by the narrator as a return to kinder times, to the age of clay, the age of earth. A novel which speaks an intimacy with death has been welcomed in reviews as an allegory where the narrator's affliction with cancer is a figure of a diseased body politic – and certainly this is a connection which her rhetoric insistently makes. But since the narrative of Elizabeth Curren's dying occupies a different discursive space from the story of South Africa's bloody interregnum, her terminal illness is detached from the demise of a malignant social order. Her salvation, effected by Vercueil, the tramp-as-figure-of-deliverance who ensures that in the disgraceful state of South Africa she will die in a state of grace, also draws attention to the absence of any prospect on another, transfigured South Africa. This withholding of the gesture to a politics of fulfilment, in a novel which does intimate a personal redemption, is made all the more conspicuous because the aspiration of the oppressed for emancipation detaches the narrator from a liberal–humanist ethic, while the text's refusal to countenance the hope for a tomorrow – 'the future comes disguised, if it came naked we would be petrified by what we saw' (*AOI* 149) – is perhaps the strongest signification yet of the fiction's urge to mark its disengagement from the contingencies of a quotidian world in transition from colonialism.

All the same, another ending narrated by *Age of Iron* has very different resonances, for in taking to its limits the only political discourse to which she has access, the narrator recites a requiem for South African liberalism. Because Mrs Curren's wrath and loathing are directed against the Afrikaners, whom she blames as the architects of the 'crime' committed in her name, she might appear to be acquitting her own English-speaking community of any culpability – as she explicitly does when speaking the customary protest of South African liberalism against an illegitimate and irrational domination which stops short of unequivocal support for radical change. Yet when she discerns the exclusions in an old photograph taken long ago in her grandfather's burgeoning garden, self-exculpation is suspended, and nostalgia for the golden days of her childhood, 'when the world was young and all things were possible' (51), is annulled:

> Who, outside the picture, leaning on their rakes, leaning on their spades, waiting to get back to work, lean also against the edge of the rectangle, bending it, bursting it in? . . . No longer does the picture show who were in the garden frame that day, but who were not there. Lying all these years in places of safekeeping across the country, in albums, in desk drawers, this picture and thousands like it have subtly matured, metamorphosed. The fixing did not hold or the developing went further than one would ever have dreamed . . . but they have become negatives again, a new kind of negative in which we begin to see what used to lie outside the frame, occulted. (*AOI* 102–3)

That this act of erasure in white self-representation cannot be restored by Elizabeth Curren's story is the burden of a narrative whose efforts to bring the blacks into representation only issues in bathos, when pastiches of a benign naturalism and moral outrage all too familiar in the South African protest novel are offered, and the exhaustion of the liberal tradition of white fiction which this signals is confirmed by the death of its author. But does not this extended metaphor of the eclipse, the silencing, the occultation of the other in the chronicle of white South Africa, have yet further reverberations which hark back to the exclusions, the holes in the narratives, 'the baffling of counter-voices' in Coetzee's own novels?

Within the current South African discussion, those critics who have argued for the oppositional energies of Coetzee's novels defend his project against those who have castigated his fictions as out of touch with the sensibilities of the times and indifferent to the existential conditions of contemporary South Africa.[15] The question of 'who speaks' in Coetzee's writing, which has been the central concern of this essay, cannot be disconnected from 'who listens' and how the novels are received. Translated into Western and Eastern European languages, as well as Turkish and Hebrew, and widely read in the Anglophone world, which of course includes many formerly colonised territories, Coetzee's fiction has won important South African, British and European literary awards, as well as the Jerusalem Prize, and has been widely embraced as a powerful moral critique of apartheid. It is also at home in the global, if restricted, discussion on the radicalism of postmodernism and the revolutionary innovations of postcolonial writing. Towards these last cognitive circles Coetzee has been hospitable, having spoken of the cultural affinities between communities in the so-called 'peripheries' of the metropolitan world, who have a title to an international language, and who share an engagement in developing a politics of writing for postcolonial literature.[16] But who, in South Africa, does Coetzee's fiction address? And whose attention has been procured? That the recent comprehensive *Bibliography* on Coetzee lists few contributions from black critics and writers[17] is a sign of how the system has until now inhibited the numbers of black literary scholars; it may also suggest continuing cultural schisms between the communities and their different interests, perceptions and concerns.

Although Coetzee, who is publicly cool about embattled South African writing, has participated in the activities of the Congress of South African Writers, he is notable amongst contemporary white writers for his refusal to be drafted into the struggle against the South African state or to offer himself as the conscience of his community. Whereas Nadine Gordimer has spoken of the white writer's forbidding responsibility to change the consciousness of white people, and André Brink has written of 'the need for literature to take arms within and against the socio-political relations of South Africa',[18] Coetzee has been concerned with safeguarding his fiction from incorporation into a critique of the South African condition. In an interview during the early 1980s with students from the University of Cape Town, where he is a Professor of Literature, Coetzee insisted: 'what I am now resisting is the attempt to swallow my novels into a political discourse . . . because, frankly, my allegiances lie with the discourse of the novels and not with the discourse of politics' (as cited in Dovey, *The Novels of J. M. Coetzee* 55). Since then, he has strongly endorsed the notion of the novel as a form 'that operates in terms of its own procedures and issues in its own conclusions . . . that evolves its own paradigms and myths, in the process . . . perhaps going so far as to show up the mythic status of history – in other words, demythologising history' (as cited in Attwell, 'The Problem of History' 101).

Perhaps the constraints of a critical environment commending functionality and demanding overt commitment has prompted Coetzee to uphold the autonomy of literature, while the coarse vocabulary of cultural agendas and the impassioned rhetoric of the liberation movements may have nourished his Olympian distaste for 'all political language'. Pondering on this proclivity in the third person, Coetzee remarks: 'As far back as he can see he has been ill at ease with language that lays down the law, that is not provisional, that does not as one of its habitual motions glance back sceptically at its own premises. Masses of people wake in him something close to panic. He cannot or will not, cannot and will not, join, shout, sing: his throat tenses up, he revolts' (Attwell, *Doubling the Point* 394).

In protesting against the predicament of writing's compliant instrumentality, Coetzee as his own critic appears determined to detach his novels from their worldly connections. While it does not follow that his novels are so dissociated, I have considered here whether a body of fiction which is at such pains to avoid playing 'the flat historic scale' does not position barriers against readings that would privilege its secular particularity. In his Introduction to the Field Day *Anthology of Irish Writing* (1991), Seamus

Deane, who rejects the truism that all writing is profoundly political, has written: 'We are concerned rather to show how this is sometimes openly acknowledged and at other times urgently concealed'. The apparent referents of Coetzee's fictions have encouraged their literal interpretation as protests against colonial conquest, political torture and social exploitation, while critics have argued that by subverting colonialism's oppressive discourses, his work performs 'a politics of writing'. What I have attempted to suggest is how a fiction which in its multivalence, formal inventiveness and virtuoso self-interrogation of narrative production and authority remains unmatched in South African writing, is marked by the further singularity of a textual practice which diverts and disperses the engagement with political conditions it also inscribes, but which remains, for all that, 'ethically saturated' (Lazarus).

Notes

References are made to the Penguin editions of Coetzee's novels, excepting *Age of Iron* (London: Secker and Warburg).

1. Although I am aware that they will continue to dissent from the revisions, I am indebted to the stringent criticisms made of an earlier version by Derek Attridge and David Attwell, which prompted me to reformulate some of the arguments.
2. See, for example, Gallagher and Penner.
3. See Dovey, *The Novels of J. M. Coetzee*; Attwell, 'The Problem of History'.
4. See *Totality and Infinity*, trans. A Lingis. On Levinas, see *The Provocation of Levinas*. For the deployment of Levinas's theories in discussions of the other constructed by colonialism, see Todorov; also Mason, *Deconstructing America*.
5. On silence as a privileged signifier of postcolonial writing, see Ashcroft, Griffiths and Tiffin. See also Paulo Freire's writings, where silence signifies a culture of defeat and resignation.
6. See Spivak, 'Theory in the Margin' (172); Huggan, 'Philomela's Retold Story' (12–23); Splendore, 'J. M. Coetzee's *Foe*' (55–60); Attridge, 'Oppressive Silence' (4–5); Castillo, 'Coetzee's *Dusklands*' (1108–22).
7. See Kristeva, *Desire in Language*; Moi, *Sexual/Textual Politics*; Moi (ed.), *The Kristeva Reader*; Jones, 'Writing the Body' in Showalter (ed.); Fletcher and Benjamin (eds), *Abjection, Melancholia and Love*.
8. Are there echoes here, as in the representation of a silent consciousness,

of Derrida's critique of Husserl? See *Speech and Phenomena and Other Essays on Husserl's Theory of Signs*: 'The autonomy of meaning with regard to intuitive cognition . . . has its norm in writing. . . . The use of language or the employment of any code which implies a play of forms . . . also presupposes a retention and pretension of differences, a spacing and temporalising, a play of traces. This play must be a sort of inscription prior to writing, a protowriting without a present origin, without an arche' (Derrida 97, 146).

9. On Gordimer, see Clingman, *The Novels of Nadine Gordimer*; Cooper, 'New Criteria for an "Abnormal Mutation"?', in *Rendering Things Visible*. The notion of the white 'post-apartheid novel' has been mooted by Graham Pechey in numerous reviews that have appeared in the *Southern African Review of Books*.
10. See *Research in African Literatures* 11.2 (Summer 1980): 253–6; *Doubling the Point* (386, 387). The question of which mode exercises the most subversive power under contemporary South African conditions has been raised by Neil Lazarus who argues for the subversive power of modernism; see 'Modernism and Modernity' (131–55).
11. For information and analysis, I am indebted to the work of contributors to a special issue of *Current Writing: Text and Reception in Southern Africa* 2 (October 1990) on *Feminism and Writing*; to the essays of Cooper, Driver and Press, all in *Rendering Things Visible*; and to Nixon, 'Border Country: Bessie Head's Frontline States', *Social Text*, Fall 1993, reprinted in Gunner and Nasta (eds), *Commonwealth Literatures*, 1993.
12. See Nkosi, 'The New African Novel: A Search for Modernism', in *Tasks and Masks* (55); Ndebele, 'Redefining Relevance' (45–50). See also Parker, '"Traditionalism" versus "Modernism": Culture, Identity, Writing', to appear; Morphet, 'Cultural Imagination and Cultural Settlement'. For an assessment of the radicalisms of Ndebele's criticism, see Anthony O'Brien, 'Literature in Another South Africa: Njabalo Ndebele's Theory of Emergent Culture', *Diacritics* 22: 1 (Spring 1992) 67–85.
13. See de Kok and Press (eds), *Spring is Rebellious: Arguments About Cultural Freedom*. My review of the above appeared in *Transition* 55 (1991). For a thoughtful piece on the culture of opposition in Central America, see Brennan.
14. *Current Writing: Text and Reception in Southern Africa*, published by the English Department, University of Natal at Durban; *Pretexts: Studies in Literature and Culture*, published by the Arts Faculty, University of Cape Town. See also *Rendering Things Visible*, *Spring is Rebellious*; Gordimer, 'Turning the Page', 'The Future is Another Country'.
15. For example, Michael Chapman, a White Professor of English, who in a review of *Foe* charged Coetzee with elitism: *Southern African Review of Books* (1988/1989): 14. See also the 'Round Table' discussion in *Commonwealth* 9.1 (1986), an issue devoted to Coetzee. For a critique of Coetzee's critics, see Attwell (1990).
16. Cited in *Southern African Review of Books* 2.3 (1989): 13.

17. See *J. M. Coetzee: A Bibliography*, compiled by Goddard and Read, intro. Dovey. One exception to the silence of black critics on Coetzee's work is a review of *Foe* by Neville Alexander, political activist, writer and educationalist, who reads the novel as politically radical.
18. See Gordimer, *The Essential Gesture*; André Brink, *Mapmakers*.

4

The Hermeneutics of Empire: Coetzee's Post-colonial Metafiction

MICHAEL MARAIS

There are obvious problems attached to the assignation of a label like 'post-colonial' to South African literary texts. Annamaria Carusi, for example, points out that in the South African context the term 'is not seen as applicable by either one in the customary coloniser/colonised opposition,' and that for the one group 'post-colonialism, as a desirable state of affairs, has been accomplished', whereas for the other group, 'to speak of post-colonialism is preemptive' ('Post, Post and Post' 80). This is true if one understands the term in a literal or a strictly chronometric sense. Other interpretations of post-colonialism are possible, however. Stephen Slemon, for example, argues that

> the concept proves most useful not when it is used synonymously with a post-independence historical period in once-colonised nations but rather when it locates a specifically anti- or post-colonial discursive purchase in culture, one which begins in the moment that colonial power inscribes itself onto the body and space of its Others and which continues as an often occulted tradition into the modern theatre of neo-colonialist international relations. ('Modernism's Last Post' 6)

In Slemon's terms, it is possible to treat South Africa as the site of such a counter-discourse.

Though definitions of the term 'post-colonial' appear to differ greatly, it is not my intention here to argue for or against either of the understandings of the term outlined above. Nor is it my intention to argue for the incorporation of Coetzee's novels into a post-colonial canon. My interest in post-colonial theory derives from the fact that it provides a useful framework for demonstrating the fallacy inherent in labelling certain of Coetzee's novels, such as *Foe* (Johannesburg 1986), postmodernist. Thus, although I would agree with Carusi that in *Foe* Coetzee makes use of those metafictional narrative strategies which are usually considered to be characteristic of postmodernism, it does not necessarily follow that this is, as she puts it, a 'blatantly postmodernist' novel ('Post, Post and Post' 88, 94 n. 4). In this regard, I find support in Helen Tiffin's point that although self-reflexive narrative strategies 'are characteristic of both the generally post-colonial and the European post-modern . . . they are energised by different theoretical assumptions and by vastly different political motivations' (Tiffin 172). Ultimately, these differences are reducible to different sites of production: on the one hand, post-colonial writing is produced by the colonial encounter and, on the other, postmodernist writing is produced by, in Slemon's terms, the 'system of writing' itself (quoted in Hutcheon 151). It is possible to draw a further distinction between these two modes of writing: while the postmodernist writers of the metropole enlist metafictional strategies to decentre the humanist subject, post-colonial metafictionists deploy similar strategies to explore the particular mode of subjectivity constituted by the discourses prevalent in the sociohistorical configurations of the colonial margins (see Hutcheon 150). In other words, they trace that 'affinity' which Gayatri Spivak detects 'between the imperialist subject and the subject of humanism' (quoted in Hutcheon 150).

Whether or not one concedes that Coetzee is a post-colonial writer, his writing is a product of the differences enumerated above; the imperialist subject is demonstrably the target of his reflexive narrative strategies. I shall argue this by tracing the occurrence, in Coetzee's work, of what is fast becoming a topos of postmodernist writers: the use of metafictional ploys to expose the notion of 'author' as an expression of subjectivity. Coetzee's use of this topos in *Foe*, for example, is evident on the very cover of the novel, which presents the reader with the names of two authors, Coetzee and (De)Foe. However, the object of critique here is not simply the humanist subject, but the particular configuration it gains in the colonies. This emerges when Susan Barton compares her own authorial activity with Cruso's attempt to clear the island of its indigenous growth and to reinscribe it with terraces and walls of stone: 'But when you see me at Mr Foe's desk making marks with the quill, think of each mark as a stone, and think of the paper as the island, and imagine that I must disperse the stones over the face of the island' (*F* 87). The point of this analogy is to cast imperialism as a form of metaphoric authorship: Cruso *rewrites* the alien terrain of the island and, in so doing, restructures this space of otherness in line with the familiar landscape of England.

This conflation of the acts of writing and imperialism is not merely confined to *Foe*; it pervades Coetzee's *oeuvre* and can be traced back to 'The Narrative of Jacobus Coetzee' (*D* Johannesburg 1974), a text which, unlike *Foe*, engages directly with South African colonial history. In fact, there seems to be little difference between Cruso's relationship with the island and Jacobus Coetzee's relationship with the South African landscape. In the novella, the colonial enterprise of legitimising an alien landscape by controlling and domesticating it is directly articulated by the narrator: 'Our commerce with the wild is a tireless enterprise of turning it into orchard and farm. When we cannot fence it and count it we reduce it to numbers by other means' (*D* 85). The coloniser imposes the closures of imperialism on the 'undifferentiated plenum' (108) of colonial space, thereby creating a closed, stable 'world' in which all threats are suppressed, and from which all contradictions are eliminated. Later in the novella, the reader's attention is directed to the authorial omnipotence which characterises this highly political act of creation: 'In his way Coetzee rode like a god through a world only partly named, differentiating and bringing into existence' (124). Here, the imperialist subject's use of language as a weapon of power in the arbitrary yet conventional creation of colonies places him in league with both the Judeo-Christian deity, who wields ultimate power by creating the world through language, and with the author of fiction, who engages in acts of linguistic creation. The more pertinent of these analogies, however, is that between imperialist and writer since, unlike the Christian God who authors the world *ex nihilo*, neither imperialist nor writer is the originator of a text. As with a literary work, the creation of the colony as text depends upon the presence of a pre-existing system of sense, an intertext of sorts or, to be more specific, the significatory matrix of the imperium. Rather than creating a world anew, the imperialist subject *derives* a world by imposing the codes of recognition of his culture on what he assumes to be the uninscribed geography of colonial space (see Slemon, 'Post-colonial Allegory' 161–3).

This analogy between the relationship of author to text and that of coloniser to colonised governs the presentation of colonial space in Coetzee's novels; it also governs their presentation of the 'native'. In *Foe,* for instance, Cruso is depicted as being both master and author of the mute Friday when Susan Barton refers to 'the new Friday whom Cruso created' (95). Moreover, Susan Barton, after Cruso's death, comes to realise that she too, through language, has become the author and determiner of Friday's existence: 'Friday has no command of words and therefore no defence against being re-shaped day by day in conformity with the desires of others. I say he is a cannibal and he becomes a cannibal. . . . What he is to the world is what I make of him' (121–2). Once again, this reflexive presentation is not confined to the highly metafictional *Foe.* In *Life & Times of Michael K,* for example, the emissaries of the Empire – the medical officer and the camp commander – refer to the spurious, but nevertheless official, account of Michael K's supposedly subversive activities on the Karoo farm as a 'story' (Johannesburg 1983, 177, 180). The point here is that the state author-ities 'write' the story of Michael K's life and times. The state creates an identity for Michael K by arbitrarily naming him and then manipulating him through language. Language thus emerges as the 'companion of empire' (Todorov quoted in Slemon, 'Post-colonial Allegory' 159).

By conflating imperialism and authorship, Coetzee also demonstrates that the dialectic of self and other informing the coloniser-colonised relationship also informs the author–text relationship; that the imperialist gesture is, essentially, an *hermeneutic* act. For example, the imperial author in each of the cases I have cited above rewrites the colonial other 'by reference to an anterior set of signs already situated in a cultural thematics' (Slemon, 'Post-colonial Allegory' 161). Cruso's authorial imperialism, for instance, is informed by the hermeneutic urge to domesticate Friday and the alien landscape of the island by integrating both into a European system of recognition. Coetzee thus presents imperial authorship as a recuperative process associated with the interpretive act. Reading, from a structuralist perspective (see Culler 134–60), is characterised by recuperation, a culturally-determined operation of making legible and scrutable the otherness of the literary text. To recuperate is to obliterate the strangeness or deviance of that which is read by integrating it into those significatory codes which culture makes available, deems acceptable, and assumes natural. In other words, interpretation is a form of (re)writing in which inherited interpretive paradigms construct their objects of observation by blocking from view whatever threatens their displacement. Interpretation is thus an author-itarian activity. So, too, is the imperial act which, as the imbrication of imperialism and authorship in the presentation of characters like Cruso and Jacobus Coetzee shows, is also informed by a hermeneutic procedure. The colonised is rewritten in terms of a particular master code: it is codified by European ideology.

The fusion of imperial authorship and interpretation of necessity politicises the interpretive act. In order to make this point, Coetzee enlists a variety of narrative strategies that raise the reader's consciousness of the political nature of the activity in which he/she is engaged. Most of these strategies are aimed at identifying the reader with characters in whom the activities of reading, writing and imperialism coalesce. In *Life & Times of Michael K*, for example, a simple but sudden shift in point of view from Michael K to the medical officer in Part Two of the novel forces the reader to adopt the position of the medical officer in relation to K (*MK* 177–229). He/she is no longer allowed to identify complacently with the victim, but is compelled instead to occupy the perspective of the interrogator. The identification thus achieved means that the medical officer's hermeneutic activity reflects that of the reader, thereby generating the analogy between literary interpretation and political interrogation hinted at in the medical officer's following words to the concentration camp commander: 'Let him be, don't haul him back and force him to die here under a spotlight with strangers looking on' (212). The hypothetical interrogators who scrutinise Michael K under a spotlight mirror the reader who scans the pages of the literary object with his/her hermeneutic gaze (perhaps aided by a reading lamp). The political interrogation of Michael K – the state's attempt to 'make sense' of his otherness – thus serves as an allegory of the reader's attempt to recuperate the otherness of *Life & Times of Michael K* by assimilating it into a literary system of intelligibility.

A similar process, in which the act of reading is cast as a form of metaphoric imperialism, occurs in 'The Narrative of Jacobus Coetzee'. The narrative levels in this text place the reader in a genealogical line of interpretive authors which includes J. M. Coetzee as the putative translator of the text; S. J. Coetzee, the putative author of the transposed Foreword which is also a critical commentary; and their putative ancestor, Jacobus Coetzee who, in his turn, authors the South African landscape by integrating it into a cultural thematics. By forcing the reader into an uneasy alliance with these characters, to whom he/she is related, if not genealogically then at least generically, the narrative strategies of identification in this text construct an analogy between the reading of the novella and the colonisation of South Africa. In the same way as the imperialist attempts to recuperate the otherness of colonial space by incorporating it into the cultural thematics of the imperium, the reader attempts to recuperate the literary object by subsuming it within an acceptable mode of literary discourse.

The various strategies of identification in *Life & Times of Michael K* and 'The Narrative of Jacobus Coetzee' are thus designed to show that the activities of reading and imperialism are informed by the same hegemonic cultural forces. Both reading subject and imperialist subject appropriate the threatening other and, thus, protect, fortify and confirm their own culturally-conferred identity.

Throughout Coetzee's fiction, this self-confirming will to power is depicted by means of the metaphor of the gaze, a metaphor which is used to portray not only the imperialist, but also the writing and reading subjects' attempts to master and possess the other. Significantly, this metaphor also occurs in an essay on landscape poetry in *White Writing*, where Coetzee argues that much early South African landscape poetry is founded on the poet's 'imperial gaze' (*WW* 167), the principal 'organ of penetration and takeover' (172) being the 'devouring, voracious eye' (173). Landscape poetry, according to Coetzee, is a colonial art linked to conquest and domination in which the poet, who occupies the 'prospect position' (173) in relation to the landscape as object, 'hold[s] the landscape in the grip of sight' (173). This metaphor of the eye as an 'organ of mastery' (172) occurs in almost exactly the same form in *Life & Times of Michael K*, where it is used to characterise the subject position the medical officer assumes in relation to K as object: 'my glittering eye would have held you, for the time being, rooted where you stood' (*MK* 225).

In the above citations, an implied pun on 'eye' and 'I' conflates the organ of sight with subjectivity. This conflation is rendered explicit by the image of the disembodied eye colonising the South

African landscape in 'The Narrative of Jacobus Coetzee':

> Only the eyes have power. . . . I become a spherical reflecting eye moving through the wilderness and ingesting it. Destroyer of the wilderness, I move through the land cutting a devouring path from horizon to horizon. There is nothing from which my eye turns, I am all that I see. (*D* 84)

Characterised by its difference from Europe, the South African 'wilderness' threatens European cultural boundaries and is accordingly assimilated by the imperialist I/eye. The master code in terms of which the open plurality of this territorial space is reduced and value-coded constructs a metaphorised identity for the landscape of otherness, one from which all contradictions have been eliminated and which accordingly fulfils the specular function of affirming the coloniser's culturally-conferred sense of self – hence Jacobus Coetzee's assertion, 'I am all that I see' (84). The identity of the subject here is not that of an individual, but that of a culture. J. M. Coetzee presents Jacobus Coetzee as the individualisation of a general consciousness, the suggestion being that the colonising subject is no more master of the discourse that he/she imposes on the colonised than is the colonised him/herself. Just as the colonised is subject to and constituted by this discourse, so too is the coloniser.[1]

The reading subject's kinship with the imperialist subject can be clearly detected when Jacobus Coetzee's description of the disembodied colonising eye/I is compared to Friday's depiction of the reading act in his sketch of the disembodied 'walking eyes' in *Foe* (147). Friday's sketch, which is a graphic evocation of the eighteenth-century literary topos of the reader as traveller, constitutes an image of reading within the text and mirrors the reading I/eye who holds the literary object in the grip of his/her 'hermeneutic gaze' (*WW* 9). This technique of internal mirroring recurs shortly afterwards when, in the novel's brief concluding section, an unidentified 'I' enters the text and, upon finding a manuscript, embarks on a journey of reading during which he/she reads the opening sentence of the novel (*F* 155). *Foe* thus ends with a striking reflection of the subject position of dominance which the reading I/eye assumes in relation to the text as other. It ends, in other words, by prefiguring its own recuperation by the reader. This metaleptic ending thwarts the expectations of closure generated by conventional literary paradigms and, by implication, criticises the reader's dependence on those literary systems of sense which govern his/her desire to foreclose on the text's otherness. The suggestion here, in sum, is that the reading subject, like the imperialist subject, is subject to and constituted by a colonising discourse – albeit in this particular case the discourse of an interpretive community.

The technique of internal mirroring with which *Foe* ends is only one of a number of strategies in Coetzee's work through which the text attempts, by both anticipating and politicising the interpretive act, to forestall recuperation and, thus, to protect its difference from assimilation into the sameness of the reader's interpretive community. The most effective of these strategies of resistance is silence, a silence which defies the self's attempt to read the other in the ideological mirror of his/her own metaphysical system.

I should stress at this point that Coetzee's perception of silence is very different to the perception which emerges from the work of most post-colonial writers. In general, post-colonial discourse recognises the relation of language to power and oppression and the crucial role that language plays in impeding the ability of the other to express self (Ashcroft *et al.* 7–9, 38–9). At the same time, this discourse underscores the urgent need for linguistic reappropriation if the re-creation of self is to be accomplished. The only way in which the represented other can be recaptured as self is by hearing itself speak, even if this means using the language of the dominant other (Hutcheon 163). Indeed, the immanence of the language metaphor in post-colonial discourse emphasises that the role of the colonial as 'historical subject and combatant, possessor of an-other knowledge and producer of alternative traditions' (Slemon, 'Modernism's Last Post' 10) can only be restored if he/she finds or creates a 'voice' with which to 'speak'. Given this insistence on the restorative and liberatory potential of language, it is not surprising that silence is viewed with suspicion by post-colonial writers and critics alike. For many of its theorists, post-colonialism must of necessity encompass a theory of agency and social change; in order to enter the sphere of political action, the reclamation and use of language as a political weapon is essential (Hutcheon 150). In this sense, to be silent is to become the passive victim of somebody else's language.

This is not the case in Coetzee's work, however, where the other, as soon as it attempts to recapture selfhood by appropriating the language of the coloniser, loses its alterior status and reinscribes itself within imperialist discourse.[2] In his representations of the silent other, Coetzee invests silence with power: silence is cast as the means by which the other preserves its alterior status against assimilation by the West. Gayatri Spivak has proposed this view of the other in her analysis of the relationship between Susan Barton and Friday in *Foe*: a relationship she reads as analogous to that between metropolitan anticolonialism and the native in which the former endeavours to give the latter voice. Spivak construes Susan Barton's apparently well-intentioned attempts to voice the other as attempts to invade the margin and suggests accordingly that '*Foe*, in history, is the site where the line between friend and foe is undone' (Spivak, "Theory in the Margin" 13–16). Significantly, Spivak concludes by indicating that all such attempted violations in the text are resisted and implicitly judged by Friday's silences (which she defines as 'spaces of withholding'):

> It is Friday . . . who is the unemphatic agent of withholding in the text. For every territorial space that is value-coded by colonialism *and* every command of metropolitan anticolonialism for the native to yield his 'voice,' there is a space of withholding, marked by a secret that may not be a secret but cannot be unlocked. 'The native,' whatever that might mean, is not only a victim, he or she is also an agent. He or she is the curious guardian at the margin. (16)

In Coetzee's fiction the other, no matter whether it manifests itself as the South African landscape, Cruso's island, Michael K, Friday, or the literary text itself, is always the guardian of the margin. Silence empowers the other as guardian; despite initially appearing to render the other vulnerable to linguistic reification, silence in fact becomes the means through which it resists the languages of imperialism. In *Foe*, this is made apparent in Susan Barton's rejection of her own claim that she has, through the manipulation of language, become the author of Friday's life: 'he is neither cannibal nor laundryman, these are mere names, they do not touch his essence, he is a substantial body, he is himself, Friday is Friday' (*F* 122). This citation hints at the political nature of silence in Coetzee's work. Silence is neither a sign of submission nor merely a strategy of passive resistance, but a counter-strategy through which the other preserves, even asserts, its alterior status and in so doing interrogates the fixity of dominant power structures and positions.

Perhaps the best example of the operation of the politics of silence in Coetzee's *oeuvre* is the interrogation scene in *Life & Times of Michael K.* In this scene, Michael K's 'stony' silence enables him to resist the state authorities' attempts to master him (*MK* 191–2). K's only response to these endeavours, however, despite the Medical Officer's repeated adjurations to 'speak', is silence: in this way, he rejects their attempts at narcissistic self-recognition, confronting them instead with precisely nothing, an absence that is entirely refractory to intelligibility. Since their position of dominance depends upon his recognition of them as masters, his silence denies them this position, and because their identity is premised on this position, his silence also challenges their very reality.

For Coetzee, then, silence is not, as Salman Rushdie would have it, 'the ancient language of defeat' (89). It is a potent political tool through which the other escapes and challenges the 'conceptual constraints of imperial cultures whose programmes of conquest and annihilation are enshrined in language' (*WW* 176). All of Coetzee's works thematise this escape. Indeed, in the case of *Life & Times of Michael K,* the very structure of the novel is informed by a recurring pattern of linguistic appropriation followed by escape. The opening sequence of the novel, in which Anna K, cared for by a midwife, gives birth to a child whom she then names Michael K, is repeated with subtle variations three times in the course of the novel. In the hospital at Prince Albert, shortly before being taken to the Jakkalsdrif camp, Michael K is attended to by a nurse and a state official (*MK* 97, 99). Similarly, at the Kenilworth infirmary, he is presided over by a medical officer and a state official (188–92). This triad recurs for the last time in the sex scene in Part Three of the novel, in which K is ministered to by the pimp and the prostitute (the latter wears a white dress (235) – reminiscent of the standard uniform of the nursing profession – and is pointedly referred to as 'the sister' (236, 238, 239, 242)). In the preamble to each of these scenes, K is likened to an infant and renamed. The act of naming here is, of course, an act of domination, an attempt to contain the threat of K's otherness, to cancel his presence as an absence. In metafictional terms, Michael K is inscribed into the texts of various author-ity figures – the principal example being the state's record of his supposedly subversive activities on the Karoo farm. In terms of the pervasive birth motif, K's identity is created anew in each of these scenes by a series of parent-*cum*-author figures. He is reborn or, on a reflexive plane, *rewritten* by being given a metaphorised identity.

As other, Michael K eludes all of these attempts at categorisation and textual containment, an escape which gains direct expression in his escape from the concentration camps and, more figuratively, in the stone motif. On numerous occasions K is likened to a stone. For example, during the interrogation scene his otherness, foregrounded by his inscrutable silence, is portrayed as follows: 'His face closed like a stone . . . he stared stonily back' (191–2). Earlier, his intractability and escape from state institutions are described in similar terms: 'He passes through these institutions and camps and hospitals and God knows what else like a stone. Through the intestines of the war' (185). Here, the stone motif serves to affirm the ability of silence to resist the imperialist imperative of assimilating, and thereby legitimising, otherness. At the same time, it underscores the manner in which Michael K's separate identity palimpsestically reasserts itself, despite previous attempts at linguistic colonisation. (This pattern of escape is perhaps best expressed in Coetzee's description of Sidney Clouts's landscape poetry: 'the thing possessed begins to mutate and shed its old name almost as soon as it is taken over by language' (*WW* 173).)

The motif of the stone reconfirms the analogy between K as other and the South African landscape as other. In an essay entitled 'Reading the South African Landscape', Coetzee characterises the South African terrain as being both stony and silent: resistant to attempts to interpret it through the 'frenzied application of European metaphor' and to the attempt to find 'a home in Africa for a consciousness formed in and by a language whose history lies on another continent' (*WW* 173). Stating that 'the true South African landscape is of rock, not of foliage' (167), Coetzee traces the gradual shift in South African landscape poetry from a 'botanical' to a 'geological' perspective (167). If one can speak of a development which Michael K, who is described as '[a] hard little stone, barely aware of its surroundings, enveloped in itself and its interior life' (*MK* 185), undergoes in the course of the novel, it is, precisely, from a botanical to a geological perspective. This change is brought about by his move from the exotic, Europeanised landscape of Cape Town – an initially alien landscape which has been legitimised or rewritten with imperial labels – to the more indigenous landscape of the Karoo:

> When he thought of Wynberg Park he thought of an earth more vegetal than mineral, composed of last year's rotted leaves and the year before's and so on . . . an earth so soft that one could dig and never come to the end of the softness. . . . I have lost my love for that kind of earth, he thought. . . . It is no longer the green and brown that I want but the yellow and the red; not the wet but the dry; not the dark but the light; not the soft but the hard. I am becoming a different kind of man. (*MK* 92–3).

K's affinity with the landscape is further suggested by the fact that he is frequently likened to underground creatures such as moles (144; 248) and earthworms (147; 248). Rather than 'betraying an attitude of denigration on the part of the writer toward the victim-as-protagonist', as Teresa Dovey (*The Novels* 285) claims, such similes suggest the fusion of Michael K as subject with the earth as object, a fusion also evident in the Medical Officer's description of him as 'a genuine little man of earth' (220). It is also significant that upon his return to the Karoo farm, K decides not to live in the deserted homestead – a symbol of settlement – but prefers, instead, to live in a burrow (137). In other words (if I can be allowed, again, to quote Coetzee out of context) K opts for 'an unsettled habitation in the landscape' (*WW* 173). He has become one with the earth.

This affinity between Michael K and the earth also emerges in those sections of the novel which are seen from K's perspective. In these sections, the South African landscape is reduced to its basic, immediate, material existence. Neutral, shorn of all presuppositions, these descriptions convey the immediacy of the relationship between subject and object, self and other. Rather than transforming the presence of the landscape, the perceiving subject is one with it and leaves it open and intact, exactly as it was before it was observed. Instead of imposing a metaphysical sense on the terrain, K is at one with its real sense, its *Dasein*: its 'being there' rather than its 'being something'.[3] In this respect, Michael K is the direct antithesis of not only the Medical Officer, whose highly reflective first-person diary entries constitute a marked shift in point of view in the novel, but also of Jacobus Coetzee, in 'The Narrative of Jacobus Coetzee', whose 'commerce with the wild is a tireless enterprise' (85) of imposing on its openness the closures of imperialism, an endeavour that is metaphorically depicted by his metamorphosis into 'a spherical reflecting eye moving through the wilderness and ingesting it' (84).

Given this sympathy between Michael K as other and the South African landscape as other, it comes as no surprise that the landscape, once it has been restructured in terms of the imperium's significatory matrix, reverts, like K, to its original identity. In 'The Narrative of Jacobus Coetzee', which deals with the period of South Africa's colonisation, the inscription of colonial space is described as a 'turning [of the wild] into orchard and farm' (*D* 85). It is therefore fitting that in *Life & Times of Michael K* (1983), which deals with a future period of decolonisation, these signs of settlement are shown to be undergoing a process of erasure: the South African landscape in the novel is marked by abandoned farms and homesteads. In this interregnum, the imperial label of the district in which the Karoo farm is located – Prince Albert – is exposed as a historically-bound sign arbitrarily linked to its referent. As in the state's naming of Michael K, the name Prince Albert can be seen as an attempt to foreclose on openness, to domesticate the other. In the time of the interregnum, however, Prince Albert becomes, like the abandoned homestead and Karoo farm, merely a relic of settlement. Its ultimate fate is prefigured by the erasure of these signs of settlement: the derelict homestead is destroyed by explosives and the farm reverts to veld (*MK* 171–2). A similar pattern can be discerned in *Foe* where, following Cruso's departure from the island, a resurgence of indigenous growth effaces the results of his endeavour to reinscribe an alien terrain with the familiar forms of the English landscape: 'Day by day the wind picks at the roof and the weeds creep across the terraces' (*F* 54).

The landscape in 'The Narrative of Jacobus Coetzee' similarly resists containment. All signs of the passage of Jacobus Coetzee, the archetypal imperialist 'I' who cuts 'a devouring path from horizon to horizon' (*D* 84), are ultimately obliterated from the South African landscape. This is made clear in the afterword to Jacobus Coetzee's narrative, where a self-conscious and exhaustive inventory – ranging from musket balls and bones to semen and smegma

– concludes with the observation: 'These relics, deposited over Southern Africa in two swathes, soon disappeared under sun, wind, rain, and the attentions of the insect kingdom, though their atomic constituents are still of course among us. *Scripta manent'* (126–7). The landscape in which Jacobus Coetzee says 'I' is an open space rather than a closed one. Like Cruso's, Jacobus Coetzee's attempts to singularise the open plurality of colonial space fail because the world on which he imposes closure is continually being transformed, displaced and decentred by time. And, as in *Foe,* the disruptive forces metaphorically linked to this instability are the elements, which are depicted as formless (and, metaphysically speaking, senseless) agents in a constant state of flux.[4]

In much the same way as Michael K, the landscapes in these novels reassert their separate identities after being named and dominated. Like him, they remain inscrutable to language and refractory to programmes of containment. In Coetzee's words: 'the real Africa will always slip through the net woven by European categories' (*WW* 165). Likewise the text itself, which slips through the net woven by critical categories. The most obvious example of textual resistance to critical strategies of containment in Coetzee's *oeuvre* is *Foe.* By positioning this self-consciously twentieth-century novel in a relation of both anteriority *and* posteriority to the eighteenth-century *Robinson Crusoe,* Coetzee not only presents his modern reader with (De)Foe's interpretive colonisation of Susan Barton's story, but also, owing to his novel's temporally ambivalent perspective, with the illusion that Susan Barton's story has palimpsestically reasserted itself. Josephine Dodd has claimed that the character Foe is to be construed as 'an agent of the institutions which inhibit [Susan Barton]' (Dodd 120): patriarchy and the literary institution. The novel's dual temporal perspective provides the contemporary reader, in turn, with the reflexive illusion that an ostensibly eighteenth-century text, after having been rewritten, has successfully defied patriarchal and literary programmes of containment, and has reinstalled its original identity.

In addition, Susan Barton's story, embedded in the primary narrative, functions as a *mise en abyme* which not only prefigures the actual reader's desire to recuperate *Foe,* but also suggests the text's defiance of such interpretive authoritarianism. What the reader-surrogates in the text refer to as 'touches of mystery' in the embedded story (*F* 83–7) mirror those lacunae in the novel proper which forestall the actual reader's quest for closure and thematic resolution. As Susan Barton's following words indicate, these lacunae are the textual equivalent of Friday's and the island's silence: 'if the story seems stupid, that is only because it so doggedly holds its silence. The shadow whose lack you feel is there: it is the lack of Friday's tongue' (117). The ending of *Foe*, which produces erasure rather than resolution and disclosure, should thus be seen as a strategy calculated to preserve the text's silence, to protect it from the linguistic colonisation of being named, described, possessed. This strategy of preservation becomes clear shortly before the end of the novel, when Friday thwarts Susan Barton's attempt to read his slate by wiping it clean (147). This image of the text's defiance of the reader prefigures the novel's ending. By establishing Susan Barton's death at a period that precedes the beginning of the novel, the final scene negates the events narraged before it: the ending effectively annuls the novel. By means of this 'strategy of erasure' (McHale 99–111), the literary object prevents the reading subject from foreclosing on its openness and otherness. It defies the reader's will to power over the text by cancelling out his/her attempt to 'naturalise' that deviant otherness which threatens the boundaries of his/her interpretive community. The text forestalls the reader's attempt to read it in the ideological mirror of his/her interpretive community and, thus, refuses to confirm his/her self-identity. Like the characters and landscapes depicted in his novels, Coetzee's texts themselves resist being named and dominated. The obvious affinities between these various manifestations of the other bring me to my conclusion.

The point of this essay has been to demonstrate that Coetzee's use of metafictional strategies differs greatly from the standard postmodernist interrogation of the humanist subject. The various reflexive strategies in the novels I have discussed are calculated to politicise interpretation in such a way that the act of reading re-enacts the political process the fiction represents, namely, the colonisation of colonial space and/or natives. The implications for the reader of this politicisation of interpretation are profoundly disturbing, all the more disturbing because they are overtly political, less abstract than, say, the standard Barthesian distinction between *lisible* and *scriptible* texts (*S/Z* 3–4): a distinction upon which theorists on the politics of reflexivity in postmodernist writing almost invariably rely. At the same time, the implications of such a politicisation of reading are more disconcerting than standard representations of political oppression in realist texts. In realist fiction, the reader is usually allowed the moral comfort of identifying with the victim and is deliberately distanced from the perpetrators of political atrocities so that he/she can, from a superior ethical vantage point, complacently condemn their actions. No such complacency is afforded the reader of Coetzee's novels. The reader of, for example, the torture scenes in *Waiting for the Barbarians*, or the interrogation scenes in *Life & Times of Michael K*, identifies, albeit unwillingly, with the *perpetrator* rather than with the victim. He/she is forced to do so by metafictional strategies of identification which extend the self-other dialectic informing the relation of oppressor and oppressed to the level of interpretation. As a consequence, the act of reading Coetzee's novels becomes a political allegory of the capture and containment of colonial space and its people.

Silence enables the other, however, to elude the self's colonial urge to integrate it into a cultural thematics. Coetzee's fiction similarly defies critical endeavours – including my own – to constrain it within a theoretical strait-jacket. Throughout Coetzee's work, the text's resistance to such interpretive strategies of containment serves as a political allegory of the colonised's escape from political programmes of containment.

Notes

1. In this respect, compare Homi Bhabha who, in his critique of the discourse of cultural colonialism, argues against 'a dialectical power struggle between self and Other' (Bhabha 153) and for 'the *différance* of the colonial presence', a radical ambivalence that makes the boundaries of colonial 'positionality' (the division of self/other) and the question of colonial power (the differentiation of coloniser/colonised) different from both the Hegelian master–slave dialectic or the phenomenological projection of Otherness (150).
2. For a detailed consideration of this problem, see Carusi, 'Rethinking the Other'.
3. See David Carroll's discussion of phenomenological concerns in the theory of the New Novel in *The Subject in Question* (11–12).
4. Compare David Carroll's discussion of Claude Simon's *Le Vent* (ibid., 76–7).

5

J. M. Coetzee: The Postmodern and the Postcolonial

KENNETH PARKER

I INTRODUCTION

As a critic, J. M. Coetzee is probably best-known for his collection of essays *White Writing* (1988). Coetzee's critical reputation is noteworthy for two features: first, that it depends most on the appraisals of European and North American, rather than South African, critics; and second, that the European and American responses tend to obscure affinities both with his fiction and with the rest of his critical output, much of which has less to do with the natal space of South Africa than with the imagined space of a Europe of the past that has never ceased to be the affective literary homeland for white writers, especially those who write in English. One objective of this paper will therefore be to seek to establish some of the connections not only between the different critical and cultural modes of Coetzee's writing, but also between the different historical and geographical locations that mark his interests.

At the outset, then, a number of general observations might be in order. The first is that several of the essays in *White Writing* date back to the beginning of the 1980s; they are the outcome of the critic's return from Britain and the United States to South Africa in the early 1970s and of subsequent critical and pedagogical concerns in English studies in white South African universities at that time.[1] Coetzee's critical interventions in the early 1970s have (with one exception) nothing to do with South Africa; his critical concerns stem, instead, out of his doctoral thesis on

Samuel Beckett, and consist, for the most part, of articles published in critical journals outside the country of his birth.[2]

It is noteworthy that these articles on Beckett pre-date the publication of his fiction: while his first novel, *Dusklands* (Johannesburg, 1974), was published in South Africa in 1974, two years after his return to that country, it was only with *In the Heart of the Country* (London, 1977) that his fiction was first published abroad. Indeed, *Dusklands* was not published in the UK until 1982 (1985 in the USA). Coetzee's critical recognition has not only been achieved in a very short space of time; it has been overwhelmingly the creation of the 'cross-border' reader, who, according to Lewis Nkosi, exists 'at the point where the South African subject of discourse attempts to interpellate the reader across these borders, from the confines of his or her own community, with its own specific values and cultural interests, in order to define his or her own unique identity'. For Nkosi, this 'cross-border' reader is 'of great importance as one of the constitutive principles in the shaping of South African literature' (Nkosi, 'A Country of Borders' 19–20).

A substantial portion of Coetzee's early critical output can be seen as having been devoted to themes and topics that loom as large as, and precede his interest in, white South African culture: those of linguistics[3] and of the broad sweep of European culture, especially as manifested in the tradition of the classic realist text.[4] Succinctly stated, one element of my argument is that Coetzee is himself the paradigm for his definition of 'white writing', a genre he categorises as writing that 'is white only insofar as it is generated by the concerns of people no longer European, not yet African' (*WW* 11).

II *WHITE WRITING*: CONTEXTS AND CON-TEXTS

The most striking feature of *White Writing* is that Coetzee nowhere attempts to define what it is to be, or to become, African. Like virtually all other critics in and about South Africa, Coetzee is entrapped by the invariably uncritical rhetoric of an overarching binarism between 'European' (in two senses: sometimes about that continent, its cultures and peoples; mostly, however, merely about white-skinned people born in South Africa who arrogate that categorisation, with its attendant cultural baggage, to themselves) and 'African'. This totalising discourse thereby marginalises what is specific about the South African experience, namely its hybridity.

In the current endeavours to forge (in both senses of the word) a post-apartheid society, it is noteworthy that what appears to connect the old discourses of racism on the part of the dominant, and the new ones of liberation on the part of the oppressed, is a rhetoric of 'authenticity' that is not only of recent creation and wholly devoid of substantiation (Gatsha Buthelezi's invention of the 'right' of Zulu males to carry 'traditional weapons' such as spears being a prime example), but is also particularly marked by being anti-intellectual, anti-academic, often deeply philistine.

In sharp contrast with his contemporaries, Coetzee shows scant interest in the privileging of the doctrine of the 'authentic'. This is particularly evident when we compare his criticism with that of Njabulo Ndebele, about whom Coetzee writes with considerable approval. What distinguishes the criticism of Ndebele is, precisely, his rootedness within a shared history of being oppressed, even when he is sceptical of some of the more extravagant pronouncements on the part of the arbiters of the culture being transformed. What characterises Coetzee's position is, equally precisely, his detachment from such a rootedness in a shared history of oppression: even his scepticism of the rhetoric of transformation is oblique, opaque, something that has to be inferred, disinterred.

It is important to be clear. My argument here is not in support of any populist belief in the myth of 'roots', especially when such attachments are invariably of relatively recent construction. My argument is that, notwithstanding its many excellences of insight and revision, this failure to define what it is to be or to become African is the most intrusive silence that marks (and indeed distorts) *White Writing*. Instead, the feature that most marks the text is how 'white South African' it is. So, although Coetzee informs us that his is a 'mode of reading which, subverting the dominant is in peril, like all triumphant subversion, of becoming the dominant in turn' (*WW* 81), Martin Trump is surely right in his assertion that Coetzee's practice, with its 'resistance to the accepting, without skepticism, of any dominant order . . . is drawing deeply from the sweetest waters of the wells of liberalism' (Trump 62–3).

The case for what might appear to be a somewhat maverick interpretation might be made in another way: if the question of identity for white South Africans is bedevilled by an unresolved tension between 'Europe' and 'Africa' (no matter how these are defined), there is increasingly an awareness of an equally unresolved tension between the claims of a dominant liberal tradition, on the one hand, and, on the other, an emergent and countervailing modernity as political culture. Coetzee, the writer of fiction, is at ease with the latter; Coetzee the cultural critic, continues to be attached – albeit resistingly – to the former. The point can be made succinctly: as inaugurator, in South African writing in English, of the break with classic realism, and as writer of postmodernist fiction, Coetzee deserves the acclaim bestowed upon him; but if a dominant characteristic of the postcolonial project is to write back to the centres, to interrogate the exclusivities of Europe's claims to knowledge, and thereby to decentre the 'authenticities' of the colonisers, then Coetzee as critic is not a participant in that counter-discursive activity. But then why should he be required to be, especially when hardly any of his contemporaries in South Africa (whether white or black) are concerned in that project? Theirs continues to be, ideologically as well as geographically, a much more restricted objective, devoted to the settlement in South Africa. Indeed, as I shall show, what is striking is how he resorts to the 'authenticities' of liberal humanism in order to attack countervailing Marxist and Black Consciousness positions. Notwithstanding, what is noteworthy is how, in recent years, Coetzee has sought to break free of these inherited shackles; expressed perhaps most vividly not only in the form, but especially the content, of his attack upon Nadine Gordimer and the Congress of South African Writers for their dis-inviting of Salman Rushdie in the aftermath of a threat to his safety by South African Islamic zealots – even before the *fatwa* against him by the Ayatollah Khomeini following upon the publication of *The Satanic Verses* (Louw 10).

It is an interrogation of the ideological and critical contexts and consequences of the common-sense distinctions between 'European' and 'African' in Coetzee's criticism that forms the burden of this essay: my argument will be that the origins of *White Writing* can be traced back to, and located in, one of the most tenacious and persistent myths of European liberal tradition, that of the 'civilising' rôle of peoples from mainly the northern and western edges of that continent.

The epigraph to *White Writing* is that section from Ovid's *Metamorphoses* 3 where it is narrated that 'Pressing his lips to foreign soil, greeting the unfamiliar mountains and plains, Cadmus gave thanks. . . . Descending from above, Pallas told him to plow and sow the earth with the serpent's teeth, which would grow into the future nation' (Coetzee's translation). What Ovid's epigraph omits is the context: Cadmus, son of Agenor, finds himself on foreign soil as a consequence of his wanderings in search of his sister Europa, who had previously been kidnapped by Jupiter. In Boeotia, the teeth of the sacred serpent he had slain grow into an army of sewn men (Sparti), who warn him against meddling in their civil war. From that war, five survivors join Cadmus to found the city of Thebes. Later, Cadmus marries Harmonia, to whom he presents a sacred robe and necklace, which will bring misfortune to whoever possesses it.

One central theme of the fable is therefore that of transformation: broadly, that of the creation of harmony and order out of chaos; more specifically, that of the founding of a future nation under the leadership of the male settler, who will be assisted by some members of the dispossessed, incorporated as junior partners in that act of dispossession. Cadmus justifies these actions by articulating the view that the land to which he had come was not only unsettled (in the sense of uninhabited, as well as marked by conflict), but also unsewn, unused by humans for profitable ends; hence the argument in support of transformation from culture in its root meaning as 'agriculture' to culture as 'civilisation', later to be developed into that well-known thesis by John Locke which asserts that 'subduing or cultivating the earth, and having dominion over it, we see are joined together. The one gave title to the other, so that God, by commanding to subdue, gave authority so far to appropriate' (Locke 252–3).

What has become known as 'South Africa' has, as landscape as well as landed property, featured historically as an object of colonial discourse that constructs it as different again from those of the New World as well as of the Orient.[5] If by colonial discourse is understood 'an ensemble of linguistically-based practices unified by their common deployment in the management of colonial relationships' (Hulme 2), the question arises: who narrates? This issue of narration is especially pertinent when considered in the context of one key theme of *White Writing*, that of the supposed uncertainty about the nature of white identity – and therefore about the conventional justifications for the rôle of dispossessor.

In the recent past, in the 'con-text(s)' of the rhetoric of a 'new

South Africa' (or is it a 'new' South Africa or even a new 'South Africa'?), this 'discovery' of 'uncertainty' has become a somewhat fashionable assertion. The history has, however, been wholly different: until recently, the dispossessor has had no doubts about the rightness of that rôle, only about its mechanisms and practices, one dominant feature of which has been the exclusion of blacks from virtually all aspects of participation in the, nevertheless common, society. The essays in *White Writing* often unwittingly draw attention to that exclusion: blacks are either obliterated from the common (especially the urban) landscape or are seen as interlopers whose presence is always conditional upon white needs.

It is only in the aftermath of recent rapidly changing material circumstances for whites, brought about by the combination of popular resistance at home, political change in adjacent African states and pressures from abroad, that the white state has sought alternative strategies for the maintenance of white hegemony. Notwithstanding many real (but mostly cosmetic) changes that have marked the South African polity since De Klerk's speech of February 1990, and the subsequent release of Nelson Mandela and some of the other political prisoners, the overriding impression of the continuing negotiations between the various parties is that these corroborate the remark made by the feudal lord to his supporters in Guiseppe Lampedusa's classic *The Leopard* (1958; translated 1960): that in order for things to remain the same, things must change.

At the heart of these discourses of transformation, in the state as well as in the contemporary fiction, there is a paradox: if the hitherto existing history of South Africa is that of racism as crucial to the needs of capitalism, the present would appear to argue its abrogation – in the interests of the needs of a modernising capitalism.

One of the silences in *White Writing*, then, is that it does not really foreground the historical specificity of these moments of transformation in black–white as well as white–white relations from the moment of white conquest and settlement in 1652. History cannot be separated from narrativity; if the former is context, the latter might be said to be con-text, not only for what it states, but especially for what it conceals. For example, what is to be deduced from a text which follows a largely linear progression that starts with the implantation of white settlement, but would appear to end in the mid-sixties of the present century?

To read that termination as the moment of the demise of 'white writing' is misleading, especially with reference to the second context: that of the moment of the constitution of Coetzee's own text – in the aftermath of radical resistance in the black townships and in the parallel development of new departures in black writing.[6]

One of the consequences of the breakdown of the certainties of a civil society characterised by white racist hegemony has been the problem it has posed for white intellectuals, the institutions in which they work and the interests they represent. Not only are these intellectuals enlisted to ensure the retention of Europe's implantations and to re-educate all sections of public opinion, but so too must the very concept of the law be enlisted to ensure that new customs, new habits can be brought into being: uncannily reminiscent of Antonio Gramsci's notion of 'spontaneous consent' (Gramsci 12–13). A number of white academics, mostly those openly committed to the national liberation organisations in the halcyon 1960s, have a distinguished record in this regard. Coetzee was never part of that commitment. To draw attention to this non-participation is not to blame or accuse; in the 1960s, Coetzee's position was the norm in white South African academia. What was singular about his position then, a position that continues to mark his responses to this day, was a highly principled and self-effacing fastidiousness.

It is partly a matter of style – Coetzee has tended to eschew the rhetorical flourish, to avoid being censorious. Above all, it is a matter of ideology: in the negotiations between the descendants of that Cadmus who came to the Cape and the descendants of the peoples those settlers encountered there, where does Coetzee fit? One conclusion is that, following on the recognition that the founding myths cannot be sustained, these myths have to be reconfigured, not only for those (white South African, as well as 'cross-border') readers, but also for those who are to be incorporated – those survivors who are to join the Cadmus-figure in the building of the new Thebes at the Cape.

Of these multiple reconfigurations by Coetzee, the one that has arguably been hardest to digest by white South African critics is the one which asserts that 'the fairest Cape' was neither part of the terrestrial paradise of the New World, nor the City on the Hill serving Europe as an example of true spiritual reformation, but rather a 'Lapland of the South'. While Coetzee has been severely taken to task by white South African critics for his supposedly 'distorted representation' (especially of Afrikaans writing),[7] his selective appropriation of the white literary record is perhaps (unintentionally) the most remarkable con-text of the book. Even if his critics are right about his selectivity, what stands out is his highlighting of the poverty of the culture of white writing in South Africa; inclusion of additional texts would not have significantly altered the conclusion that the white literary implantation and legacy is not only random and spotty, but tenuous and precarious. Coetzee's contribution to the dismantling of the myths of white South African attachments to a claimed European heritage overwhelmingly outweighs the critique to be offered hereafter. *White Writing* deserves to be celebrated as a liberatory text that has helped to free a new generation of white critics of their racist and culturally supremacist incubus.

III DEMYTHIFICATION AS DETACHMENT

Just as Ovid had done before him, Coetzee tackles particular and specific myths, and then proceeds to make connections between them in a broadly linear historical framework: from (not quite first) encounters at the Cape in the seventeenth century, via dispossessions in the hinterland in the eigthteenth century, to temporary victory of Boer over black and Briton in the more recent past. Unlike Ovid's, however, Coetzee's critical practice is to read silence in the texts – especially about people who are not white – as signs of meanings that are not only withheld from, but not open to, white interrogation:

> Our ears today are finely attuned to modes of silence. . . . Our craft is all in reading *the other*: gaps, inverses, undersides; the veiled, the dark, the buried, the feminine; alterities . . . Only part of the truth, such a reading asserts, resides in what writing says of the hitherto unsaid; for the rest, its truth lies in what it dare not say for the sake of its own safety, or in that which it does not know about itself: in its silences. (*WW* 81)

Perhaps so. But who constitutes the 'our'? Furthermore, while the critical stance is congruent with the position adopted in the fiction (the dumb Friday, the nearly-mute Michael K, the woman in *Waiting for the Barbarians* who is speechless, Vercueil in *Age of Iron* with his associations with 'verskuil': concealment; deception), what remains unclear is why. Are these, Benita Parry asks, 'figures of withholding speech as an act of resistance? Or are they the victims of textual strategies that disempower them by situating them outside the linguistic order? Does not Coetzee's own principled refusal to exercise the power of the dominant culture by speaking for the other itself paradoxically perform the discursive process of silencing?' (Parry, 'The Hole in the Narrative').

Parry's reading has especial validity when we notice the degree of self-awareness that is conferred on even the most marginal of white figures: Magda, immured in festering loneliness, can confidently assert that her 'stories are stories, they do not frighten me, they only postpone the moment when I must ask: Is this my own snarl I hear in the undergrowth?' Yet it is Magda who can go on to ponder about whether or not a speculative history is possible (*IHC* 36, 40). Much later she will go on to observe that 'This is no way to live' (190).

The most revealing example, though, is that of 'The Narrative of Jacobus Coetzee'. Compared with Foe, who is bereft of a speaking voice, and the real Jacobus Coetzee, who was illiterate and had to have his narrative transcribed, the fictional Jacobus is afforded all kinds of assistance to fashion (fabricate?) the realisation of his 'positive act of the imagination' (*D* 109). Jacobus becomes not only editor but also author, one who not only acts out the 'civilising mission' but also consciously differentiates between what he writes in his diary and what he tells the 'Hottentots' and 'Bushmen' amongst whom he finds himself: 'From the fertile but on the whole effete topos of dreaming oneself and the world I progressed to an exposition of my career as tamer of the wild' (*D* 109). By this process Jacobus begins to lose a sense of his boundaries, which, in turn, leads to his 'casting off [of] attachments'.

This notion of 'casting off attachments', of losing a sense of boundaries, has to do not only with the historiography of those encounters, but especially with the self who presents that history. For a story that has as its epigraph Flaubert's observation that 'What is important is the philosophy of history', what is to be made of the three accounts of the same journey: the 'original' first person narrative; the third person edition and commentary by S. J. Coetzee, with its editorial intrusions; the 'translation' by

J. M. Coetzee? If one assessment of colonial discourse is that it silences alternative versions of historic encounters, to what extent is Coetzee's project itself a colonising act in its imposition of elaborate layers of silencing? It is in this connection that the question of the constitution of the self is central, and Coetzee shows his awareness of that centrality by quoting from Kierkegaard:

> All versions of the *I* are fictions of the *I*. The primal *I* is not recoverable. Neither of the Words *I* and *You* exist pure in the medium of language. Indeed, after the experience of the Word in relation to one's own existence, life cannot go on as before. 'Self-annihilation [i.e., annihilation of the self] is the essential form of the God-relationship.' ('Achterberg's "Ballade van de gasfitter"' 412)

This intertextual digression on my part has been necessary in order to emphasise what *White Writing* is fundamentally about – the search for strategies by which to cast off 'attachments' to white South African myths: of origin and first encounters ('Idleness in South Africa'); of European aesthetics ('The Picturesque, the Sublime, and the South African Landscape'); of pastoral as an appropriate literary form for writing the story of white dispossession of blacks ('Farm Novel and Plaasroman': 'The Farm Novels of C. M. van den Heever'), with which is associated an appropriate language ('Simple Language, Simple People'), especially that of the overarching myth of racial 'purity' ('Blood, Taint, Flaw, Denegeration'); finally that of coming to terms with the recognition of being (in the phrase used by the poet Guy Butler) 'strangers to Europe'[8] ('Reading the South African Landscape').

For Coetzee, the coming to power of an Afrikaner Nationalist Party (1948) marks the moment of the inscription of new myths about white supremacy, as well as white writing about that supposed supremacy: 'As apartheid began to be implemented', he writes, 'moral ties were severed too; and from being the dubious colonial children of far-off motherland, white South Africans graduated to uneasy possession of their own, less and less transigent internal colony' (*WW* 11). What these rhetorical circumlocutions reveal, as I have tried to show elsewhere (Parker, 'Coetzee on Culture' 3–6), is a somewhat tendentious reading not only of the historical record of conquest and dispossession, but also of historical method. Myth-breaking though it is in many ways, *White*

Writing nevertheless ultimately suffers from the same central silence for which Coetzee (quite justifiably) criticised the late Michael Wade in a review of the latter's monograph on Nadine Gordimer: 'What is missing here is a sense of Gordimer's own existential relation to history and to fictional historiography and, in particular, a sense of the darkly prophetic stance she has now taken up' (Coetzee, 'The Agentless Sentence' 255). Whether he would agree with it or not cannot be established in any incontrovertible sense, but Coetzee would seem here to be in accordance with Fredric Jameson's notion of 'cognitive mapping': the schema whereby it might be determined how subjects are positioned in history by analysing their discursive practices ('Postmodernism' 53–92).

IV 'DARKLY PROPHETIC': HIS-STORY AS PARADOX

Alternatively stated, one theme that has exercised Coetzee as critic has been that of the conditions that might enable the emergence of a 'national' literature. Not surprisingly, the cognitive map that Coetzee draws has remarkably sharp symmetries with white South African formulations of racial identities: of so-called 'Coloureds', of black Africans, of Afrikaans and English-speaking whites. In seeking to establish the continuing impact of that symmetry, it is important to enter in a caveat: not only are the reviews on which my assertions are based few in number, they are also located in specific historical conjunctures that materially affect their production. Nevertheless, that these reviews are concerned with authors who are described as exemplary of racial identities and of political culture (Alex La Guma; Njabulo Ndebele; Breyten Breytenbach and André Brink; Gordimer and Christopher Hope) vastly modulates the qualms I have about the case I now wish to make.

Significantly, Coetzee's first major critical intervention with reference to South African literature was his essay on Alex la Guma's *A Walk in the Night and Other Stories* (1967). That essay provided him with an opportunity to range La Guma against Lewis Nkosi.[9] Nkosi had asserted that, with the exception of La Guma, whose writing he admired for its 'enthusiasm for life as it is lived', it was 'impossible to detect in the fiction of black South Africans any significant and complex talent which responds with both the vigour of their imagination and sufficient technical resources to the problems posed by conditions in South Africa' ('Fiction by Black South Africans' 71).

Bearing in mind Fredric Jameson's earlier observation about the positioning of the subject in history, it is important to look at Coetzee's observations in some detail, with reference not only to the moment of the review but also to the moment of La Guma's text. It should be remembered that *A Walk in the Night* was first published by Mbari in Nigeria in 1962, the same year in which its author was banned under the Suppression of Communism Act, and that it appeared in its Heinemann edition only in 1967, a year after the author (who had not only been detained in prison without charge on numerous occasions, but who had also been placed under house arrest that specifically forbade him to communicate with friends or family or to leave his house), had finally left for England on a one-way exit permit with his family. Because of the combination of the banning order, which remained in place even after his departure from the country, and the operation of censorship laws throughout this whole period – indeed, until only very recently – La Guma's writings were prohibited from being sold in South Africa.

Equally importantly, it should be recalled that La Guma was one of the leaders of the liberation movement against whom the 1956 arrest for 'treason' had ended in ignominious defeat for the state, when all those charged were acquitted in 1960. The three years between acquittal and banning were therefore crucial not only for La Guma's writing, but also for his political activity as one of the leaders of the South African Coloured Peoples' Congress, a constituent part of the alliance led by the ANC. It was also the period when the white state first announced its intention to remove the inhabitants of District Six, the setting for the first novel, from the centre of Cape Town, and to relocate them in the sandy waste known as the Cape Flats.

Coetzee, like most other critics at the time, appears to be unaware of this history – either of the author or of the community, whose humanity is measured in the text by acts of resilience to acts of vicarious brutality by the agents of the white state, as well as from members of that community itself.[10] He makes three interconnected criticisms about the novella from which the title derives: first, about the 'considerable weight of political statement'; second, about the origins and formal aspects of La Guma's fiction; third, sociocultural glosses on the nature of the community depicted. While the theoretical foundations of these criticisms serve to vindicate Martin Trump's detection of a liberal strain in the critic, it is important to stress that my case is not that Coetzee was part of the influential consensus of liberal–humanist criticism that dominated South African English culture (and arguably still does), but that his critical position then is an index of the difficulty of breaking with that position.

Invariably, when influential white South African liberal critics display an antipathy toward 'political statements' in literature, that should be read, not as antipathy to politics *per se*, but toward particular positions. Two positions against which liberal-humanist critics inveighed in particular were those they constructed as a Marxist politics reputedly given expression as 'socialist realism' (La Guma), and an emergent Africanist position developed initially by people like Ezekiel (later Es'kia) Mphahlele and culminating in the Black Consciousness movement of the 1970s (Mbulelo Mzamane; Sipho Sepamla; Boyd Makhoba; Mafika Gwala, etc.).[11] That there was a ferocious – but seldom admitted – battle on the part of the liberal-humanist grouping to retain control, might be judged from an analysis of the 'little magazines' of the period (Finn). It is in some of these contexts that Coetzee's assessment of La Guma should be read.

Coetzee's critique, which stems out of a deep-rooted opposition to active engagement in partisan politics is, at best, confused. The 'main line of the plot', he asserts, shows 'men overwhelmed by social forces they do not understand'. This is a misreading of the text – it is not that these people do not 'understand', it is rather that one of the consequences of the history of their oppression (which they understand only too well) has also deprived them of a language to give expression to their material situation. To therefore proceed to declaim that 'we are entitled to ask what purpose a literature serves which only chronicles the lives and deaths of little people, the victims of fates too dark for them to comprehend', and from there to conclude that '*A Walk in the Night*, despite its naturalist assumptions and its doom-laden atmosphere, contains embedded in it an analysis of the political weakness of the Coloured society in South Africa, and hence implies an explanation of the negativeness of a fiction that realistically portrays that society' is (at its simplest) perverse. By which criteria, and on what basis, is the charge of 'weakness' sustainable?

From 1947, when the white regime's very first act was to institute apartheid on the Cape Town suburban train network, through a whole range of legal measures to do with education, work, place of abode, the abrogation of the last vestiges of a franchise, the 'Coloured' community had been especially singled out for attack. What is remarkable, and a matter of public record, is their resistance – a resistance in which Alex la Guma was a leading figure. How his text can be read as manifesting the 'negativeness' of a fiction that seeks to portray that society, warts and all, can only be read as an incapacity to recognise the content of what is being articulated in the text.

That incapacity to recognise extends, as well, to Coetzee's critique of the formal elements of La Guma's text, in the critic's ascription of literary relations. For Coetzee, the 'godparents' for *A Walk in the Night* are *An American Tragedy* and *Native Son*. Not only does this ascription deny a rôle to the classic nineteenth-century Russian writers whom La Guma asserts were crucial to his formation (writers whom Coetzee himself continues to value), but in locating La Guma's precursors in the USA, rather than in Europe, Coetzee would seem to be denying to black writers from South Africa a share in the literary ancestry located in Europe that white South African writers claim for themselves.

The point must be pressed. Coetzee's argument is not that La Guma's novella is flawed because of its failure to manage the formal features of the European text; instead, for him the key flaw in the novella is that it is 'a novel without a hero: this fact is of itself the most comprehensive political statement La Guma makes'. Now, this is quite wrong-headed: like other South African Marxists of the time, La Guma believed passionately in the notion of 'the people' as hero. From amongst these, went the argument, there arose individuals who might, from time to time, assume certain short-term leadership rôles. And, indeed, the history of the struggles of that moment amply demonstrates the rightness of the theory in the emergence of Gramscian 'organic intellectuals' like La Guma himself, as well as his father before him; of trades union leaders like Johnny Gomas and Reggie September; of civil rights activists like Zainunissa (Cissie) Gool and George Peake.

Ultimately, Coetzee's misreading is the outcome of a lack of historical and sociocultural understanding that often mars his otherwise scintillating insights into white writing. In the La Guma text it is there in small details, as well as with regard to theory.

One example of the former is to categorise the thug Willieboy's fury at the visit of American sailors to the 'Coloured' brothel as 'unreasonable', and as 'represent[ing] a cultural introvertedness'. This is an observation that fails to recognise an important distinction: while those 'Coloured' males will doubtless claim their male 'right' to oppress 'their' women, their protest is a political recognition not only of how 'Coloured' women have been victims of white oppression, but also of the powerlessness of the men to resist that oppression with any degree of success.

The critic's broader general theoretical assertions are equally debatable: to say that the community 'has become a social class in a capitalist society', that 'uncertainty before the promise of bourgeois security creates a lack of cohesiveness in it', and that the community 'lacks political awareness', points not only to Coetzee's unfamiliarity with the social theories he adduces, but especially to what his assertions suppress.

The history of the community La Guma portrays will show that, whatever the tangled relations between class and colour at any one moment in history, in South Africa's capitalist phase that so-called 'Coloured' community has been a proletariat – whether urban or rural, that has been its material reality, as well as its habit of thought. And even though a fraction of the community (teachers, medical doctors, skilled craftspeople) lived ostensibly bourgeois lives, even those lives were severely circumscribed by the overriding facts of apartheid. There never was a 'promise' by the white state – neither of bourgeois security, nor of anything else except even more rigorous apartheid. Indeed, historians of the moment of Afrikaner hegemony over others in the common society might do well to look into the especial virulence with which that new ruling Afrikaner fraction set about dismantling the last vestiges of 'privilege' members of the 'Coloured' community had, and by which it could until then be differentiated from other blacks who had no rights of any kind whatsoever. To charge the community with a 'lack of political awareness' is therefore, quite simply, wrong.

That there were, at that time, considerable differences about the nature and form of the liberation struggle is a matter of record – notably between the policies advocated by the Non-European Unity Movement, and those of the South African Coloured Peoples Organisation. Also a matter of record, but suppressed in Coetzee's discourse, is the manner in which the white state sought to prevent resistance by legislation. Perhaps it is for these reasons that he is unaware of the fact – and can therefore conclude – that the community lacked political awareness. Their struggles against (for instance) the imposition of apartheid on the cape Peninsula transportation network (1947), against the Group Areas Act that designated racially specified ghettoes (1951), against the abrogation of a limited franchise in white elections (1951) and (in common with all other groups) in the Defiance Campaign against Unjust Laws (1952), are all matters of record. So, too, is their resistance to the raft of racist laws that mark the period of the early 1960s, and that inspire La Guma's writing and Coetzee's later commentary. Unwittingly, perhaps, we are back to where we started: the white liberal refrain of those times, to the effect that these people were being offered the 'wrong' kinds of political leadership.

The case might also be made from the opposite position, that of the understanding of apartheid itself, and of the means toward abolishing it. Not only does Coetzee assert that 'As an episode in historical time, apartheid is overdetermined', but he then goes on to say that, writing not as a historian but as a literary scholar, 'it is ultimately in the lair of the heart that apartheid must be approached. If we wish to understand apartheid, therefore, we cannot ignore its testament as it comes down to us in the heartspeech of autobiography or confession'.[12] While recognition should be accorded to the spirit that motivates such an approach to the unrepentant 'ignorance and madness' (Coetzee's words) of one of the formative figures of Afrikaner nationalism, it is important to insist that such magnanimity suppresses a crucial aspect about power relations in South Africa: the capacity that a white skin has to enable and to confer autonomy over self as well as others, but which a black skin disbars. To adapt an injunction, 'Look into thy heart, and destroy apartheid', will not do, if only because it is not an option that is open to the mass of the oppressed: it is only those who have power who articulate the liberal fiction of magnanimity.

Fifteen years will have passed, and an international reputation will have been deservedly gained, before Coetzee reviews the work of another black writer, Njabulo Ndebele. In view of the critique he will offer soon after about the failure of 'white writing' to become 'African', it is important to stress why Coetzee values Ndebele. Ndebele, he asserts, 'writes the clear, polished English of someone who is clearly not only at home in the language but has passed through an orthodox literary apprenticeship', an apprenticeship which Coetzee tells us is in striking contrast with what he calls a 'Soweto school', which is marked by being unliterary to the point of being anti-literary, or even subliterary.

While there is much to commend the distinction, as well as the recognition that the formal characteristics of the 'Soweto school' owes its existence as much to an affirmation of proletarian origins as to a 'segregated' (*sic*) society, the valuing of Ndebele would appear to depend upon a paradox: if white writing is in peril because it has not yet become 'African', and the 'Soweto school' is not an alternative because of the deficiencies discerned in it by Coetzee, how then to account for Ndebele? For Coetzee, Ndebele (unlike La Guma) has succeeded precisely because he has made the transition from 'African' to being 'at home' in 'English'. In other words, Ndebele has acquired, through apprenticeship, the best that Europe can offer: he has become, if you wish, 'white' by marginalising that which is 'African', most notably the oral and the popular.

As with the earlier instance of La Guma, Coetzee's reading of Ndebele exposes his unfamiliarity with text, as well as context, thus leading to a paradoxical conclusion. To annex Ndebele to the traditions acquired from Europe is not only to posit an unsubtle binarism unexpected in so sophisticated a critic, but also to obliterate Ndebele's origins in the Black Consciousness moment of 1976. Yet, when Coetzee seeks to locate Ndebele's value in the fact that, like Ayi Kwei Armah, he can be a teacher and healer of his people, such capacity must be placed in question if his practice is foreign to the experience of the oppressed as they themselves have expressed it.

But Coetzee will not have that. What makes Ndebele an appropriate interlocutor for him is because of the reverberations in the black writer of Dostoevsky – the figure Zamani in *Fools* 'in particular is a Dostoevskian holy fool, a man with a dark past – a "lovable evil".' The problem with such a reading is that it depends, fundamentally, upon a paradox: while Coetzee is mistaken about the specifics, he is fundamentally correct about the broader context when he uses his review of *Fools* to observe that it seems to him that 'a feature of the South African novel for some while has been that its writers have not known how to end what they had begun, or what the times they are representing have begun for them. It is as though the end, the true and just end, has assumed the aspect of that which cannot be imagined, that which can be represented only as fantasy. . . ' ('review of *Fools*' 36).

Stripped of the encrustations of metaphysics, what Coetzee quite correctly highlights in his reading of *Fools* is that old chestnut about the 'South African National Novel'. Writing for one of the most influential journals of state and big business opinion in the country, Coetzee remarks:

> The question is, can we find anyone who *knows* South African society well enough to present it in the depth and fullness that we (and our descendants, and the outside world) would – legitimately – demand from a Great National Novel? Or, to put the question in quite a different way: Has South African society that degree of organic unity that it can actually be known and represented from the inside out, as let us say, Tolstoy does for mid-nineteenth century society at all levels? ('The Great South African Novel' 74, 77, 79)[13]

The formulation takes us back to the central paradox that marks Coetzee's criticism (and perhaps his fiction as well): if the future for white writing is to become 'African', it will have to break with the traditions of the liberal bourgeois classic realist text; yet recourse to that tradition is imperative in order to write the Great South African Novel. While it is important to recognise that Coetzee's best work is marked by his endeavour to tease out that paradox, it is equally important to recognise that Ndebele's best work is marked precisely by his explicit recognition of hybridity. This hybridity refers notably, not to the formal elements Ndebele has acquired from Europe, but especially to the forms and practises of collectivity that are the characteristics of black experience in its resistance to an oppression that is not simply to do with race and colour: the stories are also about class ('The Music of the Violin') and gender ('The Prophetess').

There is a further paradox: because of the skills, which Coetzee approves of, that are present in Ndebele's work, it must be inferred that the black, rather than the white, English-speaking liberal writer, is best placed to effect the resolution of the 'problem' of writing the 'Great National Novel'. Is it being excessively cynical to suggest that it was ever thus: for blacks to create for white South Africa what it is unable to do for itself? Indeed, the only moments of passion in Coetzee's writing are when he offers a critique of a white liberal tradition from which he cannot wholly free himself. For instance, reviewing Christopher Hope's *White Boy Running*, he asks directly: 'Why should liberal whites have proved so fickle, so spineless? And why should so natural a liberal as Hope – middle class, individualist, pacific – have lost all faith in the relevance of liberal ideals?' The critic's answer is that we should look no further than the history of South Africa since 1960, which provides 'eloquent proof that reasonable suasion, legal argument, and peaceful protests are ineffectual against an adversary to whom *raisons d'état* are the only reason' (*WW* 37, 39).

Now, not only is this evidence of an old-fashioned and wholly untenable view that the real struggle is between the two dominant white groups, it also points again to a deformation of the historical record. The history of South Africa is marked by one overriding fact: not that of the contest between Boer and Briton, but that of the cooperation between them to impose and retain white hegemony over black. Indeed, bearing in mind that the political and cultural history of South Africa between the beginning of the ninteenth century and the end of the Second World War has been one in which traditions imported from Britain have been dominant, one of the most distinguishing features is how the rhetoric and practices of European (especially English) liberalism have been used to maintain blacks in positions of inferiority. The history of white liberalism in South Africa is not allied to a tradition of freedom, but rather to one of oppression, even though that oppression differs in form, as well as in justification, from that of its Afrikaner antagonist. Battles between Boer and Briton have historically been over strategies and technologies for the modernisation of the oppression of blacks.

It is in writing about the Afrikaner that Coetzee excels, especially when he deals with the complex dialectics that mark the work of Breyten Breytenbach. Two observations, in particular, merit citation, in that they point not only to a different trajectory from that of the past English liberal tradition, but might also have some bearing on a future literary practice. For the makers of Afrikaner cultural policy, Coetzee's observation that 'there is an interest in not acknowledging that there can coexist in a single breast both a belief in a unitary democratic South Africa and a profound Afrikaans *digterskap*, poetness. Hence the notion that the "terrorist" in Breytenbach can be incarcerated and punished while the poet in him can be let free' is absolutely spot-on (Coetzee, review of *True Confessions* 73). Equally spot-on is Coetzee's assessment of the poet: he stresses that feature of Breytenbach's poetry which 'stops at nothing: there is no limit that cannot be exceeded, no obstacle that cannot be leaped, no commandment that cannot be questioned. His writing characteristically goes beyond, in more senses than one, what one had thought could be said in Afrikaans' (ibid. 74).

V CONCLUSION: PARADOX RETAINED

The primary objective of this paper has been to show that, notwithstanding his location within a postmodernist tradition of fiction-making, when it comes to criticism J. M. Coetzee continues to inhabit the unresolved landscape of the deformations brought about by the continuing hold of an aesthetics of liberalism in South Africa.[14] If such a position can be characterised, commonsensically, as 'ambivalence', Stephen Watson has sought to account for what he calls such 'ambivalences' in Coetzee by restorting to Albert Memmi's notion of the 'dissenting coloniser' ('Colonialism and the Novels of J. M. Coetzee'). This seems to me to be quite wrong-headed. The core of Memmi's case is that *it sometimes happens* that a coloniser who is a new arrival 'refuses' and might by that, as well as other actions, become a 'moral hero' (Memmi (1990), 85, 89).

Coetzee clearly does not fit Memmi's description: he is neither a new arrival nor desirous of becoming a 'moral hero' for the dispossessed. There is, nevertheless, another and different manner in which the term 'dissenting' (without the 'coloniser' noun) might apply in his case; that, too, rests on a paradox. To the extent that he reconstitutes the ruling myths of the tribe, Coetzee is clearly a dissenter, yet it is precisely the privilege of being one of the descendants of Cadmus that empowers him to dissent. That Coetzee is arguably, along with Breytenbach and a new generation of white women who write in Afrikaans (Jeannette Ferreira, Emma Huismans, Rachelle Greeff, Marlene van Niekerk),[15] a highly principled example of the category of 'dissenter', in the restricted sense in which I use it, is worthy of celebration and should be recognised as a contribution to the struggle for liberation; but that still does not qualify him (or the other white writers mentioned) as being attached to the 'postcolonial' project. The 'post' in post-apartheid South Africa will continue to have to wrestle with the 'post' in postcolonialism, as well as the one in postmodernism. Context will have to struggle with con-text in the Manichean world of the 'new South Africa'.

One overriding reason why Coetzee's criticism, for all the problems I have sought to show mar(k)s it, is ultimately liberatory is because of his awareness of the discursive pitfalls of the terrain to be traversed, whether spatial (South African histories and cultures) or textual and linguistic. The conclusions he comes to about the comparative analysis of the first two lines of a translation of a poem by André Breton with one written by a computer, offer pertinent proof of the critic's awareness of the unresolved problem:

> We are left with a paradoxical phenomenon: two texts . . . which, if subjected to formal analysis, are describable in much the same terms, but whose background histories (to speak metaphorically) are utterly divergent. . . . In the beginning the two texts are very similar. We read one of them in terms of the intentionality of its creator, the other in terms of grammatical theory. In the course of the readings, the texts grow apart. Where we first saw likeness, we now see difference. But the truth is that neither the likeness nor the difference was inherent in the texts. Likeness and difference were meanings we did not find but created. (Coetzee, 'Surreal Metaphors and Random Processes' 30)

Notes

I should like to express my appreciation to Ms Jean Albert, formerly of the South African Public Library and the Cape Town City Library, for locating and making available to me copies of newspaper articles and reviews on or by J. M. Coetzee.

1. Of the seven chapters that constitute *White Writing*, 'Blood, Taint, Flaw, Degeneration: the Novels of Sarah Gertrude Millin' first appeared in *English Studies in South Africa* 23.1 (1980); 'Idleness in South Africa' first appeared in *Social Dynamics* 8.1 (1982) and, in a revised version, under the title 'Anthropology and the Hottentots' in *Semiotica* 54.1–2 (1985).

2. Coetzee's doctoral thesis, conferred by the University of Texas in Austin in 1969, is entitled 'The English Fiction of Samuel Beckett: An Essay in Stylistic Analysis'. Relevant articles of this period include: 'The Comedy of Point of View in Beckett's *Murphy*', in *Critique* 12.2 (1970); 'The Manuscript Revisions of Beckett's *Watt*', *Journal of Modern Literature* 2 (1973); 'Samuel Beckett and the Temptations of Style', *Theoria* 41 (1973): 45–50; 'Samuel Beckett's *Lessness*: An Exercise in Decomposition', in *Computers in the Humanities* 7.4 (1973).
3. See, for example, 'Statistical Indices of Difficulty', *Language and Style* 2.3 (1969); 'Achterberg's "Ballade van de gasfitter": The Mystery of I and You', *PMLA* 92 (1977); 'The Agentless Sentence as Rhetorical Device', *Language and Style* 13.1 (1980); 'The Rhetoric of the Passive in English', *Linguistics* 18.3–4 (1980); 'Newton and the Ideal of a Transparent Scientific Language', *Journal of Literary Semantics* 11.1 (1982).
4. See 'Nabokov's *Pale Fire* and the Primacy of Art', *UCT Studies in English* 5 (1974); 'Confession and Double Thoughts: Tolstoy, Rousseau, Dostoevsky', *Comparative Literature* 37.3 (1985); 'Censorship and Polemic: The Solzhenitsyn Affairs', in *Pretexts* 2.2 (1990).
5. See Kenneth Parker's two forthcoming works: 'Un(utterably) Other Others', in Barker, Hulme and Iversen (eds), *Writing Travels*; 'Fertile Land, Romantic Spaces, Uncivilized Peoples', in Schwartz (ed.), *The Expansion of England*.
6. A selective listing might include the following: Piniel Shava, *A People's Voice* (1989); Jane Watts, *Black Writers from South Africa* (1989); Michael Vaughan, 'Literature and Populism in South Africa', in Gugelberger (ed.), *Marxism and African Literature* (1985); *Research in African Literatures* 19:1 (1988) – special issue on Black South African Literature since 1976; *Current Writing: Text and Reception in South Africa* 1.1 (1989).
7. See Helize van Vuuren, 'Verwronge beeld van Afrikaanse letterkunde in *White Writing*', *Die Suid-Afrikaan* (1988); Hennie Aucamp, 'Skerpsinning – maar altyd wáár?', *Die Burger* 15.9 (1988); M. van Wyk Smith, review of *White Writing* in *English in Africa* 17:2 (1990); Christopher Hope, 'Language as Home: Colonisation by Words', *Weekly Mail* (July 22–8, 1988).
8. See Guy Butler, *Stranger to Europe: Poems 1939–1949* (1952; augmented edition 1960).
9. See Coetzee, 'Alex la Guma and the Responsibilities of the South African Writer' (1971). Coetzee will write about La Guma again in *English in Africa*, ed. Alan Lennox-Short (1973): 111–32, and in *Studies in Black Literature* 4.4 (misnumbered: should be 5.1): 16–23. It is tantalising to speculate on the reasons why Coetzee should have chosen to publish in *Jonala* which had originally appeared in 1966 as *Journal of New African Literature* in order to provide a facility in which black critics, mostly from Africa, might find a space to publish. Its editor, Joe Okpaku, was to argue later that the aim 'was to encourage writers to give expression to their own inclinations, no matter the straightness or waywardness of their works'. This 'New Generation'

of 'young men' (*sic*), the editor asserted, 'refused any patronage, denounced the Negritude–Tigritude debate as irrelevant, and declared that there was no such animal as 'universality' in the jungle of genuine criticism. This term *universality* was just another euphemism for *European* or *Western*'.

10. It might be useful to interpolate a personal note. Much of the factual information upon which I draw comes from participation, as a member of the South African Coloured Peoples' Congress, in some of the campaigns cited, from schoolboy involvement onwards. The interpolation is not to seek to privilege personal experience, it is merely to place on record that my friendship with John Coetzee (at university), and with Alex la Guma (in political action), dates from those years. Indeed, it is largely because of John Coetzee's interventions that, in the aftermath of the De Klerk speech of February 1990, I was grudgingly given a visa to return to South Africa for three months at the beginning of 1991 to be Visiting Professor at the University of Cape Town, where I was the recipient of many kindnesses on his part.
11. For liberal-humanist South African debates on the rôle of the writer in the period under discussion, see, in particular, the 'Foreword' by Jack Cope to the inaugural number of *Contrast* 1.1 (1960). The continuing recalcitrant force of that position might be judged by the (only marginally modified) reiterations by the present editor, Geoffrey Haresnape – see, in particular, *Contrast* 60 (December 1985), *Contrast* 63 (July 1987), *Contrast* 65 (July 1988).
12. See the essay 'The Mind of Apartheid: Geoffrey Cronjé (1907–)', in *Social Dynamics* (1991). For a further insight into Coetzee's current positions on the nature of the relationship between writer and state, with particular reference to censorship, see his 'André Brink and the Censor', in *Research in African Literatures* (1990). See also Louw, 'Satan and Censorship', *Southern African Review of Books* (1989): 13 – translated and extracted from *Die Suid-Afrikaan* (December 1988/ January 1989), which reports Coetzee's denunciation of the 'disinviting' by the Congress of South African Writers of Salman Rushdie (and of Nadine Gordimer's rôle in that act) under pressure from Islamic fundamentalists in South Africa. (Note that Islamic fundamentalists in South Africa hold a little-known world record with regard to the 'Rushdie affair': they were the first group to threaten to kill him, following the issuing of the *fatwa*; the text of *The Satanic Verses* had not even reached South African bookshops at the time.)
13. See also 'Into the Dark Chamber: the Novelist and South Africa', *New York Times Book Review* (January 1986): 13, 35.
14. See Vaughan, 'Literature and Politics' (1982).
15. See Jeanette Ferreira, *Die mammies, die pappies, die hondjies, die katjies* (1989); Emma Huismans, *Berigte van weerstand* (1990); Rachelle Greeff, *Die rugkant van die bruid* (1990); Marlene van Niekerk *Die vrou wat haar verkyker vergeet het* (1992).

Part II

6

Dusklands: A Metaphysics of Violence

PETER KNOX-SHAW

'What is important is the philosophy of history'. Standing as an epigraph to 'The Narrative of Jacobus Coetzee', Flaubert's remark serves as a valuable guide to J. M. Coetzee's concerns both in *Dusklands* (Johannesburg 1974) and in his later work. Yet *Dusklands* stands apart from the novels that immediately follow it in remaining directly answerable to history itself. For in this first novel Coetzee presents distinct historical settings (a state department of propaganda during the Vietnam war, Namaqualand in 1760–2) each replete with documentary detail, from which he allows philosophical abstraction to emerge through tacit comparison and the commentary of his narrators, while in his next two works abstraction informs even the setting. Suspended between ox wagons and flying machines that drop crystalline Spanish, the narrator of *In the Heart of the Country* (1976) inhabits a 'theatre of stone and sun', a *mise-en-scène* that assimilates both the colonial ascendancy and Cuban presence. This procedure is taken even further in *Waiting for the Barbarians* (1980) where the setting, though quite readily identified as the Namibian border by overseas readers, stubbornly retains the larger identity – as Cavafy's title and the medley of flora and fauna alone indicate – of any imperial frontier. Necessarily sparse and yet kaleidoscopic, Coetzee's universal histories are of a special order – insufficiently dense to satisfy D. H. Lawrence's dictum that the novel supplies a criticism of the doctrine to which it adheres, sufficiently unsteady to resist any systematic comparison with a particular history. *Dusklands*, however, despite its bifurcated narrative, is more traditional in conception and an approach to it as a referential text may help to clarify some of J. M. Coetzee's perennial preoccupations.

I shall be concerned chiefly with the second part of *Dusklands* and with the historical context so firmly delineated there by a variety of published records cited or quoted in the text. The documentary presentation serves, of course, as an ironic mask to what is essentially an anti-documentary polemic. Dustjacketed in mouldy watercolour and equipped with an editorial apparatus that outfusses a Van Riebeeck Society reprint, 'The Narrative of Jacobus Coetzee' enters the ranks of Africana as a slim fifth column. Fact and fiction are subtly intermeshed in the narrative, but we soon learn to distinguish fiction from historical report by the claim it establishes to a more potent truth. A wilfully obtuse commentary, translated from the Afrikaans of a chauvinist academic (identified by the author as his father), puts the finishing touches to an inside job.

Of the four documents that comprise the second part of *Dusklands*, only the last is authentic: the three-page deposition made by Jacobus Coetzee at the Castle in 1760.[1] Written up by a notary (Coetzee himself was illiterate), this bald third-person account of the elephant hunter who thought himself the first European to have crossed the Orange River and who came back with stories of a strange tribe further north, supplies an open framework for the fictional narrative of the explorer's first journey into the interior. Its sequel – the second journey to the land of the Great Namaqua – corresponds, if only in date, to a fact- finding expedition under the official command of Captain Hop but effectively led by Jacobus Coetzee, which retraced Coetzee's steps of the previous year. An uneventful though fairly detailed diary of this expedition, kept by Carel Frederik Brink, survives;[2] and it is no surprise to find that J. M. Coetzee has made use of it in reconstructing the explorer's original progress. While remaining consistent with the historical deposition, the first part of the narrative accordingly coincides at many points with the accounts of Brink. The description of Coetzee's approach to the Great River, for example, derives from the journal of the later expedition:

> Between August 2 and August 6 we covered the fifty miles to the Groene River. The going was hard. We had to force the cattle through the last day. The country is dry and sandy, nor is there game. We allowed the oxen four days to recover.
>
> Two days north of the Groene River we passed an abandoned Namaqua kraal.

On August 15 we reached the river which the Hottentots call the Koussie. Here we rested.

On August 18 we reached the defiles of the Kooperbergen and saw the date 1685 carved on the rocks.

The high ranges end a day's journey beyond the Kooperbergen and you enter a sandy, waterless plain. (*D* 67)

Monday 24 August... after a march of $4^{1}/_{4}$ miles arrived at the Groene River. .. As the veld hereabouts was better covered with grass and our draught-oxen were in general in very poor condition and eighteen of those of the Hon. Company had died, it was resolved that we remain here a few days...

Sunday 30th Aug. When we left the Groene River already mentioned...

Monday 31st Aug. We resumed our journey as far as the Klipvalley at a Namaqua kraal...

Tuesday 8th Sept. We emerged from the Aloë Kloof and pitched camp at the great Sand River [*Editor's note: 'Buffels R. or Koussie, from Nama'*]

Sunday 13th do. We passed the Kloof of the Kooperbergen at the exit of which we found the Copper Mountains which were mined by the Hon. Simon van der Stel in the year 1685.... We saw several excavations which had been made in them, the deepest about a man's length. To the right of the way, the aforesaid year 1685 was hewn out on a rock...

Friday 18th do. Resumed our journey across a sandy plain and finding no water for our cattle, saw it was necessary to continue our march farther. (*The Journals of Brink and Rhenius* 17–25)

Apart from minor recensions such as the staggering of Brink's dates and the choice of the original name for the 'Buffels' river, two departures are worth a gloss in passing. The copper mine which Jacobus Coetzee had noted in his deposition, and over which Brink on his way back expended his most detailed entry (*D* 58–61), appears in *Dusklands* merely as a date 'carved on the rocks'. The fictional narrative is distinguished throughout by a virtual effacement of economic motive. Nothing is made of the gold dust which Jacobus Coetzee gathered on the banks of the Great River and later displayed at the Castle (indeed the omission is noted).[3] Moreover, the poverty-stricken burgher of history[4] hunts in

Dusklands to satisfy a refined blood-lust (kills for 'metaphysical meat' – 85) rather than to procure the ivory for which he had been granted a permit by the Governor.

In place of the mercenary concerns that predominate in most early colonial travelogues, J. M. Coetzee allots the foreground to his explorer's encounter with primitives. Brink's Namaqua kraal appears as 'abandoned' only to preserve a fuller impact for the scene of the first meeting with the Hottentots north of the Orange River. Though this finely realised sequence follows Jacobus Coetzee's report of his unfriendly reception among the Great Namaqua, it gives dramatic substance to that liveliness which an earlier explorer on the northern route had taken for insolence and found threatening:

> They remained near us sitting round about and prating of naught save tobacco. They giggled and laughed with our Hottentots, poking fun at us, so it seemed, and had they the chance would have treated us as enemies, so that it was hardly to be endured. (from Bergh's Journal 1682)[5]

Olaf Bergh moved off; but from this point on Jacobus Coetzee is ever more closely enmeshed in a fiction that exposes his hatred of hedonism and dread of betrayal at every turn. Once in the Namaqua camp, he returns from the chief to find four of his five Hottentot servants standing disaffectedly by while his wagon is pilfered. Taking aim at a Namaqua dancer who advances voluptuously towards him (further proof of his failure to inspire awe) he fires into the dust at her feet. He heads north but his flight is shortlived – fever and further non-compliance from his men again deliver him over to the hospitality of the tribe. Inside the menstruation hut that serves him as sick-bay he hears music carried over the stream from the hippopotamus feast, delicate sounds that fill him with 'new anxiety, sensual terror' (*D* 91). Determined the next morning to reclaim his servants from new-found life, only too eager in fact to disentangle them from their night of love, he is rebuffed by all but his faithful Klawer. Yet it is the innocent mischief of the Nama children, who remove his clothes while he pollutes their river, that provokes the supreme expression of his anger: 'I screamed with rage, snapped my teeth, and heaved erect with a mouth full of hair and a human ear' (96). He emerges from the resulting mêlée to hear himself pronounced mad and unfit for society; and suffers the (traditional)[6] penalty of banishment. His servants defect to the Namaqua, with the sole exception of Klawer in whose company he sets out on foot for the Colony.

A further passage from Brink provides the basis of the sequences that follow. The drowning in the Orange River of Jacobus Coetzee's Hottentot guide is tersely reported in the journal: 'when crossing the river with his cattle, he had the misfortune to fall into the stream and was drowned' (*D* 29–31). The narrative of *Dusklands* unblinkingly provides two versions of Klawer's death, the first of which enlarges slightly on Brink's report of the incident while the second, offering a far more intricate account, contradicts it. Noticing this feature of the text in a review of *Dusklands,* Jonathan Crewe commented on the author's demonstration of 'the fictiveness of his fiction' and remarked that 'the two accounts were equally plausible' (Crewe 91).

Although this holds true, I suspect that the disjuncture is intended rather to alert us to the ease with which a sole witness may falsify facts prejudicial to his self-presentation. In this case it is only the narrator's obsessive interest in the pain of others that breaks down the reflexes of his defence. Cancelling the story of an accidental drowning, Jacobus Coetzee proceeds to linger over an episode that betrays the depths of his callousness. We hear of a Klawer who, after shivering in wet clothes on the bank, hopelessly presses himself against his companion for bodily warmth during the night; who, forced the next morning up the steep south ascent, is abandoned at last to die of exposure on the crest. While indulging in the heroic pathos of this final tableau the narrator falls a victim to the author's irony, for he is himself convicted by that indictment of brutality which he levels against Bushmen in the preamble to his journal:

> I found [an old Bushman woman up in the mountains] in a hole in the rocks abandoned by her people, too old and sick to walk. For they are not like us, they don't look after their aged, when you cannot keep up with the troop they put down a little food and water and abandon you to the animals. (*D* 63)

The narrator's conduct is extenuated neither by necessity nor by his dependant's age.

With Klawer's second death the narrative of the first journey comes full circle in a restatement of its opening theme, 'Everywhere differences grow smaller as they come up and we go down' (61). Jacobus's fear of losing racial identity in the wilderness remains latent all along in the anxious watch he keeps over his 'tame' Hottentots, since in their 'betrayal' he reads his own capacity for reversion to the wild. But only when he is southward bound through the desert, smeared with fat and equipped with a bow, does he face the choice of returning home or adapting to his new existence, 'the life of the white Bushman that had been hinting itself' (105). From this novel perspective he reviews his recent experience among the Namaqua whom he finds altogether lacking in 'true savagery' and proceeds to frame a proposition – 'Even I knew more about savagery than they' (104) – which his brutal violations of hospitality and disregard for the servant who had patiently nursed him through fever, amply substantiate. The insight appears to confirm a growing disposition for the nomadic life but, despite his having tasted the joys of ecstatic independence (101), Coetzee brushes aside its temptations. Like Marlow on the Congo River he sticks doggedly to his route, distracting himself the while with problems of mental arithmetic; but his situation differs in one crucial respect. For while Marlow and Coetzee both face the darkness they are, respectively, outward and homeward bound. Where Marlow on his way to the inner station attempts to preserve an attachment to light, Coetzee on retracing his steps reaffirms his alliance with darkness. The return to polity, that central and often highly intricate topos of exploratory fiction, receives a resolutely ironic treatment from J. M. Coetzee. Reversing the traditional scheme, Jacobus turns his back on the broad daylight of the interior to descend once more into the duskland of his familiar terrain:

> In the evening I reached the markers of my own land. Unseen I donned my clothes and buried my bow. Like God in a whirlwind I fell upon a lamb, an innocent little fellow who had never seen his master and was thinking only of a good night's sleep, and slit his throat. (106)

A radical commitment to savagery keeps Coetzee in the paths of righteousness. It is as an avowed barbarian that he remains faithful to his God, and opts for home in preference to the wild.

'New life gushed into my heart', the narrator observes on first glimpsing the border (*D* 106); but this is Dracula revived by a sundowner rather than the Ancient Mariner blessing the water-snakes unaware. Coetzee's initial response, his assault on colonial property, goes beyond the mischief of Bushmen, for its consequences are visited on their heads. The thesis of 'true savagery' finds full expression, however, only in the narrative of the second journey (subtitled 'Expedition of Captain Hendrik Hop, 16 August 1761–27 April 1762') that immediately follows.

One may wonder whether irony is a suitable vehicle for the ghastly scenes in which J. M. Coetzee deals. In the first part of *Dusklands* the narrator remarks that the 'message' of print is sadistic – 'I can say anything and not be moved. Watch as I permute my 52 affectless signs' (*D* 15). That perhaps, in view of literature's power to excite compassion, may be dismissed as the quibble of a precisian. But the idea that distanced documentary (particularly that of the camera) can corrupt response is convincingly projected: thumbing through his war photographs, for example, Eugene Dawn observes, 'I find something ridiculous about a severed head . . . like a small purchase from the supermarket . . . I giggle' (*D* 16). The hypothesis that the private life is inextricable from the public one is carried in 'The Vietnam Project' to the point of precise demonstration (Eugene Dawn's jettisoning of his wife and capture of his child corresponds exactly with his mythographic prescriptions for Vietnam; *D* 28) and this would certainly appear to include a diagnostic link between the loss of affect Dawn displays in personal relations and his work as a military propagandist. Yet the descriptions of violence in the second journey – the massacre of Nama villagers, the execution of the four former servants – are pretty much the equivalent of Dawn's footage. Nothing offsets the sadistic agency of the narrator: in so far as the suffering of Coetzee's victims is recorded, it is through the gloating eyes of their killer. The tonal range shifts from sick:

> At the foot of the hill he broke into a funny little trot with his head down and his hands stretched out behind like a running hen (*D* 111)

to glassy:

> A man, a sturdy Hottentot, began running after us clutching an enormous brown bundle to his chest. A Griqua in green

> jacket and scarlet cap came chasing after him waving a sabre. Soundlessly the sabre fell on the man's shoulder. The bundle slid to the ground and began itself to run. It was a child, quite a big one. Why had the man been carrying it? The Griqua now chased the child. He tripped it and fell upon it. The Hottentot sat up holding his shoulder. He no longer seemed interested in the child. The Griqua was doing things to the child on the ground. It must be a girl child. (*D* 109)

The tone is controlled, certainly, and the effect carefully produced – but in the absence of any other resource it must be said that the writing itself furthers the claims of true savagery. This is an art that can only re-enact.

Yet to turn back to Brink's journal of the second expedition is to experience momentary relief. It appears that Captain Hop and his party took their fact-finding mission seriously enough to trek north of the Leewens River for five weeks with limited water, in search of a tawny-haired, linen-clad nation of whom Coetzee had heard rumour on his earlier venture. There is no record of racial friction on the journey and, indeed, Coetzee himself seems not to have been without scruples, for he refused the services of much-needed Namaqua guides who offered themselves on condition they received help to fight their enemy, the Enicquas (*D* 29–31). The fictional Coetzee, needless to say, has no such compunction about the Griquas.

Debunking has its rules (Strachey was required to account even for Arnold's weak ankles) but *Dusklands* relies on other methods. Emptied of their original content, its documentary receptacles are packed with explosive material, so that an apparently innocent mission ('Expedition of Captain Hendrik Hop, etc'.) turns to shrapnel as Coetzee's fictional vendetta detonates. Not perhaps since Defoe has fiction so effectively assumed a specious armour of document. This is not to say, however, that the fiction itself is unhistorical.

Though for the most part J. M. Coetzee side-steps the corpus of Dutch Africana, he draws heavily on other travelogues. Many illustrative details (in addition to those footnoted by the narrator, Dr S. J. Coetzee) are taken from John Barrow's travels (1801), and there is much by way of analysis that coincides with Le Vaillant's commentary in his two sets of journals (1780–5, 1783–5). Neither of these writers was at all partisan to the Dutch cause.

Barrow celebrates the benefits of British rule, Le Vaillant enjoys the detachment of the *philosophe*; and both supply horrifying testimony to atrocities committed in the Cape, chiefly on the outskirts of the Colony beyond the effective rule of law. The passage from the second journey quoted above could be matched by Barrow's description of a Hottentot mother whipped while clutching her child (*An Account* vol. II, 96), or by Le Vaillant's account of a child who, having escaped from a village massacre, was shot after a contention between two burghers as to which should possess him (*Travels into the Interior* Vol. I, 298–9). There is, nevertheless, a significant difference of emphasis in the representation. For although Barrow and Le Vaillant make allowance for sadism (on several occasions Barrow indicts the 'boors' *tout court*) they are concerned to observe the social context – a situation of virtual or open conflict – in which such acts of violence occur. Indeed, Le Vaillant shrewdly identifies an economic motive behind the wholesale denigration,

> the planters every where [give] out, that these people [are] barbarous and sanguinary, in order to justify their robberies

and goes on to observe that massacres license theft:

> under pretence of their cattle being carried away, [the planters] had, without regard to age or sex, exterminated whole hordes of Caffres, plundered them of their oxen, and ravaged their lands; that this method of procuring live stock appearing to be much easier than to rear them themselves, they had employed it with so much indiscretion for more than a year, that they had shared above twenty thousand among them; and . . . had massacred without mercy all those who had attempted to defend them. (*Travels into the Interior* 297–8)

The violence in *Dusklands* is made to appear comparatively gratuitous. The narrator's motives for murder are slight (defiant servants), and even ridiculous (ants on the scrotum). His violence accordingly presents itself as a more or less unconstrained expression of his nature.

We are not, all the same, encouraged to regard Jacobus Coetzee as a monster. Whereas Voss at the outset of his career, and Ahab at the close of his, are each shown to be eccentrically placed in relation to their societies, there is nothing to distinguish Jacobus Coetzee from the type of the frontier settler. Indeed, it is essential to J. M. Coetzee's purposes in *Dusklands* that his explorer should emerge as a representative figure, not only in the context of Afrikanerdom but of Western culture as well. The procedures whereby Coetzee universalises from the particular ramify at many levels, and even a superficial analysis would have to include a breakdown of the parallels between the two separate narratives and a close look at devices such as anachronism (Jacobus Coetzee refers to Jacaranda trees, flame-throwers and Blake) and the mixing of styles; but in concluding my discussion I shall restrict myself to such examples as arise.

While the bifurcated structure of *Dusklands* metaphorically apposes contemporary America and the Dutch Colony (as the intruder), it also opposes the exotic and Western (as victim and aggressor); and this gap is widened further by a brand of naïve primitivism elliptically retailed by both narrators. The imputed absence, for example, of ritual, law and government among the Namaqua (*D* 88, 104) serves as a foil to the love of complex ritual which Jacobus Coetzee identifies both with cultural greatness and with his own sado-masochism:

> I might even have consented to die at the sacrificial stake: if the Hottentots had been a greater people, a people of ritual . . . But while it was conceivable that in a fit of boredom the Hottentots might club my brains out, it was unlikely that, lacking all religion and a fortiori all ritual, they would subject me to ritual sacrifice. (*D* 88)

The ironic comedy of Jacobus's distaste for an idyllic life that has no sadistic refinements to offer, reflects the notion that culture institutionalises the love of pain whether suffered or inflicted – the thesis advanced by Friedrich Nietzsche in *Beyond Good and Evil*:

> Almost everything we call 'higher culture' is based on the spiritualisation and intensification of *cruelty* – this is my proposition; the 'wild beast' has not been laid to rest at all, it lives, it flourishes, it has merely become – deified. (Nietzsche 140)

Whereas Nietzsche is concerned with emphasing the essential

continuity of primitive and advanced cultures, the two are presented in *Dusklands* as disjunct and antinomic. Yet if the reports of Wikar hold any truth, Jacobus Coetzee need not have deviated far from his route to have found his desires for ritualistic penetration fully satisfied.[7]

'I have taken it upon myself', Jacobus Coetzee remarks at the conclusion of his narrative, 'to be the one to pull the trigger... committing upon the dark folk the murders we have all wished' (*D* 113). His generalisation is given substance by the most emphatic parallel between the text of the two narratives. It is, significantly, not with Eugene Dawn's deranged wanderings but with an authoritative diagnosis of American hostilities in Vietnam that Jacobus Coetzee's extended meditation on violence coincides (18–19, 83–5). Placed at the climax of a process of imaginative tumescence thoroughly typical of exploratory fiction (Jacobus's fever brings on hallucinations and a pervasive sense of unreality), this passage participates nonetheless in J. M. Coetzee's inversion of traditional schemes. For in the brilliance of the desert the narrator confronts – in place of a dark, infinitely recessive self – a centre of complete emptiness. The lack of an apparent self prompts him to view his identity as coterminous with that of the external world, 'I am all that I see' (84); but in doing so he involves the entire universe in his sensation of nullity, his inner death. Hence his need for violence. For only by demonstrating his separateness – only by bringing death into the world – can he preserve a belief in external life. These are the conclusions recorded in each of the narratives:

> Our nightmare was that since whatever we reached slipped like smoke through our fingers, we did not exist; that since whatever we embraced wilted, we were all that existed. (*D* 18)
>
> The gun saves us from the fear that all life is within us. It does so by laying at our feet all the evidence we need of a dying and therefore a living world. (84)
>
> The instrument of survival in the wild is the gun, but the need for it is metaphysical rather than physical. (85)
>
> We cut their flesh open, we reached into their dying bodies, tearing out their livers, hoping to be washed in their blood. (18)

Despite the rhetorical piquancy, this is an existentialism of the armchair which, far from withstanding the desert, fails even to penetrate the text. The hare may die to save the explorer's soul from 'merging with the world' (85), but Plaatje, Adonis and the Tamboer brothers are shot precisely because of the resistance they offer to Jacobus's will. Their execution would lack all credibility were it not for the act of defiance that incites their master to revenge. Familiar principles of conflict again underlie the violence presented in the first narrative. A struggle for possession is embroiled even in Eugene Dawn's stabbing of his son, and no intimations of a reality beyond the void are vouchsafed to him either before or after the event. The margin of dissonance between theory and practice in *Dusklands* is a saving grace. For in conferring the status of a categorical imperative upon violence, J. M. Coetzee seriously depreciates the force of context. It is regrettable that a writer of such considerable and varied talents should play down the political and economic aspects of history in favour of a psychopathology of Western life.

Notes

1. The 'Relaas', together with an English translation by Dr E. E. Mossop, appears in *The Journals of Wikar, Coetsé and Van Reenen*, ed., intro. and notes by Dr E. E. Mossop (1935): 276–91. The text given in *Dusklands* (Johannesburg 1974): 131–3 is a translation by the author.
2. 'The Journal of Carel Frederik Brink of the Journey into Great Namaqualand (1761–2) made by Captain Hendrik Hop' in *The Journals of Brink and Rhenius*, transcribed, trans. and ed., with an intro., brief lives and notes by Dr E. E. Mossop (1974): 6–71.
3. By an editorial (*sic*) introduced into the translation of Jacobus Coetzee's deposition (*D* 131).
4. 'He appears, after his return, to have led a life of constant struggle and poverty for many years' (*Journals of Brink and Rhenius* 95). Dr Mossop's findings are based on the *Opgaaf* (the Stellenbosch Census Roll) and on the Company Record of Arrears. According to the census return of 1753 Jacobus Coetzee 'owned only a horse and nothing more'.
5. *The Journals of Bergh and Schrijver*, ed., intro. and notes by Dr E. E. Mossop (1931): 129.
6. In his essay 'The Nama' collected in *The Native Tribes of South West Africa*, ed. C. H. L. Hahn – a work cited in *Dusklands* (130) – Dr H. Vedder comments on 'the declaration of such people, who have been found to be a danger to the public, as of unsound mind. These were then outlawed and could be done away with, without punishment' (Hahn 143).

7. Hendrik Wikar was the first traveller to make a serious study of Namaqua rites (1779). See *The Journals of Wikar, Coetsé and Van Reenen* (65), *Dusklands* (103).

7

Game Hunting in *In the Heart of the Country*

IAN GLENN

I INTRODUCTION

Coetzee's second novel, published in 1976 in South Africa in an edition that used Afrikaans for most of the dialogue, and then in 1977 in the United Kingdom and the United States, is probably his least read and has had the least critical attention. Susan Gallagher argues that 'many readers [while] ... finding lyrical beauty in individual passages of *In the Heart of the Country* ... remain ... confused and sometimes bored by the narrative as a whole' (Gallagher 108).

The reasons for the confusion, if not the boredom, lie in the plot. Magda, a spinster living on an isolated farm somewhere in the Karoo sometime during the last hundred years, appears as the protagonist of two hundred and sixty-six numbered sections. The sections show Magda, a highly intellectual, self-conscious narrator, telling several stories or the same story in different ways. First, Magda's widowed father brings home a new wife and she attempts to murder her father and stepmother. Then, it appears, this was only imagined. The father takes Anna, the young new wife of the 'Coloured' (in the South African sense) servant Hendrik, to bed. This time Magda shoots and kills her father, apparently unintentionally as she is only trying to disturb him, and then struggles to dispose of the body in various ways. In a surreal sequence she cuts off the disturbed bedroom which floats away. She tries to find a new relationship with the servants Hendrik and Anna, inviting them into the house, but the Utopian prospects turn into disorder as the farm runs down and supplies run out. Hendrik takes a kind of vengeance by raping Magda; neighbours appear and Hendrik and Anna run off. Magda tries to communicate with airplanes going over the farm, believing them to be gods. At the end it seems her father is still alive; perhaps the action has all been in Magda's imagination.

II DIFFICULTIES AND THE CRITICAL REACTION

Most of Coetzee's critics have failed to come to grips with this puzzling novel successfully. In South Africa, the urban, industrial, mass upheaval of black scholars in 1976 in Soweto and then the rest of South Africa made it difficult to concentrate on, to appreciate justly, the rural, introspective, highly intellectual exploration of Cape feudal-agrarian life and consciousness. Suspicions of Coetzee's work stemming from this period are to be found not only in overtly Marxist critiques such as Michael Vaughan's, but also in a general uneasiness that the novel is too learned, too intellectual. Even the reading of Stephen Watson, who sees Magda as a way for Coetzee to oppose the order of apartheid, to be a dissenting coloniser, moves to the pessimistic concern that the impotence of Magda's learning and thought leads to the novel being 'a veritable museum – in fact, graveyard – of the thought and literary culture of the West' (Watson, "Colonialism" 37).

In my reading I shall argue that the political critique of Coetzee is misplaced, and that even sympathetic and generally insightful readings of *In the Heart of the Country*, such as those of Penner, Dodd, Gallagher and Gillmer, miss crucial elements of the game he is hunting, and playing, in the novel.

III AUTHORIAL CLUES AND INTENTIONS

Coetzee has given several clues as to how to read the novel. These clues have in general not been picked up or used, and in the first case the clue was damaged in transmission. In Coetzee's interview with Stephen Watson, the following exchange took place after Watson asked why Coetzee had used narrators whose consciousnesses were anachronistic:

COETZEE: I would reply to a criticism like that by saying that (a) Jacobus Coetzee is not a 18th century frontiersman and (b) Magda is not a colonial spinster.
WATSON: Who are they then?
COETZEE: I . . . figures in books. (Watson, 'Speaking' 23)

Lest one imagines this to be Coetzee's confession that 'Magda c'est moi', it should be said that *Speak* printed 'I . . . figures' for the correct 'I-figures'. Coetzee, as an expert in stylistics and linguistics, was insisting on the literary device he had used, making the point that these novels break with traditional realism. I shall explore here the ways in which Coetzee breaks with convention and to what ends he does so, but I shall also reconsider the connection between Coetzee and his protagonist.

Coetzee returns to the issue of narrative conventions when Penner asks him to comment on the unreliable narrator:

> That's another game, where . . . how shall I put it? When you opt for a single point of view from inside a single character, you can be opting for psychological realism, a depiction of one person's inner consciousness. And the word I stress there is realism, psychological realism. And I suppose that what is going on in *In the Heart of the Country* is that that kind of realism is being subverted because, you know, she kills her father, and her father comes back, and she kills him again, and the book goes on for a bit, and then he's there again. So that's a different kind of game, an anti-realistic kind of game. (Penner 57)

But the most important clue given by Coetzee is reported by Penner as a prefatory remark to a reading he was going to give from the book: 'In the course of the action people get killed or raped, but perhaps not really, perhaps only in the overactive imagination of the story teller' (56).

IV MAGDA AS WRITER

Josephine Dodd, analysing a pattern of misreadings by reviewers and critics, notes that they 'have repeatedly ignored the highly self-conscious, self-reflective and allusive nature of Magda's narrative' (Dodd 158). Dodd is quite right, but I would go further to claim that the novel announces to us dozens of times that Magda is a storyteller, both writer and character endlessly reflecting on 'my story'. Critics portraying her as the 'perhaps insane spinster' (Penner 56), as a critique of the typical Afrikaner 'vrou en moeder' (Gallagher), or as a case for cultural psychoanalysis (Paulin), have not considered how this case is complicated when we see that Coetzee's 'I-figure' is a storytelling I, a self-reflective writing I reflecting on the conditions of her writing (in terms of class, gender and colonial position), playing with narrative possibilities, wondering what the costs of her intellectual efforts are, even reflecting on herself as a product of textual work.

All of this has simply gone unnoticed by critics, to the point where Gallagher, in her recent study, claims: 'Magda does not comment on the fact that she is writing, ... but she does comment on the fact that she is thinking' (Gallagher 82). This seems to me to miss the force of the explicitly artificial structure of the numbered paragraphs, which form a kind of imaginary diary, a series of writing exercises, a set of meditations à la Nietzsche or Wittgenstein; to forget Magda's writings in stone; and also to fail to see the persistently double frame of reference of Magda's 'I'.

The evidence of Magda's role as inventor of the text is clear from the first section, where her 'Or perhaps' signals for the first time (see, for example, later sections 68, 80, 81, 236 where the *or* or the *perhaps* recur) the artificiality, the arbitrariness of the writer's imagination, where we hear of her needing 'to embroider' (a clear reference to literary artifice) and that she is typical of 'one who stays in her room reading or writing. ...'. As the last sentence of the novel also dwells on what she could have written in other circumstances, Coetzee drops clues to Magda's double role in the novel from start to finish.

The play between the I-as-narrator and the I-as-subject is one of the novel's many stylistic games. A failure to decode that game means a failure to grasp what Coetzee is doing in the novel (and, indeed, more widely in his work). It is clear from Coetzee's critical writing at the time he wrote *In the Heart of the Country* that he was highly interested both in stylistic and literary issues involved with the 'I' in literature and in highly artificial literary structures with a lot of the puzzle or game in them, as his article on Nabokov's *Pale Fire* and the major translation article on Achterberg's 'Gasfitter' sequence of poems (subtitled 'The Mystery of I and You') make clear. (The technical discussion of pronouns and 'shifters' in the latter article, which draws on Jakobson and Benveniste, should be required reading for any serious student of Coetzee.)

Early on in the novel (section 2), Coetzee makes Magda's writing deliberately mimic the prose of the neophyte writer as it takes on the effects of the school essay or literary exercise on a set topic ('The new wife') that comes out overburdened by descriptives and similes: 'The new wife. The new wife is a lazy big-boned voluptuous feline woman with a wide slow-smiling mouth. Her eyes are black and shrewd like two berries, two shrewd black berries' (*IHC*, Johannesburg 1). Magda next reflects 'She is the new wife, therefore the old one is dead' (*IHC* 1). Her imaginative start now imposes on her the need to follow the implicit story line – Magda the writer is reflecting on what the story needs, while Magda the character reflects on her past. Furthermore, Magda's reflection that the image of the mother is 'one such as any girl in my position would be likely to make up for herself' is not simply realistic-psychological, but also shows a self-awareness of her imaginative procedure as writer: of how authenticity, the plausible, are literary conventions.

Similarly, in section 4, the deliberate conventionality of the storyline of the mother's failure to bear a son and her death in childbirth because of the doctor's late arrival reflects Magda's reliance on old stories and codes, shows that this is a retelling. Section 5 ('But why did he not come on horseback? But were there bicycles in those days?') then becomes an authorial questioning of the authenticity of the detail in section 4 rather than just a question of the actual past.

It would be impossible to convey here the full range of what Coetzee tries to do through the double nature of Magda's I. She stands in the text as teller and tale, aching 'to form the words that will translate me into the land of myth and hero' (4), asking 'without liberation what is the point of my story?' More than that, she seems to know, better than her critics, that she is or becomes a textual artifice, a product of her text. When the story seems to falter on the psychology of her behaviour, she proclaims a primary rule of narrative: 'Prolong yourself, prolong yourself, that is the whisper I hear in my inmost' (5).

When Magda wants her 'story to have a beginning, a middle, and an end' (43) or predicts her 'closing plangencies' (138), it can hardly be disputed that Coetzee has played a game undetected by the majority of his critics. The game is at once amusing and centrally revealing:

> A woman with red blood in her veins (what colour is mine? a watery pink? an inky violet?) would have pushed a hatchet into [Hendrik's] hands and bundled him into the house to search out vengeance. A woman determined to be the author of her own life would not have shrunk from hurling open the curtains and flooding the guilty deed with light, the light of the moon, the light of firebrands. But I, as I fear, hover ever between the exertions of drama and the languors of meditation. (*IHC* 62–3)

We have here: Magda the character reflecting as character on her behaviour, with Hamlet wanting to bring Claudius' crime into the light as the literary counterpart; Magda as author reflecting on her inability to shape her imaginative world completely according to her desire; Magda/Coetzee warning that this may not be a real 'flesh and blood' character but one made of ink; and Magda/Coetzee reflecting on the formal and thematic limitations of the text *In the Heart of the Country* that is in the process of being created.

But what does this doubly doubled perspective add? How does it forward Coetzee's form and theme, his social analysis or psychological portrayals? Does it make the novel less vulnerable to Marxist strictures, or to several critics' uneasiness (like Cherry Clayton's, as cited by Watson) that the intellectual show is finally sterile? I would like to look more closely here at narrative form, at Magda's problems as those typical of a colonial writer, and at the problems of language, before turning to the major theme.

V COETZEE AND MAGDA: FORMAL ISSUES OF THE NARRATIVE I-FIGURE

Why should Coetzee have made Magda so learned, conscious, ahistorical, self-reflective, so much the writer of a certain type, a kind of Emily Dickinson with therapy and a thesis in critical theory? Why does she speculate so powerfully on her own condition, her own position, the relationship between her condition and her consciousness? Let me try to answer, first, by simply pointing to the evidence for Coetzee's critical interest in and creative use of 'I-figures' and, second, by recalling from memory Coetzee speaking to the tensions between critic and creator in 1974, at about the time he was writing *In the Heart of the Country*.

He spoke, at the University of Cape Town Summer School, on the difficulties the artist had in keeping topical, ahead of the critic, in an age of increasingly fast critical reaction. In retrospect, this intervention marked, to my mind, some of Coetzee the critic's challenge to Coetzee the artist. (Who wins the chase of critic and creator? How can the creator work but by keeping ahead of the best critics can do? Can the creator help but be a creature of fashion responding with a new code to the decrypter?) Coetzee's talk also highlighted the challenge his body of work was to pose, in its international assumptions, to a South African reading public and academy. How did he innovate formally here?

When Eugene Dawn in *Dusklands* (Penguin 37) announced that he was spending many analytic hours puzzling out the tricks of monologue in Bellow's *Herzog* and Patrick White's *Voss*, Coetzee marked this narrative issue as of particular interest for the writer in an analytic age. In his second novel, Coetzee's formal innovation owes something, in addition to its debts to Nabokov and Beckett, to *Herzog*. *Herzog*'s protagonist has at his disposal every insight, intellectual tool, mode of discourse, available to the writer or reader. Coetzee accepts this formal challenge in writing Magda.

Coetzee's novels persistently ask how one can judge a protagonist when there is none of the usual ironic distance between author and protagonist that protects the reader by providing us with a judgement which distances us from the protagonist. What do we do when we cannot keep an analytic distance through invoking our usual critical kits or parameters, as they seem to have been invoked already by the character concerned? Magda even resists Barthesian or 'textual' readings by repeatedly referring to her own textuality. Baffled in his/her attempts to moralise Magda's story, to give psychological readings to it or to reduce it to literary terms, even to those of avant-garde post-structuralism, the critic seems, in the end, to have no choice other than to surrender to it.

VI MAGDA C'EST MOI: THE PAIN OF COLONIAL WRITINGS

Magda as writer meditates on the limitations of writing as a way of articulating a poetics for Coetzee himself, the fellow writer writing Magda writing Magda. First, Magda allows Coetzee to meditate on his own childhood on the Karoo. Coetzee has talked of growing up, in part, on the Karoo where he was 'born in the twilight of a centuries-old feudal order in which the rights and duties of masters and servants seemed to be matters of unspoken convention, and in which a mixture of personal intimacy and social distance – a mixture characteristic of societies with a slaveholding past – pervaded all dealings' (Penner 63). Coetzee's task here is to understand and undermine that order by bringing out its inherent structural tensions and flaws.

Magda allows Coetzee to reflect on the part played by education in the wrenching apart of childhood ties in colonial situations:

> I grew up with the servants' children. I spoke like one of them before I learned to speak like this. I played their stick and stone games before I knew I could have a dolls' house with Father and Mother and Peter and Jane asleep in their own beds and clean clothes ready in the chest whose drawers slid in and out while Nan the dog and Felix the cat snoozed before the kitchen coals. With the servants' children I searched the veld for khamma-roots, fed cowsmilk to the orphaned lambs, hung over the gate to watch the sheep dipped and the Christmas pig shot. I smelled the sour recesses where they slept pell-mell like rabbits, I sat at the feet of their blind old grandfather while he whittled clothes-pegs and told his stories of bygone days when men and beasts migrated from winter grazing to summer grazing and lived together on the trail. At the feet of an old man I have drunk in a myth of a past when beast and man and master lived a common life as innocent as the stars in the sky, and I am far from laughing. (*IHC* 6–7)

The alienating effects of imported colonial education – here presumably the cosy nuclear family of the British domestic scene of the early school reader opposed to the local 'veld' and 'khamma-roots' – are painful, but that alienation is the source of Magda/Coetzee's power, of being able to 'speak like this' in the complex international linguistic and literary code we read. The power of the pre-industrial harmony presented in this case is not that of a sentimentalised tribal past, but rather that of men working together in a hierarchical colonial setting.

Another device, that of literary allusion, increases the colonial stakes in Magda's writing, as in: 'I live, I suffer, I am here. With cunning and treachery, if necessary, I fight against becoming one of the forgotten ones of history. I am a spinster with a locked diary, but I am more than that' (3).

This joint invocation of Whitman ('I am the man, I suffered, I was there') and Joyce (with his artistic credo of 'silence, exile and cunning') as literary outsiders who forged traditions to rival the metropolitan dominant marks Magda/Coetzee's communion as writer with other writers. Coetzee uses other exemplary colonials to register his investment in Magda's status as an artist, someone whose locked diary will give her (and him) a place in history.

Magda serves, then, as an *alter ego* who can explore the dilemmas of the colonial writer cut off from the landscape and its inhabitants. We need to look further at the part played by language; at the rules of address; at the problem of living in a bilingual or diglossic society.

VII THE COLONIAL AND THE PROBLEM OF LANGUAGE

Coetzee, the Nabokovian spoofer, lurks in the prefatory material of the English language editions, which read 'English version prepared by the author'. This announcement refers specifically to the original version, in which most of the dialogue was in Afrikaans while the descriptive and meditative sections were in English. This division was part of the theme insofar as Magda's distance from the world close to her – the servants, the landscape, the everyday – was marked by a switch in language. English is the language of the dictionary and the isolated bedroom, of international thought. Part of Magda's difficulty, as character and as writer, lies in the switch from home language to international language.

The issue of diglossia, of linguistic difference, is closely linked to issues of power, status and address. In the original South African edition of the novel, the dialogue moves crucially, as Magda searches for closeness to Hendrik and Anna, into a mixing of English and Afrikaans: an attempt to overcome the linguistic and political distance of colonialism and otherness. Section 203 explicitly links the code switching to the failure to attain what Magda calls 'words of true exchange' and shows Coetzee as meditator on the problem of language in colonial writing.

The sociolinguistic codes reinforce the theme of social isolation. 'Mies is die mies' is the social judgement on Magda, who is unable to move from the hierarchic distance of feudal social relationships to the I–you closeness for which she hopes. Significantly, this theme is linked to family structures, as well as to Magda's difficulty in writing.

This difficulty is at its most dramatic in the macaronic switching that takes place in a passage in which Afrikaans becomes English, and Magda turns from dialogue to monologue, the domestic to the international: 'Weet jy hoe ek voel, Anna? Soos 'n groot leemte, a great emptiness filled with a great absence, an absence which is a desire to be filled. Yet I know that nothing will ever fill me' (*IHC* 114). Magda here becomes the archetypal colonial writer cut off from her surroundings, yet struggling to dominate the language of the metropolis, to share in the cold desolation of the international:

> That is what she gets from me, colonial philosophy, words with no history behind them, homespun, when she wants stories. I can imagine a woman who would make this child happy, filling her with tales from a past that really happened, how grandfather ran away from the bees and lost his hat and never found it again, why the moon waxes and wanes, how the hare tricked the jackal. But these words of mine come from nowhere and go nowhere, they have no past or future, they whistle across the flats in a desolate eternal present, feeding no one. (*IHC* 114)

The emotional burden of colonialism lies in the distance of the coloniser whose mental universe differs from her or his physical universe; Coetzee's formal strategies embody this distance. Magda counts, reads, writes, shares in a world-wide culture; the idea of reverting to the folkloric world of African myth or tale is presented sadly and sardonically. (Hendrik cannot count, or read, and has a parodic rather than an anxious relationship to the remnants of Western culture in the attic.)

Magda's problems as writer and as character are linked powerfully in section 18 to the problems of her social and linguistic distance from her society, and also to her psychological condition:

> I live neither alone nor in society but as it were among children. I am spoken to not in words, which come to me quaint and veiled, but in signs, in conformations of face and hands, in postures of shoulders and feet, in nuances of tune and tone, in gaps and absences whose grammar has never been recorded. Reading the brown folk I grope, as they grope reading me: for they too hear my words only dully, listening for those overtones of the voice, those subtleties of the eyebrows that tell them my true meaning: 'Beware, do not cross me,' 'What I say does not come from me.' Across valleys of space and time we strain ourselves to catch the pale smoke of each other's signals. That is why my words are not words such as men use to men. Alone in my room with my duties behind me and my lamp steadily burning, I creak into rhythms that are my own, stumble over the rocks of words that I have never heard on another tongue. I create myself in the words that create me, I, who living among the downcast have never beheld myself in the equal regard of another's eye, have never held another in the equal regard of mine. While I am free to be I, nothing is impossible. In the cloister of my room, I am the mad hag I am destined to be. My clothes cake with dribble, I hunch and twist, my feet blossom with horny callouses, this prim voice, spinning out sentences without occasion, gaping with boredom because nothing ever happens on the farm, cracks and oozes the peevish loony sentiments that belong to the dead of night when the censor snores, to the crazy hornpipe I dance with myself. (*IHC* 7–8)

Magda here works for Coetzee the linguist, critic of colonial literature, colonial author, in exploring the pain of writing in a tradition not made for the place in which one lives, of not having a medium that can communicate a full range of social insights and social nuance, of being separated, as social subject and author, from the colonial other by language and power. Coetzee, as an academic widely read in feminist criticism, makes Magda self-consciously choose to be the madwoman in the closet as a way of reaching a certain bodily and expressive freedom, as a way of asserting the body to escape the father censor. But in becoming a madwoman in the study, Magda becomes more than just a female archetype; she stands for the writer and the uncertainty of the efforts of art, of the costs and effects of 'the crazy hornpipe I dance with myself'. Magda's double status persistently allows Coetzee to use her both to reflect on problems of writing in a colonial context and to examine the psychology of writing, the economies of authorship.

The trend towards a language without context, the other tongue of writing, takes its most extreme form in Magda's search for a universal language in which she might communicate with the gods, but here Magda's quest reaches some kind of completion – if only in a kind of zero degree of the 'rocks of words' she invoked in section 18, which leads her back to a search for the quotidian and a context.

I suggested earlier that Magda can be seen as an *alter ego* for Coetzee himself insofar as she allows him to explore, dramatise and exemplify the pains and difficulties of being a South African writer; even, perhaps, to expose the shortcomings of that identity. It may well be granted that Coetzee, in using and transcending Magda, is playing a more complex game with Magda than most critics have seen, but is this not simply to add mirror tricks to the basic situation? What, after all, is the basic situation that is being mirrored, and why does it matter?

VIII SEX AND RACE AS THEME

Though Teresa Dovey's analysis of Coetzee's novel as a counter to Schreiner's *Story of an African Farm* is relevant, the primary South African literary genre that Coetzee is analysing, deconstructing and contesting here is that of South African novels dealing with inter-racial sexuality. Coetzee's scholarly pronouncement in his early La Guma essay helps in foreshadowing some of the subject matter of, or terrain to be contested in, his first two novels:

> A favoured mode among white South African writers has been tragedy (though Afrikaans writers have given much time to the mythographic revision of history). Tragedy is typically the

> tragedy of inter-racial love: a white man and a black woman, or vice versa, fall foul of the laws against miscegenation, or simply of white prejudice, and are destroyed or driven into exile. The overt content of the fable here is that love conquers evil through tragic suffering when such suffering is borne witness to in art; its covert content is the apolitical doctrine that defeat can turn itself, by the twist of tragedy, into victory. (Coetzee, 'Man's Fate' 17)

Coetzee shows himself here to be suspicious of the genre for its insufficiently political analysis of the real issues at stake in inter-racial sexualtiy. What might such a political analysis involve?

The continued theme of sex across colour lines in very recent South African writing, even after the abandonment of legislation forbidding such activities, indicates that it has a significance or set of meanings absolutely central to South African writing, or at least to writing by white English speakers. In brief, the theme has the following resonance that haunts it from its beginnings: can one end one's identity as coloniser without entering into the full set of social relationships and exchanges involved in inter-marriage and kinship? Is it possible to be truly African without marrying Africa? Is it possible to be white and marry Africa?

In the Heart of the Country becomes an attempt to consider that question with a full array of intellectual and psychological complexity, rather than from the limited reaction of race or prejudice. How does Coetzee draw on the genre and the trope, and how does he transform them?

One way of seeing Coetzee's novel is as a reinvestigation of the genre as a whole. Though most critical writing on the genre has focused on novels, from Plomer's *Turbott Wolfe* (1926) onwards, which deal with the challenge of black male sexuality to the apartheid order, there are many earlier novels written by white females in opposition to white male cross-sexual transgression. These novels had strong material as well as cultural motives, insofar as the white man 'going native', withdrawing from white society (often opting for polygamy), posed a threat to the status of white women and the legitimacy of maritally based property transmissions. White female pressure was also crucial in changing legislation so that laws were changed to punish white male racial-sexual transgressors as well as white women and black men.

Coetzee, then, combines earlier issues and genres. He does not simply give the more sociologically realistic portrayal of the white male (ab)use of black women, or the more favoured revolutionary mode (a staple of Brink's and Gordimer's writing) in which a black male and white woman defy and overthrow social and political norms, but combines them by showing that the first leads to the second, and by analysing this progression within the dynamic of one particular familial setting so as to trace the psychic sources and results of the colonial sexual drama. In so doing, Coetzee focuses on the failure of the romantic mode of interracial fiction to address questions of social transmission and profound patterns of family dynamics. When, as is usually the case, such transgressive relationships fail in other novels (as in Brink's *Instant in the Wind* or Gordimer's *Occasion for Loving*), we are left short of a deep understanding why the protagonists fail to live up to the challenges of the identity conferred upon them by their new sexual partner. In *In the Heart of the Country,* Coetzee gives deep-seated psychological and social reasons for the failure of a new mode of sexual being.

Coetzee starts by making the recording consciousness that of the female protagonist. He makes her status as daughter central, with the social–colonial issues secondary, both for her and her father:

> The long passage that links the two wings of the house, with his bedroom in one wing and mine in the other, teems with nocturnal spectres, he and I among them. They are not my creatures nor are they his: they are ours together. Through them we possess and are possessed by each other. There is a level, we both know, at which Klein-Anna is a pawn and the real game lies between the two of us. (*IHC* 34)

This, at least, is Magda's judgement, though in crucial ways Coetzee seems to share it. Ultimately, it would seem, the lineal European transmission via the family prohibits union, comes between white and Africa. Father must speak to colonial daughter; all else is betrayal, evasion. Insofar as this might seem to be a problem, Coetzee backs the Freudian Oedipal mode or Lacanian Symbolic order, whereby it seems the European family has to go on reproducing its neurotic codes as surely as DNA, and the social is some kind of excrescence of this.

This seems to be the main reason for the early section in which the father marries and brings home the new stepmother. Magda is reduced to being a Cinderella or a female Hamlet by this situation; the stories belong to a Western, Oedipal tradition. The first mother is the sensual other woman of the Western psyche, opposed to the domestic taboos of the family. In moving to write colonial fiction, Magda finds that the other woman's place is taken by the Black (man's) woman, with all the consequences of that substitution.

One could certainly argue that to see the Oedipal as preceding the social hardly does justice to what has happened or could have happened in South Africa, but Coetzee's judgement on the main historical and cultural issues treated by the novel is grim. White colonial society (and Afrikaner society in particular) has built its language, its mental and cultural structures, around notions of racial separation. To break these is to break the law, to abandon the Lacanian Symbolic for 'madness'. Afrikaans, as a language which familialises other White Afrikaners in clan relationships, is (or was) an Oedipal situation extended, and this denial of equitable exchange with the surrounding world is what Magda has learned and cannot unlearn, without madness. Even the father's desire is a desire based on the illegitimacy of the desired object.

In preventing true reciprocal exchange, colonial (Afrikaner) society finds itself blocked sexually, linguistically, artistically. Coetzee makes the breakdown of language and sexual order clear in section 195, a passage where the failure of the 'father tongue' leads to a kind of fevered incestuous uncertainty of sexual status and kinship ties, with Hendrik seeing Magda and Anna as half-sisters. For Coetzee, structuralist, these linguistic, sexual, social issues are interlinked.

Why, it might be asked, does Coetzee introduce this theme by excluding Magda's mother? Gillmer and Gallagher raise some pertinent issues, but to investigate Magda's images of self would take us too far. I see the absence of Magda's mother less as a limiting condition on Magda, part of some kind of given particularity of the character, than as a way of avoiding complications to the plot – rather like the other servants who appear in section 13 but disappear after that.

Coetzee's theoretical interests at the time lead him to make Magda quarrel with her father's No and Name (to invoke the Lacanian pun). Early on, Magda is brought back to reality by the Blakean–Lacanian negation of the father whose 'eternal NO' (16) denies her story its reality, bringing her out of her first imaginings. Later, when she has killed her father again, Magda's narrating comes close to collapse when she cannot take the name of the father in the sense of real power, by signing next to the X in the post office withdrawal book, an act that would give her access to her father's name, money and power. While Coetzee persistently returns to questions of the symbolic economy between generations, he seems to be working here in a psychological mode in which the father (who stands for political power and order) produces Magda's signifying and its deficiences.

IX THE PAINS OF MODERNISM AND COUNTRY MATTERS

Coetzee's early novels thus incorporate highly self-conscious reflections on the work of art and its conditions of production. The work comes highly immunised against critical attacks and continues to understand its critics better than its critics understand it. In *In the Heart of the Country*, Coetzee's insistent questioning of the colonial, psychological, gender, and class bases of literary creation, his reflection on what we might call the sociology of literary creation, is more sophisticated than that generally found in literary criticism of Coetzee. Magda herself explicitly faces (Sartrean? Hegelian?) critical schemes in her meditations on quotations from other writings in sections 248–50 and rebuts these judgements, talks back, carries on. And the novel has, with sly mischief, warned us of this in its concluding section:

> What have I been doing on this barbarous frontier? I have no doubt, since these are not idle questions, that somewhere there is a whole literature waiting to answer them for me. Unfortunately I am not acquainted with it; and besides, I have always felt easier spinning the answer out of my own bowels. (*ICH* 138)

Coetzee's aim here is to prevent, anticipate, those answers (psychological, historical, sociological) that might allow us to avoid following Magda's spinning of her tale, that might permit us to fit her into some pre-established critical category. Considering the domestic, agricultural, colonial, familial, metaphysical, economies within which she lives, Magda writes in compensation for familial, gender, social lacks. In considering this range of issues, Coetzee places Magda and the novel beyond any simple reading. Like Schreiner before her, and other colonisers after, Magda is between systems, worlds, symbolic orders. She is a powerful surrogate, a stalking horse, for Coetzee.

In its adoption of surrealist, non-realist modes, *In the Heart of the Country* is typically high modernist in the terms identified by Anthony Giddens in his study *Modernity and Self-identity*. Giddens's study of the ways in which the modern represents a dislocation of the national and the local leaves us with the possibility, which he does not examine or explore, that the conditions of modern identity may be first found and most sharply felt in colonial situations, that the colonial, between worlds and systems, is exemplary of the modern. Coetzee's novel, his portrayal of identity, is appropriate for an age of disembodied expert systems and 'disembedding mechanisms' and 'institutional reflexivity'. In *In the Heart of the Country*, Coetzee's formal innovation is related to the colonial world experience which is modernist in all the terms Giddens enumerates. Coetzee has produced the novel of identity for the multinational age by focusing on the colonial as a kind of generic precursor of the multinational.

Finally, Magda, not surprisingly for someone who alludes to Hamlet so readily, knows that at the heart of the country lie country matters, knows it starkly with the rock image she presents to lure the gods or in her gestures to the young messenger. But at the heart of both geography and sex, in turn, lie the multiple structures and powers of language.

X CONCLUSION

Let me return by way of conclusion to my disagreement with Stephen Watson's position, or rather with one gloss that can be put on his assertion that many of the difficulties of the novels disappear when one has read the same books Coetzee has. To appreciate some of the books, discourses, influences on Coetzee may make the novels easier to understand in one sense, but the cumulative effect should rather be to suggest a density and complexity of texture which works against a notion of univocal influences that are transmitted without being transformed. *In the*

Heart of the Country presents us with a new texture in the more or less structuralist correspondences Coetzee establishes between sexual, linguistic, economic and artistic codes and their disturbances. The colonial, anthropological consciousness of this exemplary modernist text demands a further critical rethinking of the colonial and its relation to the modern and the modernist.

8

Waiting for the Barbarians: Allegory of Allegories

TERESA DOVEY

Allegories are, in the realm of thought, what ruins are in the realm of things.

Walter Benjamin

Much of the critical discussion on *Waiting for the Barbarians* focuses on its status as allegory.[1] It seems useful to clarify the various constructions of allegory being brought to bear in these discussions, to explore the modes of allegory exemplified in the novel, and to posit a reason for its importance in *Waiting for the Barbarians* in particular, when all of Coetzee's novels can, in some sense, be regarded as allegorical. Some critics validate Coetzee's choice of the mode, seeing it as a way of telling the truth in a context where oppressive censorship would prevent explicit representation of actual events (Zamora, Wade), while others have taken Coetzee to task for what they perceive to be a form of ahistorical universalism. Nadine Gordimer, for example, sees Coetzee's use of allegory as 'a stately fastidiousness; or a state of shock'. Thus she says: 'He seemed able to deal with the horror he saw written on the sun only – if brilliantly – if this were to be projected into another time and plane' ('The Idea of Gardening' 3).[2]

These very different responses to the novel are evidence that allegory is not simply an empty convention or device; that it is, as Owens points out, 'an attitude as well as a technique, a perception as well as a procedure' ('The Allegorical Impulse', Part I, 68). Allegory has been theorised in different ways, which can be broadly divided into two categories: it is either constructed as a mode which is subservient to an extra-textual reality which it simply represents,[3] or as a mode in which there is repetition of one text by another. Within both these categories, allegory can further be regarded as either conservative or subversive, according to whether it locates meaning in terms of a pre-existing transcendent truth, or master code, or whether it is mobilised on the side of resistance to an oppressive system or master code.

Paul de Man's 'The Rhetoric of Temporality' constitutes a crux in the contemporary redefinition and revalidation of allegory. De Man's construction of allegory as a more authentic rhetorical response to temporality[4] has been taken up in different ways by the discourses of postmodernism and postcolonialism. In the context of postmodernism, the allegorical mode is primarily constructed as the repetition of one text by another. Allegory thus offers a means of coping with problems of, precisely, repetition and authority, and a means of continuing to write despite postmodernity's 'crisis of representation'.[5] Allegory also allows for what Craig Owens refers to as postmodernism's fundamentally deconstructive impulse, as through allegory we encounter 'the unavoidable necessity of participating in the very activity that is being denounced precisely in order to denounce it' ('The Allegorical Impulse', Part II, 79). For postcolonial writers, on the other hand, allegory offers a way of coping with problems of historical interpretation: Stephen Slemon points out that 'allegorical writing, and its inherent investment in history' provides the postcolonised writer with a means to 'destabilise history's fixity, its giveness, and open it up to the transformative power of imaginative revision,' and also of building this into 'the structuring principle of the fictional work of art' (Slemon, 'Post-Colonial Allegory' 159).

However, Slemon's analysis does not take into account Coetzee's position as postcoloniser (as opposed to postcolonised) in the neocolonial context of South Africa. Caught in this ambivalent position, Coetzee has two histories to contend with: the history of his own discourse, rooted in the discourses of imperialism, and the suppressed history of the colonised, which has to be recuperated without being arrogated to colonial discourse. He cannot simply choose to deny the relation of his writing to prior modes of colonial discourse, and he cannot unproblematically recuperate the history of the postcolonised. (This latter is an issue which is developed in *Foe*.) The former presents him with the problem of avoiding the unwitting repetition of available modes of (colonial) discourse in his writing and the concomitant need to divest them of their authority; the latter with the problem of his writing taking upon itself an authority which it does not have, and so perpetuating the very power relations between coloniser and colonised which it seeks to avoid.

I shall contend in this essay that it is allegory which allows for a way around this dilemma, although, for the reasons I have just outlined, not quite in the way Slemon describes. For Coetzee is both a postmodern and a postcolonial writer,[6] and allegory works for him in both the ways described above. Elsewhere, I have described Coetzee's novels as double-sided allegories: on the one hand, they constitute allegories of prior modes of discourse, wittingly inhabiting them in order to deconstruct them and divest them of their authority (hence the figure of the hermit crab in *In the Heart of the Country*);[7] on the other hand, they are self-reflexive allegories which refer to their own status as speech acts engaged in a process of subject-constitution. As such, they depend upon the intervention of the reader for fulfilment – and they recognise that any form of authority which the novelistic discourse might assume will be contested by the discursive context in which the novels are read. De Man has described the time of allegory as an 'ideal time that is never here and now but always a past or an endless future' (de Man 207); in Coetzee's novels allegory allows, not for an ideal time, but for a space between past and future, taking into account both history as discourse and history as event. While wanting to avoid the assumption of power involved in the attempt to make history,[8] Coetzee's novels acknowledge their own historicity in a way in which many discourses, including most discourses of criticism, do not.[9]

Waiting for the Barbarians has been described as Coetzee's 'most' allegorical novel (Zamora 5) and, while I doubt that there can be degrees of 'allegoricalness,' the novel does seem to differ from the others in that, in addition to allegory being a structuring principle, it is dealt with at a thematic level. The protagonist, an ageing magistrate in a border town, an outpost of an unspecified empire, is preoccupied with the attempt to decipher a hieroglyphic script, written on pieces of wood which he has discovered amongst ancient desert ruins. He says: 'They form an allegory. They can be read in many orders. Further, each single slip can be read in many ways' (*WFB* [Penguin] 112), expressing a view of allegory which focuses on the act of interpretation by the reader. This finds its correlative in the Magistrate's attempts to decipher the marks and scars on the body of the Barbarian girl he has taken in to live with him. The novel traces his failed attempts to posit a meaning for both the script and the girl's suffering; it traces, in other words, a crisis of interpretation.

Herein lies the clue as to why allegory should play such an important role in this novel in particular. I have argued that *Waiting for the Barbarians* constitutes an image, in Bakhtin's sense,[10] of a particular discourse – that the Magistrate's autodiegetic narrative should be regarded as reported speech, enclosed, as it were, by quotation marks at the beginning and end. The discourse cited and subverted is liberal humanist discourse. More specifically, it is liberal humanist novelistic discourse (of, for example, Alan Paton, Dan Jacobson and the early Gordimer) as it arrives at a particular juncture in South African history: the phase of bureaucratised and increasingly militarised totalitarian control from 1948 onwards. Encountering the brutal and systematic forms of control of the Nationalist Party government, liberal humanist discourse arrives at what can be described as a crisis of interpretation. Now, it can be argued that all interpretation is allegorical, in that it involves the establishing of meaning in relation to a pre-existing code.[11] In *Waiting for the Barbarians*, allegory is thematised as a means of articulating the liberal humanist crisis of interpretation, while at the same time allegory is employed as a structural device in order to imply the inevitable imbrication of the novel's own discourse with the discourses it deconstructs. While *Waiting for the Barbarians* offers a critique of a particular failure of interpretation, it places under scrutiny its own interpretive practice and, as we shall see, that of certain discourses of criticism.

The Magistrate's narrative provides evidence of two broad areas of failure in liberal humanist discourse: first of all its failure to interpret and offer resistance to the militarised totalitarian phase of colonisation and, secondly, its failure to interpret and articulate the history of the colonised. The former is illustrated via the metaphor of blindness and sight: the Magistrate moves from a position in which he takes for granted his own superior sight or insight, commenting on the colonel's use of sunglasses in the novel's opening paragraph and asking 'Is he blind?', to a position of blindness, saying at the end: 'There has been something staring me in the face, and still I do not see it' (*WFB* 1, 155). The second is illustrated via the various facets of the Magistrate's relationship with the Barbarian girl. The allegorical and deconstructive relationship of this novel to liberal humanist discourse implies, however, that Coetzee's novelistic discourse is beset by the same failures. The difference is that, while registering its desire to interpret and resist the coloniser's discourse, and to interpret and give meaning to the history of suffering and oppression of the colonised, the discourse of this novel makes it clear, through allegory, that it cannot do these things in an unproblematic way.

The sentiments and attitudes the Magistrate is made to express represent a traditional liberal humanist position, and may be summarised as: belief in the power and efficacy of the judiciary system; belief in 'civilisation' and the continual progress of humankind; an abhorrence of violence, accompanied by an attitude of tolerance and rationality; a capacity for fairly ruthless self-scrutiny and a sense of guilt that can be incapacitating; and, more significant than all of these, a belief in individual autonomy and freedom of choice. In *Waiting for the Barbarians*, all of these attitudes are shown to be ineffectual in relation to the kind of power vested in the figure of Colonel Joll.

Failure is thus registered at this attitudinal level, but the epistemological framework provided by post-structuralism further allows the failures of liberal humanist novelistic discourse and, by implication, Coetzee's own novelistic discourse, to be located in language itself. It should be noted that this does not locate the terms of Coetzee's critique outside history, in some ideal, autonomous zone: if, as Coward and Ellis argue, language is the place in which the social individual is constructed, then one has to grant it its full materiality and historicity.[12] Coetzee's novel thus differs from the traditional liberal novel (of, for example, Paton, Jacobson and the early Gordimer) in terms of an awareness of its own status as interpretation (rather than representation), and of the problems of interpretation, which it registers by setting one mode of allegory against another. Structurally, the novel's allegorical relation to prior texts implies a third mode of allegory, which deconstructs the oppostion between the two.

First of all then, liberal humanist discourse does not recognise its status as discourse; it fails to account for the way in which the meanings it constructs are contingent upon a specific interpretive framework. This is exemplified in the Magistrate's attempts to decode the ancient script and in his desire for an intuitive experience of full meaning as he lingers among the desert ruins 'waiting for the spirits from the byways of history to speak to him' and trying to find 'in the vacuousness of the desert a special historical poignancy' (*WFB* 16, 17). It is further demonstrated in the Magistrate's attempt to decipher the scars and marks on the barbarian girl's tortured body. What he seeks is direct access to the girl's past experience and to the girl's 'being', unmediated by his own situation in the present.[13] This first mode of allegorical interpretation fails, then, in its attempt to assimilate the other and the history of the colonised other into what the Magistrate assumes is the universal perspective of liberal humanism. Interpretation here does not see itself as allegorical; indeed, does not see itself as interpretation.

One corollary to the failure of liberal humanism to see itself as discourse is its failure to see itself as located in history, inevitably contributing to it while being overtaken by it. Thus, the Magistrate is made to say: 'I wanted to live outside history. I wanted to live outside the history that Empire imposes on its subjects, even its lost subjects' (*WFB* 154). And he is shown assuming that, having oiled the slips of wood, he can simply bury them where he found them, for future generations to unearth and interpret, overlooking the way in which his own intervention is itself significant and located in history. Again, this has a parallel in the returning of the girl to her people, as though she can be restored to an originary wholeness, unmarked by the history of colonisation, to which his relationship with her has contributed.

A second corollary is the failure of liberal humanist discourse to see itself as a speech act and, thus, as engaged in a process of subject constitution which has an agenda of its own: in this case the agenda seems to have as much to do with the moral rectitude of the writer as with the fate of the victim who is its ostensible subject. (Critical discourse manifests the same blindness toward its function in this respect: much Coetzee criticism, for example, is more concerned with registering its own abhorrence of the horrors of apartheid than it is with understanding how Coetzee's writing works.) In South Africa, liberal humanist novelistic discourse frequently employs the mode of tragedy, and Coetzee has commented of this writing (one thinks particularly of Paton here): 'Religious tragedy reconciles us to the inscrutable dispensation by giving a meaning to suffering and defeat. As tragic art, it also confers immortality' ('Man's Fate in the Novels' 17). The Magistrate's relationship with the barbarian girl suggests the liberal writer's attempt to give a 'meaning' to the suffering of the victim, as he attempts to 'read' the marks of torture on her body in the same way that he attempts to decipher the archaic script. At the same time, the Magistrate's obsessive attachment to the girl illustrates the way in which the suffering victim becomes a means of establishing an identity for the liberal writer: in bearing witness to the other's suffering, and ultimately in claiming an equivalent suffering for him/herself, the writer casts him/herself in the role of seer, truth-teller, blameless one, and perhaps even of tragic hero or scapegoat.

The connection between the girl as victim and the process of subject constitution in the discourse is suggested in the parallels between the Magistrate's dreams and the figure of the girl. The Magistrate's ritual of washing the girl's feet implies the fetishising of the suffering victim in liberal humanist novelistic discourse, while, along with the repeated references to the breaking of bread, it also refers to the religious dimensions of the liberal novel in the South African context.[14]

The novel's first construction of the allegorical mode, then, implies a mode of interpretation which recognises neither the historical materiality nor the motivation of its own intervention; a mode which does not see itself as interpretation and, thus, seeks unmediated access to 'pure meaning'. The second construction of allegory is produced via the Magistrate's strategic reading of the script in Colonel Joll's presence. Having 'read' the signs on the slips as a testament of barbarian suffering and oppression, he goes on to insist that, either singly or together, the signs can be read in any way one chooses, because 'There is no knowing which sense is intended' (*WFB* 112). The potential polyvalence of the signifier is manipulated to produce a meaning for the past in the service of the present, and, one must add, in the service of the writer's presence. Thus, the Magistrate says:

> I have not failed to keep an eye on Joll through all this. He has not stirred again, save to lay a hand on his subordinate's sleeve at the moment when I referred to the Empire and he rose, ready to strike me.
>
> If he comes near me I will hit him with all the strength in my body. I will not disappear into the earth without leaving my mark on them. (*WFB* 112)

His active recuperation of the past of the oppressed is, at the same time, a gesture of defiance and provocation. As such it constructs the subject of liberal humanist discourse as innocent truth-teller and witness, set in opposition to the guilty oppressor.

Like the first mode of allegorical interpretation, then, this second mode also 'leaves its mark', although it does so knowingly and with a particular intent. However, unlike the first mode, which is subservient to a prior meaning, this second mode claims for itself a kind of freedom to make meaning. This finds its parallel in the two opposing views of history which I have described as being represented in *Dusklands* (Dovey, *The Novels of J. M. Coetzee* 75): one view sees past events as determining the present, which is continuous with, and therefore causally connected with that past, while in the other view, a strategic rupture is proclaimed between the present and the past, and the historical project claims to produce the meaning of the past, locating itself outside or on the periphery of those historical forces which constrain meaning in the present. I have argued that in *Dusklands* each of these two views of history is undermined by the opposite view, while their intersection within the novel produces a view of history best described by Jameson as not so much a text as rather a text-to-be-(re-)constructed. Better still, it is an obligation to do so, whose means and techniques are themselves historically irreversible, so that we are not at liberty to construct any historical narrative at all (Dovey, *The Novels of J. M. Coetzee* 288).

In the same way, in *Waiting for the Barbarians*, a third mode of allegorical interpretation is implied via the intersection of the first two and via the novel's own allegorical relationship to prior texts. Walter Benjamin, in *The Origin of German Tragic Drama*, suggests a parallel between allegory and modes of historical consciousness, so that for him allegory is not merely a more or less authentic response to the problem of temporality, but offers the means to undo both the reifications of history as continuity and the hegemonic power of interpretation in the present. Jameson's description of the historical project closely approximates Benjamin's critique of a particular form of historicism:

> ... historicism contents itself with establishing a causal connection between various moments in history. But no fact that is a cause is for that very reason historical. It became historical posthumously, as it were, through events that may be separated

> from it by thousands of years. A historian who takes this as his point of departure stops telling the sequence of events like the beads of a rosary. Instead he grasps the constellation which his own era has formed with a definite earlier one. (Benjamin, *The Origin of German Tragic Drama* 265)

It is, of course, not necessary to go to Benjamin for this kind of articulation of historical consciousness and its relation to allegory as both perception and procedure.[15] However, the points of coincidence between Coetzee's novel and Benjamin's view of allegorical interpretation, and the images he employs in the expression of this view, are remarkable. Consider, for example, the 'images of disinterment, of grubbing among buried ruins and salvaging forgotten remains' (Eagleton 55); the model of allegory not only as ruins, being the signs of human history within nature, but also as 'the transfiguration of a human body into meaning by its physiognomic features, the characters inscribed on its countenance' and, thirdly, 'the transfiguration of matter into signs by the act of writing' (J. H. Miller 364). Explaining Benjamin's much cited aphorism: 'Allegories are, in the realm of thought, what ruins are in the realm of things', J. Hillis Miller says

> The spatial fragmentation of objects in the ruin and the separation of the sign from its material base stand for the differential reference across time of one sign to another with which it does not harmonise. This structure of incongruous allusion is characteristic of allegory as a temporal or narrative mode. The ruin alludes backward in time to the former glory of the building and so ruins that glory metaleptically in its difference from it. In allegory naked matter shines through. It shines through as the failure of the idea to transform nature or thought.
> (J. H. Miller 365)

The building anticipates the ruin, but the ruin, in representing the fallen status of the once glorious building, implies a critique of its own origin. This is the correlative of a mode of historical interpretation which claims neither smooth continuity nor a complete rupture between past and present: the past 'shines through' the present interpretation, implying a fully dialectical relationship between the two. This is the mode of Coetzee's allegories, which, in Benjamin's words, effect the necessary 'constellation' of present with past. Through their repetition of prior modes of discourse, Coetzee's allegories recognise that they cannot remove themselves from those historically located discourses of which they offer a critique. As I have already suggested, the failures of these discourses are also, to some degree, the failure of Coetzee's novelistic discourse, and the difference is that whereas Coetzee's novels self-reflexively register these failures and imply an analysis of their sources, the earlier discourses do not.

It seems necessary, at this point, to comment on the apparent lack of self-reflexivity in *Waiting for the Barbarians* as compared to Coetzee's other novels. Because liberal novelistic discourse is characterised by its lack of self-consciousness, its refusal to recognise its status as discourse, it would have been inappropriate to construct a highly self-reflexive narrative for the Magistrate such as that of the narrators in *Dusklands* and *In the Heart of the Country*. He is made to comment on his own failures and on his complicity with the regime with a measure of self-awareness, but this is no more than an approximation of the liberal novel's capacity for self-scrutiny and its well-developed sense of guilt. Unlike Magda, the Magistrate articulates no recognition of himself as the subject of discourse. Instead, Coetzee draws attention to the status of his novel as discourse by the use of present tense narration, which signals its own 'impossibility' outside the conventions of the novel, and therefore its own fictionality.[16] Because the Magistrate is shown going to some lengths to demonstrate that he is not writing a journal or a diary, which would announce the status of his discourse as linguistic object, and because it cannot be regarded as a stream-of-consciousness or interior monologue, the novel does not allow us to posit any fictional narrative occasion.

In this sense, *Waiting for the Barbarians* is a narrative which paradoxically insists upon its own impossibility. It also refuses the finality of meaning implied in narrative closure, while its narrator continues to insist upon the possiblity of conclusive meaning. Thus, returning the undeciphered scripts to their burial place in the desert, the Magistrate says: 'There has been something staring me in the face, and still I do not see it' (*WFB* 155). As David Attwell points out, citing Foucault: 'historical continuity is both a "guarantee that everything that has eluded [the subject] may be restored," and a promise "that one day the subject – in the form of historical consciousness – will once again be able to appropriate, to bring back under his sway, all those things that are kept at a distance by difference"' ('J. M. Coetzee and South Africa' 98, citing Foucault, *The Archaeology of Knowledge* 12).

In the Magistrate's comment is implied the promise that what has not been seen or grasped may yet be understood and interpreted. It leads us as readers into the trap of saying what it is that the Magistrate has failed to see; we attempt to understand, to make his narrative meaningful through our own interpretation. The novel thus encourages us to make our own allegorical interpretations, interpretations which are inevitably subject to the same failures as those articulated by the novel itself. Thus, whether our readings appropriate Coetzee's novelistic discourse via the allegorical structures of Lacanian psychoanalysis (as my earlier reading does), or whether they attempt to situate the novel in history, reading it symptomatically, and so claiming a form of transcendence (as Attwell does), the novel's own deconstructive reading of allegory pre-empts the interpretive and allegorical activity of criticism itself.

The deconstructive activity of Coetzee's novels, then, is not an empty textual game, but a means by which they locate themselves in history without assuming the transcendence of criticism. If we choose to overlook the allegorical deconstructive strategies of *Waiting for the Barbarians*, which implicate the novel in the failures of the discourses it deconstructs, and choose to read it as a critique of the failure of liberal humanism *per se* to produce an adequate historical discourse (as Attwell does), or to respond to the systemic crisis produced in the colonial order by the militarised apartheid state (as Wade does), then we have to ask: what discourses, produced by the coloniser, could have succeeded in these ways? And, in particular, what novelistic discourses could be regarded as 'successful' in this context? One question begs another: why, and by what authority, should novelistic discourse take upon itself the task of criticising the shortcomings of political, historical and philosphical discourses, when it does not and cannot attempt to do what they do?[17]

Once again, this is not to claim that novelistic discourse can stake out an autonomous zone for itself: it is inevitably intersected by these discourses, and it is, of course, political in the profoundest sense, inevitably participating in the power relations of its historical moment. Coetzee has been taken to task for his determination to maintain the distinction between novelistic discourse and the discourse of politics and of history;[18] my own readings of his novels have similarly been criticised for locating them in relation to other novels, and not in relation to South African history and politics *per se*. The implication is that novelistic discourse is less important than these other discourses, and in this respect I have one more question to pose: why, then, do we, as critics, spend so much of our time and energy contesting the meanings of these novels?

Coetzee's novels, and his statements concerning the nature of novelistic discourse, have the virtue of being more honest, less hypocritical, than both critical discourse and liberal novelistic discourse in the mode of realism. These discourses have no way of registering their self-interest and their inevitable positioning within ideology and, as a result, they claim for themselves a power which they do not have, and assume they can simply disassociate themselves from a form of power to which they do not wish to subscribe. It is my belief that the deconstructive allegorical mode of Coetzee's writing will, in the end, make his novels less vulnerable to critique than is the criticism itself. In a way not available to critical discourse, *Waiting for the Barbarians* refabricates a temporary habitation amongst the ruins.

Notes

1. For example, see Zamora; Dovey, 'The Novels of J. M. Coetzee' and 'Allegory vs. Allegory'; Slemon, 'Post Colonial Allegory'; Wade.
2. Gordimer's writing is frequently compared with that of Coetzee, and the latter is found wanting. My analysis implies a reversal of this evaluation.
3. Traditional allegory can be seen as working in the service of transcendental and eternal truth, while modern allegories are often seen as a way of avoiding censorship when representing real conditions under oppressive regimes.
4. According to de Man:

> The prevalence of allegory always corresponds to the unveiling of an authentic temporal destiny This unveiling takes place in a subject that has sought refuge against the impact of time in a natural world to which, in truth, it bears no resemblance . . . it remains necessary, if there is to be allegory, that the allegorical sign refer to another sign that precedes it. The meaning constituted by the allegorical sign can then consist only in the repetition

> (in the Kierkegaardian sense of the term) of a previous sign with which it can never coincide, since it is of the essence of this previous sign to be pure anteriority. (de Man 190–1)

5. Thus, for example, Lyotard comments:

> The postmodern would be that which, in the modern, puts forward the unpresentable in presentation itself; that which denies itself the solace of good forms, the consensus of a taste which would make it possible to share collectively the nostalgia for the unattainable; that which searches for new presentations, not in order to enjoy them but in order to impart a stronger sense of the unpresentable. (Lyotard, 'Answering the Question' 81)

6. In my chapter on *Foe* (*The Novels of J. M. Coetzee*), I present a case for the intersection of postmodern and postcolonial discourses in Coetzee's writing.
7. The prior modes of discourse deconstructed by Coetzee's novels are in *Dusklands*, the anthropological/historical/fictional writing that can be grouped together under the heading 'journey of exploration'; in *In the Heart of the Country*, the 'anti-pastoral' mode of Olive Schreiner; in *Life & Times of Michael K*, the novel of the inarticulate victim; in *Foe*, contemporary feminist, postcolonial and postmodern discourse.
8. Gordimer complains that 'Coetzee's heroes are those who ignore history, not make it' ('The Idea of Gardening' 3).
9. In a discussion of *Dusklands* (Dovey, 'Coetzee and His Critics' 25), I argue that the novel takes into account the material conditions of its own production, whilst the criticism assumes that it is free to stand outside ideology.
10. Discussing the images of language given by Pushkin in *Eugene Onegin*, Bakhtin says:

> The author sees the limitation and incompleteness of Onegin's language and outlook, at that time still fashionable, he sees its ridiculous, abstract and artificial aspect... but at the same time there is a whole series of important thoughts and observations that he can express only with the help of this 'language,' in spite of the fact that, historically, this language as a totality was already doomed. This kind of image of another person's language and outlook, being at the same time both represented and representing, is extremely typical of the novel. (Bakhtin 215)

11. As Joel Fineman points out when he says that

> the response to allegory becomes representative of critical activity *per se*. As Frye says, 'it is not often realised that all commentary is allegorical interpretation, an attaching of ideas to the structure of poetic imagery' – as, indeed, Frye's comment demonstrates, in its presumption of global, archetypal structure, which is already

> allegorisation whatever purely literary claims he might make for it. (Fineman 27–8, citing Frye, *Anatomy of Criticism: Four Essays* 9)

12. Coward and Ellis argue that, through Lacanian theory

> The 'human' can be analysed as a socially-constituted process which plays a material role in society.... Ideology is conceived as the way in which a subject is produced in language able to represent his/herself and therefore able to act in the social totality, the fixity of those representations being the function of ideology. (Coward and Ellis 1–2)

13. Elsewhere I have discussed in detail the role of the desiring subject and of the Master–Slave relationship in the Magistrate's obsessive preoccupation with the Barbarian girl (*The Novels of J. M. Coetzee* 226–46).
14. *The Novels of J. M. Coetzee* (220–36).
15. Thus, for example, Michael Ryan points out that:

> If one accepts that the historical world is produced as a process of differentiation in which specific events are subsumed by larger chains, series, structures and sequences, then one must also acknowledge that all knowledge of it which isolates self-identical entities or events from that differential seriality is necessarily institutional, that is, conventional and constructed. (Ryan 24–5)

16. I have commented at some length on the use of the present tense in this novel (*The Novels of J. M. Coetzee* 210–17). Lance Olsen has remarked that 'The use of the present tense in a way becomes a mockery of presence in the text' ('The Presence of Absence', *Ariel* 54), and Anne Neumann focuses her entire article on the use of the present tense in the novel.
17. Wade, for example, complains that Coetzee 'has been unfortunately silent' about a class analysis of the political struggle in South Africa (Wade 287).
18. In an early interview Coetzee resists the interviewers' attempts to 'swallow [his] novels into a political discourse' (Thorold and Wicksteed 5), and in the talk titled 'The Novel Today' he resists what he refers to as 'a powerful tendency, perhaps even dominant tendency, to subsume the novel under history' (Coetzee, 'The Novel Today' 2).

9

Audible Palimpsests: Coetzee's Kafka

PATRICIA MERIVALE

All J. M. Coetzee's novels are remarkable, if oblique, parables of, among other things, the contemporary political situation in the Republic of South Africa. It is equally true that they are remarkably 'intertextual' works. I take my cue here from Stephen Watson: 'almost all the initial difficulties of Coetzee's novels vanish if one happens to have read the same books that he has' (Watson 'Colonialism' 380), even though such 'reading' is plainly only the first stage in any intertextual inquiry, and even though many subsequent stages remove only some of the difficulties. And if '"all of Europe" has gone into the making of Coetzee', as Watson goes on to say, most critics have boiled 'all of Europe' down to its synecdoche, Franz Kafka. The critical repartee among those asserting, denying or qualifying the 'Kafka Connection' is one to which Coetzee himself has contributed statements – statements, however, which go far in the direction of non-clarification: 'I don't believe that Kafka has an exclusive right to the letter K. Nor is Prague the centre of the universe' (Morphet interview, Coetzee 1987, 457); '[I] have been reading Kafka since I was an adolescent . . . in German; so it would be even more foolish for me to deny that Kafka has left his traces on me' (Sévry interview, Coetzee 1985, 5).

Kafka is, *pace* Coetzee, plainly the central intertextual problematic of Coetzee's third and fourth novels, *Waiting for the Barbarians* (Penguin 1980) and *Life & Times of Michael K* (Viking Penguin 1983), which are, as it happens, the middle pair of his six to date and perhaps, figuratively, the 'central' ones as well. Whether to be slighted (Ward, Gallagher), parenthetically refuted (Gordimer), taken for granted (Steiner, Zamora, Lazarus, and Attwell), criticised (Lehmann-Haupt: the Kafkan 'tributes' and 'borrowings' 'are overdone and call an unnecessary amount of attention to themselves'), inflated (Brink: '[Michael K] combin[es] the figures of Christ and Kafka's K'), or alternately evaded and grudgingly conceded by Coetzee himself, Kafka's work constitutes the one intertext to which almost every critic alludes. In short, there has been a lot of critical shuffling of feet, from which have emerged several handy though inevitably incomplete lists, whether of differences (Penner, Ward) or of specific echoes and general resemblances (Olson, Post, or Sévry). Sévry, having listed numerous quite apposite echoes, declares, perhaps overcautiously, 'I would not speak of actual influences' (Sévry 30). But as yet there has been no clear, forceful or conclusive comment upon the Kafkaesque in Coetzee.

Ward issues the challenge: 'Coetzee has been compared with Kafka too often, and for superficial reasons' (Ward 162). I do not pretend to be able to supply profound reasons, let alone to reduce the number of such comparisons, when so many of Coetzee's critics have noted this thorny intertextual problem only to turn aside from it. I shall, nevertheless, attempt to contextualise the Kafkan echoes in these two books, in terms of the several intertextual modes at work in Coetzee, undoubtedly one of the masters of both modernist ('read[ing] the same books that he has') and postmodernist (as in bricolagic and palimpsestic subversions which I shall be noting later) intertextual strategies.

But the most intriguing commentary on the Kafkaesque in Coetzee takes place in the long covert (and partly overt) dialogue between Coetzee and his chief rival as a fictional interpreter of South Africa to the liberal West, Nadine Gordimer. Their debate peaks in the Kafka exchange, where Kafka becomes their shared intertext, as well as the apparent provocation for their finding intertextual value in each other's work. In her influential article, 'The Idea of Gardening' (1984), Gordimer formulates her refutation of the Kafka link in *Life & Times of Michael K*: 'Michael K (the initial probably stands for Kotze or Koekemoer *and* has no reference, nor need it have, to Kafka) . . .' (emphasis added).[1] It is Gordimer's 'and', of course, which postulates a needlessly monologic[2] reading of Coetzee's image, for Gordimer cannot permit 'Kafka' to distract her from her political reading of both the splendours and the limitations of Coetzee's work. Would the Kafka reference, if conceded, be another overly aesthetic evasion of the tough political questions about, for instance, Coetzee's seeming lack of faith in a revolutionary solution, his seeming 'defeatism', that Gordimer raises elsewhere in the essay? Michael K 'is not Everyman', her oft-quoted 'Kafka' sentence concludes, but her unstated fear seems to be that 'Everyman', an allegorical and historically non-specific protagonist, may be exactly what he is.

In any case, Gordimer seems to develop a fictional rather than merely critical retort to the 'matter of Kafka' in her own later novel, *My Son's Story*, in which she shows, in her characteristically realist mode, what use 'Kafka' might actually be to a potentially revolutionary black South African – and, further, the possible limitations, and even dangers, of such usefulness:

> [Sonny, the schoolteacher] enrolled in a correspondence course. He chose comparative literature and discovered Kafka . . . – a way out of battered classrooms, the press of Saturday people, the promiscuity of thin-walled houses, and at the same time back into them again with a deeper sense of what the life in them might mean. *Kafka named what he had no names for.* The town whose walls were wandered around by the Saturday people was the Castle; the library whose doors he stood before were the gates of the law at which K. sat, year after year, always to be told he must wait for entry. The sin for which the schoolteacher's kind were banished to a prescribed area . . . was the sin Joseph K. was summoned to answer for to an immanent power, not knowing what the charge was, knowing only that if that power said he was guilty of something, then he was decreed so.
>
> This philosophizing reconciled Sonny, a profoundly *defeatist* way of staunching the kind of slow flux which is yearning. He was able to find satisfaction in the detachment of seeing the municipality and the Greek tearoom where his family could not sit down, in these terms. He became fascinated, as an *intellectual exercise*, with the *idea of power as an abstraction* . . . And although Kafka explained the context of the schoolteacher's life better than Shakespeare, Sonny did not go so far as to believe, with Kafka, that the power in which people are held powerless exists only in their own submission. (Gordimer, *My Son's Story* 17, emphasis added)

Age of Iron and *My Son's Story*, both published in the same year (1990), perhaps show these two authors drawing as close to each other as they are likely to come. This courteous dance of the two mutually respecting yet incompatible artistic temperaments and agendas represents yet another form which intertextuality can take in Coetzee's work. It is as if Coetzee took to heart the charges of distancing and obliquity to the political situation that Gordimer made so forcefully in her 'Idea of Gardening' article and, in response, made *Age of Iron* far clearer, more directly referential, more politically explicit, more available to the non-academic reading public as a text-weapon in the Apartheid Wars, than any of his previous texts and, particularly, than his immediately previous novel, *Foe*.

Despite the many similarities between these two books, we are struck by the impossibility of bridging this particular gap. It is a dialogue courteous and perhaps a little evasive on Coetzee's part (his strongest statement to date is that 'the novel is after bigger game' than can be caught by the methods of Gordimer's 'critical realism') (Coetzee (interview) 1978);[3] passionate and a trifle too literal on Gordimer's – but admiring and affectionate too, for she not only recognises Coetzee's talent (in 1986 she graciously named *Foe* as her *Observer* Book of the Year), but also realises that they are both, in the end, on the same side of the barricades.

Coetzeean intertextualities vary from book to book, exemplifying different strategies for oblique political expression. Their complexities are becoming a critical staple:[4] Dovey shows him deconstructing, in turn, all the traditional genres of South African literature; every critic of his much-analysed novel *Foe* shows Coetzee refocusing Defoe for the postcolonial world. In *Age of Iron*, classical intertexts (ones relatively easily decoded) come into play, along with a more central role for Samuel Beckett, always a hidden subtext in Coetzee's work. In *Age of Iron*, however, allusion functions primarily as a means of characterisation, with a 'mythical', hence ideological, structure operating beneath it (much as it did for the High Modernists, Virgil, Dante, and T. S. Eliot). Yet again, of course, Coetzee is in charge of the subtext; one scarcely supposes that our classicist narrator has conjured up so Beckettian a figure as Vercueil from her own intertextual repertoire. There are also, interestingly, numerous (Beckett-like) self-citations in *Age of Iron* to Coetzee's own corpus. But Kafka? Only a few allusions (*AOI* 126, 149, 157) of the sort to be found in almost any contemporary writer. Evidently Coetzee has moved on.

Leaving aside the non-Kafkan 'Europe' of *Waiting for the Barbarians*,[5] we find that a selection of the short fictions of Kafka (rather than his novels, I think, despite the centrality of the 'K' problem and Sonny's, or Gordimer's, concentration on elements in *The Trial* and *The Castle*) supplies a tradition of modernist parables (or 'allegorical fables', in Zamora's formulation – Zamora 6), fundamental to *Waiting for the Barbarians*, in one way, and to *Life & Times of Michael K*, in another. Kafka's contributions to *Waiting for the Barbarians* help Coetzee to abstract the historical process by spatialising it into the exotically liminal topographies[6] of the far-flung frontiers of empire where, time out of mind, soldiers and administrators from the distant capital have been posted to guard the empire from its enemies – the 'barbarians' – on the other side. In such parables the barbarians are only dimly, or seldom, or never, seen, which leaves their status as enemies unclear, or merely assumed, from rumour or remote tradition. These parables show the bleak, empty spaces beyond the frontier extending into never-never lands of hostile supposition, to be entered by the servants of the empire only transgressively, exceptionally, and at great risk.

Kafka's ironically mythical 'orientalist' versions of the Chinese Empire set out the basic pattern of these parables: in 'Beim Bau der chinesischen Mauer' ('The Great Wall of China'), for example, the Great Wall is revealed to be useless for its alleged purpose of defence against a rumoured but invisible enemy, the menacingly cruel, barbarously nomadic 'peoples of the north' (Kafka, *Collected Stories* 333); yet it is crucial for giving identity and a sense of purpose, however specious, to those within the wall, its builders. Their instructions reach them from that very distant, never seen, barely imaginable capital where the Emperor lives: 'aber Peking selbst ist den Leuten im Dorf viel fremder als das jenseitige Leben' ('Der Kaiser von Peking' ('Pekin and the Emperor'); 'but Pekin itself is far stranger to the people in our village than the next world'). The nomads themselves are known only through the mediation of those books and illustrations with which fathers terrify their children at the Great Wall. These illustrations show the Barbarians in much the same inhuman, horrifying light as the nomad invaders in 'Ein Altes Blatt' ('An Old Manuscript'), in which, as Lance Olsen has pointed out (110), the horrors of the barbarian conquest from the perspective of the occupied are recounted in that surviving scrap of narrative which serves to objectify the fears of those 'waiting for the barbarians'. We are at 'the borders of the Tibetan highlands' (Kafka, 'The Great Wall of China'), where vast spatial perspectives correspond to equally vast temporal ones and we are, as so often in Kafka, listening to a reflective investigator–narrator, who, like Coetzee's Magistrate, is puzzling over data from the perspective of the border, looking towards the distant capital, speaking in much the same 'voice' as the narrators of parables from the more Hapsburg-like imperium of 'Der kaiserliche Oberst' ('The Imperial Colonel') and 'Die Abweisung' ('The Refusal').

In 'Der kaiserliche Oberst', the representative of the unseen Emperor comes, like Coetzee's Colonel Joll, from the distant capital. Sitting uniformed at his desk, he dominates the citizenry by his 'gaze' alone, his slow, sweeping glance, accompanied by a strange smile which joins irony to dreamy remembrance. But in 'Die Abweisung', we see mediated imperial power in operation: the narrator receives reports of battles on the distant border, but hears almost nothing from the still more distant capital. Yet the citizens obey its commands, as delivered to them either by the highest officials (like the two colonels), who are from the capital, or by the middling officials, who are from outside the town, or by the lowest officials (like Coetzee's Magistrate), who are from the town itself ('[D]ie niedrigsten [sind] aus unserer Mitte'; Kafka, *Sämtliche Erzählungen* 356). Kafka's soldiers of occupation, small, agile, silent and significantly speaking a different dialect, silence us by their mere presence. The delegation of 'our citizens', confronting the Colonel, is intimidated by his look, by tradition and by the knowledge that a 'refusal' is inevitable, whatever the substance of the petition. This Colonel combines some qualities of both Coetzee's Magistrate (he is old and a long-time inhabitant; he serves as tax-collector) and Coetzee's Colonel Joll, whose look is powerful precisely because it cannot be seen – he wears (anachronistically) sunglasses. The Colonel becomes even more Joll-like when, in his capacity as ruler, he refuses, with the inexorable inevitability of 'die Mauer der Welt' (Kafka, *Sämtliche Erzählungen* 357), any petition or request that is brought to him. In Coetzee, as in Kafka, Imperial rule over distant segments of Empire justifies itself by appealing to the threat of attack – however amorphous – from the unknown and indeed unknowable 'Barbarians'. Imperial regimes, in these parables, must define themselves by mounting a guard at a frontier, by facing a nominally external enemy who is, in fact, only to be found within themselves. The application of this allegory to the South African situation could not possibly be clearer.

Like Kafka's Country Doctor ('Der Landarzt'), Coetzee's Magistrate is old and in search of a quiet life. But once he has taken his lantern into Colonel Joll's torture chamber, he too becomes irrevocably complicit in, as well as a victim of, Joll's uncontrollable force and cruelty: 'Einmal dem Fehlläuten der Nachtglocke gefolgt – es ist niemals gutzumachen' ('A false alarm on the night bell once answered – it cannot be made good, not ever'). As the Magistrate reformulates it: '*Justice*: once that word is uttered, where will it all end?' (*WFB* 108; Coetzee's emphasis). Both narrators find themselves, or rather lose themselves, at the conclusions of their stories, in wintry versions of a no-man's land or frontier. The Magistrate notes, epistemologically: 'the snowflakes come floating down . . . I [am] like a man who lost his way long ago but presses on along a road that may lead nowhere' (*WFB* 155–6); the Country Doctor, likewise: 'langsam wie alte Männer zogen wir durch die Schneewüste . . . treibe ich mich alter Mann umher' (Kafka, *Sämtliche Erzählungen* 145: 'we crawled slowly, like old men, through the snowy wastes . . . old man that I am, I wander astray' [I'm drifting around]). In Kafka's 'In der Strafcolonie' ('In the Penal Colony'), as George Steiner observes, the 'obscene intimacy between the torturer, the victim and the liberal witness' (i.e. Kafka's Officer, Soldier, and Explorer, respectively; *Sämtliche Erzählungen* 103), resembles Coetzee's sado-erotic triangle made up of Colonel Joll who, like Kafka's officer, believes that 'pain is truth' (Coetzee, *WFB* 5), the Barbarian woman whom he tortures, and the witnessing Magistrate.

Coetzee's 'victim' is, significantly, of a different gender, but this variation seems Kafkan as well. In 'Die Truppenaushebung' ('The Conscription of Troops'), in the course of 'never-ending frontier wars', two soldiers begin the search for a missing man who is evading conscription; in the nobleman's house an unknown girl 'from out of town, from the provinces, perhaps' is staring at the nobleman. 'Behind all the calm and friendliness she is inaccessible, like an utter stranger who is on her way home' (Kafka, *Collected Stories* 362), a fruitful hint for the figure of the Barbarian woman.

The illegible script to be written on the condemned man's back ('In der Strafcolonie') finds its analogue in the scars on the girl's tortured body, which Coetzee's Magistrate, like Kafka's Explorer, tries in vain to interpret. In Kafka's allegory of the Old Empire and the New, the torturer is part of the 'old' order now being superseded by the 'new' liberalism of which the Explorer becomes the passive ally. Coetzee seems to invert this allegory, for the Magistrate, conversely, represents an old order of would-be humanism, forced to give way to Colonel Joll's brutal new order. Numerous descriptive details in *Waiting for the Barbarians* (like the doggy soldiers and the sleeping sentry), seem to come from these and other Kafkan texts, along with Coetzee's 'Kafkan' atmosphere of diffuse hallucinated anxiety. More important, these Kafkan texts, pieced together, supply images for the strange geography of Coetzee's empire, for its political system, mediated by the representatives of the distant capital, and for the psychometaphysical effects of that system upon both rulers and ruled. That ambiguously intermediate authority figure, Coetzee's Magistrate, tries to oppose these wall-like forces of Empire with his feeble weapons of reason, learning, and good (for South Africa read: 'liberal') intentions.

As with the builders of Kafka's Chinese Wall, the liminal topography of *Waiting for the Barbarians* defines the unknown and unknowable 'other' (the Barbarians) by setting up a borderland, a no-man's land, an extended and variegated three-dimensional version of that geometrically one-dimensional line, edge or border, for which curiously vague and suppositional maps in each text provide two-dimensional warranty. All the territories into which the Barbarians swoop intermittently, which they haunt or infiltrate and then slip away from, into which imperial forces go as uneasy, endangered, incompatible aliens, are, whatever their topographical variations, liminalities. They do not, of course, define the Barbarians; they define instead the defenders of Empire.

The extended boredom of non-action in frontier garrison duty gives these individual or collective lives meaning and purpose only through the hope of invasion, thus turning waiting into the central human (in)action and non-happenings into the key events of a human life. This trope is adumbrated in many Kafkan texts, most memorably in 'Vor dem Gesetz', of course, but also 'Der Messias wird erst kommen, wenn er nicht mehr nötig sein wird . . .' ('The Messiah will finally come when he is no longer necessary'); 'Nun schien mir endlich meine Zeit gekommen oder vielmehr, sie war nicht gekommen und würde hier wohl auch niemals kommen' ('Now at last, it seemed to me, my moment had come, or rather it had not come and probably would never come . . .' ['Das Ehepaar', *Sämtliche Erzählungen* 406, 'The Married Couple']).[7] The event awaited takes place (if it takes place at all: Coetzee, like Buzzati and Cavafy, strongly implies a Kafkan anti-climax), after the end of the story and/or the death of the central consciousness. Like death itself, the Barbarian invasion, in destroying the narratorial identity of the imperial defenders, destroys the possibility of narrative. 'It will be known, but not by me, or by me, but too late', says Kafka's Burrower (Kafka, *Collected Stories* 336), of a similarly imagined siege.

Different generic patterns for parable suggest different intertextual strategies at work in Coetzee's two novels. *Waiting for the Barbarians* is suffused throughout with Kafkan echoes and elements, forming a mosaic of allusions, interpretable, on the whole, by the 'modernist' strategy of 'read[ing] the same books [Coetzee] has'. *Life & Times of Michael K*, on the other hand, plainly deploys the more 'postmodern' intertextual strategies of 'palimpsest' and 'bricolage', so that we may 'read' the tectonic plates of Kafkan episodes as they slide across each other, submerged yet legible, under Coetzee's text. The hypotextual centrality of Kafka is presupposed in the matter of the letter K itself: that far from random signifier, that most intertextual of all initials. Further, Coetzee constitutes entire episodes of *Life & Times of Michael K* by deploying the major Kafkan motifs of the 'hunger artist' and the 'burrow', rare, though not unknown, in his earlier works: 'In the blindest alley of the labyrinth of my self I had hidden myself away, abandoning mile after mile of defences' (*MK* 96). These motifs, although interwoven and overlapping, are roughly separable into the two 'burrow' settings of the cave and (more emphatically) the farm, which segue into the two 'hunger artist' camp scenes, the first of which is told in the third person, from Michael's point of view, while the second is narrated in the first person by the Medical Officer.[8] These two movements from 'burrow' to 'hunger' fill the principal gap in K's circular journey from Cape Town to Cape Town. A third such movement (abridged) occurs only in his mind, in his imagined third sojourn at the farm.

As a 'Hunger Artist,' Michael K shapes his being by negating it, by living minimally, by accepting no food. Like Kafka's Hunger Artist, he does so not out of a commitment to hunger *per se* but because, as the Medical Officer eventually figures out, he could not, in the camp, eat the food that he liked. In contrast to Kafka's existential implication, that it is impossible in this world to find 'the food that [the Hunger Artist] liked', Coetzee's politico-economic point is that Michael needs for his sustenance explicitly that food which he is free to grow for himself. Kafka's interpreter–impresario is represented here by a staggering failure in either role. A 'makeshift Medical Officer' who 'unrelentingly pressed food on you that you could not eat' (*MK* 162), he is a writer-reader for whom Michael K, '*not even* a hero of fasting' (163, emphasis added), plays the distinctly subordinate role of Text.

Particularly in the cave scene (and the end of the first farm scene, *MK* 60–9), 'burrowing' is shaped in a way intermediate between Defoe's *Robinson Crusoe* and the revisionist Cruso of Coetzee's *Foe*. Michael thinks he is in a 'pocket outside time' (60), on 'one of those islands without an owner' (61), mulling over the (lack of) interest to be found in the story of his life (67), eating an ant-nest, roots and grubs. 'But now he ceased to make an adventure of eating and drinking. He did not explore his new world. He did not turn his cave into a home or keep a record of the passage of days' (68; cf. 115: 'He was not a prisoner or a castaway, his life by the dam was not a sentence [metatextual pun?] that he had to serve out'). To negate the Crusoe experience in these explicit terms is of course to foreground it – and make it malleable for later use.

The principal 'burrow' episode begins with 'the business of making a dwelling' (*MK* 99), and supplies almost as many concrete details of this process as Kafka does. Anxious, Michael learns, like the Burrower, to 'rest by day and stay up at night to protect his land' (103). His sense of sight diminishes, but his senses of touch and hearing become sharper and, like a blind man, he 'strain[s] his ears for the noises that would herald his discovery' (105; already anticipated in a 'voice too, coming from all sides' (69)). He becomes 'more timorous than a mouse' (105), and performs elaborate mental exertions, supplying 'a thousand' (107) explanations and very little reassurance. 'I should be growing onions' (112), he says, rather than his all-too-visible surface crops, whose ripening correlates with the ripening of his anxiety. All his manoeuvres are cautious and defensive; to be spotted (or heard) is to be recaptured. He needs a 'fence . . . to stop the [counter] burrowers' (117), and suffers, like his Kafkan predecessor, from an inner enemy, headaches, and an outer one, floods. At the moment of his recapture (the moment that Kafka's Burrower, of course, cannot narratively reach), the overlapping minor motif of the Hunger Artist clicks into the major key: '"What do you think he lives on?" the soldier asked– "Flies? Ants? Locusts?"' And his purely defensive burrow, his home, the shell of his projected self, is misread by his captors according to their own expectations: '"holes and tunnels! any kind of storage site! . . . [T]he ground beneath your feet is rotten with tunnels"' (121–2).

I prefer to see Coetzee starting from parabolic (that is, Kafkan) characterisation and working up to such figures as Michael K, rather than as starting from the postulates of 'realistic' characterisation, and working down to him, as Dovey does. But Dovey deals admirably with the question of Coetzee's allegory of genre, seeing 'genre' as 'a borrowed dwelling', for temporary occupancy. I would add that, if Michael K's burrow is Kafka's burrow, then Coetzee's allegory is more than just intergeneric; it is intertextual. Where palimpsest becomes a metaphor for allegory, in Dovey's reading, I would prefer terms closer to those of its literal structure. As an example of one text which is layered over another one, and which can be seen/read through it, palimpsest provides an appropriate image of Coetzeean intertextuality, whereby Kafka's burrow-text can be read 'through' the filter of Coetzee's.

Coetzee himself proposes, in his difficult yet crucial essay on Kafka's 'The Burrow', that 'the major metaphor for the linguistic construct is the burrow itself, built by the labors of the forehead' ('Time, Tense and Aspect' 1981, 577; cf. Dovey 51). When Michael K builds himself such a structure, he too must live in anxious self-defence – 'so that he leaves no trace of his living' (*MK* 135) – in this 'makeshift . . . shelter to be abandoned' (138) on account of the 'fatal precariousness' it shares with that supposedly 'perfectly secure hideaway' ('Time, Tense and Aspect' 1981, 579, 556), Kafka's Burrow.

Thus, it is an attractive option to suppose that 'the strategies of Coetzee's texts . . . the way in which they inhabit the borrowed form, the makeshift shelter . . . [are] to avoid constructing another, alternative myth' (Dovey, *The Novels of J. M. Coetzee* 288). But I see no need to assume Coetzee's willingness to 'abandon text to successive meanings'. I would say, rather, that he counsels against treating his text, his ramshackle textual structure, his burrow (put together, by palimpsest and bricolage, out of Kafka, Poppie Nongena, Pauline Smith *et al.* (note 8), as *Waiting for the Barbarians* is put together out of 'the books he has read' – Kafka, Cavafy, Zbigniew Herbert, Gracq and Buzzati), as the start of a tradition, to be appropriated by others in their turn. Michael K is, in these terms, the survivor-hero of apocalyptic bricolage, the more affirmative Cruso(e) of Coetzee's self-referential prolepsis, as well as the more courageous (and less self-conscious) 'Burrow'-er of Coetzee's main Kafkan intertext.

There are two generic postulates to be considered in connection with *Life & Times of Michael K.* Coetzee's title seems to parody the 'Life & Times' of a famous person: *The Life & Times of a Respectable Rebel, Daniel Lindley 1801–80: Missionary to the Zulus*, for instance, might be contrasted with (it is a randomly chosen specimen of the kind of title Coetzee is guying) Coetzee's mock-heroic biography of one of the dispossessed. The Burrower's 'fundamental experience of time' (Coetzee, 'Time, Tense and Aspect' 571) becomes Michael K's exemplary 'fundamental experience' of his 'Times', which happen to be 'iron' ones, governed by 'iron laws' (*MK* 115, 151, 154), anticipating the still more apocalyptic world of *Age of Iron*.

The extended sequence of animal similes for Michael K himself (Dovey, *The Novels* 284–5) – he is, for instance, like 'a mole . . . that does not tell stories because it lives in silence' (*MK* 182) – suggests, of course, the ancient strategy of an animal fable, from which its hearers or readers are presumed to derive moral instruction. I would add that, for Coetzee, the fable form has been filtered through Kafka's remarkable development of it in his own animal-centred parables, shown by many critics (notably Koelb) to be best read as metatextual allegory, of ambiguous, if indeed of any, moral import.

In neither *Waiting for the Barbarians* nor *Life & Times of Michael K* can it be supposed that the narrator of the one (being 'out of place and time') and the protagonist of the other are at all 'responsible' for the Kafkan (among other) intertexts, in the way that Gordimer's Sonny, for instance, is responsible for taking Kafka's 'names' to name the features of his world for himself 'has no names'. The Medical Officer can, with a kind of knowingness which is one of his most irritating characteristics, wink at us over Michael's head as he talks to himself; he bears considerable – perhaps chief – responsibility for imposing Kafkan characteristics upon Michael.

The only intertextuality for which Michael K himself seems to stand warranty is the last third of the triple Disney reference, in the description of the dusty, stored garden furniture back in Cape Town: 'three painted plaster statues: a deer with chocolate-brown eyes, a gnome in a buff jerkin . . . and, larger than the other two, a creature with a peg nose whom he recognised as Pinocchio' (*MK* 180). Michael K does not recognise (nor does Dovey, *The Novels of J. M. Coetzee* [322] seem to, but presumably Coetzee assumes that we will) Disney's Bambi along with one of his Seven Dwarfs, as if Disney were the maker of icons for the subjunctive world of conditions-contrary-to-fact.

The book's cryptopastoral ending, with its ironic paean to the spirit of survival, might be Faulknerian were it not so doubtfully subjunctive: 'and in that way, he *would* say, one can live'. That same doubtful subjunctive brings about a textual rapprochement between the Medical Officer ('I would have'; *MK* 162), and Michael K ('I should have'; *MK* 183), which amounts to a kind of undelivered, undeliverable, Imperial Message. Where Michael imagines a, rather Vercueil-like, old man who will need his guidance back to the farm (*MK* 183; cf. 118), the Medical Officer says, to an imaginary, fleeing, Michael, that 'I would have come before you and spoken . . . I have chosen you to show me the way' out of the war zone, to a place 'between the camps' (*MK* 162–3). This double ending is not unlike that of Kafka's 'The Imperial Message': 'But you sit by your window and dream it all true, when evening falls'.

If the 'lesson' of Coetzee's parable is to be 'restricted to the act of reading and of writing', to metatextual allegory, as Dovey (287) seems to suggest, then it follows by many a political analysis of postmodernity that Coetzee 'implicitly endorses the system' (Dovey 287) or, in Gordimerian terms, that he has at best been occupied in 'an intellectual exercise, with the idea of power as an abstraction'. While the rhetorical stance of Kafka's fables and parables does not force an apolitical reading upon us, it does raise the question of the political implications of the Kafkan parable-form as one type of Coetzeean intertextuality, a question which, I trust, this essay has begun to formulate, if not to answer. After all, Kafka, as well as being paradoxical and metatextual, is also known to have said, 'A time will eventually come . . . [when] the law will belong to the people' ('The Problem of Our Laws') and 'Could I still endure any other air than prison air? That is the great question, or rather it would be if I still had any prospect of release' ('The Knock at the Manor Gate'). It should by now be clear that the intertextual always possesses political application. For both Coetzee and Gordimer, 'Kafka name[s] what [they have] no [better] names for'. But the difference between the stylistic, and thus the topical, import of their respective deployments of Kafka is one measure of the obliquity and indirection of Coetzee's intertextual strategies for 'naming' the political, in contrast to Gordimer's plain speaking for a wider but somewhat different audience.

Notes

1. 'Kotze' and 'Koekemoer' are 'common surnames among Cape Town coloured people' (Gallagher 13), and the resemblance of one of them, 'Kotze', to Coetzee's own surname is, despite Coetzee's onomastic play in *Dusklands*, an awkward coincidence that, until Mennecke (1991: 154) said plainly that 'Kotze' is another form of 'Coetzee', nobody wished to follow up. As for 'Michael' (a question not usually raised), Heinrich von Kleist's story, 'Michael Kohlhass' (1810), a notable intertext for Kafka, may be at least a 'grandfather' intertext for Coetzee.
2. Dovey and Gallagher quite rightly reproach Gordimer for this monologic reading, but Gallagher then goes on, with remarkable inconsistency, to reproach Lehmann-Haupt for identifying the Castle in *Life & Times of Michael K* with Kafka's – on the rather Gordimerian grounds that 'the Castle has held the Cape's administrative offices since the time of the original Dutch settlers' (Gallagher 230).
3. To a lesser degree, Gordimer too has participated in this partial rapprochement. Even apart from the Kafka scene, *My Son's Story* is unusual in the relative complexity, amounting almost to self-reflexive artifice, of its narrative structure: the story narrated by the father is in fact 'written' by the son. The two books are also chiasmically gendered: the male author writes (for distance?) in the person of a mother writing to her daughter; the female author writes (for verisimilitude?) through a father seemingly writing of his son. See Parrinder's review of the two books: '*Age of Iron* suggests the extent to which Gordimer's writings have set an agenda for her younger compatriots' (Parrinder 17). Her 1984 story, 'Letter from His Father', suggests a similar revisionary mode in dealing with Kafka. Here Kafka's father 'replies' to his son's notorious 'Letter to His Father', making the real-world case for a father doing his best, financially, emotionally and psychologically, for a son whose neurotic temperament and opaque accomplishments are crowned by that letter full of hatred, ingratitude and misunderstanding: the case, that is, for an ordinary man caged in, by propinquity, love and obligation, with an awkward genius.

4. See Brink (1984), who places Coetzee among other South African apocalyptic novelists. Other South African sources and analogues are suggested by Coetzee himself (if one chooses to extrapolate the implications of *White Writing*), by Dovey, rather programmatically, but evidently correctly, in her proposition (echoed by Gallagher) that Coetzee 'rewrites' the white liberal humanist South African novel (for example, early Gordimer). Gallagher outlines, almost equally programmatically (but more simplistically) a Coetzeean sequential allegory of South African political history. She makes cogent parallels, however, between *Life & Times of Michael K* and Pauline Smith's story 'The Pain', of which the relationship between Michael K and his mother can be seen as a revisionist reading, and (following Brink) Karel Schoeman's apocalyptic novel, *Promised Land*. Voss considers especially South African end-of-empire historical texts. All of these together perhaps play an intertextual role similar to that of the Gracq and Buzzati intertexts for *Waiting for the Barbarians* (5).
5. Three others of the 'same books', in Watson's phrase, useful for reading this Coetzee text are Julien Gracq's parabolic novel, *Le Rivage des Syrtes* (1951), Dino Buzzati's novelistic fable, *Il Deserto dei Tartari* (1945), and of course the Cavafy poem (1904) which supplies both title and epigraph. George Steiner was the first to note this three-way connection, but unfortunately he did so only to disparage Coetzee, finding *Waiting for the Barbarians* 'heavy with clichés' compared to its 'two much stronger predecessors' in this 'widespread macabre genre' (Steiner 102–3). Steiner usefully suggests some of the topographical resemblances: 'the salt flats, the haunted marsh reeds, the horizons of shifting menace which surround the settlement' resemble the setting of *Le Rivage des Syrtes*, he says, while 'the whole evocation of the avenging unknown just across the northern hills' (Steiner 103) derives from *Il Deserto dei Tartari*. 'Add to this the pervasive influence of Kafka's "In the Penal Colony" . . .' says Steiner, in his brooking-no-argument voice. In sum, many of the thematic and formal strategies Coetzee needed to make lengthy fictions from the few and brief premises of Kafka's parables are to be found in Gracq and Buzzati; they were plainly of material assistance to him in what he describes as the 'immense labor' of 'invent[ing] a world out of place and time' (Morphet interview 455). Coetzee himself mentions the imperial topographies of Zbigniew Herbert's 'To Marcus Aurelius' and 'The Return of the Proconsul' (1990–1: 161). See Merivale (1990) for a fuller discussion of these points. I have adapted part of this earlier work for my section on the Kafkan echoes in *Waiting for the Barbarians*.
6. See Jolly's excellent discussion, which I can only qualify by suggesting that her 'unfamiliar', seemingly 'unrecognisable' Coetzeean landscapes are indeed recognisable, but as intertext, not as topography.
7. As developed by Buzzati and Gracq, this motif forms virtually the whole of their fascinatingly negative plot lines. See also Henry James's 'The Beast in the Jungle', for a similar fable with a very different moral topography.

8. The Medical Officer seems to have read, in addition to 'A Hunger Artist', Kafka's 'Investigations of a Dog' (an animal who 'prize[s] freedom higher than everything else'), Melville's 'Bartleby the Scrivener' (*MK* 144–5; 'What am I to this man?' 149), Zbigniew Herbert's poem 'The Stone' (*MK* 135), possibly Nigel Dennis' *A House in Order* (on the 'idea of gardening' in a prison camp), and a great deal of Samuel Beckett. Mennecke goes much further along this same interpretive road; he suggests, validly I think and very fruitfully, that the Michael K of Parts I and III is a projection of the quasi-authorial consciousness of the Medical Officer (129–73 *passim;* 131, 135 *et al.*).

10

Oppressive Silence: J. M. Coetzee's *Foe* and the Politics of Canonisation

DEREK ATTRIDGE

I

How does it come about that a fictional work, or an *oeuvre*, is heard within a literary and cultural tradition? What does it mean for a novel to claim canonic status, or for critics to make such a claim on its behalf? What kinds of voicing and silencing are involved in this process, and how do they relate to the wider operations of voicing and silencing that characterise – and in some degree constitute – our cultural and political practices? These are some of the troublesome questions raised, internally and externally, by J. M. Coetzee's fifth novel, *Foe*.

If we characterise canonisation in a fairly straightforward way, as widespread recognition within the institutions of publication and education that a body of texts by a single author constitutes an 'important', 'serious', 'lasting' contribution to 'literature' (a characterisation I shall considerably complicate in due course), it is clear that the process is well under way for Coetzee – a volume such as the one to which this essay belongs constituting part of the evidence. In South Africa, where the political determination of the canon is more blatant, the picture is somewhat more complicated: the standing of the novels has been strongly affected by the degree to which they are perceived as hostile to the policies and practices of apartheid – and by the significance of this perception to different groups within the country. On the part of the government they have been subject to official scrutiny and delays and ignored by the state-controlled media, but they have not been banned; on the part of the liberation movements they have been championed by some but attacked by others for failing to engage more directly in the political struggle. I shall return later to this complex array of responses.

What is it about these novels that has propelled them at least into the ante-chambers of the literary canon in the English-speaking world? The answers to this question are no doubt many and diverse; since canonisation depends on the convergence of a multitude of separate decisions and actions, it is bound to be overdetermined. One part of the answer might be that through their frequently overt *allusiveness* the novels offer themselves not as challenges to the canon, but as canonic – as already canonised, one might say. They appear to locate themselves within an established literary culture, rather than presenting themselves as an assault on that culture. Sometimes the allusions are so overt that they run the risk of appearing as intrusive attempts to claim membership of the existing tradition. The narrator of *In the Heart of the Country* weaves into her text the words of a number of canonic writers, and as the novel draws to a close she hears, or believes she hears, fragments of the Western cultural encyclopedia descending to her from passing aircraft.[1] *Waiting for the Barbarians* takes its title, and one aspect of its sociopolitical dynamic, from a poem of Cavafy's (*Collected Poems* 30–3) and alludes as well to Beckett's best-known play; while the name of the central character in *Life & Times of Michael K*, often referred to just as 'K', cannot fail to recall Kafka.[2] However, it is in *Foe* that Coetzee has made canonic intertextuality a fundamental principle: the novel's manner of proceeding is to rewrite, and fuse together, the biography of Daniel Defoe and those of several of Defoe's fictional characters. The perpetuation of any canon is dependent in part on the references made to its earlier members by its later members (or would-be members), and in this respect Coetzee's novels could be said to presuppose and to reproduce the canonic status of their predecessors while claiming to join them.

It might further be argued that the *style* of Coetzee's novels also constitutes a claim to belong to an existing canonic tradition; the deliberate, chiselled prose has little to do with the exorbitance or casualness (however studied) by which texts we might characterise as 'postmodern' frequently affront the traditional valorisation of literary form. Coetzee's is writing which invites the reader to savour it, sentence by sentence, word by word, for its economy and efficiency and, although the style of each novel has its own unmistakable character, the reader receives the consistent impression in all of them of words chosen with extraordinary care. In fact, as with the use of allusions and citations, the very deliberateness of this highly literary language may for some tastes smack too obviously of canonic pretensions.

A third feature of Coetzee's fiction which is interpretable as consistent with the traditional humanist concerns of the canon is its *thematic focus*: for instance, the novels return again and again to the solitary individual in a hostile human and physical environment to raise crucial questions about the foundations of civilisation and humanity. The American military propagandist in the U.S.–Vietnam war driven to the limits of sanity and the hunter–explorer barely surviving in harsh country among 'savage' people; the self-tormenting farmer's daughter alone with her father's corpse on the isolated farm; the well-meaning state official enduring himself the barbarism on which his 'civilisation' depends; the nomadic victim of a racist society who manages to exist almost without food; the homeless derelict who squats in the middle-class backyard: these figures may appear as so many versions of Lear's experience on the heath; one poor, bare, forked animal after another. Or one might emphasise the repeated motif of masters (or mistresses) and servants – also important in *King Lear*, of course, and, in its yoking of a moral discourse of human bonds and rights with an actual relationship of economic exploitation, a recurrent source of tension in the bourgeois conscience and the novels which represent it. Once again, it is *Foe* which foregrounds this relation to the tradition: the novel of which it is a rewriting, *Robinson Crusoe*, is probably Western culture's most potent crystallisation of its concern with the survival of the individual, the fundamentals of civilised life, and the dialectic of master and servant.

This account of the canonic claim made by the novels themselves needs to be complemented by factors external to the writing which also bear on the question of canonisation. As a white male (like Daniel Defoe), Coetzee has a degree of privileged access to most canons, and as a South African, especially one who has chosen to remain in South Africa, he possesses a certain mystique: that country, for all its geographical marginality to the canonisation processes of Western culture, has a notorious centrality in the contemporary political and ethical imagination that gives its writers a special claim on the world's attention. There is, of course, another side to this advantage. It brings with it the danger that writing emanating from South Africa will be read *only* as a reflection of or a resistance to a particular political situation, whereas the high literary canon, in its most traditional form, is premised upon an assumption of universal moral and aesthetic values. But Coetzee's works seem for the most part designed to escape that danger: until *Age of Iron,* his most recent novel at the time of writing, they have either made no mention of South Africa or have been set in a South Africa distanced, by temporal or geographical displacement, from the actual country as it existed at the time of writing. An apologist for the traditional canon might argue that Coetzee's novels are not about the South African situation *per se,* which would render them contingent and propagandist, but about the permanent human truths exemplified in that situation.

Within South Africa, however, this departicularisation renders Coetzee subject to the argument that he has abused his privileges as a member of the white elite in addressing not the immediate needs of his time but a mystified human totality. If the account I have given of his work's amenability to canonisation is accurate and complete, this critique must stand as valid. The unproblematised notion of a canon is complicit with a mode of literature – and of criticism – which dehistoricizes and dematerialises the acts of writing and reading while promoting a myth of transcendent human truths and values. By the same token, however, a mode of fiction which exposed the ideological basis of canonisation, which drew attention to its own relation to the existing canon, which thematised the role of race, class and gender in the processes of cultural acceptance and exclusion, and which, while speaking from a marginal location, addressed the question of marginality – such a mode of fiction would have to be seen as engaged in an attempt to break the silence in which so many are caught, even if it did so by literary means that have traditionally been celebrated as characterising canonic art. A more careful reading of Coetzee's novels, I want to argue, shows just these qualities.

II

Foe came as something of a disappointment to many readers and reviewers.[3] The previous novel, *Life & Times of Michael K,* allowed itself to be read as, to quote the paperback's blurb, a 'life-affirming novel' that 'goes to the center of human experience', seeming to confirm those elements in *Waiting for the Barbarians* which could be taken as expressions of a spiritual and moral truth beyond politics or culturally-determined structures of signification. Moreover, *Life & Times of Michael K* satisfied those who wanted Coetzee to deal more directly with the struggle in South Africa today, while avoiding the adoption of a narrowly based political position. But *Foe* is not only further removed in time and place from present-day South Africa; it has no character whose interior life is depicted in such a way as to evoke the reader's moral sympathy (as the Magistrate's and K's do in the previous novels), and it seems to lack evidence of what one reviewer called, in discussing *Life & Times of Michael K*, Coetzee's 'tender and unwavering faith in the individual'.[4]

Instead of taking *Foe* as a swerve away from a clear and established mode of fiction and set of values, however, it is worth asking whether it can provide a perspective from which to re-examine the other works and their pertinence to the canon and to contemporary political and cultural life. We may do this by returning to the qualities of Coetzee's writing that I mentioned earlier, and scrutinising more carefully the argument that they constitute a straightforward, if dangerously self-conscious, claim to canonic status.

Although the overt intertextuality in Coetzee's novels can, as I have suggested, be read as an implicit claim to a place in the established canon, it is also possible to regard it as drawing attention to the way the text, like any text, is *manufactured* from the resources of a particular culture in order to gain acceptance within that culture, an operation that canonic works, and those who uphold the canon as an unproblematic reflection of inherent values, cannot fully acknowledge. (The most powerful upholders of the canon are, of course, those who do not acknowledge such a concept at all.) In *Foe* this process becomes inescapably evident, as the larger part of the novel consists of a memoir and several letters written by the newly-returned castaway Susan Barton to the well-known author Daniel Foe, quotation marks before each of her paragraphs reminding us continually that this is not the mysterious immaterial language most fiction uses as its medium, nor even a representation of speech, but a representation *in* writing *of* writing. And it is written not as a simple day-to-day record of experience, as in a novel of letters or diary entries, but for the explicit purpose of proffering a narrative – the story of Barton's year on an island with another, earlier, castaway named Robinson Cruso – for insertion into the canon of published English texts. When, toward the end of the novel, the quotation marks disappear, the reader is forced to ask questions which fiction seldom invites: on what occasion and by what means are *these* words now being produced, and to what audience are they being directed?

Moreover, the intertextuality of *Foe* works to unsettle any simple relation between historical report and fictional invention. The Cruso we encounter in this novel appears as the historical original of the fictional Crusoe we already know from our access to the canon,[5] yet even within the novel he is part of Susan Barton's narrative, which is clearly to some extent – but how much, and how deliberately? – a work of fiction on her part. At the same time, Barton herself is troubled by the repeated appearance of a girl claiming to be her daughter, whose reality, within the fictional world, is thrown into question by the reader's awareness that her story, and that of her maid Amy who often accompanies her, is told in another of Defoe's novels, *Roxana*.[6] From this perspective, the quotations in *In the Heart of the Country* and the name 'Michael K' seem less like somewhat intrusive claims to belong to a tradition of great writing than determined reminders – working against the skilfully contrived immediacy of the narrators' thoughts – that all cultural work is a reworking, that all representations achieve vividness by exploiting culturally-specific conventions and contexts.

Turning to the second feature I mentioned earlier, Coetzee's chiselled style can be seen not as a bid for admission to the pantheon of great writers but as drawing attention to itself in a way that undermines the illusion of pure expression; the slight self-consciousness of its shaped sentences – what one critic has aptly described as 'that style forever on its guard against itself' (Strauss 128) – goes hand-in-hand with the intertextual allusiveness to reinforce the awareness that all representation is mediated through the discourses that culture provides. Certainly in *Foe* it is no longer possible to regard this quality of the writing as an inadvertent one, an inability to achieve total unself-conscious limpidity. Whereas in the earlier novels a reader might decide that the echoes of, say, Beckett's style are an excusable failure to evade a powerful precursor rather than a calculated effect, the tinges of eighteenth-century diction that characterise the language of *Foe* cannot be anything other than a distancing device rendering us conscious of the artefact we have before us – a device which, remarkably, does not diminish the writing's capacity to produce for the reader a powerful experience of reality. Reading is usually a more complex process than we allow for in our theories of it, and one of the pleasures of reading Coetzee is realising this – and realising that this realisation need not spoil our more traditional literary pleasures.

Lastly, with regard to the thematic concerns of Coetzee's fictions, one finds that whatever accommodation was possible between the earlier novels and the humanist tradition, the isolated individuals in *Foe* function – as I hope to demonstrate – not as representatives of the motif of naked humanity granted universal insight on the stormy heath, but as compelling subversions of this motif. They demonstrate that what we call 'insights' are produced and conveyed by the narrativising agencies of culture; experience in itself is insufficient to gain credit as knowledge or truth. Even if the transmutation of experience into knowledge occurs in the privacy of the individual consciousness, it does so by virtue of internalised cultural norms, of which each of us is a repository; and without external validation, such 'knowledge' must remain uncertain and insubstantial.

III

Every writer who desires to be read (and that is perhaps part of what it means to write) has to seek admittance to the canon – or, more precisely, *a* canon, since any group approval of a text is an instance of canonisation; like languages, canons are not monolithic entities but complex, interrelated and constantly-changing systems which can be subdivided all the way down to individual preferences – 'idiocanons', we might call them. Awareness of this necessity, conscious or not, governs the act of writing quite as much as the need for self-expression or the wish to communicate. What *Foe* suggests is that the same imperative drives our self-presentations and representations; unless we are read, we are nothing. And taking together the features of this and the earlier novels that I have discussed, it would seem that it is not possible to separate the processes of canonisation that operate within the domain of high, or for that matter popular, culture from the very similar processes that operate in our everyday experience; constructing and sustaining an identity, making sense of one's own past, establishing an intelligible relationship with one's fellows, are all in part a matter of telling one's story (the story of who one is, was, and aspires to be) in such a way as to have it accepted and valorised within the body of recognised narratives – with their conventions of plot, character, symbolisation, moralisation, etc. – that are part of the cultural fabric and, therefore, part of our individual systems of judgment and interpretation. Acceptance into the canon is not merely a matter of success in the market place: it confers *value*, although the value it confers is necessarily understood as not conferred and contingent but inherent and permanent. What is unusual about *Foe* is the way that it simultaneously seeks admittance to the literary canon on these terms *and* draws attention to the canon's cultural and historical contingency, just as Barton, in seeking cultural acceptance for her story and through it an assertion of her unique subjectivity, shows an increasing awareness of the double bind which this implies.

If we extend the meaning of 'canonisation' to include these wider processes of legitimation, it might be said that the novel dramatises the procedures and problems of canonisation four times over. Cruso, who shows none of the practical ingenuity or the spiritual intensity we expect from the figure of bourgeois resourcefulness we are familiar with, has, by his isolation from culture, lost touch with its founding narratives and need for narrative: not only has he rescued very little from the wreck and made only minimal attempts to improve the quality of his life, he has kept no journal (he doesn't even notch the passing days on a stick) and has no desire to leave the island. He spends most of his time levelling the island's hill into terraces – a parodic version of the canonic castaway's taming of nature, since he has nothing with which to plant them. Most interesting for my present argument is that he appears to have lost any firm sense of the distinction between truth and fiction. Barton writes to Foe:

> I would gladly now recount to you the history of this singular Cruso, as I heard it from his own lips. But the stories he told me were so various, and so hard to reconcile one with another,

> that I was more and more driven to conclude age and isolation had taken their toll on his memory, and he no longer knew for sure what was truth, what fancy. (*F* (Viking Penguin) 11–12)

Barton herself, by contrast, feels that she lacks substance as an individual until the story of her year on the island with Cruso (who dies on the return journey) is written as a legitimated narrative, yet is barred from the domain of authorship by her gender, her social status, her economic dependence and her unfamiliarity with the requirements of published narratives. It is not merely that publication of her story will bring fame and money; she has an obscure sense that her experience will remain lacking in reality until it is told as a publicly validated narrative: '"Return to me the substance I have lost, Mr Foe: that is my entreaty. For though my story gives the truth, it does not give the substance of the truth (I see that clearly, we need not pretend it is otherwise)"' (*F* 51). When Foe goes into hiding from his creditors, she waits for his return, reminding him that '"[M]y life is drearily suspended till your writing is done"' (*F* 63), and later takes up residence in his empty house. But the longer she waits, the more conscious she becomes that to depend for her identity on a process of writing is to cast doubt on that identity: '"In the beginning I thought I would tell you the story of the island and, being done with that, return to my former life. But now all my life grows to be story and there is nothing of my own left to me"' (*F* 133). (One curious, but relevant, effect of Coetzee's strategy is that, for all the vivid first-person writing, Susan Barton does have an aura of insubstantiality, precisely because of the canonic success and consequent power of Defoe's novel.)

Foe, the professional author, makes little progress with Barton's story of her experiences on the island; he thinks of including it as one episode in the longer story of a woman in search of her daughter, or spicing it with additional material about cannibals and battles.[7] She insists that he should concentrate exclusively on the story of the island, although she becomes increasingly aware of its unsuitability for the established canon:

> I am growing to understand why you wanted Cruso to have a musket and be besieged by cannibals. I thought it was a sign you had no regard for the truth. I forgot you are a writer who knows above all how many words can be sucked from a cannibal

feast, how few from a woman cowering from the wind. It is all a matter of words and the number of words, is it not? (*F* 94)

To assess how much rewriting Barton's story of the island requires in order to render it fit for the developing bourgeois canon of the early eighteenth century we need only turn from Coetzee's novel to the novel published in 1719 as *The Life and Adventures of Robinson Crusoe* by Daniel Defoe, the more aristocratic name adopted by plain Daniel Foe in 1695 as part of *his* assault on the British canon.[8] One of the striking absences from Defoe's highly successful novel, of course, is that of any female voice: the gender requirements of acceptable narrative forms allow for women heroines in certain roles (the entrepreneur in larceny and marriage exemplified by *Moll Flanders*, for instance), but these appear not to include stories of the mastering of natural forces and the colonising of primitive cultures.[9] Within Coetzee's novel, Foe's decision to exclude Susan Barton from his published narrative altogether is not represented; but we do witness how the professional author is much more attracted to Barton's own story before and after the period on the island, involving her lost daughter, and, we are encouraged to suspect from several hints thrown out, the colourful life of a courtesan. In other words, Susan Barton's story – the one she does not want told – becomes Defoe's *Roxana*.[10]

It would be misleading to suggest that the novel uses a range of characters to lay out neatly a number of different attitudes to canonic narrative; it is itself a narrative that offers strong resistance to the masterful reader or critic, frequently becoming opaque just when a systematic or allegorical meaning seems to be emerging. But it may be possible to think of Cruso and Foe as opposites, one who no longer has any use for narrative, and the other who lives for, and through, narrative. Susan Barton, who, for all we are allowed to know, might be the author of the narratives of both Cruso and Foe, is aware of the constituting capacities of narrative and the emptiness of existence outside her culture's canonic stories, yet at the same time irresistibly (and understandably) attached to the notion of a subjectivity and substantiality which does not have to be grounded in the conventions of narrative. Yet she attempts to resist, as she must, what is implied by this self-perception: that her story is determined not by herself but by the culture within which she seeks an identity. Thus, in refusing to tell Foe of her life before the shipwreck, she insists:

> I choose not to tell it because to no one, not even to you, do I owe proof that I am a substantial being with a substantial history in the world. I choose rather to tell of the island, of myself and Cruso and Friday and what we three did there: for I am a free woman who asserts her freedom by telling her story according to her own desire. (*F* 131)

At the end of her long debate with Foe, however, she appears to move toward his position: that there are no distinctions to be made between characters invented by an author and individuals with an independent reality. In answer to Foe's question about the substantiality of the girl claiming to be her daughter, the girl from the pages of *Roxana*, she concedes: '"No, she is substantial, as my daughter is substantial, and I am substantial; and you too are substantial, no less and no more than any of us. We are all alive, we are all substantial, we are all in the same world"' (*F* 152). (For us, of course, that world is the world – substantial or insubstantial? – of Coetzee's novel.)

Foe might be read, then, as an exploration of a fact that is central to the processes of canonisation, in the narrower as much as in the wider sense that I am giving it: human experience seems lacking in substance and significance if it is not represented (to oneself and to others) in culturally validated narrative forms, but those narrative forms constantly threaten, by their exteriority and conventionality, the substantiality of that experience. A similar concern could be traced in the other novels – in the different written versions of Jacobus Coetzee's journey beyond the Great River, in the alternative stories Magda tells herself in *In the Heart of the Country*, in the Medical Officer's attempts to get a story out of the man he calls 'Michaels' in *Life & Times of Michael K*, in Mrs Curren's probing of Vercueil's past. One could thus base these novels' claim to canonic literary status in part on their critique of the traditional unproblematized notion of the canon, showing it to be the reflection of a transcendental humanism oblivious to the role of cultural production and historical materiality. This would suggest one of the ways in which these novels challenge the structures of apartheid, a political and social system whose founding narratives claim to reflect a prior and 'natural' truth of racial superiority.

IV

But Barton's reluctant conclusion that 'we are all substantial, we are all in the same world' may be too hasty; and it is perhaps significant that it is Foe, the author, who raises the possibility of an exception to this generalisation: '"You have omitted Friday"'. The presence of this fourth major figure in the novel adds to, and considerably complicates, the account of Coetzee's fiction I have just given; it also constitutes the greatest risk which Coetzee takes in the artistic and political project he is engaged upon. One could say that the inner significance of Susan Barton's experience on the island, that she senses but cannot write down and that she hopes (fruitlessly) will emerge when Foe's retelling achieves canonisation, is most fully embodied not in her story nor in Cruso's, but in Friday's. Throughout the novel, Friday is presented not in his own terms – we have no sense of what they might be – but as he exists in relation to Susan Barton. Her memoir opens with his appearance to her on the shore of the island and his carrying her to Cruso's encampment in a '"strange backwards embrace"' (*F* 6), and the narrative of her letters ends with a comparison of her importance to him with that of an unwanted child to a mother who has nevertheless reared it: '"I do not love him, but he is mine. That is why he remains in England. That is why he is here"' (*F* 111).

Friday is a being wholly unfamiliar to her, in terms of race, class, gender, culture. He may be a cannibal. But Friday's story will never be known: he has had his tongue cut out, and cannot even tell the story of the mutilation.[11] His silence, his absolute otherness to her and to her words, is at the heart of Barton's story, both motivating and circumscribing it:

> On the island I accepted that I should never learn how Friday lost his tongue [. . .]. But what we can accept in life we cannot accept in history. To tell my story and be silent on Friday's tongue is no better than offering a book for sale with pages in it quietly left empty. Yet the only tongue that can tell Friday's secret is the tongue he has lost! (*F* 67)

Later she tells Foe, '"[I]f the story seems stupid, that is only because it so doggedly holds its silence. The shadow whose lack you feel is there: it is the loss of Friday's tongue"' (*F* 117).

To put this experience of absolute otherness into words – at least any of the words Barton has been granted by her cultural experience – would be to reappropriate it within the familiar, and to lose exactly that which makes it other, and therefore of the greatest possible significance, to her. She herself articulates this process of appropriation in her debate with Foe:

> Friday has no command of words and therefore no defence against being re-shaped day by day in conformity with the desires of others. I say he is a cannibal and he becomes a cannibal; I say he is a laundryman and he becomes a laundryman. What is the truth of Friday? You will respond: he is neither cannibal nor laundryman, these are mere names, they do not touch his essence, he is a substantial body, he is himself, Friday is Friday. But that is not so. No matter what he is to himself (is he anything to himself? – how can he tell us?), what he is to the world is what I make of him. (*F* 121–2)

She has, by this stage in the novel, made strenuous but unsuccessful attempts to teach Friday a language in which he might tell something at least of his story; even music proves to be a medium in which nothing approaching communication between the two can occur. Unlike her own silence about her experiences before the island, Friday's silence, she insists in this discussion with Foe, is not a concealment. (The same could be said of her silence about Friday's silence – which is also Coetzee's silence.) Yet its powerful *effects* are everywhere. Barton tells Foe:

> [W]hen I lived in your house I would sometimes lie awake upstairs listening to the pulse of blood in my ears and to the silence from Friday below, a silence that rose up the stairway like smoke, like a welling of black smoke. Before long I could not breathe, I would feel I was stifling in my bed. My lungs, my heart, my head were full of black smoke. (*F* 118)

In Foe's view, Friday's silence is simply a riddle that must be solved: '"In every story there is a silence, some sight concealed, some word unspoken, I believe. Till we have spoken the unspoken we have not come to the heart of the story"' (*F* 141). He allegorises this depth to be plumbed by means of an imaginative interpretation of Friday's mysterious act of paddling out on a log and dropping petals on the surface of the sea, an allegory which Barton takes up and revises, concluding: '"It is for us to descend into the mouth (since we speak in figures). It is for us to open Friday's mouth and hear what it holds: silence, perhaps, or a roar, like the roar of a seashell held to the ear"' (*F* 142). For her, there can be no assurance that all silences will eventually be made to resound with the words of the dominant language, and to tell their stories in canonised narratives – not because there is an inviolable core of silence to which the dominant discourse can never penetrate, but because the most fundamental silence is itself *produced by* – at the same time as it makes possible – the dominant discourse.

Foe's most telling challenge to the literary canon, therefore, is not its insistence upon cultural construction and validation (an insistence to which we have become accustomed in postmodern writing); it is its representation, through this most powerful of non-representations, of the silence which is constitutive of canonicity itself. All canons rest on exclusion; the voice they give to some can be heard only by virtue of the silence they impose on others. But it is not just a silencing by exclusion, it is a silencing by inclusion as well: any voice we can hear is by that very fact purged of its uniqueness and alterity. Who is Friday's foe, who has cut out his tongue and made it impossible for his story to be heard? Is it perhaps Foe, the writer, the one who tells people's stories, whatever their race, gender, class, and who in writing, rewrites, driving into deeper and deeper silence that which his discourse necessarily excludes? Barton speculates near the end of the novel about Foe's efforts as an author:

> But might the truth not be instead that he had laboured all these months to move a rock so heavy no man alive could budge it; that the pages I saw issuing from his pen were not idle tales of courtesans and grenadiers, as I supposed, but the same story over and over, in version after version, stillborn every time: the story of the island, as lifeless from his hand as from mine? (*F* 151)

Yet it is important to remember that only from the point of view of his oppressors (however well-meaning) does Friday figure as an absolute absence. Included among those oppressors are Coetzee and the reader and, hence, it is only by indirection that the substantiality of Friday's own world (in which he is not, of course, 'Friday' – perhaps not even 'he') can be suggested. One example is the uninterpretable (though repeatedly interpreted) act of strewing petals on the sea's surface, another is the equally uninterpretable series of marks Friday makes on the slate when Barton tries to teach him – at Foe's bidding – to write. There is also the extraordinary final section, in which an unidentified first-person narrator makes two visits to Foe's hideaway, the second in our own time, for the house bears a blue-and-white plaque inscribed ***Daniel Defoe, Author***. In the house are the bodies of Foe, Barton, the girl who claimed to be her daughter, and Friday, but on both occasions it is Friday who commands attention. On the second occasion, the narrative blends into Susan Barton's own story of the island, as we have heard it more than once, but the now multiple 'I' achieves what neither she nor Foe had been able to achieve: the descent into the sunken wreck, 'the home of Friday' which 'is not a place of words' but 'a place where bodies are their own signs.' (*F* 157).

V

It is a necessary property of any canon that it depends on what it excludes, and since culture as we understand it could not exist without canonic processes at all levels of its functioning – including, as we have seen, the constitution of individual subjectivity – there is no question of eradicating this source of exclusion. To be made aware of it, however, is to be reminded of the violence always implied in canonisation, in the construction of cultural narratives, in the granting of a voice to one individual or one group, necessary and productive as that process is. In enforcing this awareness, Coetzee's fictions engage directly with the contemporary struggle in South Africa, doing so not primarily as political argument, vivid reportage, or moral allegory, but as an exploitation of the traditions and potencies of the novel understood as a central form in Western culture.[12] *Foe*, in particular, focuses on what might be considered the most fundamental narrative of bourgeois culture not only to examine the processes of canonisation and legitimation implicit in it and in its popular success, but also to bring forcefully to its readers' attention the silences which those processes generate and upon which they depend: in particular, a gender silence and a race silence.[13] At the same time, the novel refuses to endorse any simple call for the granting of a voice within the existing sociocultural discourses; such a gesture would leave the silencing mechanisms, and their repressive human effects, untouched.[14] Njabulo Ndebele speaks for black South Africans in these terms:

> [T]here have been diverse cultural interests to whom the challenge of the future has involved the need to open up cultural and educational centers to all races. Missing in these admirable acts of goodwill is an accompanying need to alter fundamentally the nature of cultural practice itself. It is almost always assumed that, upon being admitted, the oppressed will certainly like what they find. ('The English Language' 223–14)

Coetzee's fiction, as I read it, brings out both the necessity and the difficulty of the process of genuine structural change in a society like South Africa's. Just as canonisation inevitably involves, as a condition of the audibility of the canon, a continuous act of silencing, so political, cultural, and material domination of a social group produces, as far as the ears of the dominant class can determine, an impenetrable silence which is at the same time a necessary condition of the latter's power (and therefore a constant threat to it). Friday's tonguelessness is the sign of his oppression; it is also the sign of the silence, the absolute otherness, by which he appears to his oppressors, and by which their oppression is sustained. Foe observes to Barton: '"We deplore the barbarism of whoever maimed him, yet have we, his later masters, not reason to be secretly grateful? For as long as he is dumb we can tell ourselves his desires are dark to us, and continue to use him as we wish"' (*F* 148). What Foe is less conscious of is the cost of this inheritance of mastery, a cost of which Barton – herself subject to the logic of exclusion and silencing – is acutely aware.

But for those who find themselves unwillingly in the dominant group – and Coetzee, like most of his readers, finds himself determined in advance as a member – there is no simple remedy to be understood in terms of investing Friday with speech. If he could have his tongue restored to him, he would melt into a class which is already constituted and socially placed by a pervasive discourse. (Foe suggests that, even without the faculty of speech, he might join one of London's strolling Negro bands.) In so far as the oppressed *are* heard, it is as a marginalised dialect within the dominant language. Even those who speak against oppression from the position of the oppressed have to conform to the dominant language in order to be heard in the places where power is concentrated, as Susan Barton discovers. Effective social and political change, then, is not merely the granting or the seizing of a voice (and the power that goes with it) by one or other predetermined group; it also entails work on the part of members of both oppressed and oppressing groups to create breaks in the totalising discourses that produce and reify that grouping itself. The burden of this work necessarily falls on the oppressed, who will themselves produce the discursive transformation that will allow themselves to be heard (as part of the process of effecting the material shift of power to which any lasting discursive shift is tied). But the members of the oppressing group who seek to secure change have a role, too; not Foe's project of teaching Friday to write the master discourse with which the main part of the novel ends (though there are indications – which could never, for us, be wholly legible – that Friday is in fact *subverting* the master discourse with his undecidable graphics[15]), but Coetzee's project of representing the processes of authorship, empowerment, validation and silencing in a narrative that is constantly aware of the problems inherent in its own acts of representation.

I observed earlier that the settings of the majority of Coetzee's novels render them less likely to be read as concerned exclusively with the South African struggle, and that they may run the opposite risk of being taken as having little specifically to do with that struggle. There is clearly some significance in the fact that Friday is a black African in *Foe*, unlike Defoe's tawny-skinned creation, just as there is in the fact that the people who remain outside Jacobus Coetzee's or Magda's comprehension are South Africans excluded from white privileges. Nevertheless, the barbarians in *Waiting for the Barbarians* cannot be identified so clearly; they function as a less specifically historicised representation of otherness, upon whose necessary exclusion from its narratives and, occasionally, from its physical spaces and economic resources, the civilisation of the Empire depends. This absence of precise historical and geographical grounding is a necessary feature of Coetzee's fiction, I would argue, since the novels are addressed as much to those outside South Africa as to those within it (indeed, to be white and to write oppositional fiction in English is to restrict your readership inside the country, making access to an international canon of peculiar importance[16]). There are two relatively easy responses by outsiders to the issue of racial oppression in South Africa that Coetzee's writing inhibits, however: first, that what is at stake is a battle of universal human principles, a version of similar battles in every society and every period, another manifestation of the tragic complexity of the human condition[17] and, second, that the conflict is entirely a local matter of a particular history and a particular set of problems in need of urgent resolution by those on the spot. What these novels work to suggest instead – and again, this is a task that falls peculiarly on the shoulders of the white South African writer in English – is that the South African struggle is *part* of a wider, and entirely concrete, struggle, that it has a particular history which is continuous with the particular histories of all other countries participating in the rise of Western capitalism and the ideology on which it depends, and that one requirement in moving toward a resolution of the struggle (one of many, but one in which works of art might have a special role) is an understanding of the ways in which the cultural formations that we have inherited through those histories are, for all their indisputable value, complicit with the daily barbarities that occur in South Africa.

Turning back to the question of Coetzee's novels and the literary canon, the question that presses itself is this: can these works gain admittance to the canon without being in their turn reread (and, thus, rewritten) as stories – as the same story – of essential humanity and transcendent values, their textuality disguised, their otherness expunged, their political implications silenced? The novels themselves appear to give a negative answer, for the work of art is clearly in the same powerless situation as characters like the Barbarian girl, K, or Friday. It is the subject of stories (both before and after it appears), and only through stories – commentaries, criticism, discussion, internal reflection – does it have meaning and value for us.[18] But anything like a 'full' understanding of it would require an apprehension of what remains uncaptured in the critical and interpretive discourse by means of which we represent it to ourselves and others. It is important to recognise, however, that this is in no sense a mystical or Romantic notion; Coetzee's novels do not represent a yearning for some realm of richness and plenitude beyond language, a meaningfulness behind the emptiness of our conscious lives. They attempt strenuously to avoid both terms of the coloniser's contradiction so forcefully enacted in *Dusklands*: that the other is wholly knowable, and that the other is wholly mysterious; that the other has no boundaries, and that the boundaries of the other are impenetrable.[19]

If Coetzee's novels do gain admittance to the canon, then, it will become increasingly difficult to read them *against* the canon, since their uniqueness will be dissolved by the ideologically-determined voice which the canon grants; if they do not, it will become increasingly difficult to read them at all, since the only voice available to them is the voice granted by one canon or another. This, we have seen, is the double bind dramatised in *Foe* at the level of the individual, and inherent in any attempt to combat political and cultural repression. If I may end with a Utopian thought, however, it would be that the canonisation – however partial and uneven – of Coetzee's novels, along with other texts (fictional and otherwise) that question the very processes of canonicity itself, will slowly transform the ideology and the institutions from which the canon derives its power, so that new and presently unimaginable ways of finding a voice, and new ways of hearing such voices, come into being. Instead of canons premised upon a notion of transcendental and inscrutable value, we can hope for cultural practices and formations that encourage an awareness of the historical production of value, of the part played by axiological systems in political domination and exclusion, of the necessarily provisional and historically contestable nature of any arrangement which allows some to speak and in that gesture renders others – and a part of themselves – silent.

Notes

This is a revised version of an essay which first appeared in *Decolonizing Tradition: New Views of Twentieth-Century 'British' Literary Canons*, ed. Karen R. Lawrence (Urbana: University of Illinois Press, 1991).

1. Dick Penner, in *Countries of the Mind*, garners the allusions detected by a number of commentators on the novel; his list includes Blake,

Hegel, Kierkegaard, Heraclitus, Calvin, Pascal, Rousseau, Novalis, Stevens, Octavio Paz, Luis Cernuda, Freud, Kafka, Sartre, and Beckett (69). Another long list of authors alluded to in a Coetzee novel, this time in *Dusklands*, is given by Debra Castillo in 'Coetzee's *Dusklands*' (1115).

2. One reviewer, at least, complained about the intrusiveness of these allusions: Christopher Lehmann-Haupt, in the *New York Times*, noted the novel's 'heavy debt to Franz Kafka', including the use of 'K', the reference to the central military headquarters as 'The Castle' (though anyone who has visited Cape Town knows that this is a real enough building, with just this significance), the frequent comparison of K to insects, and K's role as a hunger artist. He comments: 'These are doubtless meant to be tributes to a master as much as borrowings from him, but they are overdone and call an unnecessary amount of attention to themselves' (Lehmann-Haupt C22).
3. Thus, George Parker asserted in *The Nation* that *Foe* was a 'wrong, if interesting step' in a novel-writing career concerned with 'the fate of conscience in the face of its own oppressive power', while Nina Auerbach, writing in *The New Republic*, complained that the new novel 'never quite comes to life'. In South Africa, the hostility was, if anything, more marked: Neil Darke of the *Cape Argus* found the novel 'often pointless, incomprehensible and tiresome', and one G. H., in *The Natal Mercury*, called it 'a literary indulgence likely to prove too oblique for any but the converted to contend with, and to estrange even some of these'.
4. Alan Ryan, in the *Cleveland Plain Dealer*; cited on the jacket of the 1987 Viking edition of *Foe*.
5. The spelling 'Cruso' is that used by the Norwich family in the hosiery business which was Defoe's most likely source for his hero's name (see Bastian 90). Alexander Selkirk has no place in Coetzee's narrative, though Barton does speculate on Foe's possession of '"a multitude of castaway narratives, most of them, I would guess, riddled with lies"' (*F* 50).
6. The hero of Defoe's *Colonel Jack* also makes an appearance in Coetzee's novel as the young pickpocket employed by Foe. Clearly, 'the reader' alluded to here is one well-versed in Defoe's fiction: Coetzee exploits the canon's lack of definite boundaries by using allusions that range from the familiar to the scholarly. The novel does not depend upon the recognition of all its allusions by a single reader, however.
7. That Foe's fictional preferences are still at work is evident from Penner's unconscious echoing of them in his criticism of *Foe*: 'One wishes that [Coetzee] had devised something more engaging for Barton to do after leaving the island than what she does. The problem with the two London sections, which comprise two-thirds of the novel, is that too little happens' (Penner 128).
8. The events of *Foe* are not securely located at an identifiable moment in Defoe's life. It is likely that the historical author went into hiding from his creditors for a period in 1692, but Susan Barton has

read *A True Relation of the Apparition of One Mrs Veal* (written, she says, 'long ago' – *F* 134), Defoe's vivid report of the appearance of a ghost to a Canterbury woman in September, 1705, which he published soon after the event. He was still trying to satisfy his creditors in 1706, and when he left for Scotland on a secret mission for Harley's ministry in that year he allowed a story to circulate that he was fleeing because of debts (see Moore 97). However, *Robinson Crusoe* (his first substantial work of fiction – received by many as a factual report) was not published until 1719. Moreover, in imagining the papers which lie in Foe's chest, Barton describes materials on which a number of Defoe's works after *Robinson Crusoe* were based (including *The Dumb Philosopher*, about one Dickory Cronke, also published in 1719) (*F* 50), and she mentions on more than one occasion the tales of thieves, courtesans and grenadiers he has worked on. One effect of this chronological uncertainty, germane to the novel's concerns, is that it remains unclear whether Foe's reputation is as a reporter of fact or, as was the case later in Defoe's career, a creator of fiction.

9. I do not mean to suggest that the properties of texts accepted by the canon are wholly determined in advance. Defoe is a good example of a writer whose work, while it clearly answered to a growing need arising from changing economic and social conditions, played its own part, once it was admitted, in transforming the literary canon. Some degree of resistance to canonic demands can itself be a canonic requirement: I have already suggested that a possible disability of Coetzee's novels as far as the canon is concerned is that they may appear to conform too obviously to its requirements.
10. Roxana's real name is mentioned once in that novel: it is Susan, as is that of the daughter who haunts her and who is murdered by her maid Amy (Defoe, *Roxana* 205). (No surname is given for either of the Susans.) The daughter in *Foe* says that her name is also Susan Barton, and her account of her mother's desertion by a husband who was a brewer (*F* 76) tallies with the events of *Roxana*.
11. To be strictly accurate, our only reason for believing that Friday has been mutilated is Barton's report of Cruso's statement to this effect; she herself has no evidence of the cause of Friday's speechlessness, as she finds herself unable to look into his mouth (*F* 85). This is of some importance to any allegorical reading of the novel – an inevitable though problematic response to it – since it precludes any simple assumptions as to the *cause* of Friday's silence and, thus, provides a more complex image of limited access to language than Michael K's hare lip. It might be thought of as connecting the *generalised* otherness produced by all representation with the *specific* otherness produced by historical acts of oppression. The challenge of the novel is to acknowledge the former without weakening awareness of the latter.
12. The relation between Coetzee's fiction and history (both the history of South Africa and the discourse of history) has been valuably discussed by David Attwell, in 'The Problem of History in the Fiction

of J. M. Coetzee' and *J. M. Coetzee and the Politics of Writing*.

13. Since my particular interest here is in Coetzee as a South African writer, I am focusing on the question of race rather than the question of gender, but I am conscious that this is to do less than justice to the novel. A longer discussion would consider the differences between the treatments of the two exclusions in *Foe*, as well as the connections that link them. (One would want to consider, for instance, the relationship between Friday's mutilation and that of female victims such as Philomela and Lavinia.) And this discussion could lead to other exclusions, such as those of class, religion, nationality.
14. See Jacques Derrida's demanding scrutiny of the question of the other (of philosophy, of politics, of literature) in 'Psyche' (339–43). For Derrida, to avoid programming the other into a version of the same, 'one does not make the other come, one lets it come by preparing for its coming' (Derrida, 'Psyche' 341–2) and this means preparing for its arrival by opening up and destabilising the existing structures of foreclosure. The relevance of Derrida's discussion to Coetzee's fictional project would be clear even without the footnote which observes: 'Racism is also an invention of the other, but in order to exclude it and tighten the circle of the same' (Derrida, 'Psyche' 336).
15. This possibility is developed by Gayatri Spivak in her strong and suggestive essay on *Foe*, 'Theory in the Margin'. Having commented on the scene of the writing lesson, she notes

    It is Friday rather than Susan who is the unemphatic agent of withholding in the text. For every territorial space that is value coded by colonialism *and* every command of metropolitan anticolonialism for the native to yield his 'voice,' there is a space of withholding, marked by a secret that may not be a secret but cannot be unlocked. 'The native,' whatever that might mean, is not only a victim, he or she is also an agent. He or she is the curious guardian at the margin. (Spivak 172)

16. To write 'modernist' fiction is to limit your audience further, of course. Lazarus argues interestingly that, since the modernist text resists reductive appropriation by the dominant discourse, 'the relative underestimation, within South Africa itself, of the work of Gordimer and Coetzee ought to be taken as an index of the oppositional cogency of this work, and not, as it is usually taken, as an index of its irrelevance' (Lazarus 136).
17. This might be a significant difference between Coetzee and two of his most potent precursors, Kafka and Beckett: Coetzee's fiction is so directly concerned with the economic and political fabric of cultural existence that it is more difficult to derive from it general statements about the human predicament. There are moments, however, when the inadequacy of representation being dramatised appears to be not so much the inadequacy of a particular set of available discourses but that of language itself; notably when the body feels

or acts in ways that exceed or escape any possible conceptualisation – as, for instance, in the Magistrate's obscure physical desires in *Waiting for the Barbarians* or K's body's refusal to eat the food of the camps in *Life & Times of Michael K.* But this does not diminish the importance of the more specific questions relating to the cultural validation of certain discourses at the expense of others, and of the price to be paid for cultural acceptance.

18. The most compelling (and therefore most occulting) of these stories are often those told by the authors themselves. It is notable that when it comes to his own interpretations of his texts Coetzee observes a scrupulous reserve, as is evidenced in his two interviews with Morphet. For instance: 'Q: Friday has no tongue. Why? COETZEE: Nobody seems to have sufficient authority to say for sure how it is that Friday has no tongue' (Morphet 462). And later Coetzee remarks: 'Your questions again and again drive me into a position I do not want to occupy. (But what legitimacy has that 'want'?) By accepting your implication, I would produce a master narrative for a set of texts that claim to deny all master narratives' (Morphet 464). In *Foe,* Susan Barton discovers the simultaneous impossibility and necessity of metanarrative commentary: '"Alas, my stories seem always to have more applications than I intend, so that I must go back and laboriously extract the right application and apologize for the wrong ones and efface them"' (*F* 81).
19. Tournier's *Vendredi,* another modern rewriting of Defoe's novel which is in productive triangulation with Coetzee's work, offers a very different view of the other of colonialism: although in both reworkings the black servant represents a consciousness radically alien to the Western mind he serves, this otherness in Tournier's work is more easily assimilated to a Eurocentric primitivistic myth. Tournier's novel surfaces elsewhere – and is perhaps gently mocked – in Coetzee's *oeuvre*: Jacobus Coetzee, alone in the veld, tries to imitate the earth fecundation of Tournier's Crusoe: 'I bored a sheath in the earth and would have performed the ur-act had joy and laughter not reduced me to a four-inch dangle and helpless urination' (*D* 95).

11

Evolution and Entropy in J. M. Coetzee's *Age of Iron*

GRAHAM HUGGAN

I wish I were not among the fifth race of men but either had died earlier or been born later.

Hesiod, *Works and Days*

The old is dying and the new cannot be born; in this interregnum a great variety of morbid symptoms appears.

Antonio Gramsci, 'State and Society'

As with all life cycles, there is no beginning in a butterfly's metamorphosis. After all, a cycle is a cycle, and who is to say that the butterfly is not the egg's way of making another egg?

Matthew Douglas, *The Lives of Butterflies*

J. M. Coetzee's novel *Age of Iron* (1990) is generally considered to be his most immediate work to date.[1] Written between 1986 and 1989, the novel is also set in that turbulent period of South Africa's history: years which were to witness the tragic deaths of three members of Coetzee's own family – his mother Vera, his father Zachariah and his son Nicolas, to whose memory the novel is dedicated – but also, in violence of cataclysmic proportions, the deaths of thousands of blacks in the cities and townships of the embattled Republic.[2] *Age of Iron* is an elegy: an attempt, through narrative, to come to terms with the grief of personal loss while mourning the collective losses of a war-torn society. To a greater extent than ever before in Coetzee's work, private and public worlds interfuse. Mrs Curren's letter to her daughter in America – a tortured confession in which we, invasive readers, are made complicit – recounts in graphic detail both the horrors of living under apartheid and the shame of living with it.

There is a raw energy in *Age of Iron*: a sense of emotional, as well as intellectual anguish that is arguably missing from Coetzee's earlier work. It would be a mistake, nonetheless, to see *Age of Iron* as representing a departure from Coetzee's five previously published novels. The novel is better seen as a continuation – indeed, in a sense, as a culmination – of Coetzee's *oeuvre*. The familiar themes are all there: the unmasking of liberal humanist ideology; the interrogation of colonial/imperial myths; the translation of a twisted cultural politics into the psychopathology of family relationships; the foundering of European metaphysics on African soil. And there are continuities, too, of form; for like all of Coetzee's novels to date, *Age of Iron* employs allegorical techniques, both to probe the metaphysical implications of history – to test the 'concrete' events of history against the 'abstract' principles of a philosophy of history – and to chart the more immediate connections between physical, psychological and linguistic disfiguration under an oppressive regime. More specifically, *Age of Iron* belongs to the genre of the apocalyptic parable. Seen through the eyes of a dying narrator, South Africa is itself presented as a 'dying' country; both deaths are implicitly deferred, however, and like many modern parables – Kafka's and Beckett's come immediately to mind – *Age of Iron* appears to gesture toward a closure it cannot quite, or does not quite wish to, imagine.[3]

The thesis that I shall present in this essay is that the tremendous, almost overpowering sense of suspense in *Age of Iron* is generated in large part by a tension between evolutionary and entropic principles. While the two principles might appear initially to be mutually exclusive – for evolution implies a process of gradual development, entropy one of inexorable decline – they are perhaps better seen as interdependent. The concept of the life-cycle (the round of changes in the generations of an organism) dictates that the old must die that the new might be born. Evolution comes about not just through a 'natural' process of biological maturation, but also through the various mutations which take place when the organism is made to confront a changing environment. The development of one species depends on the dissolution of another: those species survive which are best able both to adapt themselves to changing circumstances and to protect themselves against their natural enemies. Darwin's theory of natural selection provides the ironic framework in *Age of Iron* for a struggle for survival that plays itself out at several different levels of a characteristically multilayered text. At its most conspicuous, the struggle is a physical one. There are armies within, armies without, rebelling against the corrupt systems which constrain them. Are these armies to be seen as agents of liberation, or are they merely forces of destruction? Blurring the distinction between friend and foe – harbouring her own 'natural enemies' – Mrs Curren draws an ironic parallel here between the cancer cells spreading, uncontrolled, inside her ageing body and the rebel forces gathering in the black townships, waiting to mount their next offensive against a system whose authority they refuse to recognise: a system doomed to an imminent (if belated) extinction. To both groups, Mrs Curren offers temporary 'refuge': an act of perverse altruism, this, the attempt to aid and abet one's own 'assassins'! But the motive here is not so much to help others free themselves as to secure her own freedom. (She is exercising her right not to live, but to die and, perhaps, to live again?)

These two parallel liberation struggles, which Mrs Curren clearly intends to be seen as ironic reflections of one another, also operate at the level of ideas. Here again, Mrs Curren seems to be aware that she is fighting a losing battle. An avowed, if disillusioned, liberal humanist, Mrs Curren appears to be using her letter to her daughter as a last-ditch attempt to pass her 'caring' values onto succeeding generations. 'These words, as you read them, if you read them, enter you and draw breath again. They are, if you like, my way of living on' (*AOI* 131). It soon becomes clear, however, that the language cannot bear the weight of the ideas it seeks to express. Initially earmarked as an apologetics for liberal humanism, the letter evolves instead into the swansong for a dying creed. The ironies here are multiple, grotesque. By creating an equivalence between the cancer cells eating away at her body and the new 'children of death' – black and white alike – who 'infest the country, munching without cease, devouring lives [like locusts]' (*AOI* 28), Mrs Curren seeks to lend the story of her dying days the ringing tones of moral allegory. But the allegory rebounds against her. Like the twin discourses of Platonic idealism and Enlightenment humanism on which it is founded, the allegory reveals itself to be a 'sermon rest[ing] on false etymologies' (*AOI* 22). Having failed to adapt itself to changing times, the language now turns against itself. Faith, Hope, Charity; Beauty, Harmony, Love: it is as if the standard items of the humanist lexicon have succumbed, in *Age of Iron*, to a law of semantic entropy. The Republic of South Africa proves no match for Plato's Republic: the doctrine of Ideas dissolves into a derisory play of counterfeit abstractions.[4] Moral allegory mocks and falsifies itself. The humanist myths of the family, in particular, are mercilessly debunked: the innocence of childhood becomes as false, in the context of contemporary South African society, as the nurturing role of parenthood or the reciprocity of family ties. 'How terrible', groans Mrs Curren, her own 'children of death' evolving inside her, 'when motherhood reaches a point of parodying itself!' (*AOI* 64).

A veteran freedom fighter for truths in which she no longer really believes, Mrs Curren provides an ironic counterpoint between her own situation and that of Bheki and his youthful comrades. Committed to the cause of black liberation but hard-hearted, prematurely cynical, these adolescent rebels seem torn between a brutal present and an ideal future. For Mrs Curren, theirs, too, is a 'dying' creed: unlike their self-styled mentor, the Marxist ideologue Thabane, who believes that the future of South Africa is to be fashioned by young people, like them, who are 'prepared to lay down [their] lives for each other without question' (*AOI* 149), Mrs Curren sees in their revolt little more than a perverse instinct for self-destruction. '[Their] comradeship', she implies, 'is nothing but a mystique of death, of killing and dying, masquerading as what you would call a bond . . . it is just another of those icy, exclusive, death-driven male constructions' (*AOI* 150). Which is better, their search for the grave or her search for the womb? One shibboleth replaces another: *Amor Patris* (the collective myth of national foundation) proves no less vulnerable to parody than *Amor Matris* (the individual myth of personal origin). The high ideals of human liberation confront the ugly realities of a Darwinian struggle for social survival. Lecturing John after his latest confrontation with the police, Mrs Curren concludes, sadly, that it is 'a waste of breath to preach prudence to this boy. The instinct for battle is too strong in him, driving him on. Battle: nature's way of liquidating the weak and providing for the strong. Return covered in glory, and you shall have your desire. Gore and glory; death and sex' (*AOI* 143). Later, visualising his recovery in hospital, she is more cynical still, mapping patriarchial/ colonial tropes onto the boy's revolutionary consciousness:

> In the growing dark, the boy, lying on his back with the bomb or whatever it is in his hand, his eye wide open, not veiled now but clear: thinking, more than thinking, envisioning. Envisioning the moment of glory when he will arise, freeing himself at last, erect, powerful, transfigured. When the fiery flower will unfold, when the pillar of smoke will rise. The bomb on his chest like a talisman: as Christopher Columbus lay in the dark of his cabin, holding the compass to his chest, the mystic instrument that would guide him to the Indies, the Isles of the Blest. Troops of maidens with bared breasts singing to him, opening their arms, as he wades to them through the shallows holding before him the needle that never wavers, that points forever in one direction, to the future. (*AOI* 150–1)

'John' (the Baptist?) and 'Florence' (Nightingale?) – the Prophet of Doom and the Sister of Mercy – are conscripted into the service of a self-parodic allegory. Mrs Curren thus grants herself the right to proclaim their heroism while simultaneously debunking it. In one of the novel's most vivid dream-sequences, Mrs Curren sees Florence

> striding down Government Avenue holding Hope by the hand and carrying Beauty on her back. All three of them wear masks . . . The eyes of her mask are like eyes in pictures from the ancient Mediterranean: large, oval, with the pupil in the center: the almond eyes of a goddess. . . . Her dark coat, her dull dress have fallen away. In a white slip ruffled by the wind, her feet bare, her head bare, her right breast bare, she strides past, the one child, masked, naked, trotting quickly beside her, the other stretching an arm out over her shoulder, pointing. (*AOI* 178)

In a striking conflation of 'traditional' and 'revolutionary' iconography, Mrs Curren identifies Florence – the 'Spartan matron, bearing warrior sons for the nation' (*AOI* 50) – as a cross between the Greek goddess of pleasure, Aphrodite, and Delacroix's revolutionary heroine, Joan.[5] Identities fuse in a bizarre metamorphosis. History repeats itself in Marxian patterns: Florence, puritanical emblem of a joyless *Age of Iron,* is made to re-enact her tragic role in the context of modern farce.

What is most striking about the dream, however, is not its implicit parody of revolutionary fervour but its explicit conversion of contemporary history into the 'timeless' patterns of allegory and myth. A former teacher of the classics – a ventriloquist of the dead – Mrs Curren views contemporary South African society through the filter of a hybrid Greco-Roman philosophy in which history conforms to a pre-set pattern of eternal repetition. Her narrative is shot through with references to the epic cycles of Homer and Virgil.[6] Contemporary South Africa is a Virgilian Underworld, a Homeric Hell; her journey through it is a quest to save her soul. Myth is the medium through which Mrs Curren interprets her daily life; it is also the medium through which she prophesises a future for her divided country. Guided by the stoical philosophy of Marcus Aurelius and the diagnostic historiography of Thucydides, Mrs Curren wavers between alternative beliefs in the Myth of Eternal Return (whereby history repeats itself in accordance with the rhythms of the cosmic cycle) and the Myth of Apocalypse (whereby history comes to an end in *ekpyrosis*, or universal conflagration).[7] Both myths subscribe to an essentially entropic view of historical process in which 'the original order of things maintains itself in perfection during the Golden Age, only to begin an inevitable decay during the subsequent ages of history' (Rifkin 12).

An exemplary enactment of this process of decay is in Hesiod's Myth of Five Ages. According to Hesiod, the universe begins with a paradisal Golden Age, in which 'pure and blessed spirits . . . live[d] upon earth' and mortal people 'lived as if they were gods, their hearts free from all sorrow . . . without hard work or pain', and ends with a benighted generation, the Age of Iron, in which 'children, as they are born, grow gray on the temples', when 'the father no longer agrees with the children, nor children with their father', when 'guest is no longer at one with host, nor companion to companion' and when 'man shall give their praise to violence and the doer of evil' (*The Works and Days* 31–4). Age of Iron is characterised by disease and death, by deception as well as violence; its abandonment to vice, claims Hesiod, can only guarantee its own destruction. But as Hesiod scholars have pointed out – and it is here that we see the particular relevance of Hesiod to Mrs Curren's personal mythology – it is by no means certain whether death is to be followed by rebirth: whether the Myth of Five Ages constitutes a degenerative sequence or a regenerative cycle. Thus, while the myth appears at first sight to chart a course of progressive deterioration – to move, as it were, toward a state of entropic inertia – its schema is anything but consistent or logical (Rosenmeyer 269); nor does Hesiod offer us a recommendation as to where the myth might eventually go (Smith, 'History and the Individual' 161). The Age of Iron, in short, is as ambiguous as the greater scheme in which it functions; the critical consensus seems to be that the Five Ages masquerades as history while functioning as myth or parable.

What function does the myth serve in Coetzee's novel? At first sight, its significance appears to be minimal: Hesiod's name is nowhere to be found in Mrs Curren's narrative, after all, and in her own rendering of the cosmic cycle – which owes more to Marcus Aurelius than to Hesiod – the Age of Iron occupies an intermediary position between the 'harder' Age of Granite and the 'softer' Ages of Bronze, Clay and Earth (*AOI* 50). There is a striking similarity, nonetheless, between Hesiod's conceptual vocabulary and Mrs Curren's own. Hesiod's apocalyptic Age of Iron provides Mrs Curren with the mythological underpinnings for her interpretation of contemporary South African society. But more significantly still, it provides her with a (spurious) justification for her own inaction. In one sense, Hesiod's schema enables Mrs Curren to prefigure her own redemption – although, as the ambiguity of its language suggests, it is by no means certain whether this redemption will, or can, be achieved. In another sense, however, the myth allows her to rationalise her own inertia and to legitimate her resistance to social change.

In his comparative analysis of Myths of Eternal Return, Mircea Eliade suggests that the cyclical conception of a disappearing/reappearing humanity signals an attempt, on the part of those societies/cultures which subscribe to it, to annul the irreversibility of time.[8] Cosmic time, says Eliade, confers the illusion that 'the past is but a prefiguration of the future', that 'no event is irreversible and no transformation . . . final' and that, *in extremis*, 'nothing new happens in the world, for everything is but the repetition of the same primordial archetypes' (Eliade 89–90). Eliade claims support here from the philosopher Henri-Charles Puech. The Greeks, says Puech, 'regarded movement and change as inferior degrees of reality in which, at best, identity can be apprehended in the form of permanence and perpetuity, hence of recurrence' (Puech, in Corgin 40). Puech continues:

> According to the famous Platonic definition, the time which is determined and measured by the revolution of the celestial spheres is the mobile image of immobile eternity which it imitates by moving in a circle. Consequently both the entire cosmic process and the time of our world of generation and decay develop in a circle or according to an indefinite succession of cycles, in the course of which the same reality is made, unmade and remade, in conformity with an immutable law and determinate alterations. (Puech, in Corgin 40–1)

In subscribing to this 'cosmic' view of time, Mrs Curren hopes to justify her own political quietism. But more than that, she implicitly negates the efforts of the black majority to alter the course of South African history. Time is cyclical, history predetermined: the revolutionary potential of the struggle for black liberation – a struggle which might otherwise afford evidence of the capacity of wo/men to forge their own destinies – is neatly defused. The dialectical forces of history are reassimilated within a universal design of myth; an apocalyptic Age of Iron in which 'men shall give their praise to violence and the doer of evil' allows Mrs Curren to justify her own withdrawal from a 'dying' world, to legitimate her retreat into an imagined past, and to sanction her condemnation of the 'senseless violence' of civil war.

And there are further dimensions to the myth. While Hesiod scholars have argued over the historical ramifications of the Five Ages, they tend to agree on its basic thesis: that 'injustice arises from trying to win livelihood and wealth without working for them' (Fontenrose 12). Hesiod, an early advocate of the gospel of work, thus provides Mrs Curren with ammunition for her attack on the social irresponsibilities of idleness. Violence, in this context, becomes the result not of resistance to social oppression but rather of the misdirected channelling of unspent energies. Those who do not – or will not – work are at best outcasts (like Vercueil), at worst rebels (like Bheki and his 'delinquent' friends). Despite Mrs. Curren's vitriolic attack on the puritanical heritage of Calvin, and her ironic transference of this heritage onto the 'new fundamentalists' of the resistance movement, her own 'dissenting' liberal philosophy remains controlled, to some extent, by a residual belief in the uplifting value of work.[9]

Allied to this belief is the notion that vagrants such as Vercueil – products of a capitalist society which rejects those who fail to meet its rigorous requirements – are congenitally indolent: that they are welcomers of their own dissolution (*AOI* 8). And it is here, I would suggest, that another bizarre metamorphosis takes place in Coetzee's novel: the yoking of one paradigm of historical development, Hesiod's entropic Myth of Five Ages, to another, Spencer's evolutionary Myth of Progress. Evolution, according to Spencer, represents the change from an 'incoherent homogeneity to a coherent heterogeneity, accompanying the dissipation of motion and integration of matter' (Spencer, in Peel 171). Since society is a 'growth, not a manufacture' (Spencer, in Peel 56), the social organism can be seen as evolving – 'maturing' – in a process remarkably similar to that of biological development. Darwinian laws apply: the 'fittest' societies survive, the weakest go to the wall; it is not hard to see (as Coetzee has himself pointed out in an essay on Sarah Gertrude Millin) how such prescribed patterns of social development have been used, in South Africa and elsewhere, to justify the existence (or creation) of underclasses, to legitimate the colonisation of 'subject' peoples, and to afford 'scientific' proof of a hierarchy of races. Bound up in many of these cruder forms of social Darwinism, says Coetzee in the essay on Millin, is a 'science of degenerativity' in which degeneracy is best understood as the 'biological means whereby a legacy of evil may be passed on to succeeding generations' (*WW* 143).[10] Degeneracy is by no means an isolated phenomenon; it is rather the symptom of a widespread social disease whose 'cure' necessitates the identification, isolation and systematic purging of degenerate elements within the social body. 'Progress' depends, indeed, on these periodic purgings. The metamorphosis of the social organism – which Spencer views, significantly, as taking place within a uniform pattern of evolutionary development – consists in a series of often violent 'convulsions' (Spencer's word). These convulsions indicate that phases exist in the history of civilisation during which there are 'forcible supplantings of the weak by the strong, and systems of savage coercion' (Spencer, in Peel 22). These phases may be seen, however, as advantageous within the context of the whole.

I mentioned earlier that Mrs Curren suspects Vercueil of being 'degenerate', but in drawing an analogy between her cancer-rid-den body and the diseased state of contemporary South African society – in combining Darwinian biology and Spencerian sociology – Mrs Curren effectively converts herself into the sacrificial emblem of a 'degenerate' age. The Greek poet Hesiod joins forces with the Victorian social scientist Spencer. The Age of Iron reveals itself as malignant, mutant: an aberrant phase in the evolution of the social organism. That a Spencerian subtext should lurk beneath Mrs Curren's confessional narrative is, of course, profoundly ironic; for what could be more inimical to her egalitarian liberal philosophy than the naturalised hierarchies of social Darwinism? Spencer's scheme of social evolution enables Mrs Curren, nonetheless, to project her fears onto the revolutionary present. The Age of Iron emerges as a transitional phase: a phase in which she and her contemporaries are to be forcibly supplanted, sacrificed for the greater good of the emergent nation. In conferring victim status upon herself, Mrs Curren discovers that the genesis of the 'New' South Africa requires nothing less than her own extinction.

Yet if the Age of Iron has condemned Mrs Curren to a painful death, its punishment takes the form of a suspended sentence. In a further parody of Darwinian logic, the 'white liberal' is held up as a species which awaits – entreats – its own extinction, but which remains impelled, in spite of itself, by the will to survive; a species which wishes to perpetuate itself, but which also refuses to 'evolve' and, thus, paradoxically consents to its own destruction. Coetzee draws out these ironies in the novel by playing off the evolutionary metaphor of arrested development against the entropic metaphor of progressive disintegration. At one point later on in her narrative, her wasted body now almost entirely given over to the ravages of cancer, Mrs Curren imagines her soul as 'readying itself for further flight' (*AOI* 129). Like an emergent butterfly still encased within its life-denying chrysalis, she wishes to 'shake [herself] loose from the dying envelope' (*AOI* 129). She demands, in short, her evolutionary rights; but at the same time, she is continually forced back on the recognition of her own arrested development. Seeing herself as a creature from a bygone age – a dodo, a dinosaur – Mrs Curren surrounds herself with images which only serve to reconfirm her own obsolescence. But she also sees herself as a creature 'not properly born . . . thrown up by the sea, stalled on the sands, undecided, indecisive, neither hot nor cold, neither fish nor fowl' (*AOI* 92). Arrested at the larval stage, she has neither the strength to live nor the courage to die; instead, poised between life and death, she is a 'liminal creature, unable to breathe in water, that lacks the courage to leave the sea and become a dweller on land' (*AOI* 139). Unable – unwilling – to adapt to an age with whose rapid, and often violent, changes she cannot cope, Mrs Curren consigns herself instead to a perpetual limbo state. Torn between the contradictory desires to evolve and to resist evolution, she aspires simultaneously to emerge into the light, like the fully-formed butterfly, and to retreat into the darkness, like the unformed pupa. And, like the latter, she spins a protective cocoon around herself which shields her from the outside world, but which also suffocates and paralyses her. (Coetzee's novel abounds in such images of paralysis and entrapment.)

In her vacillating state, Mrs Curren becomes the helpless witness of her own decline: 'I grow uglier by the day. Metamorphosis that thickens our speech, dulls our feelings, turns us into beasts. Where on these shores does the herb grow that will preserve us from it?' (*AOI* 103). A coloniser in spite of herself – aware of her complicity in a regime she abhors – she reads the same symptoms of rebarbarisation in the clouded eyes of her Afrikaner 'cousins':

> A thickening of the membrane between the world and the self inside, a thickening become thickness. Evolution, but evolution backward. Fish from the primitive depths . . . grew patches of skin sensitive to the fingerings of light. Now in South Africa, I see eyes clouding over again, scales thickening in them, as the land explorers, colonists, prepare to return to the deep. (*AOI* 127)

Meanwhile, 'floating under the skin of the earth', millions of figures of pig iron wait to be raised up again (126). These are relics of another bygone age: a period in which the gradual spread of Iron Age culture into subequatorial Africa coincided with a dispersal of the Bantu-speaking peoples, forerunners of today's black South Africans (Phillipson).[11] 'When I walk upon this land, this South Africa', Mrs. Curren tells Vercueil, 'I have a gathering feeling of walking upon black faces. They are dead but their spirit has not left them. They lie there heavy and obdurate, waiting for my feet to pass, waiting for me to go, waiting to be raised up again' (125–6). The repeating patterns of Greco-Roman myth confront the accumulated evidence of African archaeology: Mrs Curren recognises that one Age of Iron must end, that another might return.

Mrs Curren's gesture toward the regeneration of a black South African nation coincides, then, with her own death-wish; yet there is no immediate sign that this wish will be granted. Her illness has been diagnosed as terminal, her death is imminent; but the moment of release continues to be denied her, and instead, along with her unlikely companion Vercueil, she remains trapped in a 'time-being . . . a hovering time . . . not eternity . . . a suspension, before the return of the time in which the door bursts open and we face, first he, then I, the great white glare' (*AOI* 176). Mrs Curren likens her situation to that of the restless souls in Virgil's *Aeneid* who wait for Charon to ferry them across the Styx to the land of the dead (*AOI* 192). Vercueil is the ferryman: the messenger whose delivery of the letter to her absent daughter will guarantee her a safe resting-place in the life hereafter. But unfortunately, Vercueil can offer no such guarantees. He promises to send the letter, but we cannot be sure that he does, or if he does, that Mrs Curren's daughter receives it. (Coetzee makes the disturbing suggestion here that this may be our fault; that our interception of the letter may have prevented it from arriving at its final destination. The letter 'lives on' in us; are we, too, responsible for Mrs Curren's continuing torment?) Vercueil, for his part, proves to be the most treacherous of allies. In French (Huguenot?), his name suggests a combination of 'ver' (worm) and 'cercueil' (coffin); in Afrikaans a conflation of 'verkul' (to cheat) and 'verskuil' (to hide). The implication is that Vercueil is more than just unreliable: he is a covert agent of destruction, a fully fledged version of the embryonic cells growing inside Mrs Curren's body. (He is described at the beginning of the novel as an insect, newly hatched out of its makeshift cocoon.)[12] The product of a malevolent Age of Iron in which 'guest is no longer at one with host', Vercueil slyly preys on his ailing companion: he is like the grub which, once hatched, will destroy the body it feeds off. But which is the parasite here, which the host? As the relationship between Vercueil and Mrs Curren develops, it assumes the proportions of a destructive dependency. At the same time, it begins to afford unwanted reminders of Mrs Curren's parasitism: of the voracious dependence of an ageing mother on her grown-up daughter. (For if Mrs Curren has little desire to survive in the here-and-now, she wishes very much to live on – insists on living on – through the agency of another.)[13]

To see Vercueil as an agent of Mrs Curren's destruction, or as her malevolent *alter ego*, is, however, to see only half the picture. For, in another sense, the two need each other in order to save each other: as Mrs Curren's grudging confidant, Vercueil grants her the opportunity to tell the story of atonement which might save her 'neophyte' soul (*AOI* 186). The unwholesome vagrant is cast in the role of ironic Messiah. Is he also the harbinger of a new age? The possibility is not ruled out, but as the Hesiod myth implies, there is no certainty as to what the future might hold. The misbegotten product of 'a time out of time' (*AOI* 50), Vercueil embodies the uncertain principles of an age of transition. Mrs Curren sees him, as she sees herself, as a misfit of evolution: 'a man left behind who cannot swim [but] does not yet know how to fly' (*AOI* 147). Unable to transform himself, he seems less than ideally qualified to bring about Mrs Curren's eventual transformation. Indeed, as his final (death?) embrace with Mrs Curren suggests, he is more closely associated with the degenerative process of entropy than with the regenerative potential of evolution. Linked throughout the novel with images of fire, Vercueil masquerades as an agent of *ekpyrosis*: his is the match that might spark the final holocaust. But his last embrace yields no warmth, still less the promise of a purifying conflagration (*AOI* 198). Instead, Vercueil and Mrs Curren are drawn together in a charade of reciprocity: in an act, which, far from providing mutual release, seems only to signal continuing bondage. It seems significant, in any case, that the novel is brought to a close by an act which is less suggestive of the development toward a new state of being than of the regression to a state of entropic inertia (quite literally, a state in which no further transference of heat is possible.)[14] It remains unclear, then, whether Vercueil is helping Mrs Curren to die (thereby expediting the departure of her soul) or whether he is preventing her from dying. Significantly, neither ferryman nor passenger can cross the threshold (*AOI* 193): Mrs Curren is condemned, once again, to rehearsing an ending which continues to elude her. As so often in his work, Coetzee invites comparison here with European writers in the existentialist and/or Absurdist tradition: Beckett's *Endgame*, Sartre's *No Exit*. 'There is no first and no last', Mrs Curren's pharmacist tells her, prescribing new pills to counteract her worsening pain. Where does the cycle begin, where does it end? Unable to retrace her origins, unable to put an end to her life, Mrs Curren must wait, in agony, for a deliverance which may never come.

'I have lived too long. Death by fire the only decent death left . . . to burn and be gone, to be rid of, to leave the world clean. Monstrous growths, misbirths: a sign that one is beyond one's term. This country too: time for fire, for an end, time for what grows out of ash to grow' (*AOI* 65). What future lies in store for South Africa, and what place will there be in it for white South Africans? Will they consent to'evolve' out of a liminal stage in which they are 'no longer European, not yet African?' (*WW* II). Will the struggle for black liberation result in the gradual development of a more equitable society, or will a violent revolution end up by eating its own children?[15] These are questions which haunt *Age of Iron*, but as Coetzee's heavily ironic, if not entirely unsympathetic treatment of his suffering protagonist implies, it is perhaps not so much that the Age of Iron represents a temporary aberration in the greater scheme of things as that the notion of a greater scheme of things may itself be aberrant. I suggested previously that two countervailing myths of historical development – Hesiod's Myth of Five Ages and Spencer's Myth of Progress – provide the context in Coetzee's novel for an unmasking of the false universals of liberal humanist ideology. Caught between contradictory aspirations – the desire for change and the desire to resist it – Mrs Curren continues, in her letter, to rail against the very social injustices she is helping to sustain. Myth provides her, in this context, with the rationale for an illusory disengagement. Hesiod's myth suggests, as Rifkin puts it, that 'if history represent[s] the continued chipping away of the original perfect state, and the using up of the original fixed bounty, then the ideal state [is] the one that slow[s] down the process of decay as much as possible' (Rifkin 12). Spencer's myth, on the other hand, contends that history evolves through a series of ritual purgings, and that each of these purgings effects the 'forcible supplantings of the weak by the strong'. In both cases, however, the myth prescribes a uniform pattern of development. History merges into the 'natural' rhythms of myth; it is as if, in the words of Roland Barthes,

> a conjuring trick has taken place; [myth] has turned reality inside out, it has emptied it of history and has filled it with nature, it has removed from things their human meaning so as to make them signify a human insignificance. The function of myth is to empty reality: it is, literally, a ceaseless flowing out, a

> haemorrhage, or perhaps an evaporation, in short a perceptible absence. (*Mythologies* 143)

Myths, claims Barthes, are 'constituted by the loss of the historical quality of things: in [them], things lose the memory that they once were made' (*Mythologies* 142). The irony of this, of course, is that myths are themselves cultural products: products which are made and remade to suit society's concerns. Throughout his work, Coetzee emphasises the – often tyrannical – power of myth: its extreme susceptibility to ideological manipulation.[16] Yet, like Barthes, Coetzee stops short of pitting the 'politicised' language of (revolutionary) history against the 'depoliticised' language of (universal) myth. Instead, through a series of self-contradictory narratives which lay bare their allegorical and/or mythical dimensions, Coetzee suggests that 'the best weapon against myth is perhaps to mythify it in its turn, and to produce an artificial myth . . . [a] reconstituted myth [which] will, in fact, be a mythology' (Barthes, *Mythologies* 135). Like all of Coetzee's novels to date, *Age of Iron* is a 'mythomorphic' text;[17] but the myths it presents are parodied, skewed, metamorphosed. (Could it be that the real *genius loci* of Mrs Curren's mythicised 'South Africa' is neither Hesiod nor Spencer, but that most iconoclastic of mythographers: Ovid?)[18] Those critics who have detected ahistorical tendencies in Coetzee's work, or who have admonished Coetzee for his misunderstanding of the dialectics of historical process, are perhaps underestimating the power of myth to shape not only the ways in which societies perceive themselves and each other, but also the ways in which those societies create and re-create their own histories.[19]

If myths, in Coetzee's work, provide strategies for the mediation of history, then the history that they mediate is one of breaks and ruptures: an aggregation of discontinuities rather than a gradually unfolding process of evolutionary maturation. Like Foucault, Coetzee appears to believe that history cannot be reduced to a single 'master code': instead of a 'discover[ing] a forgotten identity, eager to be reborn', it displays 'a complex system of distinct and multiple elements, unable to be mastered by the powers of synthesis' (Foucault, 'Nietzsche' 94).

> The traditional devices for constructing a comprehensive view of history and for retracing the past as a patient and continuous

> development must be systematically dismantled [says Foucault in an essay on Nietzsche]. History becomes effective to the degree that it introduces discontinuity into our very being – as it divides our emotions, dramatizes our instincts, multiplies our body and sets it against itself. 'Effective' history [which Foucault contrasts here with 'traditional,' or 'antiquarian' history] deprives the self of the reassuring stability of life and nature, and it will not permit itself to be transported . . . toward a millenial ending. (Foucault, 'Nietzsche' 88)

Nor will Coetzee's latest novel allow itself such easy reassurances. Coetzee has described his novels as 'rivals' to history in the sense that they 'operate in terms of [their] own procedures . . . issue in [their] own conclusions . . . [and] evolve their own paradigms and myths . . . perhaps going so far as to show up the mythic status of history' (Coetzee, 'The Novel Today' 3). But while Coetzee's novels take issue with the verifiable procedures of 'traditional' (antiquarian) history, they might also be said to lay the groundwork for an 'effective' history: a history in which it is understood that 'humanity does not gradually progress from combat to combat until it arrives at universal reciprocity, when the rule of law finally replaces warfare, [but rather that] humanity installs each of its violences in a system of rules and thus proceeds from domination to domination' (Foucault, 'Nietzsche' 85). To recognise these relations of power – to site the successive installations of humanity's violences – is to form a basis for their effective critique. Through the agency of a narrative which charts conflicting evolutionary and entropic impulses within a body multiplied and set against itself, Coetzee has demonstrated, once again, the deeply ethical nature of his fiction.

Notes

1. See Gabriele Annan's review of the novel in *The New York Review of Books;* Sean French's review in *New Statesman and Society;* in particular, Susan Gallagher's chapter on *Age of Iron* in *A Story of South Africa.*
2. For further details, see Gallagher (194–5).
3. For a further discussion of the parabolic structure of Coetzee's novels, with particular reference to Michael K, see my own essay 'Is there

a K in Africa?' in *Canadian Review of Comparative Literature.*

4. See, in particular, the well-known parable in which Socrates compares the world of appearances to an undergound cave. The benighted world of Plato's cave provides one of many classical analogues in the novel for the contemporary state of South Africa. In looking beyond the immediate world of physical appearances, Mrs Curren seeks to initiate the 'upward journey [of her] soul into the region of the intelligible' (*Republic* 231). The ironic treatment of Platonic doctrine in *Age of Iron* suggests, however, that Mrs Curren's distinction between the prison-house of the body and the liberated realm of the intellect is a false one. Mrs Curren's body turns against itself; but so, too, does the language of Eternal Ideas which allegedly 'transcends' it.
5. See Ronald Paulson's discussion of the iconography of the French Revolution in his *Representations of Revolution 1789–1820* (in particular Chapter 1). Paulson lists two basic representational alternatives, which were 'to regard revolution as a unique phenomenon for which a new vocabulary had to be invented, or to assimilate it, consider it a common occurrence, not something new and strange' (Paulson 36). Mrs Curren appears torn between these two options: on the one hand, she wishes to mediate her experience of the present through a language of the past; on the other, she recognises the inadequacy of that language to account for the unprecedented changes taking place in her society. Distortions result: as Paulson suggests, the *grotesque* emerges as a primary aesthetic mode through which the unstable events of history are 'at once shaped and falsified by their representations' (27). See also Thucydides' rueful analysis of the Corcyraean Revolution in *The Peloponnesian War* (Book 3, 82): 'words had to change their ordinary meaning and had to take that which was now given them' (189).
6. See *The Odyssey* (Book II) (Odysseus' voyage to the land of the dead); the *Aeneid* (Book 6) (Aeneas' visit to the world below). See also Susan Gallagher's brief, but useful discussion of Classical references in *Age of Iron* (*A Story of Africa*, 194–214).
7. See *Meditations* 2: 17 (on the 'putrefaction of the body'); 2: 14 (on the cosmic cycle); 10: 7, 18 (on the inevitability of change); above all, 7: 32 'about death: whether it is a dispersion, or a resolution into atoms, or annihilation, it is *either extinction or change*' (74, emphasis added). Also relevant to my discussion here are John Finley's description of the Peloponnesian war as a 'clash between a rising and a declining system, the former of which represented . . . the revolutionizing forces of the era. . . . while the latter stood for the oligarchic 'Greece of the past' (*Thucydides* 301); Charles Cochrane's assessment of Thucydides' historiography as the equivalent of attempts by modern scientific historians to 'apply to the study of social life the evolutionary canons of interpretation derived from Darwinian science' (Cochrane 3).
8. See Eliade (86–90, 112–30, 141–7). For a critique of Eliade, see also Kirk (63–6).

9. See *Age of Iron* (50–1), in which Mrs Curren conjures up

> the spirit of Geneva triumphant in Africa. Calvin, thin-blooded, forever cold, rubbing his hands in the afternoon, smiling his wintry smile. Calvin victorious, reborn in the dogmatists and witch-hunters of both armies. How fortunate [Mrs Curren reminds her daughter] you are to have put all this behind you! (*AOI* 51)

For all her vitriol, Mrs Curren has yet to disabuse herself of the legacy of Calvin, and we are left to wonder, too, about her daughter, whose 'escape' to the 'Free World' is by no means as comprehensive, or as untroubled, as Mrs Curren would have us believe . . .

10. See *White Writing* (140–9). Notice, too, Coetzee's analogy between nineteenth-century Europe and Classical antiquity: 'The practical success of science and technology in nineteenth-century Europe, the growth of industry, colonial expansion, and the dynamism of commerce convinced the broad educated public that the world was becoming a better and better place. To a minority within that public, on the other hand, the great European empires were coming to resemble nothing so much as the Roman Empire in its later years, sick unto death behind the exterior of might and opulence, their sickness betrayed by the squalor and degradation of their great cities, but also, more subtly, by the doubt and self-questioning that infected their more sensitive minds' (*WW* 141–2). Equally relevant to *Age of Iron* is Coetzee's conclusion that the science of degenerativity was bound to fail, for it 'sought a psychological and ultimately biological explanation for what was a cultural condition' (*WW* 142). In *Age of Iron*, Coetzee uncovers the 'cultural conditions' lurking beneath Mrs Curren's 'biological explanation' of the degraded state of contemporary South Africa; in so doing, he also suggests that those conditions are by no means confined to South Africa: that the 'sickness' of apartheid is a by-product of the (capitalist) West.
11. For a detailed discussion of Iron Age culture in Africa, see Phillipson (Chapters 6, 7 and, particularly, 8). My terminology here is loose: Phillipson's study, based on a careful consideration of archaeological and linguistic sources, provides a valuable corrective.
12. *Age of Iron* (3–5).
13. The host–parasite motif is a common one in Coetzee's fiction; see, in particular, *Life & Times of Michael K* (115–16). Pondering his peripheral existence at the camp at Jakkalsdrif, Michael K cannot agree with the police captain's assessment of the camp as 'a nest of parasites hanging from the neat sunlit town, eating its substance, giving no nourishment back' (*MK* 116). Instead, he thinks

> it was no longer obvious which was host and which parasite, camp or town. If the worm devoured the sheep, why did the sheep swallow the worm? . . . What if the hosts were far outnumbered by the parasites, the parasites of idleness and the other secret parasites in the army and the police force and the schools and

> factories and offices, the parasites of the heart? Could the parasites then still be called parasites? Parasites too had flesh and substance; parasites too could be preyed upon. Perhaps – [and the Foucauldian conclusion is particularly relevant to *AOI*] – whether the camp was declared a parasite on the town or the town a parasite on the camp depends on no more than on who made his voice heard loudest. (*MK* 116)

14. See Rifkin (33–43). As if in accordance with the second law of thermodynamics, Mrs Curren and Verceil have arrived at an 'equilibrium state': 'the state when entropy has reached a maximum [and] there is no longer free energy available to perform additional work' (Rifkin 36). See also Rifkin's synopsis of Heimholtz's cosmological theory (based on the Entropy Law). Heimholtz's theory of 'heat death' states that 'the universe is gradually running down and eventually will reach the point of maximum entropy or heat death where all available energy will have been expended and no more activity will occur. The heat death of the universe corresponds to a state of eternal rest' (Rifkin 44). The ironies of this 'state of rest' are not lost on Coetzee; nor is the particular irony that the Entropy Law contradicts Spencer's Myth of Progress. Instead, the Entropy Law posits that the universe is not moving from a state of chaos to a state of order, but rather from a state of order to a state of chaos. For another fictional rendering of the Entropy Law, see Pynchon's short story 'Entropy' in the *Kenyon Review* (1960). The story ends as follows:

    > [She] turned to face the man on the bed and wait for him until the moment of equilibrium was reached, when 37 degrees Farenheit should prevail both outside and inside, and forever, and the hovering, curious dominant of their separate lives should resolve into a tonic of darkness and the final absence of all motion. (Pynchon, 'Entropy' 292)

15. I am alluding here to Pierre Vergniaud's famous speech, delivered to the French assembly in 1793, in which he expressed his fear that the revolution 'comme Saturne dévorant successivement tous ses enfants, n'engendrât enfin le despotisme avec les calamités qui l'accompagnent'. Against this fear – which also seems to be Mrs. Curren's in *Age of Iron* – should be ranged St. Just's reply that the French Revolution would not devour itself, but rather its enemies. For a discussion of the implications of this exchange, see Paulson (Chapter 1). For a different perspective on the revolution eating its own children, see also Mazisi Kunene's apocalyptic poem 'The Civilisation of Iron'. Coetzee's novel clearly draws on the poem, which I reproduce here in full without further comment, with kind permission of the author:

I saw them whose heads were shaved
Whose fingers were sharpened, who wore shoes,
Whose eyes stared with coins.
I saw them
In their long processions
Rushing to worship images of steel:
They crushed the intestines of children
Until their tongues fell out.
I saw iron with sharp hands
Embracing infants
They wandered in the roads
Preaching the religion of iron.
Pregnant with those of blood and milk
I saw milk flowing
Like rivers under the feet of iron.
The earth shrank
And wailed the wail of machines.
There were no more people,
There were no more women,
Love was for sale in the wide streets
Spilling from bottles like gold dust.
They bought it for the festival of iron.
Those who dug it
Curled on the stones
Where they died in the whirlwind.
I saw the worshippers of iron
Who do not speak.

16. The best example here is Coetzee's treatment of the Crusoe myth in *Foe*. As I have argued elsewhere, the myth proves to be as enslaving as the exemplary tale of grateful servitude it relates (Huggan, 'Philomela's Retold Story'). Other enduring myths to come under scrutiny in Coetzee's work include the myth of national origin (*Dusklands*); of Edenic return (*Life & Times of Michael K*); and of imperial (civilisational) decline (*Waiting for the Barbarians*). Like Coetzee's previous novels, *Age of Iron* can be seen as a concatenation of heroic and purgatorial myths. These myths contribute to (although are by no means confined to) what Coetzee has called 'the discourse of the Cape': a discourse which has arguably allowed the white settler society of South Africa to justify its continuing hold on a land to which it has never truly 'belonged'. For a fine analysis of the 'discourse of the Cape', and an invaluable companion piece to his novels, see Coetzee's essays in *White Writing*, in particular 'Idleness in South Africa' (1) and 'Reading the South African Landscape' (7).
17. The phrase is Jacques Derrida's: see his discussion of Lévi-Strauss's work in the seminal essay 'Structure, Sign and Play in the Discourse of Human Sciences'. Coetzee, like Derrida, offers a post-structuralist reading of myth which deconstructs itself of the desire for origin. (The impact of French post-structuralism on Coetzee's work has been

noted by several of his critics, notably Teresa Dovey; I shall not pursue the matter here other than to note in passing that it is Foucault, rather than Derrida or Lacan, who seems best to underpin Coetzee's philosophical concerns.) It is an intriguing possibility to see Vercueil as a Lévi-Straussian trickster figure in *Age of Iron*: a mediator between alternative myths, as well as an intermediary figure within each individual myth who 'protects' its ambiguous (or, to use the post-structuralist term, 'undecideable') status. My argument would derive again from Foucault: what matters is not the 'undecideability' of myth (or the ambiguous relationship between one myth and another) but the means by which the myth is controlled and disseminated. As a trickster figure, Vercueil conceals the 'meaning' of Mrs. Curren's myth-laden narrative; but he also reveals the power structure that underlies it.

18. See, particularly, Ovid's variation on the Hesiod myth (Book 1) and his parody of the *Aeneid* (Books 13 and 14). Ovid's grotesquerie permeates Mrs. Curren's narrative, as does his view of life as flux. Above all, however, Ovid renders vividly 'the nightmarish quality of a world of shifting forms' (Segal): as in Kafka's celebrated story – to which there are numerous allusions in Coetzee's novel – metamorphosis conveys a sense of the 'total helplessness and strangeness of losing control over one's appearance, gesture, voice, in short all one's human attributes' (Segal 91). Ovid allows Mrs. Curren to de- and remythologise her own existence; Kafka allows her to perpetuate the myth of her own helplessness.
19. See, for example, Paul Rich's 'Apartheid and the Decline of the Civilization Idea'. In his closely argued essay, Rich contends that Coetzee's novel (unlike Gordimer's) fails to provide the 'anchoring point for a new conception of a postcolonial South African/Azanian culture' (Rich 389). Instead, it reproduces 'in a simplistic and ideal form many facets of the Western imperial imagination without at the same time being able to perceive any moral transcendence of it' (388). I shall not pursue the issue of whether Coetzee, as a 'South African writer', is duty-bound to undergo such ideological retraining. What interests me here is Rich's categorical distinction between a moribund, not to mention morally bankrupt 'Western imperial imagination' and a 'resurgent [black] nationalist history' (388). Concerned to break down a mythic opposition between 'civilisation' and 'barbarism' which is already broken down in the Magistrate's self-indicting narrative, Rich proceeds to create an opposition which itself smacks of myth. In his determination to find fault with Coetzee's 'uncommitted' politics, Rich comes close to suggesting that it is Coetzee himself, rather than the Magistrate, who manifests 'an absence of historical understanding'. The Magistrate, like Mrs. Curren in *Age of Iron*, views historical process through a filter of degenerative myth. His historical understanding, like hers, is clearly flawed, but whether there is a 'correct' historical understanding – an understanding stripped of the encrustations of myth – is another matter. Indeed, Coetzee's work suggests repeatedly that the opposition

between myth and history can itself be seen as myth: a suggestion which does not necessarily lead to nihilistic despair or, as Rich implies, to a moral dead end, but which stresses instead that the struggle to transform society must be accompanied by a constant vigilance to the legitimating strategies of power.

Afterword

DAVID ATTWELL

The position of being what the publishing trade calls a 'learned novelist' has awkward consequences. No doubt it affects the kind of investment publishers are likely to make, but it also complicates a writer's relations with readers and fellow artists. The present volume of essays represents a stage in the critical reception of J. M. Coetzee's fiction at which, after much uncertainty, a kind of equilibrium has been reached. Not that there is an established critical consensus on Coetzee; on the contrary, there are divergent and sometimes directly opposing opinions, as these essays demonstrate. But Coetzee's reputation as a major novelist is secure, though it was established unevenly in the different parts of the English-speaking world; and now readers – at least a minority on whose behalf this collection speaks – are beginning to evolve a sophisticated conversation based on their collective negotiation of Coetzee's complex, often chastening but always moving and powerful fiction.

There are now four full-length studies of Coetzee, two by South Africans and two by critics working in the United States.[1] This is the first anthology of essays. This collection, rightly, does not show the development of Coetzee criticism, but there was a period in the eighties (mainly but not exclusively in South Africa) when there were two noticeably different approaches, neither of which could do justice to Coetzee: an historicism bound by the dictates of Lukácsian realism, and a liberal humanism that was uncomfortable in Coetzee's world of formal and ethical self-consciousness. While such positions are still attempted from time to time (their ghosts appear in the corners of this volume) they have for the most part been superseded, because it is now generally recognised that in Coetzee's fictional landscapes, mandatory self-affirmations of a political or ethical kind do not easily arise, indeed, frequently the fiction explores the linguistic and historical conditions under which they are developed. Accordingly, recent criticism tries to grasp the complex interplay of well-tuned narrative strategy, theoretical allusiveness, and ethical reflection that one finds in the novels. The best of these essays exemplify such an approach.

The various constituencies of readers are differentiated largely on the grounds of how they register the contextual pressures of writing in South Africa. Noticeably, for instance, in Knox-Shaw, Watson, Parry and Parker, whose politics are divergent but who share a strong sense of the South African provenance of Coetzee's work, there is an emphasis on the ethical imperatives brought out by South Africa's history and the continuing legacy of colonial racism. By contrast, Attridge and Huggan take a longer view, one which does not disavow those imperatives by any means, but in which Coetzee's relationship with particular aesthetic and mythic traditions is explored with subtle attentiveness. The lines of demarcation between critics, however, are established not simply in terms of the old chestnut of form versus history – what Nadine Gordimer in her preface calls the 'balance between aesthetic values, regarded as transcending time, and temporal engagement, formed in and by time' – rather, it is a question of whether one sees the point of the particular, local inflections that give meaning to Coetzee's participation in the forms and traditions of European culture. In this regard, the essays by Marais, Dovey and Glenn, which examine Coetzee's adaptations of postmodern discourses, have something to teach the more politically assured arguments of Parry and Parker, who demand modes of agency from Coetzee that he might in fact be placing in question.

Nadine Gordimer finds these debates uninteresting, or worse, since she equates 'the regime of the intellect' represented in these essays with 'the regime of governments' whose role is to establish and police the forms of modern power. Coetzee is one of Us as writers, she says, while the essayists are Them. However, one of the often repeated gestures of Coetzee criticism is to confess one's own anxiety before the power of the text, that is to say, the novels rigorously examine the authority of the speaking subject, and critics frequently experience this as, among other things, a form of interrogation – of the assumptions and interests of the *critic* in the first instance. Coetzee criticism at its best, therefore, is self-conscious about how to understand the power and resourcefulness of fiction in relation to the discourses of criticism and theory. This, rather than the problem of Us and Them, would seem to be the more serious question, one which is self-evidently important in a situation such as now prevails in literary and cultural studies, namely that in the wake of post-structuralism, the boundaries of the various discourses of contemporary culture have become less and less distinct.

The question of the modern as raised by Nadine Gordimer – Coetzee's 'textual innovations' – also needs re-examination. Gordimer accuses these scholars of cultural cringe, in their wondering why Coetzee's familiarity with European traditions, that is, his postmodern ability to replay those traditions in new contexts, should be so startling when other contemporary writers are also able to traverse these traditions with ease. But it is not simply Coetzee's *participation* in the culture of postmodernism that is at issue. The deeper question behind, say, Merivale's documentation of Coetzee's debt to Kafka, or Dovey's account of Coetzee's parodic allegories, involves the *translocation* of tradition, which is also the problem of how a postmodernist self-consciousness survives in a climate like South Africa's. Marais's essay is particularly interesting in this regard, in its discussion of postcoloniality and postmodernity, the Scylla and Charybdis of the cultural and historical situation that Coetzee is obliged to navigate. The act of relocation certainly opens a different site of enunciation, giving a new historical relevance to the postmodern turn in Coetzee, but it also renders the European lines of continuity and influence curiously more visible. Indeed, since the 'modern' as a sign of Europeanness is both visible and vulnerable in Coetzee – indeed, as it is in Gordimer's own writing – surely one of the legitimate tasks of criticism is to explore this predicament?

In what direction is criticism of Coetzee likely to turn in the future? There are certain obvious possibilities. First, the question of the feminine narrators has been insufficiently explored. Feminist readings of Coetzee have been slow to develop, perhaps because Coetzee seems in an immediate way to be a powerful ally of feminism: Magda, Susan Barton and Elizabeth Curren are all displaced figures who resist pre-existing and more dominant modes of address, seeking to define themselves in worlds not of their own making. But there is more to it than this. The feminine in these narrators, as Glenn implies in his essay on *In the Heart of the Country*, serves to dramatise Coetzee's *own* self-positioning with respect to the versions of authority, both social and discursive, that compete around him. In other words, here we have the feminine as a sign for *other* kinds of difference, a situation involving tensions that need further description and explanation. Second, more work needs to be done on Coetzee's relation to psychoanalysis. Teresa Dovey has broached this subject courageously in her applications of Lacanian theory, and the relevance of Lacan is beyond question, but the relation to psychoanalysis needs to be opened up again, and from the beginning, as it were, for the traces of Freud in Coetzee are almost as significant as those of Kafka or Beckett, two literary influences whose significance is well recognised. A speaking subject driven by Oedipality, sexuality, and the fear of death; bovaristic or symptomatic language, dramatising the relation between the speaking subject and the unconscious; the question of whether the text can be read as an extension of the body: each of these things – so obviously within the domain of psychoanalysis – are to be found in Coetzee's fiction.

To conclude on a speculative note. One looks forward to more expansive treatments in future of Coetzee's relation to his European antecedents. There is a point at which tracking down this or that allusion to Blake, Dostoevsky or Eliot correctly becomes uninteresting; more significant are the *moments* of historical expression to which Coetzee returns, sometimes even without conscious reference. Coetzee's affiliations do seem postmodern in many respects, and if it were still admissable to talk in this fashion, we might speak of his willingness to rethink the modernist heritage in the context of South Africa's violent postcoloniality as a kind of heroism; certainly, one can speak of Coetzee as a courageous representative of a particular kind of contemporary cultural crisis. But I suggest that it is not only modernism or postmodernism that should sustain our interest, but modernity itself, and what I mean by this can be illustrated with a claim that will seem simplistic: Coetzee's narratives bring into creative tension the grandeur and scepticism of nineteenth-century philosophy, and the formal instability and inventiveness of the eighteenth-century novel. The broad historical vision, the semantics and ethics of colonialism, such legacies of the nineteenth century are intrinsic to the continuing search for a rational basis for society in the postcolonial context; at the same time, Coetzee's formal reflexivity – sometimes even a deceptive *simplicity* of style (as in *Life & Times of*

Michael K) whose precedent one finds most obviously in Defoe – suggests the contingency of the whole exercise, and the need to resist the projection of some new version of Utopia. One would like to believe that if criticism of Coetzee took us out of the polemical debates of the moment, into a more wide-ranging investigation of the historical processes in terms of which those debates are constituted, we would not only be richer for it, we would also have paid tribute to the work of a writer who had kept us all so busy without our fully understanding why.

Note

1. The studies by South Africans are Teresa Dovey, *The Novels of J. M. Coetzee: Lacanian Allegories* (Johannesburg: Ad Donker, 1988) and David Attwell, *J. M. Coetzee: South Africa and the Politics of Writing* (Berkeley and London: University of California Press, 1993); the studies produced in the US are by Dick Penner, *Countries of the Mind: The Fiction of J. M. Coetzee* (Westport: Greenwood Press, 1989) and Susan Van Zanten Gallagher, *A Story of South Africa: J. M. Coetzee's Fiction in Context* (Cambridge: Harvard University Press, 1990).

Works Cited

Alexander, Neville, 'A Plea for a New World', review of *Foe* by J. M. Coetzee, in *Die Suid-Afikan* (1987): 38.

Annan, Gabriele, review of *Age of Iron*, by J. M. Coetzee, in *The New York Review of Books* (8 November 1990): 8.

Arendt, Hannah, *The Origins of Totalitarianism* (London: Allen and Unwin, 1967).

Ashcroft, Bill, Gareth Griffiths and Helen Tiffin, *The Empire Writes Back: Theory and Practice in Post-colonial Literatures* (London: Routledge, 1989).

Attridge, Derek, 'Literary Form and the Demands of Politics: Otherness in J. M. Coetzee's *Age of Iron*', *Ideology and Aesthetics*, ed. George Levine (New Brunswick, NJ: Rutgers University Press, forthcoming).

Attridge, Derek, 'Oppressive Silence: J. M. Coetzee's *Foe* and the Politics of the Canon', *Decolonizing Tradition: New Views of Twentieth-Century 'British' Literary Canons*, ed. Karen R. Lawrence (Urbana: University of Illinois Press, 1992) pp. 212–238.

Attwell, David (ed.), *Doubling the Point, Essays and Interviews: J. M. Coetzee* (Cambridge, MA: Harvard University Press, 1992).

Attwell, David, '"The Labyrinth of My History": J. M. Coetzee's *Dusklands*', *Novel* 25.1 (Fall 1991): 7–32.

Attwell, David, *J. M. Coetzee and the Politics of Writing* (Cambridge, MA: Harvard University Press, 1993).

Attwell, David, 'J. M. Coetzee and South Africa: History, Narrative and the Politics of Agency', Ph.D. diss., University of Cape Town, 1991.

Attwell, David, 'The Problem of History in the Fiction of J. M. Coetzee', in *Rendering Things Visible: Essays on South African Literary Culture*, ed. Martin Trump (Athens: Ohio University Press, 1991), pp. 94–133.

Aucamp, Hennie, 'Skerpsinning – maar altyd wáár?' [Trenchant – but always true?], *Die Burger* 15.9 (1988): 12.

Auerbach, Nina, review of *Foe*, by J. M. Coetzee, in *The New Republic* 9 (March 1987): 36–8.

Aurelius, Marcus, *Meditations*, trans. G. Long (New York: Doubleday, 1962).

Bakhtin, Mikhail, 'The Word in the Novel', in *Comparative Criticism*, trans. Ann Shukman, ed. Elinor Shaffer (Cambridge: Cambridge University Press, 1980), pp. 213–20.

Barrett, William, *Irrational Man* (London: Heinemann, 1967).

Barrow, Sir John, *An Account of Travels into the Interior of Southern Africa*, vols I and II (London: Cadell & Davies, 1801–4).

Barthes, Roland, *S/Z*, trans. R. Miller (New York: Hill and Wang, 1974).

Barthes, Roland, *Mythologies*, trans. A. Lavers (New York: Farrar, Strauss and Giroux, 1972).

Bastian, F., *Defoe's Early Life* (London: Macmillan, 1981).

Beckett, Samuel, *Endgame* (London: Faber, 1958).
Bellow, Saul, *Herzog* (New York: Viking, 1976).
Benjamin, Walter, *Illuminations*, ed. H. Arendt (New York: Schocken, 1969).
Benjamin, Walter, *The Origin of German Tragic Drama*, trans. John Osborne (London: Routledge, 1985).
Bernasconi, Robert and David Wood (eds), *The Provocation of Levinas* (London: Routledge, 1988).
Bhabha, H. K., 'Signs taken for Wonders: Questions of Ambivalence and Authority under a Tree Outside Delhi, May 1817', *Critical Inquiry* 12.1 (1985): 144–65.
Boehmer, Elleke, Laura Chrisman and Kenneth Parker, (eds), *Altered State? Writing and South Africa* (Mundelstrup, DK: Dangaroo Press, 1994).
Brink, André, *Mapmakers: Writing in a State of Siege* (London: Faber, 1983).
Brink, André, 'Writing Against Big Brother: Notes on Apocalyptic Fiction in South Africa', in 'Threshold of Apocalypse: 1984 and After', *World Literature Today* 58 (1984): 189–94.
Brink, André, *Instant in the Wind* (London: W. H. Allen, 1976).
Butler, Guy, *Stranger to Europe: Poems 1939–1949* (Cape Town: Balkema, 1950; augmented edition 1960).
Buzzati, Dino, *Il Deserto dei Tartari* (Milan: Mondadori, 1985).
Buzzati, Dino, *The Tartar Steppe*, trans. Stuart Hood (New York: Carcanet, 1987).
Carroll, David, *The Subject in Question: The Languages of Theory and the Strategies of Fiction* (Chicago: University of Chicago Press, 1982).
Carusi, Annamaria, 'Post, Post and Post: Or, Where is South African Literature in All This?', *Ariel* 20.4 (1989): 79–95.
Carusi, Annamaria, 'Rethinking the Other', paper read at the *Annual Conference of the South African Society for General Literary Studies* Vanderbijlpark, 22–3 March 1991.
Castillo, Debra A., 'Coetzee's *Dusklands*: The Mythic *Punctum*', *PMLA* 105.5 (1990): 1108–22.
Castillo, Debra, 'J. M. Coetzee's *Foe*: Intertextual and Metafictional Resonances', *Commonwealth* 11.1 (1988): 55–60.
Cavafy, C. P., *Collected Poems*, trans. Edmund Keeley and Philip Sherrard (Princeton: Princeton University Press, 1975).
Césaire, Aimé, *Discourse on Colonialism* (New York: Monthly Review Press, 1974).
Chapman, Michael, review of *Foe*, by J. M. Coetzee, in *Southern African Review of Books* 2.2 (December 1988/January 1989): 22–3.
Clayton, Cherry, 'South African Writing in English, 1977', *Standpunte* 32.3 (1979): 38–48.
Clingman, Stephen, *The Novels of Nadine Gordimer* (London: Allen & Unwin, 1986).
Cochrane, Charles, *Thucydides and the Science of History* (New York: Russell and Russell, 1965).
Coetzee, J. M., 'Achterberg's "Ballade van de gasfitter": The Mystery of I and You', *PMLA* 92 (1977): 285–96.

Coetzee, J. M., 'The Agentless Sentence as Rhetorical Device', *Language and Style* 13.1 (1980): 26–34.
Coetzee, J. M., *Age of Iron* (New York: Random House, 1990).
Coetzee, J. M., 'Alex la Guma and the Responsibilities of the South African Writer', *Journal of the New African Literatures and the Arts* (September 1971): 5–11.
Coetzee, J. M., 'Alex la Guma', in *English and South Africa*, ed. Alan Lennox-Short (Cape Town: Nasou, 1973), pp. 111–12.
Coetzee, J. M., 'André Brink and the Censor', *Research in African Literatures* 21.3 (1990): 59–74.
Coetzee, J. M., 'Anthropology and the Hottentots', *Semiotica* 54.1–2 (1985): 87–95.
Coetzee, J. M., 'Censorship and Polemic: The Solzhenitsyn Affair', *Pretexts* 2.2 (1990): 1–36.
Coetzee, J. M., 'The Comedy of Point of View in Beckett's *Murphy*', *Critique: Studies in Modern Fiction* 12.2 (1970) 19–27.
Coetzee, J. M., 'Confession and Double Thoughts: Tolstoy, Rousseau, Dostoevsky', *Comparative Literature* 37.3 (1985): 193–232.
Coetzee, J. M., *Dusklands* (Johannesburg: Ravan, 1974).
Coetzee, J. M., *Dusklands* (Harmondsworth: Penguin, 1982).
Coetzee, J. M., *Dusklands* (London: Secker & Warburg, 1982).
Coetzee, J. M., 'The English Fiction of Samuel Beckett: An Essay in Stylistic Analysis', Ph.D. thesis, University of Texas at Austin, 1969.
Coetzee, J. M., *English in Africa*, ed. Alan Lennox-Short (Cape Town: Nasou, 1973).
Coetzee, J. M., *Foe* (Johannesburg: Ravan Press, 1986).
Coetzee, J. M., *Foe* (New York: Viking Penguin, 1988 (1987)).
Coetzee, J. M., 'The Great South African Novel', *Leadership South Africa* 2.4 (1983): 74, 77, 79.
Coetzee, J. M., 'Idleness in South Africa', *Social Dynamics* 8.1 (1982): 1–13.
Coetzee, J. M., interview (April 1990), *Doubling the Point: Essays and Interviews*, ed. David Attwell (Cambridge, MA: Harvard University Press, 1992), pp. 197–209.
Coetzee, J. M., interview with Claude Wauthier, *La Nouvel Observateur* 28 (June/July 1985): 69.
Coetzee, J. M., interview with Richard Begam, *Contemporary Literature* 33.3 (1992): 427.
Coetzee, J. M., interview with Tony Morphet, *From South Africa: New Writing, Photographs & Art*, special issue of *Triquarterly* 69 (Spring/Summer 1987): 454–6.
Coetzee, J. M., *In the Heart of the Country* (London: Secker & Warburg, 1977).
Coetzee, J. M., *In the Heart of the Country* (Johannesburg: Ravan, 1978).
Coetzee, J. M., *In the Heart of the Country* (New York: Viking Penguin, 1982).
Coetzee, J. M., 'Into the Dark Chamber: The Novelist and South Africa' *New York Times Book Review* 12 (January 1986): 13, 33.
Coetzee, J. M., *Life & Times of Michael K* (Johannesburg: Ravan Press. 1983).

Coetzee, J. M., *Life & Times of Michael K* (New York: Viking, Penguin, 1983).

Coetzee, J. M., 'Man's Fate in the Novels of Alex la Guma', *Studies in Black Literature* 5.1: (1974): 16–23.

Coetzee, J. M., 'The Manuscript Revisions of Beckett's *Watt*', *Journal of Modern Literature* 2 (1973): 472–80.

Coetzee, J. M., 'The Mind of Apartheid: Geoffrey Cronjé (1907–)', *Social Dynamics: A Journal of the Centre for African Studies, University of Cape Town* 17.1 (1991): 1–35.

Coetzee, J. M., 'Nabokov's *Pale Fire* and the *Primacy of Art*', *UCT Studies in English* 5 (1974): 1–7.

Coetzee, J. M., 'Nadine Gordimer: The Essential Gesture' (1989), repr. Coetzee/Attwell, pp. 382–8.

Coetzee, J. M., 'Newton and the Ideal of a Transparent Scientific Language', *Journal of Literary Semantics* 11.1 (1982): 3–13.

Coetzee, J. M., 'The Novel Today', *Upstream* 6.1 (1988): 2–5.

Coetzee, J. M., review of *Fools* by Njabulo Ndebele, in *New Republic* (December 1983): 36–8.

Coetzee, J. M., review of *Nadine Gordimer* by Michael Wade, in *Research in African Literatures* 11.2 (Summer): 253–6.

Coetzee, J. M., review of *The True Confessions of an Albino Terrorist* by Breyten Breytenbach, in *Social Dynamics: A Journal of the Centre for African Studies, University of Cape Town* 11.2 (1985): 72–5.

Coetzee, J. M., review of *White Boy Running* by Christopher Hope, in *New Republic* 13 (1988): 37–9.

Coetzee, J. M., 'The Rhetoric of the Passive in English', *Linguistics* 18.3–4 (1980): 199–221.

Coetzee, J. M., 'Samuel Beckett's *Lessness*: An Exercise in Decomposition', *Computers in the Humanities* 7.4 (1973): 195–8.

Coetzee, J. M., 'Samuel Beckett and the Temptations of Style', *Theoria* 41 (1973): 45–50.

Coetzee, J. M., 'Speaking: J. M., Coetzee', with Stephen Watson, in *Speak* (May/June 1978): 21–24.

Coetzee, J. M., 'Statistical Indices of Difficulty', *Language and Style* 2.3 (1969) 226–32.

Coetzee, J. M., 'Surreal Metaphors and Random Processes', *Journal of Literary Semantics* 8.1 (April 1979): 22–30.

Coetzee, J. M., 'Time, Tense and Aspect in Kafka's "The Burrow"', *MLN* 96 (1981): 556–79, repr. Coetzee/Attwell, pp. 210–32.

Coetzee, J. M., 'Two Interviews with J. M. Coetzee, 1983 and 1987', with Tony Morphet, in *Triquarterly* 69 (1987): 454–64.

Coetzee, J. M., *Waiting for the Barbarians* (Johannesburg: Ravan Press, 1981).

Coetzee, J. M., *Waiting for the Barbarians* (London: Penguin, 1980).

Coetzee, J. M., *Waiting for the Barbarians* (London: Secker & Warburg, 1980).

Coetzee, J. M., *White Writing: On the Culture of Letters in South Africa* (New Haven & London: Yale University Press, 1988).

Coetzee, J. M., 'Zbigniew Herbert and the Figure of the Censor', *Salma-*

gundi 88–9 (1990–91): 158–75.
Conrad, Joseph, *Heart of Darkness* (London: Dent, 1974).
Cooper, Brenda, 'New Criteria for an 'Abnormal Mutation'? An Evaluation of Gordimer's *A Sport of Nature*', *Rendering Things Visible*, ed. Martin Trump (Johannesburg: Ravan Press, 1990), pp. 68–93.
Cope, Jack, 'Foreword', *Contrast* 1.1 (1960).
Crewe, Jonathan, 'Review of *Dusklands*', *Contrast* 34 (1974): 90 5.
Culler, J., *Structuralist Poetics: Structuralism, Linguistics and the Study of Literature* (London: Routledge and Kegan Paul, 1975).
Current Writing: Text and Reception in Southern Africa, special issue on *Feminism and Writing* 2 (October 1990).
Darke, Neil, review of *Foe*, by J. M. Coetzee, *Cape Argus* 23 (October 1986).
Darwin, Charles, *The Darwin Reader*, ed. M. Ridley (New York: Norton, 1987).
Deane, Seamus, ed., *Field Day Anthology of Irish Writing* (New York: Norton, 1991).
Defoe, Daniel, *Colonel Jack* (London: J. Brotherton, 1723).
Defoe, Daniel, *The Dumb Philosopher* (London: J. Roberts, 1727).
Defoe, Daniel, *The Life and Adventures of Robinson Crusoe* [1719], ed. Angus Ross (Harmondsworth: Penguin Books, 1965).
Defoe, Daniel, *Moll Flanders* (New York: Knopf, 1991).
Defoe, Daniel, *Roxana/The Fortunate Mistress* [1724], ed. Jane Jack (London: Oxford University Press, 1964).
Defoe, Daniel, *A True Relation of the Apparition of One Mrs. Veal* (London: B. Bragg, 1706).
de Kok, Ingrid and Karen Press (eds), *Spring is Rebellious: Arguments about Cultural Freedom* (Cape Town: Buchu Books, 1990).
de Kok, Ingrid and Karen Press (eds), review of *Spring is Rebellious: Arguments About Cultural Freedom*, by Benita Parry, in *Transition* 55 (1991): 125–34.
de Man, Paul, 'The Rhetoric of Temporality', *Interpretation: Theory and Practice*, ed. Charles S. Singleton (Baltimore: Johns Hopkins University Press, 1969), pp. 173–209.
Dennis, Nigel, *A House in Order* (London: Weidenfeld & Nicolson, 1966).
Derrida, Jacques, 'Living On/Borderlines', *Deconstruction and Criticism*, ed. Harold Bloom *et al.* (London: Routledge, 1979), pp. 75–175.
Derrida, Jacques, 'Psyche: Invention of the Other', *Acts of Literature*, ed. Derek Attridge, (New York: Routledge, 1992), pp. 310–43.
Derrida, Jacques, *Speech and Phenomena and Other Essays on Husserl's Theory of Signs*, trans. with Intro., David B. Allison and Newton Garver (Evanston: Northwestern University Press, 1973).
Derrida, Jacques, 'Structure, Sign and Play in the Discourse of the Human Sciences', *Writing and Difference* (Chicago: University of Chicago Press, 1978), pp. 278–94.
Dodd, Josephine, 'Naming and Framing: Naturalization and Colonization in J. M. Coetzee's *In the Heart of the Country*', *World Literature Written in English* 27.2 (1987): 153–61.
Dodd, J., 'The South African Literary Establishment and the Textual

Production of 'Woman': J. M. Coetzee and Lewis Nkosi', *Current Writing* 2.1 (1990): 117–29.

Douglas, Matthew, *The Lives of Butterflies* (Ann Arbor: University of Michigan Press, 1986).

Dovey, Teresa, 'Allegory vs. Allegory: The Divorce of Different Modes of Allegorical Perception in Coetzee's *Waiting for the Barbarians*', *Journal of Literary Studies* 4.2 (1988): 133–43.

Dovey, Teresa, 'Coetzee and His Critics: The Case of *Dusklands*', *English in Africa* 2.14 (1987): 15–30.

Dovey, Teresa, *The Novels of J. M. Coetzee: Lacanian Allegories* (Johannesburg: Ad. Donker, 1988).

Dreiser, Theodore, *An American Tragedy* (New York: New American Library, 1964).

Driver, Dorothy, 'M'a-Ngoana O Tšoare Thipa ka Bohaleng – The Child's Mother Grasps the Sharp End of the Knife: Women as Mothers, Women as Writers', in *Rendering Things Visible*, ed. Martin Trump (Johannesburg: Ravan Press, 1990), 225–55.

Eagleton, Terry, *Walter Benjamin, or, Towards a Revolutionary Criticism* (London: Verso, 1981).

Eckstein, Barbara J., 'The Body, the Word, and the State: Torture and Interrogation: J. M. Coetzee's *Waiting for the Barbarians*', in *The Language of Fiction in a World of Pain* (Philadelphia: University of Pennsylvania Press, 1990), pp. 68–93.

Eliade, Mircea, *The Myth of Eternal Return* (Princeton: Princeton University Press, 1954).

Ferreira, Jeanette, *Die mammies, die pappies, die hondjies, die katjies* (Bramley: Taurus, 1989).

Fineman, Joel, 'The Structure of Allegorical Desire', *Allegory and Representation*, ed. Stephen J. Greenblatt, selected papers from the English Institute, New Series, No. 5 (Baltimore: Johns Hopkins University Press, 1981), pp. 26–60.

Finley, John, *Thucydides* (Ann Arbor: University of Michigan Press, 1963).

Finn, Stephen, 'The South African Short Story 1960–1989: A Comparison of Literary Magazines in English', *Altered State? Writing and South Africa*, ed. Elleke Boehmer, Laura Chrisman and Kenneth Parker (Mundelstrup, Denmark: Dangaroo, 1994), pp. 51–66.

Fletcher, John and Benjamin, Andrew (eds), *Abjection, Melancholia and Love: The Work of Julia Kristeva* (London: Routledge, 1990).

Fontenrose, Joseph, 'Works, Justice, and Hesiod's Five Ages', *Classical Philology* 44.1 (1974): 1–16.

Foucault, Michel, *The Archaeology of Knowledge*, trans. A. Sheridan Smith (London: Tavistock, 1972).

Foucault, Michel, 'Nietzsche, Genealogy, History', *The Foucault Reader*, ed. P. Rabinow (New York: Pantheon, 1984), pp. 76–100.

French, Sean, review of *Age of Iron* by J. M. Coetzee, in *New Statesman and Society* (21 September 1990): 40.

Frye, Northrop, *Anatomy of Criticism: Four Essays* (Princeton: Princeton University Press, 1957).

Gallagher, Susan VanZanten, *A Story of South Africa: J. M. Coetzee's Fic-*

tion in Context (Cambridge, MA: Harvard University Press, 1991).
Gillmer, Joan, 'The Motive of the Damaged Child in the Work of J. M. Coetzee', in *Momentum: On Recent South African Writing*, ed. M. J. Daymond *et al.* (Pietermaritzburg: University of Natal Press, 1984), pp. 107–20.
Giddens, Anthony, *Modernity and Self-Identity: Self and Society in the Late Modern Age* (Cambridge, UK: Polity Press, 1991).
Goddard, Kevin and John Read, *J. M. Coetzee: A Bibliography*, Intro. by Teresa Dovey (Grahamstown, South Africa: National English Literary Museum, 1990).
Gordimer, Nadine, *The Essential Gesture: Writing, Politics and Places*, ed. and Intro. by Stephen Clingman (London: Cape, 1988).
Gordimer, Nadine, 'The Future is Another Country: A Conversation with Stephen Clingman', *Transition* 56 (1992): 132–50.
Gordimer, Nadine, *The Conservationist* (London: Cape, 1984).
Gordimer, Nadine, 'The Idea of Gardening', *New York Review of Books* 2 (February 1984): 3–4.
Gordimer, Nadine. 'Letter from his Father', *Something Out There* (New York: Viking, 1984), pp. 39–56.
Gordimer, Nadine, *My Son's Story* (London: Bloomsbury, 1990).
Gordimer, Nadine, 'Turning the Page: African Writers on the Threshold of the Twenty-First Century', *Transition* 56 (1992): 4–10.
Gordimer, Nadine, *Occasion for Loving* (London: Cape, 1978 (1963)).
Gracq, Julien, *The Opposing Shore*, trans. Richard Howard (New York: Columbia University Press, 1986).
Gracq, Julien, *Le Rivage des Syrtes* (Paris: José Corti, 1985).
Gramsci, Antonio, *Selections from the Prison Notebooks*, ed. and trans. Quentin Hoare and Geoffrey Nowell Smith (London: Lawrence and Wishart, 1971).
Greeff, Rachelle, *Die rugkant van die bruid* (Kaapstad: Tafelberg, 1990).
Gugelberger, George (ed.), *Marxism and African Literature* (Trenton, NJ: Africa World Press, 1985).
Hahn, C. H. L., *The Native Tribes of South West Africa* (Cape Town, 1928; repr. London: Frank Cass, 1966).
H. G., review of *Foe*, by J. M. Coetzee, in *The Natal Mercury* 27 (November 1986), 16.
Haresnape, Geoffrey, 'Notes', *Contrast* 60 (December 1985): 3, 95–6; *Contrast* 63 (July 1987): 3, 95–6; *Contrast* 65 (July 1988): 3, 94–6.
Herbert, Zbigniew, *Selected Poems*, trans. John Carpenter and Bogdana Carpenter (New York: Oxford University Press, 1977).
Hesiod, *The Works and Days*, trans. R. Lattimore (Ann Arbor: University of Michigan Press, 1973 [1959]).
Hewson, Kelly, 'Making the "Revolutionary Gesture": Nadine Gordimer, J. M. Coetzee and Some Variations on the Writer's Responsibility', *Ariel* 19.4 (October 1988): 55–72.
Homer, *The Odyssey*, trans. R. Lattimore (New York: Harper and Row, 1965).
Hope, Christopher, 'Language as Home: Colonisation by Words', *Weekly Mail*, 22–28 July (1988): 15.

Hope, Christopher, *White Boy Running* (London: Secker and Warburg, 1988).

Howard, Rosalind and Ellis John, *Language and Materialism: Developments in Semiology and the Theory of the Subject* (London: Routledge & Kegan Paul, 1977).

Howe, Irving, '*Waiting for the Barbarians*', *New York Times Book Review* 18 (April 1982): 36.

Huggan, Graham, 'Is There a K in Afrika? The Modern Parables of Kafka, Laye and Coetzee', *Canadian Review of Comparative Literature* 17.1/2 (1990): 85–98.

Huggan, Graham, 'Philomela's Retold Story: Silence, Music and the Post-Colonial Text', *Journal of Commonwealth Literature* 25.1 (1990): 12–23.

Huismans, Emma, *Berigte van weerstand* (Bramley: Taurus, 1990).

Hulme, Peter, *Colonial Encounters: Europe and the Native Caribbean 1492–1797* (London: Methuen, 1986).

Hutcheon, L., '"Circling the Downspout of Empire": Post-colonialism and Post-modernism", *Ariel* 20.4 (1989): 149–75.

James, Henry, 'The Beast in the Jungle', *The Portable Henry James*, ed. Morton Zabel (New York: Viking, 1951), pp. 270–325.

Jameson, Fredric, 'Imaginary and Symbolic in Lacan: Marxism, Psychoanalytic Criticism and the Problem of the Subject', *Yale French Studies* 55/56 (1977): 338–95.

Jameson, Fredric, *The Political Unconscious: Narrative as a Socially Symbolic Act* (Ithaca, NY: Cornell University Press, 1981).

Jameson, Fredric, 'Postmodernism, or the Cultural Logic of Late Capitalism', *New Left Review* 146 (1984): 53–92.

Jolly, Rosemary Jane, 'Territorial Metaphor in Coetzee's *Waiting for the Barbarians*', *Ariel* 20.2 (1989): 69–79.

Jones, Ann Rosalind, 'Writing the Body: Toward an Understanding of l'Ecriture féminine', *The New Feminist Criticism*, ed. Elaine Showalter (London: Virago, 1986), pp. 361–877.

Kafka, Franz, *The Castle*, trans. W. and E. Muir (Harmondsworth: Penguin, 1957 [1930]).

Kafka, Franz, *The Collected Stories*, ed. Nahum Glatzer, trans. Willa and Edwin Muir (New York: Schocken, 1976).

Kafka, Franz, *Sämtliche Erzählungen*, ed. Paul Raabe (Frankfurt/M.: Fischer, 1973).

Kafka, Franz, *The Trial*, trans. Willa and Edwin Muir (New York: Schocken, 1984 [1925]).

Kirk, G. S., *The Nature of Greek Myths* (Harmondsworth: Penguin, 1974).

Kleist, Heinrich von, *Michael Kohlhaas* (1810), ed. John Geary (New York: Oxford University Press, 1967).

Knox-Shaw, Peter, '*Dusklands*: A Metaphysics of Violence', *Contrast* 4.1 (1982): 26–38.

Koelb, Clayton, *Kafka's Rhetoric: The Passion of Reading* (Ithaca: Cornell University Press, 1989).

Koestler, Arthur, *The Yogi and the Commissar* (London: Jonathan Cape, 1945).

Kristeva, Julia, *Desire in Language: A Semiotic Approach to Literature and*

Art, ed. Leon S. Roudiez, trans. Thomas Gore, Alice Jardine & Leon S. Roudiez (Oxford: Blackwell, 1981).

Kunene, Mazisi, 'The Civilisation of Iron', *A Century of South African Poetry*, ed. M. Chapman (Johannesburg: A. D. Donker, 1981), p. 244.

La Guma, Alex, *A Walk in the Night and Other Stories* (Chicago: Northwestern University Press, 1967).

Lampedusa, Giuseppe, *The Leopard* (Harmondsworth: Penguin, 1960).

Lawrence, Karen (ed.), *Decolonizing Tradition: New Views of Twentieth-Century 'British' Literary Canons* (Urbana: University of Illinois Press, 1992).

Lazarus, Neil, 'Modernism and Modernity: T. W. Adorno and Contemporary White South African Literature', *Cultural Critique* 5 (Winter 1986–1987): 131–55.

Le Vaillant, M., *Travels into the Interior Parts of Africa by way of the Cape of Good Hope in the Years 1780–5*, vol. I, trans. by M. Le Vaillant (London: G. G. & J. Robinson, 1796).

Lehmann-Haupt, Christopher, 'Books of the Times', review of *Life & Times of Michael K*, *New York Times* (6 December 1983): C22.

Lévi-Strauss, Claude, 'The Structural Study of Myth', *Structural Anthropology*, trans. C. Jacobson and B. Schoepf (New York: Anchor, 1967), pp. 202–28.

Levinas, Emmanuel, *Totality and Infinity*, trans. A. Lingis (Pittsburgh: Duquesne University Press, 1969).

Locke, John, *Two Treatises on Civil Government* (New York: Dutton, 1884 (1690)).

Louw, Chris, 'Satan and Censorship', *Southern African Review of Books* 2.3 (1989): 13; trans. and extracted from *Die Suid-Afrikaan* (December 1988/January 1989).

Lyotard, Jean-François, *The Differend: Phrases in Dispute*, trans. Georges Van Den Abbeele (Manchester: Manchester University Press, 1988).

Lyotard, Jean-François, *The Postmodern Condition: A Report on Knowledge*, trans. G. Bennington and B. Massumi (Minneapolis: University of Minnesota Press, 1985).

McHale, B., *Postmodernist Fiction* (New York: Methuen, 1987).

Mason, Peter, *Deconstructing America: Representations of the Other* (London: Routledge, 1990).

Maughan-Brown, David, 'The Anthology as Reliquary? *Ten Years of Staffrider* and *The Drum Decade*', *Current Writing* 1.1 (1989): 3–22.

Melville, Herman, 'Bartleby, the Scrivener', *The Portable Melville*, ed. Jay Leyda (New York: Viking, 1952), pp. 465–611.

Memmi, Albert, *The Colonizer and the Colonized*, trans. Howard Greenfeld (London: Earthscan, 1990).

Memmi, Albert, *The Colonizer and the Colonized* (London: Souvenir Press, 1974).

Mennecke, Arnim, *Koloniales Bewusstsein in den Romanen J. M. Coetzee* (Heidelberg: Carl Winter Universitätsverlag, 1991).

Merivale, Patricia, 'Ambiguous Frontiers: *Waiting for the Barbarians* as Topographical Parable', *Proceedings of the Twelfth Congress of the ICLA (1988)*, ed. Roger Bauer *et al.* (Munich: Judicium, 1990), pp. 272–6.

Miller, Christopher, *Theories of Africans: Francophone Literature and Anthropology in Africa* (Chicago: Chicago University Press, 1990).

Miller, J. Hillis, 'The Two Allegories', *Allegory, Myth and Symbol*, ed. Morton W. Bloomfield, Harvard English Studies 9 (Cambridge, MA: Harvard University Press, 1981), pp. 355–70.

Milosz, Czeslaw, 'The Nobel Lecture', *World Literature Today* 55.3 (1982): 403–15.

Mofokeng, Boitumelo, 'Where are the Women? Ten Years of *Staffrider*', *Current Writing* 1.1 (1989): 41–4.

Moi, Toril (ed.), *The Kristeva Reader* (Oxford: Blackwell, 1986).

Moi, Toril, *Sexual/Textual Politics* (London: Methuen, 1985).

Moore, John Robert, *Daniel Defoe: Citizen of the Modern World* (Chicago: University of Chicago Press, 1958).

Morphet, Tony, 'Cultural Imagination and Cultural Settlement', *Pretexts* 2.1 (1990): 94–103.

Morrison, Toni, *Beloved* (New York: Knopf, 1990 (1987)).

Mossop, Dr E. E. (ed.), *The Journals of Bergh and Schrijver* (Cape Town: Van Riebeeck Society, No. 12, 1931).

Mossop, Dr E. E. (ed. and trans.), 'The Journal of Carel Frederik Brink of the Journey into Great Namaqualand (1761–2) made by Captain Hendrik Hop', *The Journals of Brink and Rhenius* (Cape Town: Van Riebeck Society No. 28, 1947).

Mossop, Dr E. E. (ed. and trans.), 'Relaas', *The Journals of Wikar, Coetsé and Van Reenen* (Cape Town: Van Riebeeck Society, 1935).

Mzamane, Mbulelo Vizikhungo. 'An Unhistorical Will into Past Times', *Current Writing* 1.1 (1989): 36–46.

Nabokov, Vladimir, *Pale Fire* (New York: Putnam, 1962).

Ndebele, Njabulo, *Fools and Other Stories* (Johannesburg: Ravan, 1983).

Ndebele, Njabulo S., 'The English Language and Social Change in South Africa', *From South Africa: New Writing, Photographs & Art*, special issue of *Triquarterly* 69 (Spring/Summer 1987): 217–35.

Ndebele, Njabulo, 'Redefining Relevance', *Pretexts* 1.1 (1989): 45– 50.

Ndebele, Njabulo, 'The Ethics of Intellectual Combat', *Current Writing* 1.1 (1989): 23–35.

Neumann, Anne Waldron, 'Escaping the "Time of History"? Present Tense and the Occasion of Narration in J. M. Coetzee's *Waiting for the Barbarians*', *Journal of Narrative Technique* 20.1 (1990): 65–86.

Nietzsche, Friedrich, *Beyond Good and Evil* (Harmondsworth: Penguin, 1973).

Nixon, Rob, 'Border Country: Bessie Head's Frontline States', *Social Text* 36 (Fall 1993): 106–37.

Nkosi, Lewis, 'A Country of Borders', *Southern African Review of Books* 3.6 (August/October 1989) August/October 1989: 19–20.

Nkosi, Lewis, 'Fiction by Black South Africans', *Introduction to African Literature*, ed. Ulli Beier (Evanston: Northwestern University Press, 1967), pp. 211–17.

Nkosi, Lewis, 'The New African Novel: A Search for Modernism', *Tasks and Masks: Themes and Styles of African Literature* (Harlow: Longman, 1981), pp. 53–75.

O'Brien, Anthony, 'Literature in Another South Africa: Njabulo Ndebele's Theory of Emergent Culture', *Diacritics*, 22.1 (Spring 1992): 67–85.

Olsen, Lance, 'The Presence of Absence: Coetzee's *Waiting for the Barbarians*', *Ariel* 16.2 (1985): 47–56.

Olsen, Lance, 'The Presence of Absence: Coetzee's *Waiting for the Barbarians*', *Ellipse of Uncertainty: An Introduction to Postmodern Fantasy* (New York, Westport CO, London: Greenwood, 1987), pp. 101–13.

Ovid, *Metamorphoses*, trans. C. Boer (Dallas: Spring, 1989).

Owens, Craig, 'The Allegorical Impulse: Toward a Theory of Postmodernism', Part I, *October* 12 (1980): 67–86.

Owens, Craig, 'The Allegorical Impulse: Toward a Theory of Postmodernism', Part II, *October* 13 (1980): 59–80.

Parker, George, review of *Foe*, by J. M. Coetzee, *The Nation* (28 March 1987): 402–5.

Parker, Kenneth, 'Coetzee on Culture', *Southern African Review of Books* 1.4 (1988): 3–6.

Parker, Kenneth, 'Fertile Land, Romantic Spaces, Uncivilized Peoples: English Travel Writing about the Cape of Good Hope 1800–1850', *The Expansion of England: Essays in the Cultural History of Race and Ethnicity*, ed. Bill Schwarz (London: Routledge, forthcoming, 1995).

Parker, Kenneth, 'Un(utterably) Other Others: The Khoi at the Cape of Good Hope and Early Modern English Voyagers', *Writing Travels*, ed. Francis Barker, Peter Hulme and Margaret Iversen (Manchester: Manchester University Press, forthcoming, 1995).

Parrinder, Patrick, 'What His Father Gets Up To', review of *Age of Iron*, by J. M. Coetzee, and *My Son's Story*, by Nadine Gordimer, *London Review of Books* 12.17 (1990): 17–18.

Parry, Benita, 'The Hole in the Narrative', unpublished paper, 1992.

Parry, Benita, review of *White Writing* by J. M. Coetzee, *Research in African Literatures* 22.4 (1991): 196–8.

Paulin, Tom, 'Incorrigibly Plural', review of *In the Heart of the Country* by J. M. Coetzee, *Encounter* (October 1977): 82–9.

Paulson, Ronald, *Representations of Revolution 1789–1820* (New Haven: Yale University Press, 1983).

Penner, Dick, *Countries of the Mind: The Fiction of J. M. Coetzee* (London: Greenwood, 1990).

Penner, Dick, *Countries of the Mind: The Fiction of J. M. Coetzee* (Westport, CO: Greenwood, 1989).

Phillipson, D. W., *The Later Prehistory of Eastern and Southern Africa* (New York: Africana, 1977).

Plato, *The Republic*, trans. D. Lee (Harmondsworth: Penguin, 1974).

Plomer, William, *Turbott Wolfe* (London: Hogarth Press, 1930).

Post, Robert M., 'The Noise of Freedom: J. M. Coetzee's *Foe*', *Critique* 30 (1989): 143–54.

Post, Robert M., 'Oppression in the Fiction of J. M. Coetzee', *Critique* 26.2 (1986): 67–77.

Press, Karen, 'Building a National Culture in South Africa', *Rendering Things Visible*, ed. Martin Trump (Johannesburg: Ravan Press, 1990), pp. 22–40.

Puech, Henri-Charles, 'Gnosis and Time', *Man and Time*, ed. H. Corgin *et al.* (New York: Pantheon, 1957): 38–84.
Pushkin, Alexander, *Eugene Onegin*, trans. J. E. Falen (Carbondale: Southern Illinois University Press, 1990).
Pynchon, Thomas, 'Entropy', *Kenyon Review* (Spring 1960): pp. 277–92.
Research in African Literatures 19.1 (1988), special issue on Black South African Literature since 1976.
Rich, Paul, 'Apartheid and the Decline of the Civilization Idea: An Essay on Nadine Gordimer's *July's People* and J. M. Coetzee's *Waiting for the Barbarians*', *Research in African Literatures* 15.3 (1984): 365–93.
Rifkin, Jeremy, *Entropy: A New World View* (New York: Viking, 1980).
Rosenmeyer, Thomas, 'Hesiod and Historiography', *Hermes* 85.3 (1957): 258–85.
Rushdie, Salman, *Shame* (London: Pan Books, 1984).
Rushdie, Salman, *The Satanic Verses* (London: Viking, 1988).
Ryan, Michael, *Marxism and Deconstruction: A Critical Articulation* (Baltimore: Johns Hopkins Universiy Press, 1982).
Sartre, Jean-Paul, *Being and Nothingness: An Essay in Phenomenal Ontology*, trans. H. E. Barnes (London: Methuen, 1957).
Sartre, Jean-Paul, *No Exit, and Three Other Plays* (New York: Vintage, 1976).
Schoeman, Karel, *Promised Land*, trans. Maria Friedmann (New York: Summit Books, 1978).
Scholes, Robert, *Structuralism in Literature* (New Haven: Yale University Press, 1974).
Schreiner, Olive, *Story of an African Farm* (New York: Schocken, 1976).
Schulte-Sasse, Jochem, 'Introduction', *Modernity and Modernism, Postmodernity and Postmodernism: Cultural Critique* 5 (1986/7): 5–22.
Segal, C. P., *Landscape in Ovid's Metamorphoses* (Wiesbaden: Steiner Verlag, 1969).
Sévry, Jean, 'An Interview with J. M. Coetzee', *Commonwealth: Essays and Studies* 8.1 (1985): 1–7.
Sévry, Jean, 'Variations on the Works of J. M. Coetzee', *Commonwealth: Essays and Studies* 9.1 (1986): 18–31.
Shakespeare, William, *King Lear*, ed. H. Bloom (New York: Chelsea House, 1992).
Shava, Piniel, *A People's Voice: Black South African Writing in the Twentieth Century* (London: Zed Books, 1989).
Simon, Claude, *Le Vent* (Paris: Editions de Minuit, 1957).
Slemon, Stephen, 'Modernism's Last Post', *Ariel* 20.4 (1989): 3–17.
Slemon, Stephen, 'Post-colonial Allegory and the Transformation of History', *The Journal of Commonwealth Literature* 23.1 (1988): 157–68.
Smith, Pauline, 'The Pain', in Pauline Smith, *The Little Karoo* (London: Jonathan Cape, 1927), pp. 19–41.
Smith, Peter, 'History and the Individual in Hesiod's Myth of Five Races', *The Classical World* 74.3 (1980): 145–164.
Spencer, Herbert, *On Social Evolution*, ed. J. D. Peel (Chicago: University of Chicago Press, 1972).
Spivak, Gayatri Chakravorty, 'Theory in the Margin: Coetzee's *Foe*.

Reading Defoe's *Crusoe/Roxana'*, *Consequences of Theory*, Jonathan Arac and Barbara Johnson, eds (Baltimore and London: Johns Hopkins University Press, 1991), pp. 154–80.

Spivak, Gayatri, 'Theory in the Margin: Coetzee's *Foe* Reading Defoe's *Crusoe/Roxana'*, *Englishpost in Africa* 17.2 (1990): 1–23.

Steiner, George, 'Master and Man', review of *Waiting for the Barbarians*, by J. M. Coetzee, in *New Yorker* 58.21 (1982): 102–3.

Strauss, Peter, 'Coetzee's Idylls: The Ending of *In the Heart of the Country'*, *Momentum: On Recent South African Writing*, eds M. J. Daymond, J. V. Jacobs and Margaret Lenta (Pietermaritzburg: University of Natal Press, 1984), pp. 121–8.

Terdiman, Richard, *Discourse/Counter Discourse: The Theory and Practice of Symbolic Resistance in Nineteenth-Century France* (Ithaca: Cornell University Press, 1985).

Thorold, Alan and Richard Wicksteed, 'Grubbing for the Ideological Implications: A Clash (More or Less) with J. M. Coetzee', interview with J. M. Coetzee, in *Sjambok* (Cape Town: University of Cape Town, n.d.), 3–5.

Thucydides, *Complete Writings*, trans. J. Crawley (New York: Modern Library, 1934).

Tiffin, Helen, 'Post-colonialism, Post-modernism and the Rehabilitation of Post-colonial History', *The Journal of Commonwealth Literature* 23.1 (1988): 169–81.

Todorov, Tzvetan, *The Conquest of America: The Question of the Other*, trans. Richard Howard (New York: Harper & Row, 1982).

Tournier, Michel, *Vendredi ou les limbes du Pacifique* (Paris: Gallimard, 1967), trans. Norman Denny as *Friday* (New York: Pantheon Books, 1969).

Trump, Martin, review of *White Writing*, by J. M. Coetzee, in *Unisa English Studies* 27.1 (1988): 93–6.

Van Niekerk, Marlene, *Die vrou wat haar verkyker vergeet het* (Pretoria: HAUM-Literêr, 1992).

Van Wyk Smith, M., review of *White Writing*, by J. M. Coetzee, in *English in Africa* 17.2 (1990): 91–103.

Van Vuuren, Helize, 'Verwronge beeld van Afrikaanse letterkunde in *White Writing*' (Distorted portrayal of Afrikaans literature in *White Writing*)', *Die Suid-Afrikaan* (Desember 1988): 46–9.

Vaughan, Michael, 'Literature and Politics: Currents in South African Writing in the Seventies', *Journal of Southern African Studies* 9.1 (1982): 118–39.

Vaughan, Michael, 'Literature and Populism in South Africa: Reflections on the Ideology of *Staffrider'*, *Marxism and African Literature*, ed. George M. Gugelberger (London: James Currey, 1985), pp. 195–221.

Virgil, *The Aeneid*, trans. R. Fitzgerald (New York: Random House, 1983).

Voss, A.E., '"We Must Live As We Can": *Waiting for the Barbarians* and the End of Empire', unpublished essay, 1991.

Wade, Michael, 'The Allegorical Text and History: J. M. Coetzee's *Waiting for the Barbarians'*, *Journal of Literary Studies* 6.4 (1990): 275–88.

Ward, David, *Chronicles of Darkness* (London and New York: Routledge, 1989).

Watson, Stephen, 'Colonialism and the Novels of J. M. Coetzee', *Research in African Literatures* 17.3 (1986): 370–92.

Watson, Stephen, 'Speaking: J. M. Coetzee', *Speak* 1.3 (1978): 23–5.

Watts, Jane, *Black Writers from South Africa: Towards a Discourse of Liberation* (London: Macmillan, 1989).

Worrall, Denis, 'English-Speaking South Africa and the Political System', *English-Speaking South Africa Today*, ed. André de Villiers (Cape Town: Oxford University Press, 1976), pp. 213–22.

Wright, Richard, *Native Son* (New York: Harper, 1940).

Zamora, Lois Parkinson, 'Allegories of Power in the Fiction of J. M. Coetzee', *Journal of Literary Studies / Tydskrif vir Literatuurwetenskap* 2.1 (1986): 1–14.

Index